Saoirse McColl, a research biologist, keeps getting fired from labs for refusing to produce results the clients want. Her best friend suggests she look for a new line of work. She applies to an ad for a high school biology teaching job at an academy in northwestern Maine that promised living quarters plus salary.

Diego Vargas, a werewolf, is the principal of the academy, despite having no background in education. He has proven to the pack leader that he is dependable and detail-oriented, but he hates hiring new teachers, not knowing what to ask them.

Once Saoirse is in his office, Diego can't concentrate because his wolf loves her smell. When it turns out that she is the best-qualified candidate, Diego and his wolf rejoice, because both are convinced she's their mate. But she's not a shifter, so they need to bide their time, waiting for the right moment to inform her that she's living in a compound of mostly wolf shifters.

Can these two find happiness together, once the scientist discovers that myth is reality?

This book is a work of fiction. Names, characters, places, and incidents either are products of the author's imagination or are used fictitiously. Any resemblance to actual events or locales or persons, living or dead, is entirely coincidental.

When a Wolf Howls
Copyright © 2020 Fiona McGier
ISBN: 978-1-4874-2674-3
Cover art by Martine Jardin

Published by eXtasy Books Inc or
Devine Destinies, an imprint of eXtasy Books Inc

Look for us online at:
www.eXtasybooks.com or www.devinedestinies.com

When a Wolf Howls
Northwest Maine Academy
Book 1

By

Fiona McGier

DEDICATION

Some of us are lucky enough to find our mates.

CHAPTER ONE

"Well, this sucks." Saoirse McColl scanned the multiple internet links for appropriate jobs she could apply for.

"Can't apply to some of them because I know people who work there, who might sabotage my application by talking about me. Can't apply to others because I already know what it would be like to work there, and setting myself up for another failure is stupid. And the rest don't need my special skills, so they won't pay what I'm worth. What to do?"

She sighed and glanced around the empty room, discouraged. She was staying with her long-time best friend, so none of the furniture was hers, and she still felt like an intruder, even when the two other residents weren't home.

"Guess I'll have to keep sending out resumes and pestering HR departments for interviews. I need some kind of income-producing thing, and soon, or I'll be tossed out of this dump and have to live on the street."

"Why are you calling our home a dump?" Her longtime friend and roommate walked through the door, tearing off his nurse's uniform top as he strolled through the room into the kitchen.

"Oh, hey Freddie. Because I don't have any money to contribute to the bills, so I feel like a loser. I guess I'm taking my bad attitude out on everything around me."

"If you stay, I'm not any worse off than I was before you moved in." Freddie poured some chardonnay he pulled out of the fridge into a glass, then entered the living room and sat on the couch.

1

"But if I move out, you and Jorge can let one of your other friends move in . . . hopefully, someone who can help you pay the bills."

"When you moved in, you were helping."

"Yeah, but then I got fired again. *Insubordinate,* they called me. Just because I was following correct lab procedures, which made the tests take longer. So they said they had to let me go. I refused to cut corners, and I absolutely refused to fake data to produce the results their clients wanted. Hell, if even science is going to lie for corporations, then there's no one left to trust anymore. Right?"

Freddie took another sip from his glass, then shrugged. "I guess. You know I don't know anything about what you do at work. Or why you care so much. But that's a part of your charm, I guess."

"Your friends didn't appear to be nearly as taken with my charm as you are." She sighed. "Last night, when you had some people over, they seemed kind of uneasy that you have a female living with you. Almost like I'm some kind of different species."

He smiled. "Some of my friends are uneasy with anyone who is straight listening in on our conversations. Nothing personal."

"No, but some did tease you a lot about turning straight because you're allowing a woman to share your place."

"Then I explained that we've been friends since grade school and that ended, right?"

"Well, kind of. At least they stopped being actively rude to me."

"I seem to remember you saying you had to go meet some friends, and you left after about an hour."

"I lied. There are acquaintances that I used to work with, but you're the only friend I have in this city. My family is mostly all back in Chicago. You know us Irish . . . we tend to stay where we landed when we got here. And Chicago is a city of neighborhoods, where even in the middle of urban crowds you can choose to live among people who look like you."

"Yeah, you can even find places where people think like you. I liked Chi-town's Boystown for a while. But when I got the offer to move out here to Boston, I realized that you can find like-minded folks everywhere. You just have to be open to finding them."

Freddie stared at her, serious for a moment before smiling. "Maybe that's your answer, Sam. You need to be open to new people and hope the universal karma will toss in folks who think like you, and who will appreciate you, your way."

"And just how am I supposed to do that? It's not like heading into the local gay bar to find other gay folks. There aren't any science bars where geeky researchers hang out. Where am I supposed to go to find people who believe in doing the best job they can, and who don't let money issues dictate what to research? People who want to help people improve their lives through science, but who still want to be able to afford to pay the bills?

"Even when I was working full-time, I barely had enough to pay a third of the rent on this place. I was just lucky that you and Jorge were all right with me crashing on the air mattress in your spare room when I was desperate for a place to stay. And that you took pity on an old friend and let me mooch off your good nature."

He got up and pulled her out of her chair for a big hug.

"Honey, you know I'd do anything for you. We go way back. Remember when you beat up Danny O'Toole when that snot called me a faggot in fourth grade?"

She nodded, smiling. "Yeah, he didn't expect a girl to be able to hit so hard. I guess he didn't know that I had six brothers who made me fight them frequently, just to keep

3

themselves in shape. I guess they did teach me how to protect myself."

He laughed. "And others. Danny ran away crying, with blood gushing from his nose. I don't think he underestimated girls after that."

"At least not me, anyway." She smiled and sat back down. "I didn't even know what a faggot was back then. I was just pissed that he was insulting my best friend."

Freddie resumed his position on the couch. "And honey, I sure was glad we were besties, especially since other guys thought twice about messing with me after that."

"Well, it was never fair that they would gang up on you, either because you were Black, or because you were gay. They needed to know that you had a crew who would fight with you. Even if your crew only consisted of one girl with a red-head's temper."

Saoirse was lost in thought for a few minutes, reminiscing.

Then Freddie broke the silence. "No luck with the job search today, then? Is that why you're in such a pissy mood?"

She sighed. "Yeah. There are only a few labs around doing the kind of research I'm interested in doing. Most of them I've either worked for or know people who work there, who would advise their bosses not to hire me. I don't know what to do anymore."

Freddie tapped his phone and began to scroll through things quickly. He stopped after a few minutes and looked back up. "Why don't you think about something completely different?"

"Like what?"

"Well, here's an ad for a high school biology teacher."

She snorted. "I can't even get along with adults. What makes you think I could get along with teenagers?"

"You're very good with troubled people. I can't think of any time in my life when I was more troubled than in high school. You talked me out of a whole lot of stupid mistakes, and you picked me up and helped me recover after the bad ones I did make. Maybe that's your calling?"

"I don't have any teaching certification."

He scanned the ad again. "It says teaching experience preferred but not required. It's a private school, up in northwestern Maine. See?"

He passed his phone over, and Saoirse read the ad.

"Hmm, it says you would have to live on the premises, but living quarters are provided. It also says that the school lab needs to be updated and remodeled, so the new teacher would be expected to help with that project. I would really love the chance to design a lab myself. I have so many ideas about what to put into it, and what not to."

"And you have a master's degree in biology, right? You're a researcher. If anything, you're probably over-qualified. But as long as the salary is decent, them supplying you with a place to live would enable you to not have to pay rent anywhere."

"Yeah . . ."

"Honey, what can it hurt to apply?"

"How will I be able to afford to get up there to interview?"

"You have a birthday coming up, right? I can pay for you to fly up there and rent a car to get to the place."

She smirked. "Just so you can get rid of me?"

He tossed a pillow at her, which she just barely avoided by ducking in time for it to fly by her head.

"No, silly bitch. So I can repay you for all of the times you held my hand when I needed a friend."

Saoirse shrugged. "I grew up in a big family, remember? Lots of people around all the time, many of whom needed a listening ear followed by hugs . . . or a slap upside the head. It's not any special kind of skill."

"No, but damn few people know how to do it as well as

you. So apply, already."

She picked up her laptop and typed in the e-dress that was listed in the ad. "Okay, it's worth a shot, I guess. I wonder what kind of area it's in. Northwestern Maine is pretty rugged, right? No big city pollution up there. Worst-case scenario is I don't hear anything back from them."

"A better case is you get to fly to a state you've never been to and rent a new-ish car to drive into the countryside. You like that better than city driving anyway, right?"

"Uh-huh." She was distracted by filling out the application form.

"Let me get you a glass of that sparkling wine you like . . . I think there's an open bottle in the fridge, right?"

"Uh-huh."

"Good luck, girlfriend."

CHAPTER TWO

"Why so glum, old buddy?"

Diego Vargas looked up from his desk to the man who strolled casually into the room as if he owned it. John wasn't a tall man, but he bore his confidence with quiet pride. Since he was a high-ranking member of security for the academy, he wore the usual khakis and a polo shirt with an elaborate insignia on the breast pocket, but he had an additional patch of authority on his sleeve. His light brown skin, along with his black curly hair, was evidence of his bi-racial heritage, but his skin was lighter than Diego's.

The sun was beginning to set, and rays of golden light were streaming through the window of the office, reflecting on the word *Principal* printed on the glass panel of the heavy wooden door.

Diego frowned. "Hey, John. I hate having to find new teachers. Since I'm not a teacher myself, I never know what to ask them. And since I've only hired one other teacher since I got here, this is still a new and daunting project for me."

"You'll be fine, Diego. Just go with your gut feeling, like you did with Zack. He's been an excellent boys' phys ed teacher since the day he got here. The kids love him, and he's really good at keeping even the most boisterous boys in line."

"Yeah, but he just dropped into my lap. Remember, I was in the process of reviewing the applications I'd chosen when Zack made an appeal to the big guy for pack membership. When we asked him what his skill set was and he said he was a gym teacher in a middle school, I was thrilled that I could

7

stop my half-hearted attempts at interviewing prospective teachers."

"Maybe someone will apply to the pack again, and you'll get a new biology teacher the easy way."

Diego snorted. "And maybe pigs will grow wings, and we'll all have to wear umbrella hats. No, I'm afraid I'm going to have to actually carry out the interviews I've got scheduled."

"So you've had some applicants already?"

He nodded. "Yup. A couple have years of experience but are looking for a change in schools. I haven't had the time to check out any references yet, but I'll have to do that before they get here next week."

"How do you do that? Contact the schools?"

Diego shrugged. "Who knows? I guess I'll start with emailing the principals to see how to proceed. They won't have heard of our school, but the word *academy* in the title should get me some serious attention. But I'm not sure about the other two applicants. One is a local boy from Augusta, who just got his teaching certificate, so he hasn't worked in any schools yet, except as a sub. I don't know who I can contact about him. And the other one is a researcher who lives in Boston, and her only experience is in labs. She's got a master's degree in biology, so she's sure over-qualified for what we need. I guess I'll contact the last lab she worked at."

"You're only going to interview four people?"

Diego sighed. "I only got five applications. One wasn't interested when she found out what a remote area our school is in. She's a city gal who hates the outdoors. Two more came in weeks ago, I got one last week, and the lab rat just applied today. I'm going to fit her into the day I've set aside for interviews, and just hope for the best. Hopefully one of them will work out."

He sighed and leaned back in his chair, massaging his

temple. "We've been so lucky up to now. All the other teachers are either pack members or married to a pack member. I'm almost afraid of letting four non-pack people onto the grounds, but I have no choice. We really need a biology teacher, and I can't just wait for one to magically appear."

"You could interview them in a hotel, to weed out the ones you think won't work out. That way, only the ones you are interested in need to come here."

"Yeah, but then they won't have any idea just how remote we are. I want them to know what they're applying for from the start.

"Okay, boss. I'll make some arrangements so the applicants won't know how to get back here. Tell them they will be picked up at the Augusta airport, and I'll send Nathan out in the limo. We'll ask them to turn off their cell phones at the airport, so the GPS won't be able to locate where we are. The windows on the limo are almost black, so it's hard to see where you're going anyway. We'll let them use the limo's TV. That should be enough to get most people to not pay attention to the countryside. And after your interview, we'll drive them back to the airport and drop them off at the hotels near there."

Diego nodded. "I plan to do an initial interview with all of them, then if I think any of them might work out, I'll have them come back the next day to teach a sample class to some of our kids. That will allow me to watch them in a classroom situation, to see how they handle what our kids might dish out."

John snorted. "I take it you'll pick the kids you know won't cause too much trouble? No shifting in the middle of the lesson and all?"

Diego grinned. "Yeah. But I do want them to test the teachers. I don't want to go through all the bother of hiring someone and moving that person into the mansion, only to find he or she freaks out at some of the, shall we say, idiosyncrasies of our students."

"Dude, I don't envy you having to do all of this. Part of the reason I like being in charge of security is that what I have to do is cut and dried. Keeping the pack safe is a natural urge. And being a member of the pack leader's family makes me want to protect everyone, not just my family. But having to make decisions about adding a new, non-pack person to our world? I'm glad you're the one who has to do that."

"Do you think your dad will want to sit in on any part of this?"

John shook his head. "I don't think so. He's having a good day today, but there have been more bad ones lately. Just because you're a werewolf and have an extended life span, doesn't mean you don't die eventually. And cancer is hard for even our enhanced bodies to fight."

"Doctor Chan has been here a lot lately."

"Because his cancer doesn't seem to be in remission anymore. It's flaring up, and the doctor's not hopeful it will subside again."

"I'm sorry. When will the pack be told?"

"Soon. He wants to do it himself, which is only right. As the pack leader, he's the one who presides at the weekly meetings, so he's the one who should be letting everyone else know that there will be a need for a new pack leader soon. Not today, and hopefully not tomorrow. But soon. That's actually what I came in here to talk to you about."

Diego gaped in surprise. "Me? Why?"

"Might you be interested?"

"But I'm not a blood relative. I'm an outlier. You're blood. Aren't you going to apply for the upgrade?"

"Me? Aw, hell no. I like doing security. Lots of responsibility, but none of the paperwork. Beating up bad guys, I'm very good at. Dealing with other pack members and their personal problems? Uh-uh. Dealing with the leaders of other packs and their issues? And the paperwork? No way, *José*! No, I'm happy where I'm at. If the new leader allows me to continue in my present function, I'll be a happy camper."

Diego lowered his voice, even though no one else was in the near vicinity. "You know, once he's gone, you won't have to hide who you are anymore. I don't think anyone else will care."

John grimaced. "But packs are still very conservative in their morality. It's only recently that anyone who is pack would even admit to being gay. And I only know that from rumors about other packs. Nobody in this pack has admitted anything. And no one will accept a gay leader, even if I wanted the job . . . which I don't."

Diego shrugged. "If you say so. I didn't think anyone would accept me having such a high position in the school, but your dad thought I could do the job, and no one questions the pack leader's choices. It's not good for one's longevity."

"You have a strong personality, Diego. You don't make rash choices, you think things through, and when you make a decision, you stick with it. You're an honorable guy. That's what my dad saw in you, and that's why I think he might be considering you to replace him."

"Honestly? I'm very flattered. But there are lots of others who've been pack here much longer than me. If my name is on his list at all, I'm honored. But I'm not expecting to make a change in my position around here. After the past couple of years, I've gotten comfortable with being the principal. Now that I have some experience under my belt, I think I'm doing a better job. I'd hate for the school to be in chaos again if I got moved."

"You could keep being the principal, at least part-time." John shrugged. "Well, I just wanted to give you a heads up. That's all. And I'm hoping the doctor is right and Dad's got at least a few more months left."

"I think I'd better email the hopefuls and let them know about the arrangements. They'll have to book a hotel room for the night if they're not local. But they won't need to rent a car, since the limo will be picking them up."

John got up in a fluid movement full of grace to walk toward the door. When at the threshold, he turned back. "You'll need to give Nathan the list of names, so he'll know who he's picking up."

"Will do. And thanks for the vote of confidence."

With a small salute, John walked out and shut the door behind him.

Diego shook his head. *Joe would think of me to be pack leader? Me? Only a few years ago, I was a homeless man wandering the streets of Augusta with no direction to my life. I was afraid to seek out a pack, since the ones I'd been a part of were such disasters. I don't understand why so many feel being different means they have to choose a criminal lifestyle. There are other ways to cope with knowing you can do something that most of the humans around you can't do.*

He leaned further back in his chair, reminiscing on how he'd found his new home.

I was running through the woods with no destination in mind. I was enjoying the freedom of being in such a remote place, with the sights and smells of the wilderness surrounding me. When I heard other wolves howl, I almost jumped out of my skin. But I had to find out where they were . . . and if they were like me. When I got to the fence, I could sense it was electrified. But there were large wolves on the other side, looking back at me. I freaked out at how many there were! And I could tell they were all shifters.

I knew who the alpha was when the pack parted to let him through. He beckoned to me to get closer and sniffed me for a while. Then he nodded. Another wolf stepped forth to incline his head for me to follow. We trotted along the fence for what felt like forever since we were moving so slowly. When we finally got to the gate, I figured that was the end of things. I was shocked when the wolf nodded at the guards, and they opened the gate to let me in.

After I walked through, they locked the gate again. I expected to be tested . . . to have to fight. But there was none of that. Once the alpha nodded, the others accepted his decision and let me hunt with them that night. Then once we had all had our fill of the night, they gave me a guest room to sleep in. The next morning, I officially met Joe and John and petitioned to join the pack.

Was it really only three years ago? Diego smiled as he looked out of the window behind his desk. *I've never felt so at home anywhere. Now I'm even under consideration to be the next pack leader? I'm a lucky man.*

His cell phone buzzed to let him know he had a text. His reverie disturbed, he glanced at it. It was a message from the researcher, wondering what arrangements to make for the interview.

I'd better get to explaining to all of them how this is gonna work. It will be easier if one of them is like us. But if not, I guess I'll just have to use my intuition to figure out if any of them might feel comfortable here. Back to business.

CHAPTER THREE

Saoirse smiled at the clichéd manner in which they were being greeted. A tall blond man wearing khakis and a polo shirt with an intricate emblem on the pocket stood holding a sign that listed four names on it. Since he was so tall, the placard was easily seen, even over the heads of others exiting the airport. There were already three other people milling around the man, and when she headed over, they faced her as one.

"Um, is your name on the sign?" the man asked.

She smirked. "Not willing to even try to pronounce it?"

He gave her a sheepish grin. "Um, nope. Miss McColl, I hope?"

"Yes. And it's pronounced *Sir*-sha. It's Irish. Don't blame me for the spelling. Gaelic folks are not big on doing things phonetically."

"I know. I'm the English teacher at the academy. You should hear the students bitch when we do Shakespeare or anything in *Olde English*. You'd think it was a foreign language the way they carry on."

The older man of the group moved near the limo, calling out, "We're all here, right? Shouldn't we get moving?"

The tall man nodded and addressed them all.

"My name is Nathaniel Taylor. As I said, I'm the English teacher. It's going to take about an hour and a half to get to Bingham, then another half hour or more to the academy. There's a TV in the limo, but no wi-fi. I'm afraid where we're going is way too remote for any signals to be reliable. Please turn off your cell phones to conserve your batteries, because they'll be useless where we're going.

"Since we are a private institution, we ask that you leave your phones in the limo. They'll be undisturbed while you are on the grounds, and I'll lock the vehicle. We don't allow pictures or recordings of any kind, since there are children on our campus.

"There are water bottles in the fridge and some snacks in the basket next to the fridge. Help yourself to anything you want."

Nathan opened the rear car door before moving around the limo to get into the driver's seat. The older man gestured to a woman, who looked to be close to Saoirse's age, to precede him. Then he turned to wave to her also.

"Ladies first?" she asked. "Thanks."

She slid onto the seat next to the other woman. He got into the car and moved along the bench to allow the last person, a young man wearing a suit and tie, to get into the limo.

The window to the front was open, and Nathan turned to face the group. "Are we all in? Good. I'll leave the window open in case anyone has any questions. Like I said, it'll take a while to get there. Enjoy the ride, everyone."

When the car started moving, Saoirse relaxed as the others leaned back in their seats.

"We might as well get to know each other, right?" The older man leaned over to grab a water bottle out of the fridge, then settled back into his seat. "I'll start. My name is Tom Healy. I've been teaching for the past ten years at a school in Boston. I'm originally from Upstate New York, where I taught for a few years out of college, but I moved when I got married and the wife's job moved her. We're now divorced, and I'm looking for a new challenge in life. I figure this academy might be an interesting career change."

The other woman spoke up, "I'll go next. I'm Helen White. I've been teaching for twelve years in a big school district in

Augusta. I'm tired of dealing with administrators who won't allow for any deviations from their set agendas. I'm hoping for some leeway in how things are done, so I can be more creative in my labs."

Saoirse nodded to the other man to go next.

"I . . ." His voice squeaked when he started, and he coughed before continuing. "I'm Otis Williams. I just graduated with my teaching degree in December, and I've been subbing in Augusta schools since then while living with my parents. I'd really like a bigger school, but they want you to have experience. If I get the job, I could teach for a few years, then apply to some bigger schools, maybe out of state. I'd really like to teach and live in a big city like Boston . . . or maybe New York."

"And I'm Saoirse McColl. I've never taught, other than running entry-level labs when I was a TA working on my masters. I got my master's in biological research, and I've spent the past ten years working in labs. I'm from Chicago and worked there for a while. Recently, I decided to travel around to see more of the states." She turned and nodded at the younger man. "Now I'm looking for something to do with my degree that isn't research-based. I'm tired of being told what my results should be before the testing is even done. I mean, if you can't trust science to tell the truth, who can you trust?"

She could feel the others judging her as the weakest link, so she changed the subject. "I wonder what's on TV out here?"

The older man grabbed the remote from the shelf under the screen and began to flip through the channels.

Fine. I already know I don't belong here even trying for this job. But damn it, I don't have many other options. Maybe I can catch a quick power nap while we drive. I didn't get much sleep for the past couple of nights, worrying about whether or not this is a good idea. Screw them all, with their education degrees. This way, at least, I'll appear rested if not experienced.

She closed her eyes and pretended to be napping. Before long, she drifted off for real, lulled by the gentle rocking of the limo as it devoured the miles.

CHAPTER FOUR

Diego leaned forward in his chair, resting his elbows on the desk and rubbing his temples in exasperation as the door closed behind the most recent applicant.

Shit! Three out of four down, and I have no idea what I'm doing! They'd probably all do well enough, but none of them smell like shifters. I'm on my own here, and I have to make a decision based on what? A gut feeling? My instincts? I wish there was someone else willing to help me do this. The first two were condescending, and even the kid right out of college appeared to think my questions were odd. Probably not what he was led to believe he'd be asked when he was still in college.

He took a long drink from his water bottle, then shrugged at his situation. Resolutely, he stood and walked over to the door to open it one last time for the final applicant.

"Miss McColl?"

He was dazed by the sunlight glinting off the bright auburn of her hair as the woman got up, smiling, and swept past him into the office. He barely managed to nod at the other three, who were all paging through magazines in the waiting area.

Something . . . He sniffed. *Something smells really good!*

He closed the door and saw that the woman had sat in the chair in front of his desk and turned expectantly to watch him. He walked toward his seat, breathing deeply, trying not to be too obvious as he passed her.

Make that someone smells really good! Like wildflowers and grass.

He sat down and opened the file in front of him, trying to concentrate on the words while his nostrils flared, drinking in the scent of the woman.

"Um, exactly how do you pronounce your name, Miss McColl?"

She grinned. "I can assure you, this isn't the first time I've been asked that . . . not even the first time today. It's pronounced *Sir*-sha. It's Gaelic. Me da and mam were from the old country."

Diego raised an eyebrow in question.

She chuckled and clarified her statement. "Ireland. They were already married when they decided to try their luck across the pond, in the colonies."

He smiled. "The pond? I never thought of the Atlantic as a pond."

"Well, that's what folks in the British Isles call it. My parents jumped the pond and ended up in Chicago. It's got a large Irish faction, including many of the local politicians. That's where they raised all ten of us. And yes, we're Catholics. No need to make any jokes when we make them ourselves first."

He shook his head. "I wouldn't dream of it. I want to talk to you about why you applied here. It says on your application that you don't have any teaching experience. Why do you want to teach here at the Northwest Maine Academy?"

She leaned forward conspiratorially. "Actually, it was the bit in the want ad about helping to redesign the lab that got my interest. I've been working in labs for the past ten years, and I got sick and tired of being told I have to make do with what's there whenever I made a suggestion about how things could be better. I'm also done with being told what my results will be before I've even finished the testing. I think science should always be honest and truthful, not tied to the corporation paying for the research."

He moved his chair closer to the desk to lean his elbows on it. He tried to ignore his cock, twitching to get his attention, expressing interest in the delicious scent coming from the woman. "What makes you think you'd be any good as a teacher of teenagers? Some of our kids are challenging, to say the least."

"I was raised in a family of ten kids. I was third, and the oldest girl, so I helped to raise the younger ones, which is traditional in Irish families." She shrugged. "I helped my adolescent siblings deal with their traumas and issues, and I helped my cousins deal with theirs. Most recently, I've been living with an old friend from grade school, and he reminded me that I often helped him deal with his problems in high school. In fact, he was the one who found your ad and told me I should apply."

Diego struggled for control when his wolf began to stir, growling softly, asserting its jealousy of this unknown man the nice-smelling woman had been living with. She continued speaking, oblivious to his dilemma.

"In fact, he gave me the money for the plane ticket as a birthday present. I used the rest to rent the hotel room, since I didn't need to rent a car. This way, if I get to do the second interview tomorrow, I'll be well-rested. If not, at least I'll get a chance to explore a city I've never been to before."

Diego cleared his throat. "He's a most generous friend. I'm surprised you'd consider moving so far away from him."

She shrugged. "If I get the job, he and Jorge can rent their spare room to someone else. No big deal."

Gay man. No threat. His wolf calmed, placated by the information.

He shifted in his chair, trying to appear professional but afraid he was failing miserably in the presence of this woman. He couldn't even remember any of the questions he had prepared, so he punted.

"Is there anything you'd like to ask about the school?"

She nodded. "Why is it in such a remote area? Do the students live here too? Away from their families, year-round? And why do you need a biology teacher? Is someone retiring?"

On safer ground, he took a deep breath, then regretted it as his body reacted to her scent again. Once more, he struggled with his wolf for control.

"Yes, our current biology teacher is retiring. He's going to be seventy this year, and he and his wife want to do some traveling while they're still young enough to enjoy it. His retirement has put us . . . well . . . me into an awkward position.

"And yes, the students and faculty all live here, but there are others as well. This is actually a small gated community, and we don't often admit strangers to join us.

"As you noticed, we are in a remote, wild area of the state. There are no close towns to visit, so if you're looking for nightlife, this isn't the place to live. We grow a lot of our produce on the grounds, and everything else gets picked up by the staff when they make regular supply runs. We pay all our employees with direct deposit, but you are always welcome to borrow one of the company cars to run to the bank or do other errands."

He shook his head and gave her a weak smile. "I'm sorry. I know I'm not asking the kinds of questions I should be asking. I don't have a degree in education . . . in fact, I barely got through two years of junior college. But the owner of the school trusts me with running it, and the faculty works well with minimal supervision.

"Our students have often had . . . um . . . difficulties, in other, more conventional schools. We offer them the freedom to be themselves, and for the most part, they do well. Many of them revel in the liberty of having the grounds to roam around on, and some discover they have abilities that would be useful here, and they stay on even after they have graduated. Those who move on, often contact us later to thank us for the quality education they got that allowed them to do well in whatever colleges or universities they attend.

"So you see, we're not really looking for a traditional teacher. We're looking for someone to pique their interest in science . . . biology, primarily. But we'd expect you to be able to teach at least basic chemistry, and if any students are interested, anatomy as well."

Saoirse nodded. "No problem for me. I got an anatomy minor, since I originally wanted to be a doctor. And I took an AP chemistry class in high school and a couple more chem classes in college. I don't know how much I remember, but I'm a quick learner, especially when it's things I've learned before. How big is the lab space?"

He smiled. "You'll see it tomorrow. It hasn't been updated for over twenty years, so you might be kind of disappointed."

"I have so many ideas about how I'd like to do it . . . Wait. You said I'll see it tomorrow? Does that mean I won't get to explore Augusta? I'll be back here?"

Diego nodded. "As long as that's okay with you . . ."

"It's more than okay. That's great!"

Diego stood when she did and leaned forward to shake her hand. He was pleased with the strong grip she gave him and ignored how much his hand tingled when he touched her skin.

"Tell the others I'll be out in a few minutes to explain what I expect from you all tomorrow."

Her face reflected disappointment when he mentioned all four candidates would be returning for the second interview, but she quickly corrected it to a smile.

"Okay. Thank you for the chance to prove myself tomorrow." She moved to the door and left the room.

Diego sat back into his chair and worked to quiet his mind. *Yes, she smells good and feels good, too. But I can't base my decision on that alone. I must determine who will be the best teacher for the school. I can't just hire her because I want . . . What do I want? No! I can't think about that.*

He stood and walked into the bathroom in his office. He turned on the cold water and splashed his face, then dried off and glared at himself in the mirror over the sink. *Focus, man, focus!*

He took a deep breath, reentered his office, and walked out to address the applicants in the waiting room. "Tomorrow, you will all have the chance to teach a mini-lesson to some of our students. The limo will pick you up at eight from your hotels. You will all get a total of thirty minutes in front of the kids. It's your choice what the lesson will be about, and how you want to present it. We don't have smart boards, but we do have computers in the classroom. You can do a *PowerPoint* presentation if that's your choice. Afterward, I'll make my decision and share it with all of you. Good luck, everyone. See you back here by eleven."

Saoirse mentally noted the tense atmosphere in the limo on the ride back to the airport. The other applicants appeared to be silently planning their presentations for tomorrow. When she tried to ask a few general questions, the attitudes of the others made her decide to join them in silence.

She already knew what she was going to do with the students. It was an experiment that she'd had success with when introducing new students to lab procedures. She'd captured their attention with it and taught them a few things about her expectations. She had to pick up a few things, but they were the kinds of things usually available at a grocery or department store . . . both of which were near the hotel she was staying at.

Okay, then. May the best one of us win tomorrow!

CHAPTER FIVE

The students who had been chosen as guinea pigs for the applicants were a mixed bunch. There were honor students, and some with average grades as well. Diego made sure there were at least a couple who enjoyed disrupting classes with their antics. He gathered them all together in the classroom next to the lab and made sure they were seated before the prospective teachers arrived.

The students all had paper and pencils, and were instructed to test the teachers, but not too much. They were also to take notes on anything they noticed, whether it was a good or bad thing, so he could discuss their opinions with them afterward. They were excited to learn they would have a say in the new teacher, and he had high hopes they'd provide the kind of insight he needed.

He decided to have the teachers present their lessons in the same order he'd interviewed them the day before. He pulled one of the desks to a back corner, so he could watch and listen, both in the classroom and the adjacent lab area.

Nathan escorted the educators to the same waiting room they'd spent time in yesterday, then accompanied them, one at a time, down the hall to the science classroom. The first to present was Tom Healy, the older, experienced teacher.

The students were all chatting among themselves when Tom walked in and settled behind the teacher's desk.

He greeted them with a hearty, "Good morning, class!"

The kids looked at him briefly, then returned to their discussions.

"That's not how you would treat each other, so don't be rude to me," he snapped. "I have a lesson to present, and you will need to pay attention, so you don't miss anything."

Tom had the students accompany him into the lab area. He did a quick demonstration of the chemical properties of baking soda and vinegar, resulting in a lava eruption from the jar he'd brought with him. While he was doing that, one of the students slipped out of the room unnoticed. When Tom looked up to gauge their reactions, he was startled at seeing a medium-sized black wolf walking up the middle aisle, to end up sitting on the floor next to one of the boys.

"What the hell . . ." Tom began.

Then he apparently remembered Diego was in the back corner and took a step backward, looking confused.

"Why is there a wolf in the lab?" he demanded.

"He's my comfort animal," the boy replied. "I need him to be with me in case I get anxiety attacks. Your demonstration made me get excited, which can lead to an attack. I hope it's all right with you."

"Um, I guess. It's a bit out of the ordinary, but okay."

"You're not afraid of wolves or anything, are you?"

Some of the other boys sniggered.

"Shouldn't he be on a leash or something? I mean, I assume he's tame, but still . . . wolves are wild animals."

"No, he'll be fine as long as you don't make any sudden movements."

With Tom's concentration obviously blown, and his attention centered on not moving quickly, his second demonstration didn't go as planned. The man was sweating profusely when Diego tapped his watch to signal the end of his time.

When the erstwhile teacher left the room, the students turned to see if Diego was amused. He shook his head in exasperation.

"You said to test them." The boy who had claimed the wolf

defended his actions. "Don't you want to know how they react around wolves?"

"Are you going to pull that stunt with all of them?"

There were multiple nods, making Diego sigh.

He addressed the wolf directly. "Very well. But no jumping at any of the teachers. Do you understand?"

The shaggy head bobbed up and down in agreement. The non-furry students all filed back into the classroom and sat back down to await the next presenter, while the wolf left the room by the back entrance.

When Helen White walked into the classroom, the students looked at her with interest, since she was carrying a large bag of candy-coated chocolates. She introduced herself and told them there'd be no need to go into the lab since she was doing a quick demonstration of genetics. She invited them all to approach the teacher's counter, where she began the lesson by emptying most of the candy onto a large sheet of paper. While she was separating them into piles based on colors, she noticed that some of the boys were sneaking pieces of candy and hiding them . . . in their mouths.

She got upset, berating them by pointing out that she'd bought the candy with her own money, and that it was incredibly rude of them to be eating the candy before the demonstration. She also mentioned her intention of letting them all split the candy after the lab was done.

One of the girls blurted, "After your sweaty hands have been all over them? Ew!"

The rest of the demonstration went poorly, even before the wolf sauntered up the aisle. At the sight of him, Ms. White shrieked and ran toward the door. She cringed, shaking, with her hand on the doorknob.

Her gaze found Diego in the back of the classroom. "Do something! Get that filthy animal out of my classroom! How am I supposed to teach with that thing ready to attack me?"

Diego turned to see the wolf sitting quietly next to the student who had claimed him before.

"He's my comfort animal," the student announced.

"I don't care! I can't teach under these dangerous conditions!"

With that, she opened the door and lunged out into the hall.

There was a moment of silence, then the students descended on the candy and divvied it up quickly, making sure to save some for the wolf, who would eat his when he had resumed the shape of someone who could digest chocolate.

Diego sighed, more heavily this time. "Guys, the wolf might not be a good idea."

"But look at what a good job he did of exposing her as *lupophobic*!"

"I guess so. There are two more applicants. Keep in mind, if none of them work out, we'll have to go through this process again. I, for one, don't want to have to do that."

There was general grumbling about the unsuitability of any teacher to take the place of their beloved Mr. Hoffman. The students settled back into their chairs in the classroom, and the door opened to admit the youngest applicant.

It was evident to anyone with a wolf's enhanced sense of smell, which was some, but not all, of the people in the room, that he had been smoking. Diego sat back patiently to watch.

Once again, the young man was wearing a suit and tie. Some of the girls smiled and leaned forward, perhaps finding him more attractive than their fellow students. This made some of the boys sit back and cross their arms over their chests in obvious disapproval.

"Hi, everyone," the young teacher began. "My name is Otis Williams. You can call me Otis if you want to, because I just graduated in December. So if any of you are seniors, I'm barely four years older than you. No need to be formal about things."

Diego noticed the introduction went over well with the girls, and not so well with the boys. He wrote a question mark next to the young man's name in his notes.

"I'm going to show you how to make a smoke bomb. I mean, who doesn't like blowing things up? It's a simple process and can be done with common ingredients. But it makes a helluva noise that can really freak out anyone who doesn't know it's harmless. So let's move into the lab and get started."

Thirty minutes later, all the overhead fans in the lab were running full blast, and some of the students were still coughing from the smoke. The wolf had made a brief appearance, but the teacher was too involved with blowing things up to notice. Once the smoke got oppressive, the wolf left the room to protect his more sensitive nose.

Some of the girls said, "Goodbye, Otis," as the young teacher walked through the door when his time ran out. He turned and winked at them, grinning as he left.

Diego added a note next to the teacher's name. *Too young. Not enough age difference between him and the students.*

Resigned to having to repeat the odious process again, he was discouraged as the last applicant entered the classroom.

Saoirse appeared all business from the moment she entered the classroom. She set a bag of supplies on the front desk and addressed the students. "Hi, class. I'm Miss McColl. I've never been a teacher, but I was a TA for a while, back when I was working on my master's in biology."

One boy raised his hand.

"Yes?"

"What's that? I mean, I know what T *and* A stands for."

There was general snickering around the room from the boys. Some of the girls turned to glare at the offender.

Diego sat back and watched with interest.

Saoirse waved dismissively at the offender. "Oh, of course you don't know what it means. You're too young to have been to college yet. It means *teacher assistant*, which means I helped the professor with her entry-level biology classes by grading papers and running labs for the students."

Diego smiled, writing a note next to her name. *Didn't rise to the bait. Answered without hurting any feelings. Emphasized age difference.*

Saoirse continued. "I'm going to run a lab for you that I used with all the students for their first lab. So it's a college-level lab, but I think you can handle it. First, I need you to count off in fours. There will be four lab groups, with two of you in each one. When you're done, we'll move to the lab area so you can help me set up the microscopes. You'll also need to bring paper and something to write with."

The students counted off and followed her into the lab. A girl showed Saoirse where the microscopes were kept in a cabinet, and four of them were taken out and set up at different stations. The students gathered into their groups and turned to her awaiting instruction.

"There has been stuff in the news about how well hand sanitizers work at killing germs. Every lab I've ever worked at has dispensers filled with it at every door, to minimize germs being able to contaminate our research. But do they really work? And if so, is there a cheaper alternative? Now, everyone work with your partner and write down your answers to both questions. Meanwhile, I'll come around and give you some of your supplies."

When the students all had answers written down, Saoirse continued.

"The first thing you're going to do is one partner will scrape a tiny sample from his or her palm with the wooden stick, then smear it on a slide. Look at it and draw what you see. Then, using the hand sanitizer I gave you, that partner will wash his or her hands well, then repeat the test to see if the germs have been removed."

The wolf walked into the lab while the students worked,

then sat near the boy who had claimed it before.

"Uh, why is there a wolf in the lab?" Saoirse asked.

"He's my comfort animal," the boy stated. Then it was his turn to wash his hands with the sanitizer. He appeared more interested in what he was doing than with the wolf who sat quietly, staring at him, then at the teacher.

"Is he now? Most people would pick a dog or a cat. Maybe a hamster or mouse or something more portable. Well . . . whatever. As long as he's housebroken, I guess it's okay. He seems well-behaved."

She walked over and tentatively put out a hand. "If he sniffs my hand, can I pet him? I've never felt a wolf's fur before."

The boy looked up from writing his notes. "Yeah. He's good with people."

"Especially hot girls," a low voice said. Some of the boys snickered.

Saoirse spoke without looking for the offender. "I've been over eighteen for many years, dude. I'm not a girl."

She patted the wolf's head, then turned to correct the procedure one of the boys was using. "No, that's not how we adjust the microscope. Don't take off your glasses first. Just bend down over the scope and adjust it that way.

"Everyone have their results? Great. Now I want the other partner to come up to the front to measure out and mix together two-thirds cup isopropyl alcohol, one-third cup aloe vera gel, and eight to ten drops of the clove oil. Mix it together with your stick, then repeat your lab using the other partner's hand. Put your pencil down and sit quietly when you're done. Then we can compare notes to discover if the homemade one is as efficacious as the commercial one."

"Effen-what?" one of the girls blurted.

"Efficacious. It means having the same beneficial effect."

"Why compare notes?" one of the boys asked. "Is there

going to be a prize if we get the right answer?"

Saoirse smiled. "Just like in a real lab, there really isn't a right or wrong answer. There's just data to be analyzed. But if you all do the lab correctly, I'll let each group ask me a personal question. Of course, I reserve the right not to answer if it's too personal."

Diego stopped taking notes and just watched her now. The sun coming in through the windows made copper highlights glint in her auburn hair. Her skin looked translucent, and she moved around the lab like she belonged in it.

While the students were busy, she was efficiently wandering around, commenting on their work, while also checking out what was in the other cabinets, and noting how everything was arranged.

Five minutes later, she returned to the head table. "Well? Which group wants to go first?"

She smiled when all the students' hands shot up. "Okay, we'll just go clockwise, from my left. You two, what were your results?"

As the team spoke, she walked over to check their notes and nodded approvingly. She repeated this with each of the other three groups, then returned to stand in front of the class.

"Great job, everyone! You all followed correct scientific procedures and got similar results. The homemade sanitizer worked as well as the commercial one but was less convenient. But now you all know why having hand sanitizer at the door of a lab, and using it before you start, is a good idea, right?"

Heads nodded in agreement.

"Okay then, the first group who spoke gets to ask the first question. Talk with each other, then ask away."

There was a low murmur, as each group conferred on their question.

The boy in the first group raised his hand. "Are you Irish?"

She grinned. "Guilty. What gave it away? The red hair? Or my last name?"

Diego smiled, then raised his hand. She noticed it and pointed at him.

"If you think her last name sounds Irish, you should hear her first name." He chuckled.

"What is it?" a boy blurted out from the second group, as his female partner punched his arm.

Saoirse laughed. "That doesn't have to be your question. It's this . . ." She walked over behind the big desk and wrote her first and last names on the whiteboard. "It's pronounced *Sir*-sha," she explained. "But some of my oldest friends call me Sam since my middle name is Anne."

The girl from the second group now raised her hand. "You're so pretty. Why aren't you married?"

Saoirse smiled and curtseyed. "Thanks. Probably because I'm too bossy. Most guys want to run things, and I don't follow orders well."

Some of the girls gave each other knowing looks. Some of the boys rolled their eyes.

The next group was two boys. One bent lower to the wolf, then sat up. "You smell really nice. What kind of perfume do you wear?"

Diego frowned. That was coming dangerously close to letting her know the wolf could communicate with the boy. She didn't appear to notice though.

"Thanks, but I'm not wearing any perfume. The scent might be my deodorant. I use a natural one that has no dangerous chemicals in it. I've seen what some supposedly *safe* chemicals can do in a lab, and I don't want to be spreading them on my skin. I guess if I smell nice when I'm nervously sweating, it must be working well."

She gave a nod to Diego before turning to the last group.

The girl who had helped her set up the microscopes asked

her group's question. "If you're Irish, do you come from a big family?"

"Ah, you know about us, eh?"

There was snickering around the classroom.

"Yes, I'm third of ten kids."

Murmurs greeted that comment.

"People don't have big families like mine anymore, mostly. But it was fun growing up in a big mob of kids. I have two older brothers and four younger ones, along with three younger sisters. My brothers taught me to fight when I was young because they needed a sparring partner when they got bored beating on each other. When I was young, I used to get in trouble for physically fighting other kids, and not just the girls. I guess that's part of why I'm so bossy, huh?"

Diego noticed Nathan standing in the doorway of the classroom, which made him glance at his watch. He cleared his throat audibly. "I'm sorry, but you've gone over your allotted time, Miss McColl."

"It's okay. I'm done."

The students called goodbye to her as she left the classroom.

There was silence for a heartbeat, then the students all turned to Diego and spoke at once.

"She's the best one!"

"Did you notice she said we did the lab the best?"

"I always wondered if hand sanitizers were any good."

"Have you ever heard of such a big word? Efficacious. I love it!"

"You're gonna hire her, right?"

Diego frowned. "I have to think about it. I'm going to speak with Mr. Johnson to get his opinion. I'll let him make the announcement at tonight's meeting. For now, all of you need to clean up the lab and put everything away."

The students got right to work. Diego chuckled when he

overheard one boy chatting with the wolf.

"I'll show you how we did the lab later. Okay, okay . . . next time I'll be the wolf, and you get to be the student."

When the lab was tidied up, he ushered the students out of the classroom door and locked it behind him. He walked down the hall to call his pack leader to discuss his decision.

CHAPTER SIX

"**N**o shit! You got the job?"

Saoirse laughed. Freddie had just walked in the door from work, and she'd greeted him with a huge smile on her face.

"Yup! You're looking at the new biology teacher for the Northwest Maine Academy."

"This calls for a celebration! I'm gonna open another bottle of sparkler, then when Jorge gets home, we'll go out to dinner to celebrate both your thirty-third birthday and your new job," Freddie called over his shoulder as he headed into the kitchen.

"Won't that be expensive? You already gave me my present when you paid for my ticket and the room. I'll be eternally grateful to you for that, sweetie!"

There was a loud *pop* as the wine bottle was opened. Freddie walked back into the living room with two glasses in one hand and the bottle in the other. He sat on the other side of the couch from Saoirse and poured some bubbly liquid into both glasses before handing one to her and picking up the other one.

"A toast. To my oldest and bestest bestie, who now has a chance to start a new chapter in her life. You'll be the best bio teacher ever!"

They clinked glasses together, then both took a sip.

"Ooh, yummy!" Saoirse turned the bottle to look at the label. "This is that pinot noir cava you were telling me about?"

"Uh-huh. Only the best for you, honey. Now tell me all

about it."

"Well, the interview was really strange. There were four of us, and I was last to be called in. The guy who interviewed me didn't seem to know what kind of questions to ask, but he did let me ask some questions . . . and the place is really interesting."

Freddie leaned forward. "Just the place? Or the man, too? Come on, you can tell your old friend. Is he hot?"

Saoirse blushed despite herself as she tried to look stern. "Come on, now. He's my new boss. The last thing I need is to get involved with my employer. Then if things don't work out, it would be incredibly awkward to work there, and I'd end up having to leave. Been there, done that, threw away the t-shirt."

Freddie was still leaning forward. He poured more wine into her glass and looked at her expectantly.

"Okay, okay. He's got sexy down to an art form. His name is Diego Vargas, and he's dark-skinned and has longish black hair. It was held back in a ponytail, but it looks so silky I'd never get tired of running my fingers through it. He's got what I always call *flashing dark gypsy eyes* since they look almost black. When he smiles, his lips do this really sexy move, that I could watch all day. He's not that much taller than me, but then I'm tall for a woman."

"Don't I know it! With big feet, too." Freddie chuckled. "Remember the first time I took you into a trannie clothing store, and you were so excited to be able to get size eleven shoes that were fashionable?"

"Shoes in size eleven are rarely available, and if they are, they're usually old lady-ish, *sensible*, walking shoes. You know how much I hate having big feet."

"Yes, but with you being close to six feet tall, you'd look really stupid with teeny, tiny baby feet. You'd probably fall over, unable to keep yourself in balance."

"I'm only five-foot-ten." She sighed. "But yeah, he's probably six-one or six-two. And muscular? Dude, the guy must work out every day to look so good in his clothes."

"Let me know if you ever get to see him without his clothes! Then we'll really have something to talk about."

"Freddie, you're terrible! What would Jorge say if he could hear you?"

"He'd ask you to come right on back here and tell us how sexy this man looks without his clothes on."

Saoirse blushed again.

"See, see? You're already imagining it."

She frowned at him. "Do you want to hear the story or not?"

"Okay. I'll be good. So the interview went well?"

"Uh-huh. Then he told me I was invited to come back the next day to do a thirty-minute mini-class for some students, so he could observe my style. As you well know, I've never taught in my life . . . well, I mean not since I was a TA. Not teenagers, anyway."

Freddie got up to go into the kitchen, still visible through the pass-through opening between the rooms. "Go on, I'm just grabbing some cheese and crackers."

"Then I found out that all four of us who interviewed were coming back, so I didn't feel so special. And during the limo ride back to the hotel, no one was talking. I think they were planning their labs and afraid to talk for fear someone else would use their ideas."

"Sounds like a bunch of douche bags." Freddie put a cutting board with cheese slices and some crackers on the coffee table next to the couch.

"There was an older man, who was kind of bossy, as if he figured since he was the oldest, he was in charge. The other woman looked like she was close to my age, but she seemed nice. They both had years of teaching experience. Then there was a kid who just graduated. The ink wasn't even dry on his diploma yet, so his only experience was subbing. I think he was trying to flirt with me, but I was thinking like, dude, seriously? I'm way outta your league! So I ignored his feeble attempts to catch my eye."

Freddie laughed. "Honey, you are too fussy! Lots of men have flirted with you, and you always shut them down. You're never gonna find a man that way."

Saoirse shrugged. "Too bad. I have to figure *me* out, first, before I have the time to deal with a man."

"So, go on."

"Oh yeah, it was kind of weird. The limo driver was the school's English teacher, and he said we needed to turn off our phones and leave them in the locked limo when we were on the grounds. Something about security for the kids on campus."

"Sounds like they take their responsibility for the kids very seriously. Nothing wrong with that.

"You don't think so? I guess not. So then I bought some stuff I needed to do the lab before I went back into the hotel. I ordered myself a pizza to be delivered. And when I was going through my clothes, I found the half-sized bottle of Prosecco you hid in there. Thanks a million! It went really well with the garlic and mushroom pizza. I toasted you when I opened it."

Freddie nodded. "Yeah, I got your text. But I was out partying, so I didn't answer."

He leaned over to pour more wine into both glasses and settled back on the couch, munching on his crackers. "So what happened the next day?"

"We got picked up early, then driven back to the academy. It takes about two hours to get there, from the airport in Augusta. Then we left our phones in the limo again, and we had to go sit outside the principal's office. At least there were a few new magazines added to the collection on the end tables."

"Thoughtful," Freddie noted while chewing.

"Yeah. We each had a half hour to wow the students and the principal. I was interviewed last, so I went last. But it was really weird when the other woman came back to sit down. She was shaking like she was afraid of something. But she wouldn't talk about it. She just said she wanted to go home and then she concentrated on a magazine."

"Nerves? Stage fright?"

"Who knows? Finally, it was my turn. I think the kid before me made smoke bombs, because the fans were running, and the place still smelled like sulfur. Dumb move, to make them inside. He should have moved them outside for that."

"So what did you do for your class?"

"What I used to do with each new class of beginning bio kids on the first day. That lab with the hand sanitizer."

"Ah. That went well?"

"Yeah. The kids loved it. There was one kid who had a comfort animal join him, though. And I thought it was kind of weird that it was a wolf."

Freddie choked on his cracker. He coughed and took a quick drink. "I'm sorry, I thought you said wolf."

"I did. It was a big brown wolf, who strolled in like he belonged in the lab. He just sat next to the kid while he did his work. I even worked up the nerve to pet it. Wolf fur is kind of stiff, not soft like a dog."

"Okay . . . no cell phones and a wolf in the lab. Not hardly weird. Then what?"

"It went so well that I went over my time. Then when I rejoined the others in the waiting room, I got some nasty looks. I think they all figured that since I was in there longer, I had gotten the job. Which I had, but I didn't know it. We'd been sitting there in awkward silence for another twenty minutes or so when the principal—"

"Mr. Hottie," Freddie interjected with a leer.

"Mr. *Vargas* came into the room and told us he'd made his decision and said the delay was for him to clear it with the owner of the academy. He thanked all of us for taking the time to apply and interview but said he was giving the job to me. I was so surprised I almost fell off my chair!"

Freddie shrugged. "Why? I told you you'd be a natural with teenagers."

"Yes, you did. I guess you were right. Anyway, he said the limo driver would take the others back to the hotel, then come back to get me. The others got up and left, and I was alone with my new boss."

Freddie leered and growled.

"Cut that out! I really need this job, so I don't want to screw it up! If anything happens with him, it's going to be some time way in the future. I need to concentrate on learning how to be a good teacher first. Oh, and redesigning the lab."

She mused about the lab for a moment, then shook her head. "Anyway, he took me back to his office to sign some official paperwork, then we went back into the lab to talk about how to remodel it to be a more useful space. He liked my ideas and told me all I had to do was make a list of supplies and give it to him. He also would send a carpenter over to talk with me about anything major that needed to be changed.

"Then we had lunch out on the porch. There were about six tables out there. All of them were full when we got there, so I got introduced to a lot of people whose names I forgot already. You know what I'm like with names. But one of them was a son of the owner of the place. I got the feeling that he's gay, but not out even to himself . . . wound tighter than a drum. You know the type."

Freddie nodded while rolling his eyes.

"And I met the chef, who turned out to be the owner's wife. They all had *J* names, to go with the last name of Johnson.

40

They all seemed very nice and welcoming."

"Go on."

"After lunch, the principal—"

"Come on! You don't expect me to believe he told you to call him *the principal,* or *Mr. Vargas.* You're equals, right?"

Saoirse blushed yet again. "Okay, he did tell me I should call him *Diego.*"

"Um-hmm."

"So then Diego took me to see the suite that will be mine while I teach there."

"The suite? Not just an apartment? A suite? How lah-de-dah."

She ignored Freddie's attempt to tease her. "Yes. It's got a smallish sitting room, with a couch, coffee table, and end table with a lamp on it. There's a tiny dorm-sized fridge, a micro-wave, and a bar sink on one end of the room, with cabinets for storing munchies next to a small kitchen table with two chairs. Then there's a bathroom, with a small *Jacuzzi* tub and a shower stall. And the bedroom is really nice! There's a queen-sized bed and a huge closet. There's even a balcony with two chairs and a tiny table, so you can sit out there and enjoy the view of the forest."

"Wow! Sounds palatial! Do they need any nurses? I could use a change of scenery."

She scrutinized his serious expression for a moment.

Then he grinned.

She smiled and sighed in relief. "You had me going for a minute."

Freddie shook his head. "Honey, you know I hate the great outdoors. I always say that's why it's called *outdoors,* because it belongs out *there,* while I live in *here.*"

There was the sound of a key in the lock, and Jorge walked in.

Freddie got up to greet him with a kiss, then walked into

the kitchen to get another champagne glass. "Sam got the job! We're going out to dinner to celebrate!"

Jorge took the glass and clinked it to hers and Freddie's and took a drink, then sat with Freddie on the sofa.

"But we can't stay out too late," Saoirse said.

"Why?" Jorge demanded. "After all, it's karaoke night all around town."

"I have to come back here and pack up my stuff. I've got to be at the airport again very early tomorrow. I have a nine o'clock flight back to Augusta. Then I'm moving in and starting my new job. The flight takes about an hour, so I'll be there by lunchtime. The chef promised to make corned beef and colcannon in my honor."

"Col-what?" Jorge asked.

Freddie wrinkled his nose. "Potatoes, cabbage, and leeks boiled in milk and water, then mashed until they're unrecognizable, and drowned in butter."

Saoirse grinned. "You say that like it's a bad thing. I love colcannon!"

He shrugged. "As long as I don't have to eat it."

Jorge got up. "Didn't someone say we're going out for dinner? I'm grabbing the first shower, so you two need to plan where we're going."

Freddie turned back to her. "My treat, your pick. Where do you want to go, honey?"

"How about that Mexican place that you guys love so much? The last time I was there, the Chili Rellenos tacos were to die for!"

"Ooh, and their sangria? I'm salivating already. And their Mariachi band guys are always so sexy! I can feel the music already." Freddie did an imitation of a cha-cha as he followed Jorge into their room.

So the three of them spent the evening partying, making sure Saoirse's last night in Boston was memorable. When they got home, she packed her meager belongings and arranged for a ride to the airport. She got to bed late, but since she didn't plan on sleeping, due to her excitement, she figured it didn't matter. Surprisingly, she was asleep before she had a chance to count her blessings.

CHAPTER SEVEN

Saoirse was so tired from her move she thought she'd fall asleep instantly as she crawled into her bed in her new apartment. Instead, she lay awake, unnerved by the absence of street noises and other human sounds, plus the silence of the forest that surrounded the estate. Her thoughts raced around in her head like squirrels as she reviewed the day's activities.

The early morning flight got me to Augusta quick enough, but I had to wait around for a while until the limo got there. I just read the news on my phone. When Nathan — as he told me he preferred to be called — arrived, he was overly apologetic, so it was okay.

I asked him if I could sit next to him on the drive back, and he let me. The view of the countryside we drove through was gorgeous! Rolling hills, forests . . . no sign of man around for miles and miles. Then when we got to the grounds, I was surprised to see an electric fence surrounding it, which I hadn't seen from the back of the limo before.

There was a metal sign hanging on the locked gate that said Northwest Maine Academy. *A guard checked out who we were before he opened the gate. Once we were through, I was even more impressed by the scenery of the grounds. Wow! The forests appeared untouched by anything mankind has ever built. Nathan told me the original owner had made a fortune in logging, before he had an epiphany of sorts and realized trees are not simply commodities placed on this planet for us to cut down and make into stuff. They are living creatures deserving the right to live. So he invested his money into buying a huge chunk of virgin forest land and built himself a mansion in the middle of it.*

Nathan pointed out the mansion and explained other buildings around it now. Some are barns and garages and service buildings. There's also housing for the other people who live here full time. Some are like dorms for single men or women, who provide services here, like security, cooks, maids, and farmers. And other houses are for families who spend their whole lives living in the wild splendor of the area.

Remembering the beauty that surrounded the academy, Saoirse rolled onto her back with a heavy sigh. *I think I'm going to really like it here, where the forest is so omnipresent. I can't wait to discover if there are paths to run along since I haven't been able to do much running lately. Boston is just too crowded and smelly where Freddie's apartment is, and I hate running in traffic. Out here, there is no pollution.*

She took a deep breath to enjoy the clean air and returned to the musing of her day.

The mansion is now the main building, which holds the living quarters for the owners and their family, the school, dining areas, kitchen, the dorms for the students to live in, and the teachers' quarters. Nathan mentioned that having to live close to their teachers helps the students learn that they are always expected to behave themselves, despite their parents not being there. I'm not sure how I feel about being that easy for the students to access, but then I guess this is a different kind of school, and we're teaching them to be good people, not just good students.

Since all I own fit into my two bags of clothing, along with my laptop, I was able to carry my own stuff upstairs when Nathan dropped me off. I'm glad the apartment is fully furnished.

Diego had left a bottle of Prosecco in the fridge with a note that said how happy he was that I joined their staff. It mentioned how eager the owner of the estate is to meet me. It also asked me to join him for lunch on the veranda again, and it mentioned joining the owner and his family at the main table that night for dinner.

Of course, I started obsessing about not having any formal kind of clothing to wear for a fancy dinner. But when I asked Diego over lunch what I should wear to meet the owner, he said anything I chose would be fine. The policy is pretty casual about what the teachers wear when not teaching — that extends to the students as well. When we're in front of a class, we're to wear nice skirts, slacks, or jeans with the school-provided polo shirts. Bleah! I didn't think it was a good time to tell anyone I believe polos are the ugliest shirt styles ever invented!

Saoirse rolled over to her side, speaking to the empty room. "At least, thank God, they don't expect us to tuck them in like I had to do when I worked in retail. That just looks so *twee* if you ask me. And the shirts are a pine green color — green always looks good on me. I shudder to think how awful it might have been if they were orange or yellow, or some other color that makes my skin look putrid."

After lunch, I got to spend a few hours in the lab, poking around. I tossed out lots of old samples and specimens of things that had ossified over time. But I grabbed one of each of the textbooks I found on shelves in the classroom. And there were catalogs on the main desk, from science supply places. I grabbed those, too, so I can start figuring out what kinds of things I want to use to refit the lab to be able to do real research. Because that's what I figure I could do with the classes. I'd like to give every student the feel for what it's like to make real discoveries and actually do real science. They might not all choose to become scientists, but at least they'll be aware of the important contribution that science makes to our lives.

At dinnertime, Diego met me at the door to the main dining area and walked me over to the table where the Johnsons were sitting. I was so nervous even I could smell my deodorant! Darn kids, pointing it out to me, and now I'm aware of it. But the Johnsons were all so nice and welcoming.

The owner of the estate, Mr. Joe Johnson, is an old man, though I couldn't guess his age, and he's obviously not in very good health. But I can tell he was an attractive man when he was younger. His body still looks athletic, and his handshake was strong. And he has those piercing blue eyes that make you feel like he notices everything.

Even things you don't want him to see — like his principal just hired a teacher who has no idea what she's doing!

His wife, Janine Johnson, is the head chef and looks to be quite a bit younger than her husband. She's a tall, regal-looking black woman whose hair is just starting to go gray. Since he's white, their kids — sitting next to the couple — are a gorgeous blend of both races.

Their son, I think his name is John, is the head of security. He's the man I told Freddie about, who set off my gay-dar. Everyone seems so accepting, so I'm sure he's going to decide, sooner or later, to come out. He's got curly brown hair, brown eyes, and skin the color of café au lait.

His sister, Jerene, is one of the math teachers at the school. She wears her hair in a fro and is a much better dresser than I'll ever be! Her cute, simple dress made me feel like mine hung on me like a bag. Her husband is Arnold, and he's an accountant who takes care of the finances for the school. They have two kids, but I can't remember either of their names. Both are being home-schooled by their mom since they're too young for the academy.

Over dinner, we talked about all kinds of things. We discussed world politics, the economy, the role of science in society, and the importance of exposure to nature, especially for children. When they asked about me, I was embarrassed to admit that I'd never taught before, except for being a TA. But they didn't seem to care. Joe said he trusts Diego's instincts. Diego told him I'm a natural with the kids. I sure hope he's right!

Saoirse rolled onto her back again, her mind still buzzing too much to fall asleep. *Maybe I should get up and do some work, like reading the textbooks. No, I don't want to be half-asleep doing that. I want to be fully awake when I'm figuring out what I can and can't use in class.*

She had left the door open on the balcony, and a gentle breeze came in through the closed screen doors.

Maybe I'll go sit outside and admire the forest and the night sky with a glass of that sparkling wine that Diego left for me.

She got up and padded barefoot to the fridge. She found a

flute in a cabinet and opened the bottle screw top, smiling to herself.

How thoughtful he was! With a regular cork, I'd feel I had to save the bottle until I planned on drinking it all, or most of it since it goes flat so easily. But with a screw top, I can have a glass at a time, and it will keep. Smart man!

She walked back into the bedroom and to the open door. She opened the screen door and closed it behind her, then went over to the railing to lean her elbows on it. She took a sip of the wine, then breathed deeply as she gazed around at the natural beauty on display.

There's a full moon! Or at least almost full. How cool is that? The forest is so beautiful in the moonlight. I can't see many stars, but I'm sure once the moon sets, I will be able to see lots of them. I wonder if I'll see any Northern Lights up here. I think we're far enough north, and I know we're far enough away from any city lights. That would be so cool . . .

Movement at the edge of the forest caught her attention. She leaned out further and squinted, trying to see better in the semi-darkness. A large, black shape had moved then stopped. As her eyes acclimated, she realized what it was. *That's a wolf sitting there! An enormous, black wolf!*

Wow! I mean, we're on enough grounds that I suppose there might be a pack out there somewhere. But it's pretty nervy of him to be so close to human habitats. I wonder if he's related to the comfort wolf that kid had in class.

As she continued to stare at it, she became aware it was staring back at her. *What the fuck?*

Her heart beat rapidly with excitement, tinged with a hint of fear, as the wolf continued to look in her direction for a few moments. Then it turned its face upwards and howled. The sound was eerie and primal. A chill ran down Saoirse's back, as though a racial memory was being stirred. Suddenly there were answering howls from deeper in the forest. Others were joining in until there was a chorus of howling. The sound was mesmerizing.

With a sudden flick of his tail, the wolf bounded into the woods and was gone.

Saoirse sat down heavily on one of the small chairs and took another long drink from her glass. *I know it's stupid, but I feel like he was welcoming me to this place. Is this the kind of experience that I've read about in cultural anthropology books, where native tribal folks talk about having been contacted by beings in nature? Wild animals communicating with humans? Spiritual guidance coming from a wolf?*

She sat on the balcony for a long time, watching the woods and listening to the sounds of howling as it got further and further away from the clearing. She drank the last of the wine, then realized she had achieved her goal and she was finally sleepy. She went in, careful to close and lock the screen door, then she put the glass on the nightstand and crawled under her sheets again.

And when she finally fell asleep, her dreams were confusing and vague, punctuated by the howling, which continued into the night, and inhabited by black shapes that kept trying to tell her something.

CHAPTER EIGHT

Saoirse sighed in frustration. She had been trying to get onto the internet for twenty minutes but kept getting a message telling her *unable to connect, click here for suggestions.*

Crap! I found a lab video with graphics yesterday, and now I can't get back online to verify that it can be used by schools without paying. It does a better job than I could, explaining the procedures I want them to try.

She looked at the clock above her desk and realized how long she'd been working. *Oh man, it's after four. Probably no one left in any of the classrooms. But it's worth a shot to see if I can find anyone to help me with this screwy wi-fi they have in this place.*

Grabbing her laptop, she left her classroom and walked down the hall, hoping to see an open door. She spotted one and headed for it. When she peeked into the classroom, she saw that it was one of the math rooms, and Jerene was perched on a stool at the teacher's desk, tapping away on her laptop.

"Hey Jerene. You're online? How did you do that? I've been trying to get on for, like, forever!"

Jerene looked up and grinned. "Oh, hi, Saoirse. Yeah, it can be wonky. But since I was one of the people who set it up years ago, I know some shortcuts. Come sit by me, and I'll show you."

Saoirse grabbed the other lab chair that was in the corner and pulled it over to sit next to Jerene at the raised teacher's desk. "Was this ever a science classroom? Most of the other rooms don't have a high desk for the teacher, like this one."

"Yup. This was the Engineering classroom back in the day. Since we don't have anyone to teach that anymore, I converted it for my math class. That way, I don't have to share my room with the other math teacher."

"You only teach a few days a week, right?"

"Uh-huh. I teach my own kids on Monday, Wednesday, and Friday. Then my husband takes them on Tuesday and Thursday, so I can teach here."

"There's only one teacher for most of the other subjects. Why two math teachers? I mean, besides the fact that you're the daughter of the owner and you only want to teach part-time."

Saoirse cringed, realizing she'd made it sound like the other woman was taking advantage of her relationship to the big boss. She quickly tried to make amends. "Oh no! I didn't mean to suggest that you have this job due to nepotism. Or that they wouldn't make arrangements for any other teacher. I'm sorry . . ."

Jerene shook her head and smiled. "No need to apologize. Others have made that suggestion, and not as politely as you, I might add. But yeah, I didn't want to give up teaching entirely, but I also wanted to home-school my own kids until they're old enough to enroll here. Mike, the other math teacher, is married to my cousin, Bernice. He had been doing odd jobs, rewiring stuff, and keeping small engines running . . . that kind of thing. But she knew he had his degree in math, so when I had my second kid, she approached me about giving him a chance. We have so many students with limited math skills that it just made sense to keep the classes small and give them lots of extra attention. That is a big part of what their parents send them here for."

Saoirse breathed a sigh of relief. "Thanks for not taking offense when none was meant."

"No problem. Now, what kind of message are you getting

when you try to go online?"

Saoirse worked with Jerene for a while until she was successfully online. She found the video she had been looking for and downloaded it, just in case, so she'd have it for her class.

"Thanks. I'm so relieved. I was afraid no one else would be here this late."

Jerene looked at her watch. "Oh! I didn't realize it was getting so close to dinner time." Her expression turned bemused. "Are you always here this late? I mean, we know you're dedicated and all, but still. You don't have to work such long hours."

Saoirse shrugged. "It's just that I really wanted to be able to show this video, since I used it when I was a TA. The university had a paying arrangement with many scientific sites, so I never bothered to check if it was okay to use it before. But now I want to be extra sure that I'm not leaving the school or myself open to charges for showing it in class. And I usually stay late because I have the least experience of any teacher here. I'm determined to do my best to repay Diego for giving me a chance here."

"I must admit, I was a little surprised that he chose someone with no teaching credentials. But once I met you, I realized how passionate you are about science and how smart you are . . . and what a good storyteller you are. Must be the Irish in you, huh?"

"Yeah. My parents can both talk your ass off and keep you laughing so hard you won't mind that you never get a word in edgewise."

"Arnold's like that. I've never had that gift. I'm happier being a listener."

"How lucky for your kids, to have both in their parents."

Jerene tilted her head with a wry smile. "Diego says you're a natural with teenagers. That's what we really need here. Some of our students had difficulties fitting into other schools. Some are Special Ed and weren't getting what they needed. Some have emotional issues that get taken care of mostly by our counselors. And some are so gifted they were bored to tears. We don't place them by age here . . . just by interest and experience."

"I have noticed the age disparity in some classes. But it's no big deal, as long as the kids want to learn."

"Diego also says you've been having them do actual research in the lab. That's such a great idea! For some of them, it's the first time they've ever felt that what they do in school is important . . . that it has some use beyond getting them a grade."

Saoirse nodded. "That's how I always felt in school. I wanted to learn important things, not memorize a bunch of crap that I could find quickly with a search on my phone. I wanted help in learning how to think, not just how to remember. Besides, doing science is the most interesting thing I've ever done, and seeing the kids get excited about it is really gratifying. I'm trying to single-handedly create more science majors, especially girls, who might not have ever met a real scientist before, and most probably not a woman."

Jerene shrugged, waving a hand dismissively. "Diego is always talking about you, about how well you're doing, and how glad he is that he hired you."

Saoirse couldn't suppress her surprise. She scrutinized Jerene's expression for a long moment before she spoke. "Some people have told me I'm too direct, but I can't help it. I don't like to play games. Are you suggesting that he might be interested in me?"

A small smile played on Jerene's lips. "I don't like games either. Diego's only been living with us for a few years, but he's proven himself time and time again to be trustworthy, and the hardest worker we've ever had as a principal. And he's become a good friend to many of us. I'm just saying that he talks about you a lot, and you can make what you will of that. But he's a good man."

Saoirse shrugged. "I don't want anything to interfere with my job. You don't know how important it is to me to finally have a place where I can use my skills and not get canned for doing the right thing . . ."

She stopped, horrified at what she'd revealed. She covered her mouth with her hand, hoping the floor would open up and swallow her.

But Jerene just smiled serenely. "Don't worry. We know about your past experiences at the last few labs you worked at. Diego contacted them. Schools are usually pretty close-mouthed about giving out much beyond verifying that someone worked there and for how long. But he says your lab ex-bosses were eager to discuss your independent streak, which didn't allow you to produce the required results, and your propensity to disobey orders."

She chuckled and patted Saoirse on the arm before she continued. "But what they didn't know is that is just what we were looking for. We're not a traditional school by any definition. We don't want to produce graduates that unthinkingly follow orders. We want to produce thinkers who will make decisions for themselves. And who will try to change things that aren't right."

Saoirse took a deep breath. "I wasn't trying to hide anything from you. It's just that I needed a job so badly. I felt like such a failure when I couldn't fit in anywhere. I'm really enjoying being here. I feel . . . I don't know . . . appreciated."

"Good. That's how we want you to feel. And forget I said anything about Diego. He's a big boy and can take care of things himself. But I'm really glad you came in here today. I don't have any close friends, since there aren't a lot of female teachers here. And I think others avoid me because I'm the big boss's daughter. Or maybe it's just that I don't usually talk much, so they think I'm unfriendly."

"I don't think you're unfriendly. I'm glad I found you here, too. Not only did you solve my internet issues, but I think I've found a friend. I'm so new here that I've been spending all of my time working and not allowing myself any time to socialize."

"That's not good. All work and no play . . . and all that. What do you like to do in your off time? Any hobbies?"

"I read a lot, mostly e-books since they're easier to cart around than physical books. And I like to go running. I haven't been able to do it for a while. When I was working, I had very long hours. And when I was unemployed, I was living with an old friend in an urban area of Boston. The streets were crowded with traffic, and I hate to run while breathing in exhaust fumes."

"Well, you're in luck. There aren't any exhaust fumes around here."

"Are there any trails that I could run on? I've been spending all of my time inside, so I haven't had any time to go exploring."

Jerene's expression turned guarded. "There are a few trails. I'd be glad to go running with you to show you where to go, but you don't want to do too much exploring . . . at least not by yourself. I'm sure you've realized that there is a wolf pack that lives on the property, and you need to be aware of where you are, so you don't go too far away from the buildings. And don't ever go running after dark. I know that's a pain in the late fall and winter when it gets dark really early. But we want you to be safe."

Saoirse nodded. "I've gotten used to falling asleep listening to the howling. I find it kind of comforting, in a weird way. It's a whole lot better than hearing car alarms honking, and the urban sounds of arguments or gunshots. I'd much rather hear natural sounds like wolves any time."

Jerene seemed pleased with her answer. They both looked up when Diego poked his head into the classroom.

"Are you ladies bucking for a promotion by working so late? Because I happen to know the boss is leaving, so you've already stayed longer than him. Or are you skipping dinner because you don't like fried chicken?"

They both turned to look at the clock.

"Wow! It's a lot later than the last time I checked," Jerene said as she started to log off her laptops.

"I'm sure your mom will be pleased that it's not her cooking keeping you from the dining room." Diego grinned at Jerene, before turning to Saoirse. "And you, young lady, need to stop skipping meals. I know you're trying to suck up to the boss, but there's no need for that. I already think you're the best hire I've ever made . . . of course, you're only the second hire I've ever made. But still, you should stop working so much. Don't you have any hobbies?"

Jerene spoke up before Saoirse had a chance to respond.

"Yes. She likes to run. I'm going to go with her to show her the trails that are safe for running . . . at least during the daylight hours."

Saoirse felt things deep inside of her react when Diego smiled. She gritted her teeth. *Can't let him see how he affects me.*

He nodded at Jerene before turning his attention back to her.

"You're a runner? Great. I'd like to go running with you also. I've found some amazing places that don't take that long to get to but are really scenic. I like to go there and paint what I see. I'm not very good, but it relaxes me."

Saoirse stared, momentarily stunned. "You like to paint? Me too . . . but I haven't had time to do any painting for years."

"Why don't we all go downstairs and eat, and we can talk more about running and painting," Diego said.

He gestured toward the door, to indicate they should precede him.

CHAPTER NINE

The warm, early fall sunlight was streaming in through the windows as Saoirse looked around in satisfaction. Four months ago, she'd first walked into the lab and felt a thrill of ownership that she'd never felt before. Now the stations had been redesigned to meet her specifications, and the equipment she wanted had been added. This was the freshman bio class, and the students were all busy working on a research project. Each group had their own thesis, and the steady hum of their conversations let her know they were actually working, not just wasting time.

Even though I never wanted to be a teacher, I'm happier doing this than anything I've ever done before!

Suddenly one of the boys stopped working and stood still, staring off into space. The girl he was working with poked him in the arm, then in the ribs, and got no reaction from him. "Um, Miss McColl? I think there's something wrong with Caleb." The girl looked panicked when he bent over double and began to moan.

Saoirse rushed over to check on Caleb, horrified to hear repeated cracking sounds. "Oh my God!" She ran back to her teacher station to push the red button that Diego had shown her. He'd explained it was for emergencies only, and help would come quickly.

Within seconds, Diego pushed the door open and came into the room. "Are you all right?" he asked.

She gestured toward Caleb. "He's having some kind of seizure, I think . . ."

He glanced quickly at the boy, then spoke into his walkie-talkie as he walked over to the student. "Need a med-security team to the science lab ASAP. Student in *first* trouble."

Diego cleared students and furniture away from the boy. He was blocking Saoirse's view, so she couldn't see what was going on. She moved for a better look.

Diego turned to her and shook his head. "Don't worry. We got this."

The door burst open as three security guards rushed in with a stretcher. They got the student onto it with some difficulty, since he was moving around a lot while moaning loudly. Together with Diego, they surrounded him and carried him out of the classroom.

Saoirse looked around in shock. Noticing all the students' tense faces, she realized it was up to her to say something. "Um, I'm sure Caleb will be fine. We have excellent medical care here, and Mr. Vargas took prompt action. The best thing you can do is get back to your research."

"Will he be all right, Miss McColl?" his partner asked.

"I hope so. We'll find out as soon as Mr. Vargas has something to report."

Reluctantly, the students returned to their work. Saoirse went over to the girl who was Caleb's partner. "Why don't you explain to me where you two were in your research, so I can help you with it for a while?"

"Um . . . okay."

The end of the class period seemed to take forever to arrive. Finally, the bell rang for the end of the school day. The students were subdued as they cleaned up the lab and gathered their things to depart. Saoirse was walking around checking to be sure that all the equipment had been put away and everything was unplugged.

She was in the back of the lab when she saw Diego walk into the classroom. "I'm back here," she called out. She moved quickly over to him. "Is Caleb all right?"

He nodded. "Yes, he'll be fine. He's never had this kind of seizure before, but the nurse said he appears to be out of any danger now. We called the doctor and his parents, and he's resting quietly now."

"Can I go see him?"

He shook his head, "Not yet. Let's give him time to sleep. It's the best thing for him right now."

Saoirse leaned against a student desk and hugged herself. "It was so scary. I've seen epileptic seizures before, and I've seen junkies having over-dose reactions that were pretty intense. But I've never heard anything like the bone-cracking sounds that were coming from Caleb."

"Bone-cracking? Maybe he hit an arm or leg on the desk. That's probably what you heard. I'm telling you, he's okay now. The danger is over."

"I guess . . . will you let me see him when he's able to have visitors?"

"Of course. You look kind of stressed. The school day's over. Do you want to go for a run with me? We've only done the shorter trails before, since you said you hadn't run much lately and wanted to work your way back up to doing more distance. But you've been running consistently for a while now. I think I'll show you the special place that I like to go when I'm in the mood for painting. We don't have time to paint today, but we can still admire nature's bounty. There are lovely flowers and trees all around the shorter trails, but the view along this one is spectacular."

When Saoirse looked undecided, he approached her and patted her arm, speaking gently. "Come on. You've been working too hard, and now you've had a bad shock. Doing a good, long run with some scenic views to admire will help you recover. You need to take better care of yourself. I don't want my best bio teacher burning out from exhaustion." He leaned closer. "I haven't shared this place with anyone else, you know. It will be our little secret."

She gave him a grim smile. "Okay, I guess that might be a good idea."

"Excellent! Lock up, get changed, and meet me out front in, say, twenty minutes?"

Just shy of twenty minutes later, Diego stopped in his tracks, not even remembering to breathe. His body reacted to seeing a great deal more of the woman he was craving.

Saoirse was in her running shorts with an oversized tank top on over her jogging bra. She was bending over, doing some preliminary stretches, so luckily, she didn't see his expression when he walked out the door. He groaned quietly when her tiny shorts rode up, exposing the rounded curves of the top of her thighs.

Gradually he became aware that some of the grounds crew, who were out working on the flowers nearby, had stopped cultivating and were also unabashedly enjoying the view. His wolf growled softly. Not loud enough for her to hear, but loud enough for the more sensitive hearing of the gardeners to notice. They glanced at him before quickly returning to their work. He took a calming breath before approaching the woman of his desires. "That's one of the things I like about you." Diego hoped he managed to keep his voice sounding conversational. "You're so prompt."

Saoirse shrugged. "You said twenty minutes. It didn't take me that long to change, since I've been running with Jerene on Tuesday and Thursday afternoons and with you on Saturdays. Plus I've been doing some cross-fit stuff like weights and stretches in the gym on alternate days. So my work-out stuff hasn't been getting put away."

"That's okay. That's Pearl's job, anyway. She takes care of

your wing in the mansion."

They began to walk across the grounds, heading for the edge of the forest, where the trails started.

Saoirse shook her head. "You know, I was freaked out the first couple of times she let herself in with the passkey when I was in there. I was even more unnerved when I'd get back to find that someone had rearranged my things while I wasn't there. I'm a big girl . . . I don't need someone cleaning up after me. After the first few times she surprised me while I was doing yoga, or taking a nap, I asked her to just come into my place only once a month. That's often enough for her to change the sheets and clean the bathroom. Other than that, I can dust and put things away myself."

Diego shot her a sideways glance, "You really are an independent sort of woman, aren't you?"

She nodded. "Does that bother you?"

"*Díos mio*, no. I find it refreshing. My mom was the epitome of old-fashioned femininity, a kind of southern belle, even though she wasn't from the south. She'd lie around on the couch, complaining to the nanny about how exhausted us kids made her, then yell at the maid when her cleaning woke Mom up from her nap."

"Wow! You could afford a maid growing up? My mom *was* a maid for a while, until she took enough classes to get certified as a secretary. Then at least she could sit while she worked, and the hours were more regular.

"Being the eldest daughter, I was expected to do all the housework at home. I used to resent the boys who only had to do the sporadic stuff, like mowing the lawn or shoveling the snow. Once Mom decided she was a feminist, though, that changed for my brothers, to their eternal unhappiness. That's when the chores got divvied up on a rotation schedule. I got to sometimes enjoy the smell of grass when it's being mowed, and the boys got to have cracked fingernails from washing dishes by hand."

They had reached the start of one of the trails, but Diego kept walking along the edge, heading them in a different direction than they had run before. When he reached his destination, he stopped and pointed.

Saoirse's eyebrows rose. "That's the trail? It looks like a deer path . . . hardly wide enough for us to run together."

"We'll have to run single file. Since I know where we're going, I'll go first. Trust me, the view will be worth it. It's a longer run, but it's been a rough week. We both have some tension to run off. We do want to be back by dinner, so I'm going to go at a fast pace. Is that all right with you?"

"Lead on, boss."

Saoirse realized she wasn't paying much attention to the flora and fauna around her after a few minutes of trotting along behind Diego. *You sure were right about the view! Dude, if those shorts got any shorter, they wouldn't qualify as suitable to be worn in public! But I don't mind at all. I already knew you have really muscular legs, to go along with the rest of you. But your ass? Holy shit! The view is already definitely worth it!*

He kept increasing the pace until Saoirse had to concentrate fully on her breathing and keeping up with him. She was glad she'd been running regularly, both with Jerene and with him. Otherwise, she wouldn't have been able to maintain that kind of pace for long.

She had no idea how long they'd been running when he slowed down so quickly that she bumped into the back of him. "Sorry!" she squeaked, wondering if she'd be bruised from running into the solid wall of muscle in front of her.

He turned to speak over his shoulder. "No, my fault. I just thought you might want to go at a slower pace for a while since this is where the scenery starts to get really beautiful."

He was right. There was a stream running parallel to their

path, with wildflowers growing in profusion on both sides of it. Ahead, giant rock formations promised enterprising climbers would be able to see for miles around if they were willing to do the work required to get to the tops.

After trotting along at a leisurely pace, he slowed to a stop, this time making sure he gave her advance warning by waving at her. "Just past these trees over here, then we're at my special place."

They walked through the trees to end up in a glade, with the stream burbling through it and the sounds of nature caressing her ears. All around her bugs were buzzing, frogs croaking, birds singing, and the distant sound of a woodpecker looking for a meal.

Diego gestured for her to sit and gracefully folded his legs to end up sitting cross-legged on the grass. Saoirse plopped down, panting, her legs sprawled out in front of her.

"Phew! That was quite a run! I'm sure glad I've been gradually increasing my time running, or I'd never have been able to keep up with you."

He grinned. "That's why I've never taken you this way before."

He reached into the fanny pack he had around his waist and pulled out a couple of water bottles and a paper bag. "Water?"

She nodded gratefully. "Yes, please."

After handing her a bottle, they both drank about half of the water. Then he reached into his bag again. "Cookie?"

"What? Did you raid the kitchen before we started?"

"Guilty as charged, ma'am. But I figured we'd need the energy. Plus, I can never get enough of Janine's oatmeal walnut chocolate chip cookies, since everyone else likes them, too. So I grabbed a few off the dessert table as I cut through the dining room to get outside." He leaned forward conspiratorially, looking around furtively. "As long as she doesn't have spies out here, and you don't rat me out, we're fine."

She giggled. "No, I won't tell on you. As long as you give me another cookie."

"I brought four, so there're two for each of us."

Saoirse chewed the second one more slowly and drank a bit more of the water. She scooted over to lean her back against a nearby tree and sighed with satisfaction. "It's a gorgeous afternoon, those were great cookies, and it's been a good run, so far."

"I didn't go too fast and leave you behind? You seemed to be keeping up."

"No, it's fine. I enjoyed it."

He stretched his legs out and leaned backward, supporting himself with his elbows under his shoulders. Saoirse tried not to stare at the six-pack that revealed itself under the shirt, now wet with sweat and clinging to his torso. When she looked back at his face, she was surprised at how intent he looked as he spoke.

"So, how do you feel about the job, now that you've been here four months?"

Saoirse met his gaze with equal intensity. "I've never been so challenged in my life. But I've also never enjoyed myself so much at any job. I'm spending lots of time finding projects for the students to research, and I've found a couple that I'd love to work on myself if only I could spare the time. Part of why I designed the lab the way I did was to give myself a space to do real research also." She looked away guiltily, then gave him a small smile. "If that's all right with you."

He nodded. "I knew you were dedicated to research when I spoke to your former employers who bitched about you refusing to find what they wanted you to find. And when I spoke to you, you were honest about wanting to redo the lab. I figured it was because you were hoping to find a project to interest you in your spare time. Presumably, you will be able

to carve out more time for yourself once you're more acclimated to the demands of the teaching life."

"I hope so. I never expected to enjoy teaching so much. The
students keep me on my toes, and sometimes they amaze me
with their insights. Or they make me laugh. So to answer your
question, I'm happy with my job." She looked down to flick a
bug off her leg. "Are *you* happy with the job I'm doing?"

"I'm totally pleased with it. I've spoken to a lot of the students, and they all agree that you are more demanding than
our old bio teacher was, but that they are enjoying learning
how to be scientists from you. And you're *chillaxed* with
them—though I had to ask them what that meant."

Saoirse grinned. "It's a *portmanteau*—when you combine
two words to make a new one. Like combining spoon and
fork to make *spork*. Or ecology with tourism to make *ecotour-
ism*. Or information with entertainment to make *infotainment*.
So they combine chilled with relaxed. "

"Yeah, that's what they told me. They even used the word
portmanteau. That's another thing. Nathan tells me the students have begun using words he's never heard before, and
when he asks them where they got them, they always say
from you. So the bio teacher is also expanding our students'
vocabularies to include complex words. Good job."

Saoirse shrugged, "I've always been a voracious reader,
and that's how you expand your vocabulary. Plus, my parents
never talked down to us, but used multiple-syllable words,
expecting us to ask them if we didn't know what it meant.
Dad was a carpenter and Mom a secretary, but they both took
online college classes as a hobby, teaching us to regard learning as a lifetime challenge."

"Good idea. Jerene and Mike have both said that some of
their more reluctant learners are asking for extra math help,
because they say they need it to be able to complete their labs
for you, and they're embarrassed to let you know they're

having trouble. So you're inspiring them to do better in math, as well. Excellent job. Joe is really pleased that he's hearing such good things about you."

"How's he doing these days? He hasn't been down in the dining room the last few days. Is his health taking a turn for the worse?"

Diego grimaced. "Unfortunately, yes. It's got everyone on edge since he's been in charge around here for so long. Some are worried about the upheaval there will be when he finally succumbs to his cancer."

"You are all so healthy, I'm surprised that anyone even gets sick. I've never seen anyone more than mildly overweight, and everyone seems to be seriously into running and using the gym. If I didn't know better, I'd wonder if this was some kind of cult . . . dedicated to fitness training."

He smiled as if she had said something amusing. Then he sat up, plucking a long blade of grass to swat a bug off his arm. "We all just love the outdoors. In the summer we're all running and swimming in the lake. In the winter, we all wear snowshoes and hike around until the snow is packed enough to resume running. There aren't any big enough hills for downhill skiing, or we'd be doing that, too. But there are cross-country skis in the big shed, for anyone to use. And of course, if you want to be warm, there's the indoor pool in the gym building that's available for year-round use."

"What kind of cancer does Joe have?"

Diego grimaced again. "The kind that many of the first re-sponders got from digging through the rubble of nine-eleven, in New York. He led a team of volunteers from here to go help when the call went out. They spent three weeks there, trying to save as many lives as possible. The after-effects took a while to manifest. When they did, we had to call in Dr. Chen from Portland. She's an expert in respiratory cancers and has treated many of those now suffering from their bravery."

"Wow! I already admired him for how well this place is run since he's in charge. Now my opinion of him has increased exponentially! And to think, at his age, he'd have gone down there."

"How old do you think he is?"

Saoirse shrugged, "I don't know . . . maybe seventy-five or eighty?"

Diego shook his head, "He's ninety-eight."

"What? So he was in his late seventies when he went down there?"

"Yes. You could attribute it to good genetics, or to the healthy lifestyle we all share around here. But without the cancer, he'd probably still have another ten to twenty years left in him."

"Wow! Just another reason for me to keep at my fitness routine."

"How old do you think I am?"

"About twenty-five? I know you're younger than me."

"Not by as much as you think. I'm thirty-one."

"I can only hope moving here is as healthy for me as it obviously is for all of you."

They were both quiet, for a few minutes, drinking from their water bottles, until Diego broke the silence with another question. "How do you feel, personally, about living here? Are you adapting to the silence and the isolation?"

She grinned. "I don't get much silence when I'm in class with the kids. They're noisy all the time. I wish I could bottle their energy . . . I could make a fortune selling it. So when I do get time off, I enjoy not having to interact with anyone, unless I want to. I mean, the meals are communal, but I usually enjoy that."

"You can always ask for something to be sent up to your room if you don't feel like talking to anyone. That's why you have a dining area in your suite."

"Thanks. That's good to know if I ever feel like eating by myself. I have a lot of solo hobbies, like reading, and I like to do yoga in my room. Plus, now that I have access to some art supplies, I've been doing some painting again, which I haven't been able to do for years. So yeah, I've been enjoying living here."

"I know we don't have much in the way of nightlife. There aren't any clubs for attractive young women like you to go partying the night away. The closest town is Bingham, and they roll their sidewalks up after dinner and turn out the lights."

"I never did get much into clubbing. I mean, I went with Freddie and Jorge when I was living with them, since their friends were all into that. But it's not really my scene. Don't get me wrong, I do like to dance and party, but not as much as I did in my younger, more rebellious days. Ten years ago, I'd have thought this place was too remote. Now I like the peace and quiet."

He was sitting right in front of her, and she watched his face. His lips quirked upwards briefly before he glanced away. She sensed some hesitation in his silence.

"Is there anything else you want to ask me?"

He was silent for just a heartbeat, before turning to stare directly into her eyes. "Would it be all right with you if I kiss you?"

She boldly returned his gaze, "I wish you would."

He leaned closer, and she closed her eyes as their lips met. The tingles she felt from that tiny connection with him surprised her. It was like an electric jolt that traveled down her throat, making her nipples tighten with excitement. The sensation moved lower, warming her abdomen, to zero in on her clit, newly alive and throbbing. With a low moan, she leaned into the kiss, wanting more.

Diego moaned at Saoirse's response to the kiss. Internally, he was fighting a battle for control with his wolf. It was fully awake and making demands in a language that only he understood.

Take her now! She belongs to us!

No! She's not pack. She doesn't know what that would mean.

No matter. She will learn. She will be pack.

Not yet!

Hear her? Smell her? She wants. Take her!

No!

He was startled by the sudden noise of branches being trampled nearby and a growling sound.

Diego pulled back from the kiss to turn his head in the direction of the sound and inhale deeply. Instantly, he reached out with the hand he'd been caressing her with and covered her mouth. He shook his head, silently asking her to not make a sound.

A mama Black Bear with two cubs emerged from the brush only a few feet away from them. The family lumbered by them, heading for the stream. Once she was downwind from them, she turned and saw them. She regarded them gravely, grunting a warning to her cubs as she took a step nearer to where he and Saoirse sat.

Diego made a low growling sound in his throat, and the bear stopped. She turned back to the cubs and headed up the stream, herding them along with her, quickly put distance between them.

When Diego was satisfied that the danger was over, he took his hand off Saoirse's mouth. "Are you okay?"

She nodded weakly. "I've never seen a bear that close. I've never seen a bear not in a zoo before. That was terrifying and exciting, all at the same time!"

He stood up and offered her a hand to pull her up. "The danger is over, for now. Just the same, it's getting late, and we want to be back in time for some dinner."

"How did you do that growling thing that convinced her to leave?"

He shrugged. "You live around here long enough, you learn ways to convince the locals to leave you alone. We were intruding on her home territory. I tried to let her know we were leaving. So we need to make good on that promise. Are you ready?"

"Wow. Just, wow. Maybe you can teach me that someday?"

Diego didn't know how to respond, so he turned back to the path they'd come on and walked quickly towards the woods. When he didn't hear her footsteps, he looked back to see Saoirse watching the bears in the stream. He cleared his throat to get her attention. She turned toward him with an expression he couldn't read, but she followed him back to the part of this wilderness where they belonged.

CHAPTER TEN

Saoirse stuck her tongue out at herself in the mirror, "Get a hold of yourself, Sam! You've spent all week obsessing over one little kiss. Diego hasn't been avoiding me, but he hasn't gone out of his way to be alone with me either. I think he enjoyed it as much as I did. His pulse was racing, even before the bear appeared. I could feel it in his fingertips when he touched my face. I wonder when I'll ever get another chance with him."

She continued getting ready for her classes by applying the minimal makeup she usually wore, a few dabs of powder to tone down her freckles and a trace of peach lipstick to complement the green color of her polo shirt. She pulled a brush through her thick hair, noticing how long it was getting. "No way to get a haircut out here unless I want to drive into Bingham. And my unruly curls always defeat stylists until they get the hang of working with it. I guess now is as good a time as any to grow it out and see if I like it long."

Satisfied that she was presentable, she winked at herself in the mirror. "Happy Friday." She grabbed the notes she needed for the day and locked her door on the way out.

When she got to the dining room, she was surprised by the air of expectant excitement that seemed to have gripped all the other residents. Even people who were usually taciturn were smiling. When she went up to the buffet to get her breakfast, she overheard a few others saying things like *Happy day,* and *It's going to be a good one, I can tell.*

She, on the other hand, was greeted with the same

pleasantries she'd received since she first moved in. People greeted with the usual *Good morning*, and *It looks to be a nice day, today.*

She decided she must be imagining things and sat down to eat her breakfast. Jerene and her kids joined her, and the antics of the little ones were enough to make her laugh, which chased away any questions she might have had.

Her classes all went well, with the students even more cooperative than normal. A few of the older students seemed more excited than normal. Otherwise, her day was uneventful. When it was time for the last period students to file in, she was pleased to see a familiar face had returned. "Caleb! So good to see you. Are you feeling better?"

He nodded with a big smile. "Of course, Miss McColl. That's why I'm here."

"Did you ever find out what happened to you?"

His face became guarded. "Yes. It wasn't any big deal. Nothing to worry about. I'm fine . . . really. Can you give me the work I missed all week?"

She got involved with filling him in on what he had to make up. Then she explained to the others what they were going to work on that day. The hour flew by, and soon the students were cleaning up their labs and walking out the door.

"Bye, Miss McColl. Have a great weekend!"

"See ya, Miss McColl. Hope it's a good one for you."

After they had all left, she did her usual walk around, checking to be sure that everything had been unplugged, cleaned up, and put away. Then she went to the front of the room and sat on her stool, making notes about how the period had gone.

When she was done, she stared off into space for a moment. *I was so glad to see Caleb back. He looks great. Even healthier than before. But one thing was weird. The other kids used to ignore him unless they had to partner with him. But today, everyone seemed to be treating him with newfound respect. It was almost like he did something special. I guess it could be because he survived whatever it was that gave him that seizure. But still . . . I wonder what's up.*

After she locked her door, she purposely walked by the principal's office, hoping Diego would want to run with her, as he often did on Friday afternoons. But his door was shut and locked. She was glad there wasn't anyone else in the hall to see the disappointment she was sure her face reflected.

She walked back to her suite, meaning to change right away and go for a quick run before dinner. But she remembered she had a letter from her parents, so she sat down and read it, savoring news from home. Soon she was laughing at the descriptions of things her nieces and nephews were doing to irritate their parents. All of which her parents were very much enjoying, now that it wasn't *their* kids doing the misbehaving.

When she finally looked up, it was getting close to dinner time, but she still wanted to run. She changed quickly, then went downstairs and checked with Janine in the kitchen. She asked if she could have a dinner plate sent up to her room in about an hour and a half.

Janine gave her a disapproving look. "Why? You're not planning on running for that long, are you? It's getting late."

Saoirse nodded. "I'll be careful," she said as she grabbed a water bottle from the drinks fridge and headed out to hit the medium-length trail.

The weather was perfect since it was still warm-ish, but there was a slight breeze to keep the late seasonal bugs away. The run was so enjoyable that she extended it a little bit further than she had planned on doing. *Oh well. If I get back to find my dinner has cooled off, I can reheat it in the microwave. No harm done.*

When she was on her way back, near the beginning of the trail, she stopped to finish off her water bottle. It was then she looked around and realized that it was getting dark. The sun had already set, and the night was rolling in much quicker than she had expected it to. *Damn! Diego warned me about this . . .*

Suddenly she heard the unmistakable sounds of wolves howling, and they weren't from a distance. They sounded like they were right next to her! Or around her! Or in front of her!

Fear gripped her heart, and she ran faster, willing herself not to panic. She desperately searched for the clearing that was right before the tree line that signaled the edge of the forest, and the beginning of the human habitat area. Finally! She raced into the clearing and stopped dead in her tracks.

It was slightly lighter in the clearing now that she was out of the woods. The large, black wolf she'd seen a few times at night was sitting there, staring right at her as if he had been expecting her. She was so unnerved she barely noticed what covered the circle of benches and the ground all around him. She could feel her heart pounding so quickly that she worried that she might be having a heart attack. And the drumming was so loud in her ears that she was sure the wolf could hear it also.

She spoke out loud, partly to try to control her own anxiety, and partly hoping to calm the savage beast with a steady voice . . . as she might do with a large dog. "Hey there, I've seen you before, haven't I? You're the one who sits at the edge of the forest at night and appears to be looking up at my window. I know, crazy, right? Why would you care where I am? What makes me think I'm so important?"

She sidled along the edge of the clearing, giving the wolf a large berth, trying to make her way past him to the last line of trees before she'd be out of the woods entirely. "You almost look like you understand what I'm saying. But that's silly, right? Just like those piles of clothing that are near you. There are shirts and pants together with shoes . . . even underwear. Like people had stripped naked and left them where they could find them again when they came back. But that's insane! Came back from where? And it's night, so it's getting chilly. Who wants to be wandering around on a cold evening, naked? It's not like it's a good night to go skinny-dipping or anything."

The wolf still watched her closely but had not moved. She was almost to the trees. "I mean, you have fur and all, so you're not cold, right? If I had fur, I'd be happy to be out here, naked. Because then . . ." Her eyes grew wide, her mouth dropped open as an extraordinary epiphany popped into her head. Right behind the wolf, where she could clearly see it now, was the t-shirt she had seen Diego wear many times when they were running together. It was folded neatly on top of a pair of jeans, with his running shoes next to the pile. She froze in her tracks, unable to move, or even to breathe, as she stared at the wolf's eyes . . . dark brown eyes . . . the same color as Diego's eyes . . .

The wolf stood up, breaking the spell. With a gasp, Saoirse took off running toward the trees. She ran as if her life depended on it. In minutes, she was at the end of the trees and burst through them into the grassy area that began the academy grounds.

She didn't stop running until she reached the front steps leading up to the entrance. She pelted up the stairs and quickly opened the door, slammed it behind her, and turned to run up the stairs to her suite. With her heart chugging like a train engine, she frantically felt in her bra for her key, then opened the door and fell through it into her room. She slammed that door also, locked it, and put on the chain, which meant no one, even with a passkey, could enter. Then she ran into the bathroom, locked that door also, and she collapsed onto the toilet and burst into terrified tears.

CHAPTER ELEVEN

Saoirse didn't get much sleep that night. After her terror-induced tears, she'd stripped and taken a long, hot shower, trying to ease her aching muscles. Then she'd wrapped herself in a fluffy robe and opened the door, peeking outside to be sure no one had entered the suite while she was in the bathroom.

The place was, of course, empty. She noticed the balcony door was open, as usual, to let in the cool night breezes. She didn't know much about wolves, but she didn't think they'd be able to jump up to the third floor, so she controlled her panic enough to leave the door open.

She found a note on the table telling her that her dinner was in the fridge with instructions on how long to heat it up. She grabbed the meal, placed it in the microwave, and started it. She took out the bottle of Prosecco that seemed to magically replace itself each time she finished a bottle. She poured herself a glass and went over to sit on the couch. She pulled her legs up and protectively wrapped her arms around her knees. She sat like that while waiting for the food to heat up.

I don't know why I'm even bothering. I don't even feel hungry. I may never feel hungry again. I don't know what to think or feel anymore. What I suspect is so absurd I can't even put it into words . . . even in my own mind. It's not possible. It would be a scientific anomaly, and those are extremely rare. But this borders on the paranormal, therefore it can't be possible. The only explanation that makes sense is that I imagined it all. There can't have been clothing there. It must have been just piles of old stuff . . . maybe meant to be given away.

The ding from the microwave let her know her food was ready. Reluctantly, she rose and went over to pull out the plate. She breathed in the smell of veggie lasagna. The mixture of tomato, garlic, and cheese wafted through the air, making her stomach growl.

Too bad I can't do that sound in my throat too . . . just in my stomach! She choked back a laugh that threatened to turn to hysteria. Her mind presented her with images out of horror movies, juxtaposed over the familiar face of the man she had been hoping to get to know much better.

She managed to eat some of her dinner, then finished the rest of the bottle of sparkling wine. She tried to read for a while, but her thoughts raced around in her mind like squirrels on amphetamines. She gave up and walked over to sit out on the balcony. She was out there a long time, listening to the formerly comforting, now newly menacing sounds of the wolves enjoying the forest at night.

Eventually, her eyes drooped, and she almost dropped the glass, waking up with a start. She moved into the room and put the glass on her nightstand. She took off the robe and put on a nightgown, then crawled between the sheets and lay there, staring up at the ceiling, until the wee hours of the morning. She knew there was no way she was ever going to feel the same about anything. She cried bitter tears, heartbroken at the idea of having to give up her dream job, along with her hopes and dreams — and returning to Boston and starting a job search all over again.

She had no idea when she finally fell asleep.

Saturday morning Saoirse woke slowly. She hadn't set the alarm, since she was normally awake by seven. Her usual habit for the day was to eat an early breakfast, then go for a run with Diego before she started her planned activities. However, this couldn't possibly be a normal day, now that she knew what she did.

She recalled waking a few times during the night, always with a sense of fear from some unremembered nightmare. When she opened her eyes to bright sunlight, she rolled away from the balcony to shield her from the light and maybe get more sleep.

Suddenly, the noise that must have woken her started again. She sat up quickly and listened. *Someone's knocking on the door! What am I going to do? I don't want to talk to anyone! I just want to be left alone. I want to sleep until I can wake up and have this whole nightmare be over . . . and I can laugh about how foolish I was.*

The pounding did not let up. In fact, it got louder. She rose out of bed and pulled her fluffy robe on over her nightgown. She slowly walked toward the door, hoping against hope that if she stalled long enough, the person knocking would go away. They didn't. She leaned her head close to the door and asked, "Who is it?"

"It's Diego. You slept through breakfast, so I brought some food and coffee up for you. Please let me in."

"I don't want to see you."

"Saoirse, please. We need to talk."

He knows! Oh, my fucking God! He knows! I was right! How else could he know that we need to talk? She tried not to sound as frightened as she felt. "Just leave the tray outside the door. I'll get it later . . . when I'm feeling better."

"Saoirse, I'm not going away. And I'm trying to be polite here, by telling you I borrowed a passkey."

She glanced at the chain on the door, realizing with relief that it was still attached. "You wouldn't dare . . ."

"Yes, I would. And if you think that tiny chain is going to stop me, think again."

She backed away from the door, trembling, and leaned against the side of the couch. "Promise you won't hurt me?"

Diego let out an audible sigh from the other side of the

door. When he replied, he sounded exasperated. "If I meant you harm, why would I bring you your favorite muffins and jam, along with strawberries, whipped cream, and coffee?"

Might as well get it over with. Better to die with a full stomach, than hungry. Taking a deep breath to screw up her courage, she resolutely walked over to open the chain and the lock, then scampered back to the couch. Once again, she pulled her legs up and wrapped her arms around her shins in a protective crouch.

Diego walked in and closed the door behind him. "I'm not going to lock the door. It's just closed because I want our talk to be private. Is that all right with you?"

She nodded, her eyes wide open, her heart pounding a mile a minute.

He walked over to the coffee table and placed the tray in front of her. He pulled a chair over from the kitchen table and sat with the coffee table between them. When she didn't move, he sighed and poured some coffee from the small thermos into a mug, stirring in some creamer that he'd also remembered to bring. He leaned across the table to hand her the cup, but she still didn't move.

He sighed heavily again and put the mug on the tray, then leaned back in the chair. "I knew this conversation was coming, but I didn't expect it to be so soon."

She merely stared at him, her fear keeping her mute.

"What do you want to ask me? I will tell you everything, but you have to ask. I know you're confused, so I want you to lead." When she didn't respond, he pleaded in a gentle voice. "Please, Saoirse. Have some coffee. Eat something. Say something."

She slowly reached down to pick up the coffee. Her hand shook as she brought it to her lips and took a sip. She cradled the mug, its heat warming her hands. When she tried to speak, her voice cracked, so she coughed, then tried again. Her voice was so raspy from crying that it was almost a whisper. "Was it really you in the woods last night?"

"Yes."

"And all of the other nights when I saw a wolf watching my room? That was you, too?"

"Yes."

"Why?"

"To be sure you were safe."

"From what?"

"From anyone and anything. Just to be protective."

"Why?"

He looked into her eyes. "Just . . . because."

She stared at him, then took another sip of her coffee. She broke off a tiny piece of the muffin and chewed it slowly before taking one more sip. Then she put the mug down and sat up straighter. "Are you a werewolf?"

He nodded. "Yes."

She jumped up and paced over to the window and back again, wringing her hands. "How is that possible? Am I still asleep, and this is a nightmare? Or is it some kind of delusion, and you're trying to get me to share it? Werewolves don't exist. It's a myth . . . like vampires . . . or ghosts. It's not scientifically possible."

"And yet, here I am."

She walked back over and sat on the couch. He smiled, obviously pleased when she tucked her feet next to her and leaned over to pick up the coffee again.

She shook her head. "Are there others here?"

He nodded.

"Everyone?"

He shook his head. "No. Most of the adults are pack. Others are related to or married to one of us."

"Is that even possible?"

He smiled. "Of course. It's encouraged, because otherwise there would be too much inbreeding. You know more about genetics than I do, so you know the science behind what we've always tried to avoid."

"I've been living here for four months. Have you all been walking on eggshells, trying not to let anything slip in front of me?"

He shrugged. "Kind of. I was told I had to be the one to tell you, since I brought you onto the grounds when I hired you. But you were so perfect for the job that I had no other choice. We usually try to add only pack members to our population, but we needed a science teacher quickly. As I told you in the interview, our old biology teacher wanted to retire, but he didn't give me much advance notice. And there isn't a werewolf network where we can advertise for special skills. After all, the internet isn't really safe from spying, and we would be in danger if our . . . ahem . . . secret were to get out. We tend to keep a really low profile in any kind of public space."

She looked down at her hands on the mug, taking a deep breath before looking up into his eyes. "Am I in any kind of danger?"

He smiled. "No, I promise you. Despite my nightly watching of your balcony, there really isn't any harm that could come to you here. You've made a lot of friends since you moved in. Everyone has been anxious for you to accept us as we are, so we could stop worrying that you'd discover our secret and run away."

She dipped a small strawberry into the whipped cream, then chewed it slowly. "In the interview . . . the kids were testing me for my reaction when the wolf walked in and one of them said he was a comfort wolf, right?"

"Yes. They did that to all of the teachers to see who they thought could handle it."

"What about Caleb?"

"It was his first time. He's young for it to have happened already, so we didn't expect it yet. The initial change can be traumatic, especially when it happens during the day, unexpectedly."

"It doesn't need to be during a full moon then? Or even at night?"

He shook his head, "No."

"When I asked to see him, you wouldn't let me. He wasn't really sleeping, was he? He was . . . furry?"

Diego chuckled as he nodded. "Yes, he was furry. Some of the other adults accompanied him on a quick run, so his wolf could enjoy his newfound freedom."

"I did hear bones cracking, didn't I?"

"Yes."

Her scientific interest had been piqued, and curiosity was taking over. "How does that work? Does it hurt?"

He grimaced. "Think about it. You've seen human skeletons, I presume. Have you ever seen a wolf skeleton?"

She nodded.

"There are a whole lot of joints that need to break and reset. Bones need to lengthen or shorten. Organs need to change and rearrange themselves. The whole process is immensely painful. You learn to bear it because you have no choice."

"Then why do it?"

"Change? Because, believe it or not, it hurts more if you don't."

"Why?"

"Because the wolf wants to get out and will make you suffer if you don't let it."

She furrowed her brows, "Then it's like you have a split personality? There are two of you, living in your head?"

"Yeah, kind of. Living in harmony with your other half becomes easier when you realize that since you're stuck with each other, you need to compromise. Both of you get a chance to be in charge. The wolf will usually be happy with an occasional run in the woods at night. The human gets to run things the rest of the time."

"Did you still understand me when I was talking to you?"

"Yes, but of course, I couldn't answer you. Different vocal cords and all."

She was fascinated and appalled at the same time. "So is this whole compound for the pack?"

"Yes."

"Why run a school?"

"Because we never know which kids are going to become one of us until puberty hits, and it either manifests itself or it doesn't. People wanted a safe place for their kids to learn while knowing that if it happened here, we'd know how to safely guide them into being able to control themselves."

"Couldn't their parents just take care of it?"

"Twenty-four-seven? While they were in school? With two-income families who have to work long hours? No. Besides, sometimes it skips a generation. And sometimes it appears out of nowhere. Two *weres* can have normal kids, and two normal parents can produce a *were*. There's no way to predict who it will happen to."

"Seriously? You have no idea? It's got to be a recessive gene, somehow. Or maybe it's something in the blood."

He shrugged. "Who knows? But it's not the kind of thing you can go to a doctor for answers about. Nor are there any of us willing to go public about wanting to do research into the biology of werewolves, since we're not even supposed to exist."

Diego slowly began to rise. "I'm going to get up now. I'm telling you because I don't want to spook you. I think you have enough to think about for now, so I'll leave you to finish your breakfast. Of course, we all want you to stay. But we'll understand if you don't want to. Let me know what you decide." He walked over to the door, turning when he got his hand on the handle. "Let me know if you have any other questions. You know where to find me."

He opened the door and stood there for a long moment, head bowed, before turning back to look at her. "Saoirse," he began hesitantly, "I'm sorry for putting you through this. I . . . I really hope you stay." He went through the door, pulling it closed behind him.

Saoirse got up and walked over to lock the door. She smiled to herself at the futile gesture when she put the chain back on also. Then she walked over to finish the rest of her breakfast and do some serious thinking.

CHAPTER TWELVE

After breakfast and a long, hot shower, Saoirse was once again sitting on the couch. She had finished the coffee and started drinking ice water to get herself hydrated enough to go running sometime later in the day. She was still in her robe, with her hair wrapped in a towel. She was rereading the letter from her parents, but not really seeing the words. Her thoughts were racing again, trying to force new patterns on her brain.

There was a light knock on the door, and a voice called out, "Saoirse? It's Jerene. Can I come in? I was wondering if you want lunch sent up, or if you'll be coming down to eat with us."

Saoirse went over and unlocked and opened the door to let her friend in. She was surprised when Jerene pulled her close for a big hug. She relaxed and returned the embrace. When they released each other, Jerene gave her a big smile, grabbed her hand, and led her to the couch. They both sat facing each other.

Jerene took a deep breath, then spoke quickly. "Diego told me he'd talked to you, so I know you're dealing with a shit-load right now. We never meant to turn your world-view up-side-down. But there really isn't any good way to tell some-one you care about that not only do werewolves exist, but you're living in a compound full of them. Oh, but there's nothing to worry about. Any questions?"

Saoirse smiled, feeling herself really relax for the first time in many hours. "Are you?"

Jerene nodded, "Yup. Everyone in my family is except my older sister. She's a lawyer and lives in Portland. She handles any legal issues that the pack might have. Arnold isn't either, but when we met in college, it was combustion at first sight. We were inseparable from then on. I was terrified to tell him, for fear I'd lose him. But when we were getting really serious, and he had taken me to meet his family, I knew I'd have to get it over with. So I went backpacking with him, way up north in Michigan's UP. After dinner one night, I told him I had something to share with him. I told him what I was. Of course, he thought I was joking, or maybe just a touch crazy."

"I know the feeling." Saoirse snickered. "Go on."

"I went to the other side of the campfire from him and shifted. Scared the fuck out of him! Literally. When I shifted back again, he said he was afraid to sleep next to me that night. I shifted again, then ran off into the woods and stayed out all night, howling my pain to the moon. When I got back the next morning, I was afraid he'd be gone, and I'd return to an empty campsite. But he was still there, making coffee. We spent all day talking. At the end of it, he decided that he could accept me as I am if I was willing to do the same for him. There were a lot of tears that day. But that was eight years ago, and here we are."

"What about your kids?"

"They're still too young to know. I'm sure Diego told you that's the whole reason for the school. Puberty is usually the onset of the syndrome—when the wolf first wakes up and starts talking to its host."

Saoirse shook her head. "As a scientist, this is all so unbelievable. But I'm not as freaked out as I was last night when I felt like I'd been hit by a bus. Now I'm starting to get interested in the whole thing. And the idea that no one knows how to tell who inherited it and who didn't? That tells me someone needs to do some research with a lot of blood samples to see

if there are any markers that will allow for accurate predic-
tions."

Jerene smiled broadly. "That would be icing on the cake if
you could find anything out. But the most important thing is
that you feel comfortable enough to stay. We've all been really
happy with your teaching style, and the kids adore you. Some
parents want to shake your hand, to thank you for inspiring
their kids to actually care about science and all their other
classwork. And Dad is thrilled that Diego has found . . ." She
stopped talking, looking embarrassed. "Oops. I didn't mean
to say that. Forget I said anything."

Saoirse reached over and took a drink from her water bottle. "What's the deal with Diego? He hasn't told me much
about himself other than he grew up with a maid and a mom
who didn't want to have much to do with her kids. My mom
was a maid for a while, and kids ruled in our house, since we
outnumbered the adults. So I can't relate in any way to his
upbringing."

Jerene seemed glad to change the subject. "Don't you know
who he is?"

Saoirse shook her head.

"Didn't the last name Vargas give it away?"

"Not really."

"His mom's not as famous now since she's getting older.
But when she was younger, everyone knew who Valerie Vargas was."

Saoirse was surprised. "Oh! You mean the singer who got
her start on that kids' show, then went solo when she got
older, doing shockingly sexy videos to announce that she was
changing her image? Then, when she wasn't in the news anymore, posed naked for *Playboy*? *That* Valerie Vargas?"

"Yup. He left home when his body started to change. He
fell in with some bad packs for a while, then wandered solo
for a long time. He found us almost four years ago. At first,

Dad wasn't sure where to assign him to work, but he has a way of understanding what kids are saying, even when they aren't sure. He started out as a counselor, helping some of the more troubled kids. But when our old principal died, he was the natural choice to take over. And he's proven to be even better than Dad had hoped."

Jerene looked at her watch. "If we're going to make it down in time to get any lunch, we'd better head down soon. Are you coming, or do you want me to have something sent up for you?"

Saoirse got up. "Just give me five minutes to put on some clothes. Then I'll come down with you."

"You're sure?"

"Yeah, I think so. Of course, now I'm going to be looking around at everyone, wondering who is and who isn't. But I'm over the initial shock now, and I want to try to return to my normal routine. That's why I want to go running sometime this afternoon."

"I'm sorry, but I won't be able to go with you. It's our daughter's fourth birthday, and her other grandparents are coming out to the compound for the afternoon party and then staying for dinner. So I'll be busy with them for the rest of the day."

"Do they know?"

Jerene shook her head, giggling. "Oh, Lord no! They're really conservative people. They'd totally lose it! Probably try to rescue their son and their grandkids. Everyone keeps a very low profile when they come here a couple of times a year for the kids' birthday parties. And we make sure they're off the grounds before nighttime."

Saoirse went into the bedroom and changed, then returned wearing jeans and a t-shirt. She found her flip flops under the coffee table and used a banana clip to pull her unruly hair back from her face. "Let's go show everyone I can roll with the punches when I have to. After all, us McColls put up with a lot in the old country, and we had to learn to adapt again when we crossed the pond to get here."

"Good thing you're so flexible, honey."

They walked through the door, and Saoirse locked it. They made their way down the stairs.

"You know, some of my oldest friends call me Sam, because my middle name is Anne, so my initials are S.A.M. Saoirse is a handful of a name. I don't mind."

"Sam? I like it. And you can call me Jerry if you want. Arnold does."

"I don't want to use his pet name for you."

"Oh, believe me, that's not what he calls me during *those moments*."

Saoirse put her hands over her ears. "Don't tell me what he *does* call you! Too much information!"

They were both laughing when they entered the dining room to find it less than half-full, since they were catching the tail end of the lunch hour. They got their food from the buffet and joined Arnold at a big table, where he was trying to get their kids to keep their clothing clean until their grandparents got there.

Saoirse was touched by the number of people who stopped by their table to exchange pleasantries with her. Some she'd barely met before, yet here they were, letting her know with their presence that they knew she was now aware of their secret, and that they were all hoping she could accept it and remain. She grinned, watching the antics of the kids and their parents' comical attempts to control them, and felt like the huge icicle that had formed inside of her was melting.

She wasn't surprised when she felt Diego's presence before she saw him. He walked up to the table from behind her, but somehow, she knew he was there. Jerene looked up, exasperated, but smiled when she saw him.

"Diego! Have you come to dole out some principal-style punishment to my kiddies, who are driving their parents crazy right now?"

"You look like you've got things under control." He grinned, despite the food on the table, the floor, the walls, and the clothing of everyone close to them.

Saoirse felt her heartbeat start to speed up at his nearness but tried not to let it show. She casually flicked a piece of mashed potato off her shirt. "They're just being recalcitrant children because they're excited about the birthday party later. All kids are like that when they're looking forward to something."

"But putting them down for a nap is going to be damn near impossible," Arnold said with a grimace.

"Then don't." Saoirse grinned evilly. "Let them stay up and vibrate with excitement. They'll probably fall asleep with their faces in their food at dinnertime. But at least they'll have enjoyed their day . . . their way."

The adults all laughed.

"Good idea, Sam," Jerene said. "I keep forgetting that even though you're not a mom, you had so many younger siblings that you have years of experience with this sort of behavior."

Jerene and Arnold now wrestled their kids out of their chairs and trundled them off, herding them out of the room, presumably to clean them up again before their grandparents arrived. Diego sat at one of the semi-clean places at the table and looked expectantly at Saoirse.

"What?" She asked him.

"Recalcitrant?"

"Willfully disobedient."

"Ah. As a principal speaking to parents, I'll find that one useful. You know, we missed our run this morning. Do you still want to run today?"

"I did just finish eating. I'll need some time to digest."

He nodded and looked at his watch. "And I've got another hour or so of paperwork that I need to get done. How about if we meet by the trailhead at two?"

"Sounds good to me. I got a letter from my parents that I want to answer. They want to know all about my new job . . . and my living arrangements."

His expression turned serious as he stared at her. "What are you going to tell them?"

She gave him a withering look. "Not everything, duh! They'd be sending a paddy wagon to take me away in an attractive jacket that ties along the back. I have no intention of spending any time in a padded room just because I've found out that some people are very different from others. We Irish can roll with the punches. I'll tell them how much I like teaching, and what a beautiful area this is to live in. And I'll leave it at that."

He got up, nodding. "Then I'll see you soon."

"It's a date," she said. She blushed when he turned back to stare at her in surprise.

His lips curved upward, "Yes. It is." Then he turned and walked out of the dining room, heading in the direction of the school.

She enjoyed watching his ass as he walked away, then headed upstairs to write . . . and to ponder the eccentricities that life continued to amaze her with.

CHAPTER THIRTEEN

When Diego reached the trailhead, he once again found Saoirse stretching her legs before the run. His wolf, who always perked up whenever they were near her, began to growl softly with desire. He tried to ignore it, hoping his cock would calm down before he started running. Because just looking at her was enough to make his recalcitrant organ misbehave. He smiled to himself. *She's got me using her big words now, too. There's so much more I want to learn about you, Saoirse. And so much I want to tell you about me. I just hope you'll stay, so I get a chance to let you know how I feel about you.*

"Ready?" She asked when she noticed he was near.

"Yes. Do you want to do the longer trail that we did the last time or one of the shorter ones?"

She frowned. "I'm not sure I'm ready to do that one again . . . yet."

He nodded and hid his disappointment because he understood. She was asking him to back off while she processed the shock she'd received last night. But she appeared, at least for now, to be staying!

"Of course. Then let's do one of the medium-range ones, so we can get a good distance in, but it won't take as long."

Saoirse loped alongside Diego in an easy rhythm. She noticed he had his fanny pack on again, so she knew he had brought water and maybe a snack for them to recharge with at the halfway point. She also noticed he was not wearing the t-shirt she'd seen on the ground last night. Nor was he wearing his usual running shoes. She smiled to herself, grateful that he was taking such care with her feelings. *I need to let him know that I'm coping better than I was this morning . . . and certainly better than last night!*

Since they had run this trail many times, Saoirse knew they were getting close to the place where they would stop and rest before returning. She put on a burst of speed and surprised Diego by beating him to the grassy area, which was matted down from years of runners stopping there. With a happy sigh, she plopped herself down and leaned her back against a tree. "Phew! It may be fall, but it's pretty warm out for October."

She covertly enjoyed the view of Diego opening his fanny pack to take out two water bottles and hand one to her. He opened his and took a long drink, his Adam's apple bobbing as he swallowed. Then he pulled out a couple of giant cookies, which were partially crumbled. "Cookie?" he asked as he handed her the bag.

She looked at what he was holding and asked, "Oatmeal?"

"Peanut butter chocolate chip, with oatmeal so you can call it health food. Another of my favorites."

"Ooh, mine too!" She took a bite of the crunchy cookie and chewed slowly, savoring the taste. "I love the *mélange* of flavors. Is there any better combination than peanut butter and chocolate? A marriage made in heaven!"

He shook his head, grinning. "*Mélange*? I feel like I'm in English class when I'm with you. If I didn't know better, I'd think you were an English teacher. But I know you're a scientist."

"S'okay," she said with a mouthful of cookie. "All of the McColl kids got teased at school for our use of words that even the English teachers didn't know. Plus, we sometimes pronounced things with the Irish accent we'd all acquired from our parents, so we were also told we talked funny and should go back to where we came from."

"That's typical of how cruel kids can be," Diego observed.

"No matter. My brothers and I usually ended the discussion by punching someone. Nothing like a black eye, bloody nose, or split lip to convince them they should keep their opinions to themselves."

He snorted a laugh. "Really? You're so beautiful that I find it hard to think of you as a scrappy little girl, punching some boy in the face, with your long, red curls bouncing in the wind."

"That's how Freddie and I got to be such good friends. He got called *faggot* and *gay*, and sometimes the n-word, back when I didn't even know what those things meant. What I did know was that my best friend was being insulted, and that some boys were threatening him. So I let them know he had a crew of his own, even if that was just one angry Irish girl who knew how to fight."

He scooted back to lean against a tree across from her, mirroring her position.

"I could have used a friend like you, back then."

"Why?"

"Have you ever heard of Valerie Vargas?"

She nodded. "Child star on a TV show turned solo singer when she hit puberty. Then posed for *Playboy* soon after that."

He nodded soberly. "Yeah. Talk about being harassed by other kids? Try having bigger boys tell you they whacked off every night to the fold-out of your mom. They'd talk about her tits, her privates . . . anything to get me pissed off enough to hit someone. Then they'd beat the crap out of me when I tried to defend her. And when we got dragged to the principal's office, they'd all insist that I started it, since I was the one to always throw the first punch."

"Is that when you learned how *not* to behave as a principal?"

He gave her a startled look. "I . . . I guess so. I never thought about it that way. But I spent the better part of my school years in trouble, in one way or another. Middle school was especially rough."

"Amen to that. Middle school is rough for everyone . . . but particularly for those with some difference that others find exploitable."

"High school wasn't much better. By then, Mom had had a couple more kids with different men. I have two half-sisters who are much younger than me. They're both blonde, so we don't look anything alike. And since they were younger and cuter, not to mention blonde and marketable in the tabloids, I was pretty much ignored. When my wolf started to speak to me in my head, I was sure that I was going crazy."

"Wow! What a load of shit to deal with as a young teenager. It's hard enough to change into an adult without finding out that you will be doing other changes as well."

They sat in silence for a few minutes, then Saoirse asked, "Did you ever meet your dad?"

He nodded. "I looked him up after I graduated with my two-year Associates of Sciences degree. He's Hispanic. Mom named me Diego after him since I looked so much like him, even as a baby. But he left her right after I was born. He'd been a dancer on one of her videos when she was in her *slut* phase, doing all her songs half-naked.

"Looking back on it, I don't fault her, since no one really knows what they're doing when they're young and stupid. But she should have given me up for adoption. She was too young and irresponsible for a baby. I was raised by nannies and maids, most of whom were also Hispanic. They felt sorry for *el niño*, the little boy whose mom was too busy being famous to take care of him."

"Is that where you picked up the *español* that you toss into your sentences sometimes?"

"*Sí, señorita.* She paid so little attention that she didn't even realize I was being taught by the hired help to be bi-lingual."

"It's amazing that you are so well-balanced now. You managed to grow up into a responsible person. Jerene says that her dad trusts you a lot, and he's glad that you're here to help him out so much."

She listened attentively when he resumed his story. He talked as if he was compelled to tell her everything about himself.

"After I found my dad, I hung out with him for a while. But it was man-to-man, not father-to-son. He still wasn't married and hadn't taken responsibility for any of the kids he'd fathered. He wasn't even sure how many there were.

"One night, I finally got both of us drunk enough to work up the courage to ask him if there was anything different about us. He growled at me, then began to shift in front of me. I was terrified, because I'd never shifted while drunk before, but him doing it in front of me encouraged my wolf to take over, too. We were in his dinky apartment in the middle of LA, so we had to run a long time before we found any woods. We hunted together, eating what we caught. We fell asleep, and when I woke, I was naked in the woods, and my father was gone. I haven't seen him since that night."

"What a shitty way to treat your own son." Saoirse wavered between anger and sympathy. "You're a credit to your own strength, then, since no one seems to have helped you grow up. You had to do it all by yourself."

"I did find a few packs to belong to, during the years I was wandering around. But I can't for the life of me figure out why they always wanted to live a criminal lifestyle. I would leave when they wanted me to steal things or deal drugs. Just because I can do something that most other humans can't is no reason to think of myself as better than anyone else. And I certainly don't want to prey on others just because they can't do what I can. Live and let live."

"How did you find this place?"

He shrugged. "Just lucky, I guess. I was wandering around the country, trying to find somewhere to belong, but convinced there wasn't any place I'd be able to fit in. I had no job and no money. I was homeless and miserable. But at night, when I shifted, I felt free. I could just be an animal enjoying the smells of the night, and the feel of the grass under my paws. I almost ran right into the fence because I was trying to find where the other wolves' howling was coming from. I saw them on the other side of the fence, and they cleared a path for Joe to come up to the fence to smell me. He nodded, and John had me trot along the fence next to him until we got to the gate. The guards knew who he was and what he wanted. They opened the gate to let me in, and the pack let me hunt with them that night. The next morning, I petitioned to join."

"And the rest, as they say, is history. Joe depends on you. And you're a respected member of a community that just happens to include a lot of people who have wolves living inside of them."

He watched her closely, taking a deep breath before he spoke again. "You . . . ah . . . seem to be taking things a little better than this morning. Certainly, better than last night."

Saoirse chuckled at hearing Diego's opinion of her initial reaction to her discovery. "Just to be clear, I've never been so shocked in my life! All of a sudden, I had to accept something I'd always thought was a myth, was real. And furthermore, that one of them was . . . um . . . the man I'm attracted to."

His eyebrows rose to his hairline, and he gaped for a moment. "Did I just hear what I thought I did?"

"Yes."

"But you didn't want to go on the long run today. I thought . . . I thought you wanted me to back off."

"The more I think about it and talk with people who treat

it like a perfectly normal variation in life, the easier I find it to deal with. The essence of being a scientist is that when you are presented with facts, you have to put aside your preconceived notions and accept them. Especially when they're not the results you were expecting. I'm not done processing yet, but I'm coping. It may take me a while to completely digest the knowledge I've been presented. But I'm working on it."

"I don't know how to behave around you, then. I don't know if I should keep my distance, or what."

"That makes two of us, señor. I don't know how to act around you either. But don't worry. When I'm ready, you won't have to ask. I'll let you know."

She glanced at her watch. "Now, I think it's time for us to start heading back, isn't it? I want to shower before dinner."

He rose up gracefully, in one fluid motion, and offered her a hand. When she stood up, he pulled her hand up to his mouth and kissed the back of it. The feel of his lips on her skin sent tingles traveling all over her body again.

"I'm a patient man, Saoirse. I've always had to wait for what I want."

She smiled. "Good."

With that, they both began to trot along the trail, heading back for dinner.

CHAPTER FOURTEEN

The next two weeks were filled with surreal moments. Saoirse would look around in the communal dining areas and try to imagine what the people around her would look like as wolves. She already knew that Diego's black hair was repeated in the black fur that covered his wolf. And that his eyes were remarkably similar. She wondered what color fur blonds would have, and if blue-eyed people made for blue-eyed wolves. Other than Alaskan Malamutes, she'd never seen a dog with blue eyes.

She observed Caleb closely in class, since he was the only student she knew for sure was a werewolf. But there was nothing unusual about him or his behavior. The only difference was that, as she'd noticed the first day he returned, he got more respect from his fellow students. But when his partner was a girl, he was still just as tongue-tied talking to them as he had been before. Obviously, having a wolf living inside of you didn't make it any easier for you in life . . . even in a setting where you didn't have to hide your lupine nature.

It was cooler outside now, and it was also getting dark much earlier. Saoirse still kept her balcony door open to enjoy the sounds and smells of the night, but she'd added a hand-made afghan and a feather quilt to her bedding. She had found them both left in her room on the bed, neatly folded, when Pearl had done her monthly cleaning visit. She decided to leave the woman a nice gift for Christmas, for being so thoughtful.

Nothing else really changed. Life proceeded in an orderly

fashion, despite her recent discovery. Her shock had been replaced by a desire to learn all she could about the *lupine syndrome*, as she privately referred to it. Not only was she living in the middle of a large group of people who shared the syndrome, but she had also fallen in love with a man who had a wolf living inside of him. The only ones she felt comfortable enough to ask questions about it were Diego and Jerene. Until, unexpectedly, she made another friend.

Jerene's brother, John, joined them at dinner one night. She could sense his curiosity when he asked her about where she had been living before she moved to the compound. She told anecdotes about living with Freddie and Jorge and dealing with their friends. She recounted feeling prejudice from the other men, who thought she'd judge them since she was hetero. To counter the possibility, they treated her rudely. She bemoaned being unable to punch anyone to settle things, as she had done when she was younger. She added a few funny stories about going to gay bars or drag clubs with Freddie and Jorge, where everyone was impressed at how perfect her drag was since they all assumed she was a man.

Besides her and John, the only other ones at the table that night were Jerene, Arnold, and Diego, so she didn't feel disapproval from anyone. But she could sense John's anxiety, and his hunger to hear about others like him who were accepted fully as they were.

You have really been dealt a raw deal, my friend. You have to deal with two differences, either of which could break most people. You're a shifter in a world that would hunt and kill you if they knew you existed, and you're gay in a culture that thinks that one difference is enough for anyone to have. I hope I can somehow help you accept yourself enough to present who you are to your family. Your sister, at least, seems to already know. So who is it you can't risk losing? Your parents?

Another week had passed, and it was getting close to

Halloween. The students had festooned the school halls with themed decorations of witches and black cats, vampires, and of course, multiple images of werewolves. There were also Saturday movie nights, with classic werewolf movies shown back-to-back.

The first time Saoirse walked into one of the movies in the auditorium, sudden silence traveled through the previously boisterous crowd of mostly teenagers. Many of them stared at her, probably wondering how she would react. She looked around and spotted an older student with whom she'd formed a friendship because the girl wanted to become a chemist.

Saoirse called out loud enough to be heard by everyone there. "Hey, Kristin! Okay if I sit by you? I've heard you guys yell at the characters and make fun of the way Hollywood always depicts your relatives. I want to throw popcorn at the screen along with everyone else."

Relieved chatter instantly echoed throughout the theater.

Then she heard Diego's voice. Looking around, then up, she saw him in the room above them in the back, where the equipment was. Apparently, he was acting as a chaperone for the students. He turned to the man next to the projector and smiled. "See that, Randy? Best hire I ever made."

The other man nodded in agreement.

When Saoirse got close to Kristin, the girl jumped up and high-fived her, then moved over one seat to make room for her. She chuckled to herself when she heard random comments from the crowd.

"Coolest teacher ever!"

"I'm so glad she's staying."

Everyone settled in to watch Lon Chaney Jr. get schooled by Maria Ouspenskaya.

Saoirse volunteered to be one of the chaperones for the

students' Halloween costume party. She dressed as a gypsy, wearing an old flower-print skirt and a peasant blouse, which she wore loose enough for one bare shoulder to be exposed. She wore large hoop earrings and lots of gold bangles on her wrists. She tied a scarf around her head, which left the rest of her hair to look as if it was wildly escaping from the multi-colored fabric. It was a costume she'd used before, with parts that could be worn on other days, just not together.

Diego was also there, of course, as another one of the chaperones. He was dressed as Zorro, wearing all black. He had on skin-tight black pants, a black shirt that laced up the front, and a black hat over the black mask that covered the upper part of his face. As usual, he'd tied his black hair back, but in a nod to the character, he'd used a red ribbon instead of his usual rubber band. He carried an obviously toy plastic sword, which made the students laugh at the incongruity—his costume all black and his sword a bright orange.

One look at him had Saoirse wanting to beg him to take her captive. She tried not to drool too openly over how his perfect ass was displayed by the pants or the glimpses of dark chest hair that peeked out through his open shirt. The fact he was being true to his word and keeping his distance was driving her to distraction. She was long since over her shock at discovering what he was, and anxious to learn more about how they would be together. She knew the onus was on her to let him know that, but she wasn't sure how to do it.

Both she and Diego had to circulate constantly, to break up pairings of students feverishly groping each other in dark corners. And to make sure that no one repeated last year's folly of dumping a bottle of rum into the fruit punch. They had to push through the dancing throngs to end any obvious grinding and to encourage students to behave themselves. They barely got to smile at each other across the room for most of the party, which was scheduled to run from seven to ten on

Friday night.

Just after nine, a couple of security guards stopped by the party after their shifts had ended. One of them had a son at the party, so they both helped themselves to some snacks and punch and helped with the chaperoning. Saoirse took the opportunity to use the bathroom since she'd been trying not to leave Diego alone with the kids. She was just walking back in when a hand grabbed her from behind a curtain and pulled her onto a balcony.

Her momentary confusion changed to delight when she realized it was Diego. He had obviously taken the opportunity to grab a few stolen moments in the dark now that their chaperone services were temporarily augmented.

He leaned against the wall next to her, stroking her cheek with his knuckles, the moonlight reflecting in his eyes. "How could I resist such an attractive gypsy woman?" he murmured in a low, husky voice.

She smiled coyly, batting her eyelashes. "Why, sir, are you bothering with a lowly peasant woman like me?"

Using one finger, he tilted her head upward until their gazes met. "Because if I don't kiss you, I'll never forgive myself." With that, he brushed his lips against hers in a light caress.

The tingle that ran through her body made her blood boil. She leaned against him, enjoying the feel of the hard muscles under his skin. He increased the pressure of his lips, and she met him with equal fervor. With a low moan, she opened her mouth, and their tongues caressed, tasting each other's passion.

He pressed her against the wall, using his hips to capture her, introducing her to the indisputable bulge throbbing against her body. Her heart was already racing, but feeling how much he wanted her increased her arousal. Her hands explored his chest, heading up to his shoulders. Imagining how it would feel to be pressed down by their strength made her dizzy. The thought of becoming better acquainted with his rock-hard erection increased the tingling sensation all through her body.

Diego had to fight harder than ever to control his wolf.

Take her now!

I can't! We're in a public place . . . we're the adults. We have to go back to the party.

Take her now! Taste her. Smell her. She belongs to us. We need her!

This was not the first time Diego wished he could give in to his wolf's desires. Everything was so simple to the wolf—take what you want, and to hell with the consequences. At that moment, he was willing to risk anything to plunge himself into this woman . . . to give them all what they wanted. Yet he knew it wasn't the right time.

What started as a minor buzzing in his back pocket, got steadily more insistent. Apparently, even Saoirse noticed the vibrations, since her hands were caressing his butt cheeks.

She drew back slowly from their kiss, her eyes glazed with desire. "Shouldn't you answer that?"

"Um-hmm," he answered as he buried his face in the curls around her neck.

The buzz sounded again, loud enough for them both to hear.

"It might be important," she said in a ragged voice.

With a massive sigh of impatience, he leaned back against the wall, pulling the offending technology out of his pocket.

He jabbed at it angrily and gasped when he read the text.

Joe having trouble breathing. End could be near. Come immediately.

He swore softly, leaning forward to rest his hands on his knees. He took some deep, cleansing breaths. Saoirse grabbed the phone from him, moaning when she read what was there.

Chapter Fifteen

The next few hours were filled with increasing anxiety. Saoirse talked one of the security guards into staying with her until the party was over, since Diego had to leave. The one whose son was there remained to serve as the other chaperone. The other took off right after Diego did. Apparently, both the guards had received texts telling them to return to duty. But Saoirse didn't want to end the party early, since it only had a half-hour to go.

"Let the kids have their fun," she told the dutiful father.

He nodded, "Who knows when things will get back to normal?"

She was going to ask what he meant by that, but a fight had broken out between two boys, and he had to apply some discipline and break them up.

After the party was over, everyone left the premises. Saoirse detoured to walk through the dining room, hoping to find someone who could give her some news about the ailing patriarch . . . but it was deserted.

As she headed for the stairs leading to her quarters, she heard voices coming from a side door. It was the same guard that had been at the party and left soon after Diego did. She recognized his sandy-haired crew cut. He was talking in a low tone to another man she didn't know, but the woman's voice she knew. It was Pearl, the maid.

She snuck over to stand behind some nearby curtains, ignoring her spark of shame for eavesdropping.

"Who d'ya think he's gonna give it to?" the unfamiliar man

asked.

"There are rumors that it'll be the principal. That Mexican is too sneaky for my tastes. Moving in here like he did, then sucking up to make the old man like him more than some who've been here for much longer. Too bad we can't report him and get him deported."

Saoirse was astounded a security guard had said that. *How could anyone misread Diego so totally? Besides, he was born here.*

Pearl spoke up. "I heard he got a text before everyone else did. The old man asked for him. I'll bet he's got it all sewed up."

"Well, that's it then," the unknown man said.

"Not if there's a challenge," the security guard replied.

"Who's gonna challenge him?" Pearl asked. "He's solid muscle. Besides, you know what *those* people are like—they're all gangbangers. They fight dirty."

"Maybe someone who's a better man should think about it," the unknown man said.

There was some murmuring agreement from all three. Saoirse saw another guard walking toward the group, doing the usual perimeter check that was done every hour. Pearl and the other guy quickly faded into the darkness of the deserted dining room, leaving the sandy-haired guard alone by the door. Saoirse shrunk even further into the folds of the drapes to avoid detection when the approaching guard got closer.

She was shaking, almost angry enough to report what she'd overheard to the new guard. Instead, she decided to tell Diego what she'd discovered. She stood straight and quietly made her way to the stairs without either of the guards noticing her.

When she got to her suite, she unlocked the door and went in, locking up behind her. She went over to the fridge and poured a glass of sparkling wine, then sat on the couch. Her thought relived the fevered groping she and Diego had shared before reality so rudely intruded upon them. *God! I wanted him before, but now I can't even think about anything else! When he touches me, it's magic. Every part of me tingles with arousal. It's like his cells are speaking to my cells, and our bodies are desperate to join together. I wonder if that's because of his wolf?*

She jumped when she heard a single wolf's howl close to her open balcony. She walked over and peered outside, seeing the grounds covered with wolves. Every one of was them silently staring at the west wing where the pack leader's family lived. She kept her vigil for a while, sympathizing with their anxiety over their alpha, their pack leader.

Eventually, she was too tired to remain, so she went in to take a shower. While under the water, her body became hyper-sensitive. She spent some time enjoying the extra sensations she got from applying the creamy bath gel on her various parts. Remembering Diego's touch, and the feel of what he had to offer pressed intimately against her, she quickly brought herself to orgasm. Her legs struggled to hold her up as she rode the spasms of pleasure.

Afterward, she wore only her towel as she went to her bed. She hung it on a nearby chair and slipped naked under her sheets. Sleep eluded her for a long time. She stared at the ceiling and wondered at the anxiety that she felt.

Is it because I haven't been laid in so long? Or because I want Diego so much? Or is it because I can feel the anxiety of the wolves down there, worrying about their leader? Or is it because of what I overheard? I have no idea who Joe will name as his successor. I would assume it would be one of his kids. But what does it mean if there's a challenger? Do they have to duel or something? It can't be a legal challenge. I can't imagine that wolves sue each other in court.

She comforted herself by saying some prayers, asking for God's blessing on Joe's soul, and His mercy in easing the grief of the bereft family.

Eventually, she fell asleep. Her dreams were haunted by a

large, black wolf she kept trying to touch. Every time she got close to him, she was blocked by something—other wolves, trees that grew out of nowhere, human females who laughed at her because who would ever want a freakishly tall, ugly, freckly ginger like her? Then they shifted into wolves with blonde fur and blue eyes, and they easily jumped barriers she spent the rest of her dreams trying to climb over.

When Saoirse woke the next morning, she was more tired than when she'd lain down. After getting dressed, she headed downstairs for breakfast. She knew that Joe's wife, Janine, was the main chef, but figured there must be a large, well-trained staff that could manage without her for a while. The buffet table was decked out with the usual choices, but there was no special quiche of the day, which was always labeled as *Chef's Choice*.

She helped herself to bacon and scrambled eggs and one of the muffins she liked so much. She got her coffee, then looked around for someone to eat with. The tables were filled with somber-looking people. Some of the women were sobbing, while friends tried to comfort them. She felt guilty intruding on anyone's grief. She'd almost decided to carry her tray upstairs when she noticed Nathan waving at her from a far corner.

She walked over to join him, relieved for the company. "What's going on?" she asked as she began to add cream to her coffee.

"Joe passed on early this morning," he replied. "He fought a good fight, but even he couldn't stop such an aggressive cancer."

"So it only happened a few hours ago?"

Nathan nodded with tears in his eyes.

"No wonder people are so affected. I'm sorry for the loss of your leader. He was a good man."

"He took good care of the pack. He was always fair, and you knew where you stood with him. We'll all miss his wisdom."

Saoirse picked at her food, finding she wasn't as hungry as she thought. "Um . . . did he, um, choose someone?"

Nathan nodded. "Diego. There's going to be a naming ceremony tonight, in the auditorium. It's a formality, but it's the way things have always been done. The family and the council will convene on the stage and announce who has been named as the new leader."

"What if there's a challenger?"

Nathan glared at her, speaking sharply. "Why? Do you know someone who's going to try?"

"No. I was just wondering what would happen if someone wasn't happy with Joe's choice."

Nathan shrugged. "Everyone likes Diego. I don't think it was much of a surprise to anyone."

She pushed her plate away, suddenly not hungry at all. "Do you know where he is? I'd like to congratulate him."

"I don't know. He was with the family all night. He might have gone back to his quarters for some sleep sometime this morning. But if I were him, sleep is the last thing I'd be able to do. It's a huge responsibility to take on, being named the pack leader. So much to learn, so much to do."

"I think I'll go check out his office," Saoirse said. "He might be in there."

"I'll see you later," Nathan said. "We'll all be expected in the auditorium at seven, after dinner."

"Won't I be an intruder there? I mean . . . since it's pack business and all."

Nathan gave her a grim smile. "No. You live here, so you're honorary pack. You should be there to see what goes on in an orderly transfer of power. As a teacher, you'll be a calming influence on the students. They'll all be nervous right now, and so will the rest of us. This hasn't happened in damn near seventy years. Most of us have never seen anything like this, either. We weren't here when Joe took over."

"Okay. I'll be there."

Nathan got up to leave also. They walked together over to the garbage cans and dumped most of their food into the compost collector. They went their separate ways out of the dining room.

Saoirse headed to the school wing, to check for Diego. He wasn't in his office. She knew where his quarters were but had never been there. *He's probably in shock and could use a friendly face.* Then she argued with herself. *The last thing he'll be thinking about now is sex. He's probably with the family, making plans. What kind of plans? Who the hell knows? They're wolves. Wolf-y plans.*

She went for a run before lunch but didn't see any sign of Diego on the trail she chose. When she got back, she ate a salad for lunch, then went up to her suite to try to take her mind off her anxiety. She opened a book she'd been meaning to start and got a few chapters into it before she fell asleep. When she woke from her nap, she felt irritable as she usually did after naps. She decided a soak in the *Jacuzzi* tub was just what she needed, and she took the book with her.

When she got out, she wrote letters to all her siblings, and to Freddie. Then she looked at her watch and sighed. *Still over two hours to go. I can go down for dinner soon. But chances are I still won't have much of an appetite. Oh Diego, where are you? I hope you're all right.*

CHAPTER SIXTEEN

At seven, Saoirse left the dining room and walked along with the crowd of people heading for the auditorium. She nodded at the students she saw along the way and hugged some of the girls who were crying. Even the boys grabbed for her hand as if seeking some reassurance that things would be all right. By the time she got there, few seats were left. She decided to stand along the back of the hall, to keep an eye on her students in case anyone needed her, and because she was too nervous to sit.

A large, brown wolf walked onto the stage and howled. Everyone quieted down. No one took much notice of what happened next, but Saoirse was transfixed, staring in amazement. The wolf began to change. The bone-cracking sounds were so loud she could hear them plainly from the back of the room. When the face became that of a man, it was set in a grimace of pain, but she recognized John. He was on all fours, panting, then he straightened and stood. Once the shift was complete, John was given a pair of pants and an academy-logo polo so he could get dressed. Meanwhile, other people came onto the stage and sat in the semi-circle of chairs that had been set up.

There was a respectful silence as the crowd waited for the appearance of the people for the last two chairs. Saoirse looked in the direction the others had come from and saw Janine enter with Diego by her side. People began to rise from their seats with respect for the widow. Janine acknowledged it all with nods to each area of the room. There were tears in her eyes, but she maintained her dignity.

What a classy woman. She's so strong. I wonder why she didn't want to be the pack leader? Maybe they don't allow females.

Saoirse turned her attention to Diego and was alarmed at the haggard look on his face. He hadn't shaved, and a black shadow covered the bottom half of his face. But his eyes looked haunted. She fought a strong urge to run onto the stage to give him a hug.

John tapped on a hand-held microphone that was on a stand in the middle of the stage so that when any of them spoke, it would be amplified. He spoke to the crowd, now settling back into their seats.

"As second for the Northwest Maine Pack, I, John Johnson, call this meeting to order. Are all of the other council members present?"

A tall, regal-looking Black woman, whom Saoirse had been introduced to but not seen much after that, stood up.

"I, Monique Martin, third for the Northwest Maine Pack, am present and a witness."

Nathan stood. "I, Nathaniel Taylor, fourth for the Northwest Maine Pack, am present and a witness."

Then Janine stood. "And I, Janine Johnson, widow of Joe Johnson, recently-deceased pack leader of the Northwest Maine Pack, and fifth in command, am present and a witness."

John nodded. "Then we are all present. Were all of us witnesses at the passing on of our esteemed pack leader, Joe Johnson?"

Everyone on the stage nodded their heads, including Diego, who was sitting quietly.

"Did Joe Johnson name a successor to be the new pack leader of the Northwest Maine Pack?"

The council members all answered in unison. "Yes."

"Then it is my honor to announce that the new pack leader for the Northwest Maine Pack is Diego Vargas."

There was applause from many in the audience, but not everyone seemed to be pleased with the decision.

"Are there any objections?"

There was silence for a few minutes as John glanced around at the assembled pack members.

Suddenly a voice rang out. "I claim the right of challenge!"

Saoirse's stomach clenched when she recognized the man who stood as the guard she'd overheard last night.

"I, Virgil Tate, claim the right to challenge Diego Vargas, for the leadership of the Northwest Maine Pack."

A buzz of excitement went around the room as people reacted to this. Saoirse watched Diego as he straightened up, drawing himself up to his full height, and locking eyes with the challenger.

"So it shall be," John announced. "The funeral arrangements are pending, but the leadership position cannot be undecided. Tomorrow night at six, on the west lawn, the challengers will meet in combat. May the strongest leader prevail."

He looked around at everyone. "Thank you for your attention. This meeting is adjourned."

The conversations raged all around Saoirse as she was swept out the door by the rest of the crowd. Once in the hall, she was beset upon by students who gathered around her, clamoring to be heard.

"Did you see Mr. Vargas? He didn't look well."

"Mr. Vargas is the new pack leader? That's so cool!"

"I don't like that security guard who challenged him."

"Who do you think will win, Miss McColl?"

"I'd put my money on Mr. Vargas. Have you seen the muscles on that guy?"

"But the other guy's a guard. I'll bet he knows some moves."

Saoirse found it all surreal. She was a scientist, surrounded by children demanding her attention because they were concerned over a challenge to the leadership of their werewolf pack. But the idea of Diego having to fight someone for an important position was making her so frantic that she had trouble thinking of anything else. "Kids, kids, please. I'm sure that Mr. Vargas appreciates your concern and your pride in him. But I can't tell you much, since this is all really new to me."

"It's new to us too! No one has ever seen a pack leadership challenge."

"Then, we'll all watch and learn tomorrow night, right?"

Some of the students nodded and began to walk away.

Saoirse's nerves were on edge, but she knew she had to do something to help the kids. "Right now, I think you should all do something to relieve your anxiety. Do something physical. Go for a run. Go swim some laps. Go work out in the gym. Sweat those stress hormones out of your body. You'll feel a whole lot better."

Another student walked up to the group, asking everyone, "Did you hear that Mr. Johnson said there's a communication black-out?"

This was enough to increase the murmurings around the group.

"You mean I can't call my mom?" a girl asked, looking worried.

"Nope. He says it's for security reasons," the new student replied. "No talking with anyone outside the pack until leadership has been decided."

There were grumbles about how to cope with the lack of social media for twenty-four hours. Saoirse had to smile, despite herself. Their abject panic at possibly missing something important seemed to quell some of their worries, even though the most important thing to affect their lives was going to happen in real-life tomorrow.

Saoirse shook her head and called out, "That's it, guys. I'm heading up to my quarters to take my own advice. I might see you on a trail or in the gym. Or I may decide to take a long bubble bath. But I need to chill as much as you do. So I'll see you later."

She was heading for her suite when she decided to take a last-minute detour. She went into the academic wing and walked down the now-familiar hallway. The door to the principal's office was closed, but there was a light clearly visible in the crack between the door and the floor. *Did he leave the light on, or is he in there? Either way, I have to find out. I have to talk to him if I can. And let him know I support him.*

She grabbed the door handle, and it turned easily. She knocked with her other knuckles, speaking as she opened the door. "Diego? It's Saoirse. We need to talk."

"Come in." His voice sounded tired and strained.

She entered the office and locked the door behind her, then turned around.

CHAPTER SEVENTEEN

Saoirse held back a gasp when she saw Diego sitting at his desk. He looked even worse up close than he had on the stage. His face was tense with anxiety, and his eyes were dull with fatigue. His clothes were crumpled and mismatched like he'd thrown them on haphazardly. His hair was loose, finally letting her see the full shoulder-length, straight mass, but it was in tangles as if he'd been running his hands through it. He had a mug of black coffee in front of him. He'd been leaning on his elbows with his head in his hands when she walked in. Now he looked up to greet her with eyes more haunted than tired.

She perched on the edge of one of the chairs facing his desk. "Diego! What can I do to help?"

He shook his head slowly. "Nothing."

"Would it help if I just listen while you talk?"

"There's no hope. I'm so screwed."

"What do you mean? Because of the challenge?"

"Yes."

"But you're younger and stronger than he is, right? You can take him."

"For pack leadership, we don't fight as men. We fight as wolves."

"Well, I haven't seen his wolf, but I've seen yours. You're massive as a wolf, and you look like you can do major damage to anyone who fucks with you."

He sighed heavily. "He's ex-army. His brother, Vernon, and sister-in-law, Pearl, have been with the pack for ten years.

118

He joined us about six years ago when he got out of the service. Everyone here works at what they're good at, so Joe made him one of the security guards. He's had training that I haven't."

"But you said you fight as wolves. Army training won't do him any good when he has paws that can't hold a rifle or even a knife."

"True. But he has another huge advantage over me."

"What?"

He rose up to stand with his back to her, staring out the window behind his desk, his voice an exhausted monotone. "Before a fight this important, wolves use . . . um . . . sex, to enhance their testosterone and get them into peak fighting mode. Virgil has always had a way with the ladies, so I'm sure he's fucking non-stop already, to get himself primed."

"Then you need to do that too. That's not a big deal, is it?"

He whirled on her. "Yes. It is."

"Why?"

"Because my wolf won't let me fuck just anyone. It wants only one woman."

She stopped breathing for a heartbeat, then whispered, "Who?"

He stared deeply into her eyes. She got the impression of two beings looking back at her — the man and the wolf. *I must be going crazy!*

His gaze intensified with his reply. "You!"

She smiled as she got up and moved to his side of the desk. "That's not a problem then. I'm . . . uh . . . willing to take one for the team."

His growl stopped her advance. She tried to retreat but found her way blocked by the edge of his desk. She worried he might be losing control over his wilder half. She could sense — almost feel — his internal struggles.

"You don't understand." His voice became more gravelly with each word he spoke.

"Yes, I do. You and I have been dancing around each other for a while now. It's time for the dancing to stop. I'm only too willing to do what I've been fantasizing about doing since you hired me. And if it gives you strength for the fight tomorrow night, so much the better."

He shook his head. "No. You still don't see."

He moved closer, and she had to look up to meet his eyes . . . those tortured, dark windows to his soul, with the long, black eyelashes. His hands were at his sides but fisted, and his arms were shaking from the strain.

Her body responded to his nearness. Her breathing grew quick and shallow, and her heartbeat sped up. She licked her lips but regretted it when a low growl escaped from deep in his throat. She swallowed hard before asking, "What don't I see?"

"It won't be enough for either of us . . . the wolf or me . . . to have you only for one time. Or one day. There can't be any limit."

Her eyes widened. "Wh-what do you mean?"

"You have to know what you're committing yourself to if you say yes."

In a hoarse whisper, she asked, "What?"

He advanced even closer. The heat from his body radiated to her very core, and his intent gaze burrowed its way to her soul. She felt the flush spreading across her face, and the sweat trickling down her face and back.

He growled again. "Wolves mate for life. I don't want to just fuck you, Saoirse. I have to mate with you. Both of us do."

She gaped at him. "Hey, I draw the line at bestiality. I want to have sex with you, but not with your wolf . . . no offense."

His lips curved slightly upward. "I don't mean that. But once I have you, I won't be able to let you go. You'll belong to me . . . to us."

They stared into each other's eyes for a long moment, the

only sound from the gentle hum of the small fridge in his office.

With a small nod, she whispered, "Yes."

A low growl rumbled in his throat as he closed the small gap between them, pinning her to the desk with his hips, his insistent erection pressing against her mons. Both hands reached out to grasp her shoulder. He spoke with difficulty, obviously fighting his wolf for control. "Are you sure? This can't be taken back. You have to be sure. Once I let go . . . I don't think I'll be able to stop."

In response, Saoirse pressed herself closer and wrapped one hand behind his neck to pull his head down for a kiss. Her other hand was trapped between them when he held her tighter, trying to meld their bodies together. The heat from his lips crushing hers set her on fire! The tingling electricity flew through her body, exciting every nerve ending, setting every cell aflame.

Then the wolf in him seemed to take over as he began to wildly tear at her clothing. He pulled her shirt open, and buttons flew in every direction. He pulled it behind her and growled as he buried his face in her neck, inhaling deeply. The buttons on the sleeves defeated him, so he tore the shirt to shreds and discarded it. Her pants were more of a challenge, but he tore the front open and yanked hard enough to shred the seams. Her matching lace bra and her thong were the only barriers left.

He backed away for a second and was even more brutal with his own clothing. Saoirse's desires intensified, with just a little frisson of terror as he ripped the material, quickly exposing his fully naked and aroused body. She admired his sculpted chest, with dark black hair that continued down his abs, pointing to what she'd been imagining. Her breath caught in her throat and her pussy clenched when her gaze locked onto his rampant erection for the first time. It was a dark bronze club, jutting out from a nest of black hair. The veins on it were so engorged she could see his rapid pulse beating in time with her own.

He grabbed both sides of her thong and shredded it, then lifted her onto his desk. With a frustrated growl, he ripped off the straps of her bra and pulled it down, exposing her to his gaze. Her breasts ached for his touch, and her nipples peaked with her passion, inviting him to explore. He fastened his mouth on one and sucked deeply. She almost lost consciousness from the feeling of being devoured.

He ran one hand along her back, from her neck down her spine, making her jump with the tickling sensations until he stopped at her hip, holding her still. He used the other hand to tease her with his cock, smearing her juices around, adding what was leaking out of him to her own lubrication.

Then he raised his head, staring into her eyes as he rammed his hips forward and entered her to the hilt. It was a tight fit and bordered on painful for her. He seemed to sense her discomfort and stilled for a moment. The look of wonder and amazement on his face as she adjusted to the girth made her smile. Feeling his pulse throbbing against her clit increased her arousal. He slowly pulled back and then proceeded to impale her over and over again, each thrust making more room for himself as he enforced his claim on her. Both of his hands dug into her hips as he pursued the inevitable outcome. His movements sped up and grew shallower.

The sensations drove Saoirse higher than she'd ever been before. It felt like she was climbing a huge hill, going further and further up, never quite reaching the top. Then he changed his angle slightly, hitting her secret spot. She screamed as she tripped over the edge, free-falling into monumental spasms that made her inner muscles squeeze him harder and harder.

He pulled her tightly against himself and exploded with a howl that was part man, part wolf, and all male.

CHAPTER EIGHTEEN

Diego leaned against Saoirse, trying to keep most of his weight off her. Their breathing slowed, no longer in unison, as they struggled to become separate beings again. Suddenly Saoirse's body began to tremble, her shoulders and torso shaking.

Diego lifted his head from her mass of curls and looked into her eyes, which were filled with tears. "Are you crying, my love?" He feared the worst. "Did I hurt you?"

She shook her head. "No. I'm crying happy tears. That was not only the hottest sex I've ever had, but my emotions were firing on all cylinders. It wasn't just a meeting of our bodies, but . . . like . . . our souls as well."

His whole body flooded with love and adoration. "Are you sure you don't have a wolf inside of you?"

A slow smile played across her lips. "I don't think so. But I feel like I'm on a first-name basis with yours now."

He smiled. "You are. You are mated to both of us now. As long as I live, I will want only you."

She looked around and giggled. "Well, I think we're gonna have to clean up the office before we leave. Not only does it smell like sex in here, but we knocked everything off your desk."

He shrugged. "Who cares? *Mañana, querida.* We have less than twenty-four hours to enhance my strength so I can beat that *pendejo* tomorrow. And if I can't, then it won't matter."

She glared at him. "Don't say that. I don't even want to think about that. I just had the most life-changing experience of my entire existence. I don't want to think about it ever ending."

"Neither do I. Let's go back to my quarters so I can ravage you in my bed, over and over again. Then maybe in my *Jacuzzi* . . . or on my couch. Maybe even on the balcony if it's dark enough."

Her eyes twinkled. "Small problem, señor. You ruined all of our clothing. I'm not really sure how close your quarters are to here, but I have no intention of streaking all the way there."

He pulled his still semi-erect cock out of her and straightened up, bemoaning the loss of her moist heat. "I have a few pairs of running shorts and t-shirts around here somewhere."

Her eyebrows rose. "For when you entertain ladies in your office?"

"Um, hell to the no. I've never had sex with anyone in here before. In fact, I haven't had much sex at all in the time I've been living here. It's tricky with us. You think you're just messing around, then one of your wolves decides it's a mating, and you're stuck with someone you maybe didn't expect to choose for a lifetime, and your wolf is not happy. Makes for some really strained dating relationships."

He pulled out a file drawer and dug around behind a pile of books. "I keep running clothes in here for when I decide that I absolutely need to go running. The stress of being a boss can do that to you."

He handed her a pair of shorts and a t-shirt, then dressed in his own shorts.

"Not going to be very fashionable, but at least they will cover my naughties." She snickered.

He nodded. "That's all that's required. You're not a shifter, so no other man can ever see you naked again. Wolves are very possessive lovers."

"Yeah, I got that."

He moved closer and wrapped one hand in her hair, then turn her face up to meet his. He covered her lips, hungrily invading her mouth with his tongue. His wolf rejoiced with him when she responded eagerly.

He drew back slightly, leaning his forehead on hers. "But I promise you, I will make it worth your while. You'll be so exhausted from our couplings you won't be able to think of any other man."

"Let's get to that bed of yours quickly!"

Her breathy voice added to his urgency.

He grabbed her hand and led her to the door. He poked his head out and looked both ways. Satisfied there wasn't anyone else in the hall, he pulled her out with him. They walked quickly to the stairway that would lead them out of the school area, and into the corridor that led to his quarters.

Hours later, Saoirse sighed happily as she leaned back in the large *Jacuzzi* in Diego's bathroom. She took another sip from the dark pink wine that was bubbling in her fluted glass. "What did you say this was?"

Diego was relaxing, sitting across from her, his feet caressing hers under the water. "It's a pinot noir sparkler, from Spain. French ones are the only ones that can be called Champagne. Italian ones are Proseccos, and Spanish sparklers are Cavas. This one is a nice change from the white ones. I'm glad you like it."

"I appreciate the bottles that you've had sent to me to stock my fridge."

He smiled wickedly. "I've been stalking you since you moved here . . . very stealthily, of course."

She snorted. "Yeah, so stealthily that I wasn't even sure at first if you were interested in me. Or if I was imagining things because it had been so long since any man expressed any interest in me at all."

He shook his head. "Now *that* I find hard to believe. You have a beautiful face, the lightest blue eyes, a runner's body, and miles of creamy white skin, with the most adorable freckles I've ever seen. How could any man resist you?"

She frowned. "I'm also bossy as hell, and a ginger with a meaner-than-usual, red-headed temper. I don't like to obey orders, and I insist on doing things my own way. And thanks to my brothers, and my height, I can deck anyone who gives me trouble. None of that has ever endeared me to any man."

"Before now. All those things you listed are why I'm so in love with you. I'm too quick to follow orders, even those I disagree with. I'm always trying to get along with others. And I always feel like an outsider who wants to be accepted."

"Well, you've been accepted into this pack in a major way, don't you think? Joe could have named anyone as his successor, but he chose you . . . even over his own family."

"Janine says she's too old for the twenty-four-seven responsibility. Jerene didn't want it because of her kids since it's such a large time commitment. John didn't want it either . . . and he told that to everyone, including his father."

"Because he's gay?"

He gave her a sharp look. "Did he tell you that?"

"No. It's obvious to someone who grew up with my best friend, Freddie. He knew he was gay from a very young age. Do you think John was afraid of his dad's reaction, and that's why he hasn't been open about it?"

Diego shrugged. "Probably. But on his deathbed, Joe beckoned for him to bend down to hear what he had to say. I think it was an acceptance, because John was crying when he straightened up."

"I hope so. Considering that you are all *different*, in the eyes of normal society, I'd think you'd be *more* accepting, not *less*."

"But that's not how things work. We are very slow to

accept changes. That's why everyone is so concerned about the lack of certainty about a pack leader. That's why the challenge has to happen soon. So things will be settled, one way or the other."

"I expect you to win tomorrow. But if you think you still need some energy, I'm feeling up for that challenge. After our crackers and cheese snack, I think I'm sufficiently recovered and able to provide that for you. It's a sacrifice I'm proud to make for my new pack leader." She batted her eyes coyly.

He reached over and tickled her most private place. "Oh, you are, are you? Then why don't you sit on the ledge here, and let me have another taste of you?"

She giggled when she slid off the ledge the first time due to the scented oil in the water. Then she propped herself on the edge of the *Jacuzzi* and held on. "Like this?"

He moved closer and knelt in front of her, spreading her legs wide. He caressed her knees, then slid his hands higher, setting the nerve endings in her upper thighs on fire.

With his head between her thighs, he inhaled deeply. "I will never grow tired of smelling your scent. You are addicting. You smell like wildflowers and grass, and woman . . . my woman."

He lowered his head and began to lick her from her perineum to her clit and back again. He slid his tongue inside her, and she fought to not fall off the ledge again as she trembled from his ministrations. She spiraled into multiple orgasms — one, then another, then another. And still, he continued.

"Stop!" she squeaked with a voice hoarse from the noises she'd been unable to stop herself from making.

"Never," he growled.

Suddenly, he stood and pulled her into his arms, as graceful and agile in human form as he was in his wolf's. He stepped out of the tub, miraculously without slipping, then carried her to the bed, tossing her into the middle of it. Then he began to crawl over her, his eyes once again those of a hungry wolf ogling his favorite prey.

She opened her legs in invitation, and he plunged himself into her again. Then there was no more talking as they moved together in perfect rhythm, further cementing their forever relationship.

Saoirse sighed happily as she lay on top of her man. She had been riding him like a prize horse only moments before until they both exploded into ecstasy, her screams almost as loud as his howling. Then they had both collapsed in exhaustion. She had to smile since she was still impaled by his cock, which seemed to never get tired.

She peeked up to see his eyes closed, a supremely self-satisfied look on his face. The early rays of dawn were beginning to appear through the windows in his bedroom.

"Are you asleep, my love?" she whispered.

He shook his head with his eyes still closed. "No. I'm enjoying the feel of you on me. We are one. I'm happier than I ever dreamed I could be. Especially while in human form."

"I just want to let you know that no matter how much I love my teaching job here, if" — she hesitated — "if you lose, I will leave with you and live with you anywhere in the world. Where you are, there is my life."

He opened his eyes to stare into hers. "Your eyes are so beautiful. I've never seen such light blue eyes before. And I've certainly never seen such love in any eyes directed at me. I'm honored, *querida*. But if I lose, I won't be moving anywhere."

"They'll let you stay? I guess it would be hard to replace you as the principal since you're so good at what you do."

He shook his head slowly. "No. What I mean is that a challenge is only over when one of the wolves is dead."

She pulled herself off him and sat up. "What?"

He sat up, pushing himself back to lean on the headboard

of the bed. "I thought you knew. That's why I have to be as strong as possible. Either I win and remain as pack leader, or I die."

"Oh, my fucking God! No! Then you can't do this, Diego! You can't make me love you like this, then leave me!" Tears were running down her face, and she shook with the intensity of her fears.

He reached out his arms, and she crawled into them to be cradled by the warmth of his body and his love.

"Then I can't lose, *mi amor.*"

"Promise?" she sniffled.

"I promise I will fight as hard as I can, because you are worth fighting for. I will be fighting for a life with you. Nothing else matters as much to me."

"Can't you talk it over with that guy first? Maybe decide that when one of you assumes the surrender position, that the other has to stop?"

"I don't think so. But I *am* uncomfortable with the idea that I have to kill someone. Hell, I've left packs before when all they wanted me to do was steal or deal drugs. I never expected to have to commit murder. Especially here, where I have made a life I want to keep."

"I will love you no matter what you do . . . ever. But I'm even more afraid for you now. I don't know if I'll be able to watch. But at the same time, I'd be too petrified about what was happening if I didn't."

"That's your decision to make, *querida.* You aren't a wolf, so I will accept your choice, either way."

"Do you think we should try to get some sleep?"

"Probably. That little nap we had hours ago was refreshing, but we've expended a lot of energy since then. I'll scoot down, so I can keep holding you while we both try to sleep."

"Okay. I don't want to let go of you either."

Saoirse remained awake for a while, consumed by the

turmoil of her thoughts. Eventually, she heard Diego's gentle snoring, satisfied he was finally getting some much-needed rest. She said a prayer for his protection, then succumbed to her own exhaustion.

Chapter Nineteen

Saoirse groaned at the sound of a discreet knock on the door in the late morning hours. Diego got up and went to see who was there, returning a few minutes later with a large covered tray. As he carried it to the table, she padded over, as naked as he was, and lifted the cover to see what was there. Apparently, they didn't have to order breakfast, it had just magically appeared.

There was a coffee pot with two mugs and cream for her on one side, and a small pitcher of fresh-squeezed orange juice, with two glasses, on the other. In the center was a platter with two omelets oozing cheddar cheese and a large dish of bacon on the side, along with a bowl of fried potatoes. There were muffins, too, Saoirse's favorite kind, and the jam she liked to spread on them.

"Um, I guess there's no keeping anything secret around here, huh?" Saoirse grinned, feeling a little embarrassed.

Diego set their breakfast on the table and gestured toward a chair. "Not when the ruling family is aware of my feelings for you. Joe was very pleased that I had found a woman to love. He and Janine had been after me for a while to commit to someone. Sex is such an important part of keeping the wolf happy and quiet. They were concerned when I didn't seem to care about anyone."

Chewing on a piece of bacon, she smiled and winked. "Especially when Joe was thinking about making you his successor. Isn't the pack leader required to be mated?"

He took a long drink of orange juice, then put the glass

down. "Yes. There are pack leaders who are not mated, but they usually choose someone within the first few months. It settles a community down, to have a mated, and therefore happy pack leader."

"I'll bet that Janine put this all together, since she's obviously thought of what I like, as well as added extra bacon to satisfy your cravings."

"She *is* the head chef, you know. And she'll remain that as long as she wants the job. The widow of a pack leader often chooses to stay on. She acts as a steadying influence for the new leader, and a bridge to the old ways for those who are unsettled by change."

Silence reigned at the table as they both directed their full attention to eating. Saoirse was famished from their earlier activities and assumed Diego was as well.

Diego finally pushed himself back from the table with a satisfied burp, smiling. "I don't think I could eat another bite."

Saoirse giggled. "Me, neither. Which is lucky for us, since there's nothing left!"

She took Diego's offered hand, and he led her toward the balcony in his bedroom. He wrapped her in one of his robes and pulled her close for a long, lingering kiss, before they went out to the chairs, putting their coffees on the small table.

Saoirse's thoughts started to niggle with worry about the upcoming challenge. Her concern must have shown on her face, because Diego leaned over and tapped her knee.

"None of that, now, *querida.*" He spoke in a gentle voice. "I'm even more worried about tonight than you are. But I don't want to ruin our time together with sad thoughts."

"Then what should we talk about while we digest all of that food?"

"How about planning our future together?"

"What do you mean?"

"My wolf is already satisfied, but the human in me needs

you to become my wife."

Saoirse took a deep breath. "I thought we settled that last night when I said *yes*."

"Do you still agree?"

She laughed out loud. "After all of the hours of acrobatics we just shared, you have to even ask? Good Lord, man, I've done things with you I didn't even know I was capable of doing—and I enjoyed all of them! So yes, of course I want to marry you. But doing something in front of God and the community will be just a formality. We're already a mated pair. Right?"

His smile reflected relief and love. "Yes."

She wrinkled her brow. "But how do we invite my family? Do we let all those non-pack members know where we are located? I mean, I can vouch for my family, for the most part. But I don't know who some of my siblings are dating recently, and they might be someone we don't want to attend. And what about your mom and sisters? Won't inviting them be endangering the pack with the onslaught of paparazzi that will inevitably be following her?"

He stretched his legs out in front of him, crossing them at the ankles and sighed heavily. "There are a lot of details that I hadn't really thought of. We need to ask Jerene how she and Arnold handled getting married. They were already married with two babies when I joined the pack. Hopefully, she and Janine can give us pointers on how to stage a large party. We'll need to accommodate all the pack members who'll want to attend, as well as your large family."

"And a few friends. I can't possibly get married without Freddie being there. Not only is he my oldest friend, but he was the one to suggest that I apply for the teaching job here, so he has to come."

They sat in silence for a while, enjoying the crisp air warmed by the late fall sunshine.

"Why don't I go fill the *Jacuzzi* again?" Diego rose and picked up his coffee cup.

"Why, señor, are you recovered already?"

He smirked. "I thought you realized by now that between my wolf and me, we are all but insatiable."

Saoirse leered at him, waggling her brows. "As I found out over the past few hours, apparently, so am I."

"Then shall we?"

She got up, her coffee cup already in hand, and followed him into the bedroom. She threw off her robe once they were in the bathroom and the water was filling up the *Jacuzzi* for a long, luxurious soak.

Diego's alarm clock kept buzzing, interrupting their smooth, passionate lovemaking. He hit the snooze button a few times, cursing it, grumbling that he needed just a few minutes more with his lady.

He finally roused them out of bed at four-thirty in the afternoon. They both showered, then Saoirse put on the shorts and t-shirt he'd given her so she could return to her suite and change into her own clothes. At the door, she turned, then ran back for a long, tight embrace. Her shoulders shook against his chest. He lifted her head with one hand, then kissed both of her tear-filled eyes.

"None of that, *mi corazón*. I will do my best. You have given me the inspiration that I need . . . a reason to want to continue living. I want to make love with you until you can't walk anymore. I want to see my seed swell in your belly with our children. I want to grow old with you and love you until the breath finally leaves my old, withered, and used-up body."

She smiled through her tears. "I want all of that, too."

"Then go change into something that will be comfortable for you. I will think you are the most beautiful woman in the world, no matter what you wear. Then you will be my most important cheerleader. The only one I really need to see."

"I wish I could do more . . ."

He shook his head. "Seeing your lovely face there is all I will need."

She nodded decisively. "Then, of course, I'll be there."

She turned, and he gently slapped her on the ass before she made it out the door.

"And afterward, you'll be in my bed again."

"Sí, señor," she teased over her shoulder.

He admired the sway of her hips, sauntering down the hallway in *his* tiny running shorts. Then he closed the door and began to ready himself, literally, for the fight of his life.

CHAPTER TWENTY

When Saoirse left her suite, she was surprised there were no other people in the hallway. She walked quickly in the direction of the stairs. She glanced at her watch and saw it was five-forty-five.

"Fifteen minutes to go," she said softly, "Diego, I'm praying as hard as I can. Please, God, don't take him away from me like this. Please let us love each other for a very long time."

She walked quicker as she got closer to the door that led outside. Once outside, she saw others making their way to the grounds on the west end of the front lawn. There was already a crowd there, both human and lupine.

There was an informal *fence* of wolves around what was obviously the fighting arena. Diego was in one corner, and the challenger in the other. John was standing next to Diego, talking earnestly to him. Diego kept shaking his head, obviously disagreeing with what John was saying. Virgil Tate had his brother by his side, and they were both laughing. She got the distinct feeling this was something they had been looking forward to for a long time.

Saoirse tried to catch Diego's attention but found her way blocked by those jockeying for a better view. Suddenly, someone grabbed her elbow, and she turned to see Jerene beside her. Jerene smiled grimly, then forcefully guided her through the crowd of bodies, over to stand near where Diego and John were arguing.

Janine was already there and nodded. "Ah, you found her. Good. He said he wanted to be able to see her face . . . for inspiration."

"Thanks," Saoirse said. "And thanks for the excellent breakfast. And for not having it delivered until later in the morning."

A small smile played around the older woman's lips. "You think I don't remember what it's like, to be chosen by one meant to become the pack leader?"

Jerene shook her head. "Please, Mom. You know I don't like to hear about what you and Dad were like when you were young and crazy wolves." She turned. "Is there anything worse than hearing your parents reminisce about the good sex they used to have?"

Saoirse nodded emphatically. "Yes, there is. Living in a small house and hearing them having it right over your head—or from the next room. That's much worse!"

She laughed along with Janine and Jerene, glad for something else to think about other than what was going to be happening very soon, right in front of them.

Saoirse glanced at her watch. *Oh, God no!*

Once again, John started things off. He walked to the center of the gathering and did a human imitation of a wolf's howl. The crowd began to quiet down.

Diego frowned as he watched Virgil and his brother laughing on the other side of the arena.

Suddenly, Virgil yelled loud enough to be heard by everyone in the crowd. "Hey, Diego, I was glad to hear that you finally got laid by someone. Been a long time for you, huh? But too bad it had to be a human. No chance to fuck together as wolves. I guess getting something is better than none. I'll find out how good she is after I win and claim her for myself. Then I'll fuck her as a human *and* a wolf . . . whether she wants to try it or not."

Some male laughter traveled around the crowd, but most of the males were either already wolves, or were not willing to take sides by reacting.

Virgil continued his taunts. "I spent my time fucking anything with a pulse, both humans and bushy-haired with tails. I lost count of how many females wanted bragging rights about getting laid by the next pack leader."

He glanced around the crowd, smirking, making sure everyone was listening to him. "But I did manage to squeeze in time for some porn. You know, the kind starring Valerie Vargas. I was kind of grossed out by the fact that you'd nursed from those big tits of hers, and you were born through that manicured blonde cunt. But I'd still love a chance to stab that, no matter how roomy it is now. If it was too big, I'd turn her around and fuck your madre wolf-style, in the ass. Now that would be really something."

Diego had been growling throughout Virgil's diatribe. He was now shifting, quickly, dropping to the ground onto all fours, and grimacing with pain.

Virgil high-fived his brother, then dropped to the ground to begin his own shift.

Diego's huge black wolf and Virgil's stockier, light brown wolf moved cautiously toward the center of the arena. They began to circle each other, each looking for an opening to attack.

Suddenly, Diego lunged at Virgil, and the battle began.

Saoirse trembled at the violence displayed by both animals, each fighting for their lives. Jaws snapped, and blood covered both wolves. Chunks of black and brown fur covered the grass where they fought.

At one point, Virgil was getting in some savage bites that had Diego howling in pain. Saoirse automatically moved forward, needing to somehow help Diego. Janine grabbed one of her arms, and Jerene grabbed the other.

"Sam, you can't! This is his fight. You can't interfere. No one can," Jerene insisted.

"But I love him!"

Janine nodded sadly. "I had to watch this twice. When Joe first took over the pack, then again many years later, when some young buck thought to take over. It's never easy. But he needs to know you're here. You give him strength."

Saoirse felt helpless, tears flowing down her face as she sobbed, "How?"

"Just by being here, my dear. He loves you. He's fighting for a life with you."

Saoirse turned her full attention back to the fight, horrified by the amount of blood on the grass and on both combatants. It was impossible to say which of them was hurt more, since they were both slowing down, showing signs of tiredness from their continuous battle.

Suddenly, Virgil lunged, with jaws opened wide, for Diego's throat. Saoirse shrieked in alarm. Diego twisted at the last minute, and instead of his throat, Virgil's jaws closed around Diego's tail. At the same time, Diego's jaws clamped onto Virgil's back leg and bit down hard. The bone-crunching was audible to everyone, followed by a hideous howl as the leg was rendered useless by Diego's teeth.

Virgil fell back weakly and tried to assume the position Saoirse had seen the wolves use for shifting. Diego shifted quickly. One minute he was a wolf, and the next, he stood tall while Virgil was still trying to finish his transformation. Once Virgil was fully human, it was obvious one of his legs was a broken mass of visible bones with lots of blood.

Diego moved forward and grabbed Virgil's hair, pulling his head up. He punched him hard in the face, making Virgil fall over backward, unconscious.

Diego stood unsteadily, next to Virgil's body, turning to address everyone in the crowd.

"I will not kill!" he announced in a booming voice. "But I, Diego Vargas, am pack leader for the Northwest Maine Pack.

Virgil Tate is now banished from our pack. He is not allowed on the grounds for any reason, or he will be hunted and killed. He has no place here, ever again."

He whirled around to stare at Virgil's brother, Vernon, who cowered under his glare.

"Any who sympathize with him are ordered to leave with him. He will be taken off the grounds and driven to a hospital, where he will be left in the ER. His belongings will be sent to him in that hospital. I, Northwest Maine Pack Leader Diego Vargas, order it to be so."

Vernon bowed his head and bent one knee, to show his acceptance of Diego as the new leader. Those who were still wolves bent one leg and lowered their heads in a show of respect for their new alpha. As they shifted, they joined the others already in human form, joining in the murmuring of discontent.

Saoirse didn't care about anything other than the fact that Diego was still alive. Janine and Jerene finally let her go. She pushed her way through the crowd and ran into Diego's arms. He staggered slightly, but she held him up, her arms encircling his waist, her face pressed to his blood-covered chest.

The crowd parted for them as they left the area, walking slowly to accommodate Diego's slight limp. A small group of people followed them back to the mansion and up the stairs to Diego's quarters. Some were still nude, but no one seemed to care. Besides John, Janine, and Jerene, Saoirse also recognized Monique from the council meeting. At least *she* had managed to pull on a pair of running shorts and a t-shirt after shifting back to her human form.

Once inside the room, she led Diego over to the bed. He collapsed flat onto his back, his skin a mass of bloody scratches and bites. Saoirse tried to stop a woman from approaching him, but John grabbed her arm, shaking his head.

"Rachel's the pack doctor. She needs to get those wounds cleaned and bandaged quickly. Our bodies can heal some damage when we shift, but anything bad enough to still be there after shifting has to be given prompt medical care."

Saoirse collapsed onto a nearby chair, body trembling and teeth chattering. "But it's . . . it's all over now, right? He's the pack leader, and it's done?"

"There are quite a few who are not happy that he let the challenger live. It's not our way," John replied in a measured tone. "It might . . . invite another challenge if word gets around that our pack leader is . . . squeamish. Some might think that makes for a weak leader. And there are always lone wolves who think of themselves as alphas, who're just looking for a pack to take over."

"That's ridiculous! He's just not a murderer! You should be glad of that, not upset with him for that."

"The pack leader is not just a man. He's also a wolf. He needs to be the strongest and most ruthless wolf to protect the pack."

Monique interrupted the conversation. "Let her be, John. Time will tell if he made the right decision. But for now, we have a new pack leader who needs to rest. We have all seen that he is being patched up, and his mate is here with him, to help him heal."

John nodded. "As second, I will stay outside his quarters all night, to be sure he's not disturbed."

Monique bowed her head slightly, and the two of them began to clear the others from the room.

Eventually, the only other person left in the room was Rachel, who was finishing up cleaning the wounds on Diego's back. Saoirse winced at the sight of her man with so much damage to his magnificent body. But Rachel's skills were impressive. She had assessed the worst injuries and dealt with those first, then took care of the others, one by one. She had most of the blood cleaned off Diego, and he was now covered with stitches and bandages.

Finally, Rachel straightened up. "I've done all I can. The rest is up to his body's ability to repair itself. Either he will be able to, or the wounds will get infected. You need to text this number immediately if he gets feverish, or if you can't wake him up."

Saoirse took the slip of paper with shaking hands. "Isn't he all right now?"

Rachel shrugged. "Probably. But just in case I missed anything, you should try to stay awake for as long as possible."

"Thanks for everything," Saoirse said, fighting back a sob.

The woman nodded. "He's our pack leader. It's his due." She gathered all her things, tossing the used items into the trash, and made her way to the door. "Remember — a fever, or he won't wake up."

Saoirse nodded. "I'll watch him." Then she was alone with her man.

She pulled a chair closer to the bed and curled up in it, so she could watch his restless sleep. Whenever she nodded off, some random sound he made would wake her. He moaned in his sleep, and she wasn't sure if it was because of his dreams, or if the pain he was in had followed him into his slumber.

She startled awake when he uttered her name. His eyes were open, and though dull with pain, they didn't look feverish. She bent closer to check on him, and he held out his arms in a mute gesture of supplication. Ignoring the blood still covering parts of him, she lay on her side next to him, and he draped his arm around her body. He sighed, and within minutes, she heard his regular breathing again as he drifted back to sleep. She lay very still and prayed very hard for his swift recovery.

Then she finally succumbed to her own tiredness and allowed herself to sleep.

CHAPTER TWENTY-ONE

"This is great," Saoirse remarked the next day. John had just left after informing them that he and Monique would handle things until Diego felt better.

"This gives us time to figure out some things, like where to live, and how we are going to be able to get married while keeping the pack safe."

Diego phoned Janine to ask her up to talk over some details. She agreed to bring up their breakfast once she was done in the kitchen.

"I'll eat with you, and we can talk over some pack business—informally, of course," Janine said.

The breakfast smelled good, so Saoirse and Diego were both glad when Janine insisted that they eat first.

"After all, I think better on a full stomach. I'll bet you do too," Janine added.

Once they were enjoying their coffee and digesting, Diego cleared his throat to get attention. "Janine, we know that tradition dictates that the penthouse is the pack leader's home. We don't expect you to move out any sooner than you want to. But we wanted to talk about this, since it's part of the changes we all have to make."

Janine nodded. "I figured that's what you wanted to talk about. I've already started boxing up Joe's things and separating out what I want to keep handy, versus what I'll put into storage. After all, I don't need such a big place anymore," she pointed out. "Joe and I raised our three kids in that penthouse.

But it was too big for us once they all moved out." She grinned at them. "Now, it can be too big for you — until you have your own kids to fill the extra rooms."

"Where will you move to?" Saoirse asked quickly to hide her discomfort at the turn in their conversation.

Janine waved around her. "In here. This is one of the biggest single apartments. I've always loved the eastern view of the sunrise, since I'm an early riser. I think I can be happy here. Of course, I'll have to decide what I really want to keep, and get rid of some furniture — unless you might want some of it?"

"Why don't we stop by soon, to look at what you don't want to keep, and we can decide then, okay?" Saoirse suggested.

Janine nodded. "That's a wonderful idea. Some of the things are very nice, but I don't need as much stuff for just me. In fact, I'm kind of looking forward to down-sizing. It will help me get used to my new position in life as a widow."

Saoirse reached her hand over to cover Janine's. She couldn't imagine what the woman was going through. "I'm sorry," she whispered.

Janine's eyes filled with tears, but they remained unshed. "Thank you," she said with a small, sad smile. She got up and started to put the dishes back onto the cart she'd wheeled up to their apartment.

"Let me help you with that." Saoirse stood and began to place plates and silverware onto the cart.

Once Janine had left, Saoirse sat on the couch, staring at the door, feeling sad for her friend.

Diego looked up from checking his emails, then moved over to sit next to her. He threaded his hand into her hair, turning her face up to look at him. "A penny for your thoughts, my love."

Saoirse gazed into his eyes. "I already can't imagine my life without you in it. I can't even begin to understand how Janine must be feeling after being married for over fifty years to her man."

Diego leaned over to place a gentle kiss on her lips. "If it makes you feel any better, I don't plan on going anywhere. You give me a reason for living. So it works both ways."

Their lips met again, and their love expressed itself with passionate kissing, that led to a quickie encounter on the couch.

Afterward, Saoirse giggled. "I don't think we should leave this couch for Janine. I'm sure she has one that has memories for her, as this one does for us."

Diego nodded solemnly. "Now we need to talk to Jerene next, right? To find out how she was able to get married to a non-were without compromising the safety of the pack."

"How about we invite her up here for lunch?"

"I think we should invite her kids to come also." Diego smiled.

Saoirse regarded him with raised eyebrows. "Why?"

"Because it's her day off, so she'll be watching them today. If she knows they're welcome, she'll be more apt to agree, because she won't need to find someone else to watch them."

A few hours later, Saoirse sat with Jerene's children, encouraging them to provide her with some artwork for her fridge. Jerene pushed herself back from the table, smiling at her kids busily drawing pictures.

There was a knock on the door, and Saoirse got up to answer it, letting Rachel into the apartment.

"Diego, I must ask you, as my pack leader, to allow me to check on the status of your wounds. Your body has surprised me in the past, at how quickly you recover from injuries. I won't be surprised if I already have to remove some stitches."

Diego walked over to sit on the couch across from where

the children were drawing. He took off his shirt and leaned back to allow Rachel to check on his chest.

Saoirse drew in a breath as she stared at her man. She heard a choked giggle and turned to see Jerene stifling a laugh.

"What?" Saoirse asked, walking back over to sit at the table and poured more coffee into her cup. She deliberately ignored Jerene's smirk. "So we've been talking about getting married, to make the mating legal and all."

"Not a moment too soon, either, from the look on your face!"

In reply, Saoirse stuck out her tongue at her friend.

Diego spoke up. "How were you able to have a ceremony and reception that involved non-weres who are still oblivious as to what kind of woman their son married?"

"Easy! We had a destination wedding. After all, they're all the rage these days, don'cha know!"

"Where did you go?" Saoirse asked.

"Ours was in Montreal, since some of Arnold's relatives are from up that way, and they were pleased as punch to be able to host other members of his family who weren't locals. Plus, they knew where the best places were to host things like the rehearsal dinner and the day-after champagne brunch. Then we snuck off and did some camping in the backwoods. So everyone was happy."

"I've never been to Canada. I don't even have a passport," Saoirse mused out loud. "And most of my relatives are still in Chicago."

"How about Boston, where your friend Freddie lives?" Diego asked.

Saoirse turned to him, a small smile spreading over her face. "I suppose that might work. Getting a flight from Chicago to Boston would be fairly cheap. There are a lot of hotels downtown that offer luxurious accommodations. Especially for disgruntled relatives who will grouse about having to leave home when there are so many great places in Chicago for weddings."

"Just explain to them that you live in Maine now. Many of your new friends would not be able to travel that far, but they would still like to help you celebrate your marriage," Jerene suggested.

"And there's your friend, Freddie, who would be thrilled to suggest local places for dinners and such," Diego added.

Saoirse smiled. "I assume you'll have a bachelor party here, before we leave then, right? But Freddie is my closest bestie, so he'll probably insist on hosting the bachelorette party in Boston. I guess I'll have to fly out there a couple of days earlier than you to party down . . . Freddie-style."

"Well, that was easy," Jerene remarked.

Saoirse and Jerene watched Rachel removing the last of the stitches from Diego's body.

"Speak for yourself." He grunted as the forceps removing sutures tore off a scab that promptly began to bleed again.

"I'm amazed at how quickly you healed," Saoirse said. "Especially considering how you looked right after the fight."

Jerene chuckled. "Part of our heritage, along with longevity, is an enhanced immune system. We rarely get sick, and we heal quickly. I think it's because our bodies are used to rebuilding us whenever we shift."

Saoirse gaped at her friend. "Really? So instead of tiring you out, your changes build up your energy?"

Jerene nodded. "Yup." She looked toward her kids, who were now poking at each other and giggling. She sighed. "I knew this was too good to last. I'd better rally the troops and get them back to their schoolwork, or they'll keep escalating until there's a major fight going down."

Diego nodded. "Good idea. There's been enough serious fighting around here to last for quite some time."

Rachel stood and grinned, patting Diego on the shoulder.

"What? You'll be back to full health and ready for another smack-down in a few days. You're already further along than I'd expected you to be. Keep it up, and you can assume all of your duties by Friday."

She cleaned up the supplies she'd been using and packed her medical equipment back up, then turned toward Jerene. "I'll walk out with you. Maybe we'll catch Arnold in your apartment, and I can finally jab him with his flu shot. My feelings would be hurt, thinking he was avoiding me if I didn't know how much he hates to get shots. He's worse than your kids."

The two women corralled the two kids, and they all left.

Saoirse fixed two large mugs of coffee and walked over to the table next to Diego.

"No! I don't want to stay sitting down. You heard Rachel. I'm almost healed. I want to take a shower and sit on my balcony. Judging by the sunlight coming through the window, it's fairly warm out there for mid-November. I want to enjoy what little sunshine there is and admire how your hair gleams like copper in the light."

Saoirse gave him a sly look. "You may need some help reaching those pesky areas of your back that are itchy. Maybe I'd better join you in the shower . . . you know . . . to help out."

He leered back at her. "What a great idea! Race you there!"

Diego got under the steamy water first, moaning as the hot liquid soothed his aching muscles and broken patches of skin. He'd left the door open, so he could watch Saoirse remove her clothing. She caught his gaze, then proceeded to prolong his agony—and enjoyment. She turned her back to him, bending over to slowly remove each shoe, one at a time. She slid her pants down, giving him an eyeful of the rounded globes of her glutes. She continued her sensual display by arching her back while she removed her t-shirt and stretching further as she reached back to unhook her bra. She teased him by holding it to her chest as she'd slipped her arms through the straps.

She sauntered slowly toward the shower. "Enjoy the show?"

He nodded mutely, beckoning her closer to him.

The shower was built for double occupancy, with two shower heads above them, and one coming out from each side of the roomy stall. A bench along one side provided Diego a perfect spot to sit and crook his finger again, inviting her to come nearer.

Once Saoirse stood right in front of him, she dropped to her knees.

"Is there something I can do for my pack leader, to take his mind off his pain while he recovers?" she asked, a small smile curving her lips.

"What did you have in mind, *querida*?"

She used her hands to spread his legs wide enough to fit in between. She lowered her head, kissing the top of one thigh, then licking her way up to his belly button and down the other side to kiss the other thigh. Her wickedly delicious tongue created a trail up his shaft to lap gently at the head of his cock, which bobbed eagerly to get her attention.

"Is *this* what you want, señor?" she purred just before swallowing him whole.

He felt the back of her throat relax as she engulfed his entire length, burying her face in the nest of hair at the base. She inhaled deeply and swallowed forcibly, making him groan as her throat massaged him. She pulled back before lowering her face to swallow him again — over and over again.

"*Mi amante*," he whispered. "No other woman can do what you do to me. I am a slave to your love."

He wrapped his hands in her hair and pulled her head up

so he could see her eyes. They sparkled with mischief, and her swollen lips curved upwards as she met his gaze. He tugged gently on her head, and she rose to stand in front of him. He slid his hands down, caressing her shoulders and then her breast, cupping one in each palm. She edged forward, and he attached his mouth to one nipple, his tongue circling the rigid peak, eliciting a needy whimper from Saoirse. He twisted and pulled on the other one, then switched positions to provide equal treatment for both enticing globes, enjoying the flush that spread under her translucent skin.

He continued to tease her with his mouth, his hands traveling down to her hips. His hands were large enough for his fingers to knead her hips while his thumbs massaged her labia, spreading them wide. He grasped his shaft with one hand to tease the mouth of her pussy, spreading their juices around. He pushed his hips forward to impale her but stopped when the mushroom head was barely inside. He rotated his hips, spreading her wider, making room for the rest of him.

All the while, the water cascaded down on them, making it seem like they were having sex under a waterfall. She eased herself down onto his cock, inch by inch, until she was sitting on his lap. He locked his gaze on her eyes and watched as passion played across her face. Her hips synced with his in an erotic dance of love, stimulating him to the edge of ecstasy.

Suddenly, Saoirse's face froze and her eyebrows rose, then she exploded with muscular spasms. Diego rode out the roller-coaster ride with her, continuing his movements. He sensed her passion rising again when she leaned forward and took one of his nipples into her mouth and sucked hard.

Diego felt ready to explode. He pulled Saoirse close, holding her firmly as his orgasm shimmered just beyond reach, then crashed over him with the force of a tsunami. He howled his release, and they both rocked back and forth, riding the waves of mutual pleasure, enhanced by the sensory feel of the pulsing water that continued to rain down on them.

CHAPTER TWENTY-TWO

After the shower, Diego wrapped himself and Saoirse in robes. He led them through the kitchen to refresh their coffees and then to the balcony to enjoy the warmish sunlight.

Once they were both comfortably seated with their coffees on the small table between them, Diego asked the one question circling in his brain. "How soon do you think we can get married?"

Saoirse leaned back in her chair. "I don't know. Can't we just go to a courthouse and have a judge do the honors? I mean, I've never been the kind of girl who dreamed about a big wedding. Honestly, I've been to so many in the family. They just seem like a whole lot of work, for a day that becomes a disappointment after all the anticipation. No day can live up to that kind of build-up. And besides, some of the biggest, most extravagant weddings I've been to ended in divorce. I'd rather keep things simple and keep the focus on our love. And I don't want a ring that costs a year's worth of salary. In fact, I don't want a diamond at all. I'd rather have something that you pick out because it reminds you of me."

He chuckled. "You're a scientist, for sure."

"Why? Because I don't want to waste money on something that isn't necessary? Look at me. I don't wear any rings. I wear a simple Celtic knot on a gold chain around my neck because my parents gave it to me when I turned eighteen. And I have gold hoop earrings to match. But that's it. Why would I want a clunky ring that will be in the way when I'm doing my lab work? Besides, then I'll have to keep track of where I put it.

Knowing me, I'll lose it somewhere."

"Okay. No diamond. I'll pick something else out for you. But we will need wedding rings."

"Just simple gold bands?"

"Sure. But when?"

Saoirse shrugged. "Next year sometime?"

"I was thinking more of before the end of the year."

"What? It's already mid-November!"

"I know. But the students only have finals the first week, then they go home for the holidays. That way you won't miss any classes. Besides, if we're just doing a courthouse ceremony, then we can probably still book it. And we won't need a church. Just a small hall of some kind."

"Small? With all of the pack members who will want to attend? And my big family?"

"Oh. I was forgetting that." Diego furrowed his brow. "Also, other pack leaders will no doubt want to show their respect for *the changing of the guard*, and at least make an appearance at the reception."

"What day is it? Thursday? It's Freddie's day off. Let me call him and see what he thinks."

"Okay. I'll just close my eyes and enjoy the warmth of the sunlight and listen to the melodic sound of my lover's voice."

Saoirse snorted. "Melodic? Me? Boy, you've really got it bad, señor!"

He couldn't help but smile. "Sí. Yes, I do."

She went into the apartment, and by the time she was back on the balcony, she was already on her phone, talking to Freddie. Diego leaned back, closed his eyes, and listened.

"Fine, I'm doing just fine. Hey, I wanted to ask you something. I want to get married, and I wondered if you could help me set things up so the wedding can happen in Boston."

Diego rejoiced in the joy he heard in her voice.

"Thanks. Yes, it is kind of sudden. But believe me, when

you see this man, you'll know why. He's very persuasive."

He swelled with pride to hear his woman talking with such certainty.

"When? Actually, he was thinking the sooner the better. Is there any way things can be thrown together for sometime late in December?"

Diego's curiosity got the better of him now. With his enhanced senses, it only took a bit more focus to hear both sides of the conversation. He almost chuckled at Freddie's shocked response.

"December? Sam, did you go and get knocked up already? Is that the reason for the rush? I mean, it's no big deal, but wow! Not like your usual, responsible self."

Diego smiled inwardly, reassuring his suddenly stirring wolf. *Not yet, but soon . . . very soon.*

Saoirse almost shouted her response. "No! Of course not! Jesus, what gave you that idea? Just because we want to do things quickly doesn't mean there's a bun in the oven."

"Well, that's a relief. Because that would really put a damper on the smokin' bachelorette party I plan to toast you with. We're gonna party so hard they'll have to carry *both* of us back to my apartment."

"Okay. But what do you think? Is it doable?"

"Let me make some calls. I've got a friend who owns a banquet place that usually does gay weddings. But I could probably talk him into doing a cis wedding, making an exception for my bestie. Do you care if it's a weekday? 'Cause I'm sure the weekends are booked through at least the next six months."

"A weekday would be fine. See, part of the deal is that I have three weeks off school in December. As for my relatives, they'll have the choice of rearranging their holiday plans to include a quick few days in Boston, or not."

"I need to check on hotels also. See if there's anyone I know who can get a deal on rooms for a crowd. Oh, and I know this woman who does non-denominational ceremonies. I've been to a few she's done, and she's great."

"That's cool. We *were* planning on doing the deed at a courthouse."

"They're probably also all booked through next year. I'll hang up now and make some calls and get back to you."

"Okay."

"Hey, why aren't you in classes today?"

Diego listened more intently. After all, her response could have an impact on the whole pack. To his surprise, she replied with an airy, dismissive voice, lying with a facility he hadn't known she possessed.

"It's an institute day. The kids are off classes, and I'm supposed to be doing grading and planning."

"Oh. Good thing, since you have a *little thing* like a wedding to plan. Girl, this is going to be so much fun! Too bad Jorge is in Mexico."

"What's he doing there?"

"His grandfather passed away a couple of days ago. The family will probably try to talk him into moving back down there to take over the family business. But he plans on coming back up here. He got a two-month leave of absence approved for family reasons. But he won't be back until mid-January at the earliest."

"Well, you make those calls and get back to me, okay?"

"Sure thing, Sam. And congratulations. He must be some man to have captured your heart so quickly."

Saoirse nudged Diego's leg with her toe. He opened his eyes to find her smiling, clearly aware he'd been listening the whole time.

"Oh, he is, all right. Wait until you meet him. But he is definitely *not* open to anything you might suggest, mister."

"Sam! I would never put the moves on your man! Not

unless you *forced* me into trying a *ménage*. Now if he has a brother, maybe. Or a best friend who'd like to try a walk on the wild side."

"You are too much, Freddie!"

"Yup, too much for one man to handle, that's for sure! Talk to you soon, Sam. Love you."

"Love you, too. Bye, Freddie."

She nudged Diego with her toe again. "You don't have to pretend that you didn't hear every word. I know you have super-hearing on account of your wolf-y faculties. I'd call it eavesdropping, except I knew you'd be listening."

Diego couldn't help a small smile. "Besides, we have no secrets from each other, right?"

"Right."

"And at this bachelorette party Freddie's going to throw for you, can you assure me there won't be any eligible men there that I need to worry about?"

Saoirse snorted. "Uh, nope. All the male guests will be gay. The other women there will have to arm-wrestle the gay men to grope any male strippers. Besides, it takes two to tango. I'm done with other men. Otherwise, I wouldn't have agreed to marry you, silly man."

"And Freddie doesn't swing both ways?"

"Diego! You're amazingly open-minded for a principal."

He shrugged. "I spent quite a few years bouncing around on the streets. There's not much that can surprise or shock me. Besides, when I was a kid, there were always men hanging around Mom. And being in the music business, many of them were . . . shall we say . . . *fluid* in their sexuality."

"Dude! Anything Freddie and I ever wanted to do together, we did many years ago when we were inexperienced teenagers, and he was still exploring whether or not he was indeed gay. But he is. So no worries."

"I thought you said he was living with Jorge. Why would

you think he might try to hit on me?"

"Because you're such a gorgeous hunk of man? Freddie's a sucker for strong, muscular men with dark skin. You qualify for all of that. But you're also *my* type . . . and *my man*. So he's outta luck," she stressed. "Actually, he and Jorge are just good friends. Friends with occasional benefits, that is. When they're together in bars, they both feel free to explore other options. That's the nature of their relationship. Neither of them is committed to each other—just to having fun. And they're such close friends that if either of them met someone special, the other would back off."

They both looked up when there was a discreet knock on the door.

"I'll go see who it is," Saoirse volunteered.

"No, I want to let whoever it is see how quickly I'm recovering."

Diego got up and strode to the door. He opened it to find John standing there with a smile. With a quick nod and a wave of his hand, he led John into the kitchen. Saoirse joined them, placing their empty coffee cups on the table.

"Hello, Saoirse. How are you today?" John greeted.

"Just fine. And yourself?"

John threw his hands into the air. "Oh fine, just fine. Trying to cope with planning Dad's memorial service, keeping Mom's spirits up, and looking into the details of the ceremony passing on pack leadership to Diego. Being the Pack Second has never been this much work before."

He turned to Diego. "So, boss. Are you going to be able to dig into your new responsibilities tomorrow?"

Diego waved toward the table, inviting John to sit. "I'm ready to start now. What should I know about first?"

John laid a file on the table with a heavy sigh. "I was hoping you'd say that. Let's get started."

Saoirse's phone buzzed. "I'm going back onto the balcony,

guys. Freddie's calling back."

Saoirse rolled her eyes when neither man acknowledged her, but no one saw that either. She took her phone out of her robe pocket and answered it on the way out to the balcony.

"Hello, Freddie. What's up?"

"Sam, have I got news for you! You know that guy I was telling you about, who owns the banquet place? Like I figured, he's all booked solid for weekends through June. But he says he was planning on closing after Sunday, the nineteenth, because no one plans stuff for a few days before Christmas. I asked him if he would be willing to keep his staff working for one more event. He said he'd be thrilled to do it. That way, they would all get one more day's pay before they go finish their shopping.

"So I figured we could do your bachelorette party on Saturday, the eighteenth, and spend Sunday recovering.

"The rehearsal dinner will be on Monday night, which is usually a slow night at most places. I called around and found a couple of places that have specials going for Mondays, so we can talk about that, depending on what kind of food you want.

"Then the wedding itself will take place on Tuesday afternoon at the guy's banquet hall, under a nicely decorated arch of flowers, with the reception right afterward.

"Wednesday will be the day-after brunch, then you and your honey can head out on a honeymoon late Wednesday, and the rest of the guests can travel home either then or Thursday. Everyone will be home in time for Friday, which is Christmas Eve. What do you think?"

"I'm amazed at your mad planning skills! It hasn't been that long since I talked to you. You got a lot done in such a short amount of time. I'm thrilled!"

"I'd try to be humble, but you know me too well. So thanks. Oh, and I called around and found a few hotels that are willing to set aside a chunk of rooms starting on Monday, for as many nights as folks will need. Getting a couple rooms for any female relatives of yours that want to attend the bachelorette *soiree* and don't want to crash on the floor at my place won't be a big deal. So what we need to do now is talk about what kind of culinary choices you want to offer for all three meals — rehearsal dinner, reception, and day-after brunch — so we can put down some deposits, and things will be set. Then you can get those invitations out and go shop for a dress."

"Freddie, what would I do without you?"

"You'd muddle through somehow. Oh, and I called another guy I know, who's just about the best DJ around. He's booked for weekends and usually doesn't work on weekdays. He's willing to do a Tuesday night as a favor for me."

"What do you have to do in return for all of these guys bending over backward to accommodate me?"

"Bend over backward myself? Actually . . . no, I'll bend over frontward, so my ass is accessible."

"Ha, ha. Seriously, I don't want you owing favors to a bunch of people on my account."

"Girl, there's no limit to the dicks I'm willing to suck to make sure you have the bestest wedding ever! You know that. Besides, I've been waiting my whole life for a chance to pay you back for protecting me all those years ago. This is it. After this, we're even."

Saoirse giggled. "Honey, I never kept score. But yes, we'll be even. Oh! I almost forgot. I want you to be my maid of honor. Or man of honor. Whatever you want to call yourself."

"Sam, seriously? With all your sisters and sis-in-laws, you'd choose little ol' me?"

"Who has been a continuous part of my life through all of my trials and tribulations? You, Freddie. Who else could I choose? Besides, if I picked any of them, the rest would be jealous. This way, I avoid any family issues and can have my bestie play a crucial role in my wedding."

"I'm touched. No, really. I never expected such an honor. But yeah, I'll be your person of honor. I just hope you find me a hot man to stand up with."

Saoirse glanced at John through the balcony door, who was in serious discussion with Diego.

"Oh, I think that can be arranged."

"Good. Now let's talk about gustatory choices, so I can get this nailed down. Then we need to come up with an estimated number of people. The banquet hall can serve up to two hundred, but even *your* family isn't that big. Does your man have a big family too?"

Saoirse grinned. "Don't you remember? His name is Diego. And no, not family. But there are a lot of people at the school who will want to attend. And he said some distant friends might want to show up. Once I get off the phone with you, I'll talk with him about the possible number of people and get back to you. God, I haven't even told my parents yet! Of course, Mom will bitch about it being so close to Christmas, and Dad will ask the same thing you did because it's such short notice. But seriously, I'm not knocked up. We just want to get this taken care of, so we can get on with our lives together."

"I never thought you'd fall so quickly for anyone, Sam. But as long as he's good enough for you, I'm okay with signing my name to the marriage certificate. But I'll have to judge him for myself—just to be sure."

"Fine. Now, what are the meal options?"

They were on the phone so long Saoirse had to find her charging cord and plug her phone in when the battery got low.

Then she called her parents.

CHAPTER TWENTY-THREE

Saoirse woke up Sunday morning, loath to open her eyes. She rolled over and got comfortable again as the details of the last few days tumbled through her mind.

The students had only been given Monday – the day after the fight – off from school. I stayed out until Thursday, worrying and taking care of Diego. Rachel volunteered to fill in for most of the biology classes, with her nurse, Max, covering the rest. By Friday, I was ready to return to my classroom, and Diego began his duties as pack leader full time.

We agreed to save the news of our wedding for the Sunday night pack meeting when everyone would be assembled in the auditorium for an update about the transition. That gave us time during Diego's convalescing to finalize details, make deposits, and sign contracts online with the places that needed them.

I ordered the invitations on Saturday. But before that, after talking with my parents, I put up advance notice on the McColl family Facebook page, so any relatives who wanted to attend could start making their plans.

Saoirse rolled over again to rest her head on the cooler side of the pillow as she continued to review.

Friday night, we were both so exhausted after our very full first day back at work that we went to bed early. At least we did fit in a quickie. She sighed aloud, remembering her bliss. *Even our quickies are earth-shaking. I definitely do not intend to let this man go . . . ever.*

We both slept late on Saturday, catching up on much-needed rest. Diego had plans to make and speeches to write, so after ordering the wedding invitations, I spent a few hours grading the work that had

161

been done in my absence. I also planned the next week's lab assign-
ments. After an early dinner, we spent the evening with the John-
sons, getting advice and tips on how to survive the relentless pres-
sure of being in charge of such a diverse group of people. A group
united only by either being someone with a wolf cohabitating in their
body or being married to someone who does.

Now that she was fully awake, she held off getting up by
keeping her eyes closed, dreading the intense pressure of the
day. Joe Johnson's memorial was scheduled for ten, to be followed by a luncheon. It would be held in the chapel on the
grounds, which Saoirse had been to when she sporadically at-
tended Sunday masses.

When Diego came in and *woke* her with a kiss, she tried to
pull him down, but he shook his head.

"No, honey. There's too much to be done today for us to
spend time enjoying each other. I have to assume the mantel
of responsibilities that I never dreamed I'd ever be given, and
I need you by my side to support me."

With a sigh, she drank some coffee from the cup he'd
placed by her head before reluctantly sitting up, sliding her
feet onto the floor, and traipsing to the bathroom. She showered and dressed quickly while Diego was talking on the
phone. When she reached the dining area, she was pleased to
see there was still breakfast left. She ate sufficiently, knowing
that she had to maintain her strength to be strong—for both
of them.

The chapel where the memorial service was to be held was
a small, pleasant building behind the main mansion. It had
numerous windows to let in natural lighting and multi-de-
nominational images on the walls. From the artwork, Saoirse
figured the people who lived in the compound were a mix of
religions. Some were Christians, some were Jewish, others
were Muslims, and there were Hindus represented as well.
There was even Druidic imagery depicted.

She and Diego arrived at the chapel ahead of time, since

Diego had to prepare for the ceremony. She took the opportunity to study the smaller paintings she'd overlooked and discovered that some of the artwork celebrated the ability to change into wolves. She marveled at the realism, which accurately depicted pain on the faces of the shifters as they changed.

Diego led the service, introducing himself to the visiting leaders of other packs, as well as to those who were only loosely affiliated with their pack. He thanked everyone for attending, then spoke about his own personal relationship with Joe, ending with expressing his gratitude for the honor of becoming the new pack leader.

The oldest Johnson sibling, Jennifer, stood up to speak first. She introduced herself as the one whom genetics had cheated of the opportunity to have a dual personality. She mentioned she lived in Portland. Far enough from her family to not have to face her difference daily, but close enough to be able to handle the pack's legal matters and visit her loving family. She spoke of her love for her father, who had always treated all of his children as special to him. She shared the respect she had for the fairness and impartiality he had shown when his children fought, as well as when there were pack issues to be settled.

John spoke next, his voice cracking several times, as he expressed his love for his father, along with his respect for Joe's position as pack leader.

Jerene, the youngest sibling, sobbed openly through her words praising her daddy, resulting in few dry eyes in the crowd, even among the males in attendance.

When it was Janine's turn to speak, tissues were passed along the rows of attendees. She spoke of the love she had shared with the man who had become pack leader when the previous leader had chosen him. She emphasized the necessity of trusting the instincts of leaders, whose wolves help them to choose a successor. She shared her joy of raising their family together, and of their love for all of their children—whether or not they inherited their parents' shifting abilities. She talked about Joe's determination to help others, which guided his passion for his pack. She mentioned his volunteering after the nine-eleven tragedy that kept him and other pack members in New York for weeks. And she bemoaned that his giving of himself was what caused the cancer that even his superior physical shape couldn't fight. In closing, she thanked him for over sixty-five years of being happily married and for sharing himself with her. Then, in tears, she told him good-bye.

When Janine sat down, Monique said her piece, then Nathan. A few other pack members also stood to talk of special moments they shared with Joe. They were followed by leaders from other packs, who had come to show their respect for one of their own and to pledge their allegiance to the new leadership.

After all of those who wanted to speak had their say, Diego let go of Saoirse's hand and got up to thank everyone for attending and for sharing their memories. Then he invited everyone to join them at the luncheon.

After the meal was over, they said their farewells, and Saoirse held onto Diego's hand as they walked back to their apartment.

"I assume you'll be busy working on tonight's speech, right?"

He nodded. "It's the most important speech I've ever given. I have to set forth my visions and plans for the future of the pack and introduce some new procedures and ideas as well. Some won't be happy with any changes. I'm just hoping that they'll give me a chance."

When Diego closed the door behind them, Saoirse took the opportunity to wrap her arms around him. She rested her head on his chest, inhaling deeply as her hands rubbed his back.

She turned her head and met his eyes, smiling at the question in them. "I want you to know that I love and support you while you write. I'm going to get on my phone and call some family members. Apparently, my parents feel that everyone should get a personal invitation, as well as the chance to grill me on the state of my non-pregnant body."

He leered lasciviously. "We can change that, easily, can't we?"

She shook her head vehemently. "Hold on, cowboy! We're not even married yet. Let's take our steps one at a time."

He lowered his head, capturing her lips with his. The intensity of his passion surprised her, considering they both had work to attend to.

After a few feverish moments of groping, he reluctantly pulled back. "Go make your calls. I have to work on my speech. We can celebrate our love later when I can relax again."

Janine took care of their dinner, sending up a pizza so they could both continue to work as they ate.

The monthly pack meeting was set to start at eight o'clock as usual. The time had been selected to allow for everyone to be done with dinner, also allowing time for the kitchen staff to complete the cleaning up tasks. People began to gather in the auditorium right after they finished eating, to get the best seats, and to socialize beforehand.

Saoirse held Diego's hand as they headed toward the back door to the stage area. When he tried to pull her in through the door with him, she shook her head.

She held out her hand to forestall any argument. "No, I'm not lupine. I'm not part of the pack leadership, so I don't need to be up there."

When Diego still appeared ready to argue with her, she gently patted the side of his face. "I promise I'll stand close to the stage, off to one side. You'll be able to clearly see me from up there. I want to watch as my man becomes the leader he was meant to be."

She entered the auditorium from a door in the front, next to the stage. She was warmly greeted by a few of her students, who were standing nearby, leaning against the wall. They all exhibited various nervous mannerisms, like tapping their feet or bouncing and swaying. She spoke briefly to them, trying to project calmness when she heard a howl as John started off the meeting the way he'd done before. He trotted on stage, howling again for quiet. Once that was achieved, he shifted and pulled on shorts and a t-shirt, then joined the others sitting in the semi-circle.

During the business part of the meeting, Saoirse noticed a few people who seemed unhappy with Diego as their new pack leader. There wasn't anything said that she could hear clearly, but murmurings and whispers followed almost every point he made about things that were to change under his rule.

When Diego finished his speech, he asked if anyone had questions or comments. "I want to start a new tradition of allowing the general membership to feel free to add their input to these meetings. Your voices and opinions matter, and there is no better way to know that, than to have you react to things you liked or didn't like, about what has been said."

A few people, both men and women, stood up to shout out questions, which Diego either answered smoothly, or noted who it was from so he could work on their issues, then get back to them.

He's a born leader. He leads by consensus yet reserves the right to make the final decisions that will affect everyone. She beamed with pride in her man.

Finally, Diego announced there was one more piece of

business before closing the meeting. He looked around and smiled when he saw her standing at the side of the stage. Saoirse felt the warmth of his gaze in her entire body. She knew she was blushing, but for once, she didn't care and smiled back with all the love in her heart.

"There is one last thing to announce. I, Diego Vargas, your new pack leader, have chosen a mate. I will marry Saoirse McColl in December in Boston."

Saoirse heard a quick intake of breath, along with a small cry of "No!" She looked for the source and found a woman regarding her with intense dislike. The woman glared at her, as Diego continued speaking. She returned the woman's stare, trying to figure out where she had seen her before. *She's not a teacher. Not a maid. Not someone who works in the mansion. I know I've seen her, but I don't recall a name, or what she does around here.*

She looked back to the stage when Diego asked everyone to join him in celebrating his marriage as a sign of stability for the pack. There were muted cheers and applause in response. Many people turned and smiled at her, some moving to congratulate her, and others giving her the thumbs-up sign.

She was looking for the unhappy woman when she felt the air move behind her and turned to see Monique standing there.

"You won't see her here anymore," Monique said. "She left when Diego started giving the details of your wedding."

"Who is she, and why is she so unhappy?"

Monique sighed heavily. "Doesn't anyone tell you anything about things that happened before you got here? I mean, really. Even when it concerns you?"

"How?"

"I'll fill you in later. Right now, I'm to lead you to Diego, so you both can accept congratulations from your people."

"My people?" Saoirse squeaked.

"Of course. You are going to marry the pack leader, which

makes you, by definition, a part of the ruling family. Your status has been elevated to the point where security will always need to be aware of where you are and who you are with. Didn't Diego tell you that?"

"I'm not sure he was even aware of it . . ."

"Hardly possible." Monique huffed as she guided Saoirse onto the stage through the crowd of well-wishers.

The next hour was a blur of faces. People she had never met wanted to shake her hand, and she was introduced to more people than she was aware even lived at the complex. She knew the teachers from the school and the people who worked in the main mansion. But she didn't know how many others lived in the smaller houses situated in various neighborhood enclaves on the grounds. Other faces belonged to those who were affiliated with the pack but didn't live on the grounds. She even met a few of the leaders from other packs, who joined in offering their congratulation.

At ten o'clock, the crowd thinned out, and Diego caught her attention. "Go with Monique. I will run tonight with the pack and other pack leaders. I'm not sure when I'll be back. You may already be asleep by then. But Monique will make sure you have anything you might need."

He leaned over and kissed her before turning to walk off the stage with John and Nathan following close behind. Saoirse stood and watched as they walked out a side door.

Monique drew her attention with a touch to her elbow. "Are you ready to head back to your suite?"

"Is this what you meant about security watching me now? Am I going to be under constant surveillance?"

Monique shrugged as they started walking toward the living quarters. "For a while, at least. It's always dicey when there's a change in leadership. Some members might not be happy, but most won't act on it. It's the few that might you need to be protected from. For now, you'll be escorted around. That way, everyone can see that you are being guarded closely. Once some time has passed, it probably won't be necessary."

When they reached her door, Saoirse asked, "Will you come in, please? I can make some coffee, or I have wine. But I'd like to ask you a few things, since you seem to know a lot more about this whole situation than I do."

Monique nodded. "I do, and I'll be glad to. Coffee would be great. I'm technically on duty, so no alcohol allowed. Plus, I don't like drinking much. The occasional stout is about all I ever have."

Monique closed and locked the door behind them and did a quick walk around the suite, checking out dark corners and closets. Saoirse busied herself with the coffeemaker, then got a few cookies out of the freezer. She put them onto a plate and placed it on the table. By the time the coffee finished percolating, Monique had seated herself at the table, her back to the kitchen, so she was facing the door. Saoirse brought two mugs of coffee, along with a small tray carrying the creamer, the sugar, and two spoons.

"Thanks," Monique said as she stirred cream into her coffee.

Saoirse sat across from her and leaned forward. "So who is that woman, and why was she glaring at me?"

"Did Diego tell you anything about when he first joined the pack?"

"He told me how he found the pack and how he joined the next morning."

"When he got here, he had been a lone wolf for a long time. I don't think he'd ever even met a female shifter. There are some very attractive single women here, and he . . . um . . . sampled a few of them. One was that woman who was looking daggers at you."

"Because he's going to marry me?"

Monique nodded. "Yup. She tried to convince him that they were mates, and he denied her. I don't know if her wolf really meant it, or she was just trying to get him to commit to her because she sensed leadership abilities in him. But since he was totally uninterested, she had to let it drop." She leaned forward. "What kind of cookies are these?"

"Irish shortbread," Saoirse replied. "I made them in the kitchen last week and froze them. It's an old family recipe. They're not too sweet, and they're great for dunking in your coffee."

They both enjoyed a cookie before Saoirse spoke again. "Diego did tell me that it's kind of weird with you wolf-people. He said that sometimes one wolf thinks it's a mating, but the other doesn't. He said it can make for very awkward encounters. I didn't know he was speaking from experience."

"Her name is Stacy, and she's an LPN that helps out when Rachel needs more than one nurse. She's also had some experience as a midwife, so she helps new moms, too. She joined the pack a few years ago when her therapist suggested she seek employment here."

Saoirse raised a quizzical brow.

Monique chuckled. "Yes, a lot of us go into therapy when we first start hearing another voice in our heads. Being schizophrenic is actually preferable to many people, as opposed to accepting that there's a whole other creature sharing your body with you. Some of us try to drug ourselves into not hearing the other voice. Therapists are quick to write prescriptions for anti-psychotic drugs for patients who claim a wolf is living in their heads."

Saoirse shook her head. "If you'd have told me a year ago that I'd be having this conversation with you, I'd have figured *you* needed therapy . . . and drugs. Now it seems like a normal topic to discuss. How did her therapist know to send her here?"

"Dr. Sullivan's an affiliate. He's not a pack member, per se, but a lone wolf who likes to be able to run on the grounds, and who pays a nominal fee to be affiliated with us. Often, our kind chooses where to live based on having pack hunting grounds somewhere nearby. He lives in Bangor. So when a patient tells him they hear another voice in their head, or more specifically a wolf, he pays close attention. He checks how they smell, and listens carefully, to be sure they really are shifters. Then he advises them accordingly."

"Is that how you came to live here?"

Monique shook her head. "No. I was married to a pack leader in Michigan. That's how I learned the ins and outs of pack politics. I've always been into fitness and lifting weights, so I was a very active fifth in leadership. I learned to fight when I was just a kid from my older brothers."

Saoirse smiled. "Me, too."

"We had three kids, and life was good. Then he got challenged by a wolf who brought a crew with him. It was a fair fight, and my Timothy lost. I waited until after the challenger started celebrating his good fortune, then snuck our kids out with me in the middle of the night. I didn't want to chance that anyone might think I'd try to challenge the new leader. But I knew I didn't want to live there under new rules created by the man who had killed my husband. Plus, I had to protect my children."

Saoirse felt her stomach clench. "Oh, my God! You mean things like that really happen?"

"Of course. That's why a pack needs a strong leader. Tim was strong, but the other wolf was stronger. There's always that possibility."

"I don't know if I'll be able to sleep at night anymore."

"We're in a very remote area up here," Monique reassured her. "My old pack was fairly close to Detroit, and there were always lone wolves looking to prove they had what it takes to be an alpha, trying to take over. Until now, there hadn't been a challenge up here for more than fifty years, with Joe in charge. Things feel unsettled now, but I'm confident that Diego will be able to prove himself. If Joe trusted him, then I do, too. The natural, wild beauty of this compound is a part of its charm, and it's far removed from any major metropolitan area. Those are the kinds of places where lone wolves congregate. They try to blend into the crowd. This is a safer place to raise my kids, and I like having the high school right here. My oldest one is heading into ninth grade next year, so you'll have him in one of your classes. Then I'll only be home-schooling the other two."

Saoirse leaned back in her chair, shaking her head. "I really had no idea what I was getting into when I took the teaching job here. Having to accept that shifters exist was weird enough. But now, here I am, a non-shifter, and I have to learn to navigate pack politics. And keep on doing my job as the biology teacher. I hope I don't disappoint everyone."

"You won't. Just like I trust Joe's judgment, I trust Diego's also. He and his wolf both chose you. That's good enough for me."

"Did you and him ever . . ."

Monique snorted. "Oh, God no! He's not my type. I like my men to be tall, skinny, and blond. I just trust Diego because I've seen him achieve great things with the school. Plus, he's always kept his word, and he works hard. He's a good man. You made a wise choice."

"I didn't choose him," Saoirse murmured.

"No, but you said *yes* when he asked you. That took strength and a willingness to open yourself up for new challenges. I think you'll be fine."

Monique got up from the table. "I'll be right outside your door until Diego gets back. I think I'll get myself situated out there now."

"You can stay in here if you want to."

"No. The whole point is to make it obvious that you're under pack protection. If no one can see me, it's not as effective."

"Okay." Saoirse went into the kitchen and brought out the coffeepot. "There's still about a cup left. Do you want it?"

"Thanks. I'm not really tired, but it's good coffee. Can I take those last two shortbread cookies, too?"

"Sure. And the next time I feel inspired to make some, I'll be sure to send you some of them."

"Cool. I'll hide them, so my kids don't eat them all." Monique grinned. "You should try to get some sleep now. There's no telling when Diego will get back. He's running with some other leaders who've come long distances to show their respect. They may not get in until dawn."

"Thanks for the heads up. I'll try."

"Lock the door behind me."

"I will."

Monique walked over to the door and opened it, then went through and settled on the couch across the hall.

"Do you want a book or something?"

Monique shook her head. She reached down and picked up a book from the couch and showed it to Saoirse. "Crosswords. I love to do crossword puzzles. I left the book here earlier so it would be here when I needed it. It'll keep my mind active and focused."

"Okay. Goodnight, Monique. And thanks for schooling a newbie like me."

"No problem. Oh, and Saoirse?"

"Yes?"

"No one except the ruling family knows about where I lived before this. I'd like it to stay that way."

Saoirse nodded. "Of course."

"Good night."

Saoirse shut and locked the door, then went into the

bathroom to take a long, hot shower. When she was done, she walked over to stare out at the woods beyond the balcony window. *Diego, I hope I don't disappoint you. I love you and will try my hardest to be the best pack leader's wife that I can be. I'm sure Janine will help, and I know Monique will also. I just hope I'm up to the challenge.* She opened the door to take a deep breath of the cold night air. In the distance, she heard the howling of many wolves. *Funny, that sound never frightened me here. Now I find it downright comforting.*

She walked in the darkness to the bed and turned on the reading lamp. She picked up her e-reader she'd left on the nightstand and got back into her book.

When Diego returned, the first faint glimmers of dawn were creeping across the sky. He found his lady asleep with the reader on her chest. He picked it up and put it on the nightstand. Then he went into the bathroom and took a quick shower. After drying off, he walked to the bed and stood for a moment, gazing silently down at her. *With you by my side, I can accomplish anything.*

He leaned his head back and gave in to an enormous yawn. *We're both tired. It was a good run. Time to sleep.*

He listened to his wolf and crawled into bed next to his love. She seemed to sense him and snuggled her backside closer to him. He pulled her into his arms. It wasn't long before his snoring joined with hers.

CHAPTER TWENTY-FOUR

Saoirse decided it wasn't worth telling Diego about the re-
sentful woman. *After all, he has a lot on his mind. That's one
detail he doesn't need to concern himself with. Besides, I know how
to take care of myself. I've fought men who were bigger than me and
won. No jealous woman is going to scare me.*

She continued with her project of having the senior students do actual research now that she had taught them the
basic rules and procedures. She planned to have Rachel and
Max get more blood samples from shifters and non-shifters.
She supervised the students as they attempted to see if there
were any discernible differences. She had no idea if the key
was to be found in the blood, or in any of the various other
bodily fluids humans were awash in. But at least she was going to try to find something. *And any students who participate
in the research will get a glowing recommendation letter from me to
any university science department they might be applying to join.*

Last-minute details for the wedding were made during her
spare time. Finding a dress turned out to be easier than she
had thought it would be. Jerene and Monique went with her
on a shopping trip to Augusta. She managed to find something that looked suitably formal but was an off-the-rack
dress. It had multiple layers of cream-colored lace and an off-
the-shoulder style that showed off her freckles. *I've always
found them to be annoying, but Diego likes them, for some strange
reason. So he'll probably like seeing me in this dress.* She also
bought cream-colored pumps to match.

On a whim, she stopped in a lingerie store and bought a

lacy bra, thong, and garter belt, along with nylons to match the outfit. She got a lot of ribbing from her companions but told them that she'd never thought much about the actual wedding but had big plans for the wedding night.

Finals kept her extra busy during the first week of December. With a real feeling of accomplishment and exhaustion, she logged out of her account after inputting the last of the students' final grades. *There! My first semester of teaching done. Wow! Has it really only been one semester? I feel like a real teacher now, not a pretender. And I've made a place for myself in this new life – and found a man to love. Things are moving right along for me. Time to give thanks.*

She made her way out of the mansion, walking carefully to not slip in the snow, and headed for the chapel. The doors were always unlocked, so she went in, dipping her fingers in the Holy water to cross herself. She made her way to a pew about half-way up the aisle. She knelt, crossing herself again as she'd been taught so many years ago in her catechism classes. She repeated her prayers solemnly, then offered gratitude for the many blessings in her life.

After a short while spent in quiet contemplation, she rose and walked up to the altar to genuflect respectfully, then turned and made her way back down the aisle to the door. On the way out, she caught a glimpse of some other people in the shadows. But since she preferred to be left alone to talk to God, she figured the other people would feel the same way.

The day arrived for Saoirse's trip to Boston to stay with Freddie and enjoy his idea of a *bitchin' bachelorette bash.* Jerene and Monique traveled with her again, mostly to keep her protected.

Or, as Monique put it, "To keep you out of trouble."

Jerene added, "And to have some *nasty fun* far, far away from our families, so no one will be shocked."

Freddie picked them up at the airport in a limo, crushing

Saoirse in a hug when she ran over to him in the airport. He warmly greeted her friends, and they got into the limo for the trip back to his apartment.

Saoirse, Monique, and Jerene all brought their bags into the apartment. They barely had time to unpack and hang up their formal dresses, when Freddie insisted they needed to change to get ready for the *party of a lifetime.*

All three of Saoirse's sisters had checked into their hotel earlier in the day. Freddie had the limo swing by to pick them up so they could join the soirée. They met the rest of the partiers at the first stop of the evening.

The rest of the night was a blur, and not just from overconsumption of alcohol. Saoirse had been working long hours with very little sleep for weeks. With her tiredness, combined with her lowered tolerance, she got giddy from just the first drink. She was glad Monique was there to lend a hand when she stumbled more than once. Especially when her heels threatened to twist an ankle or pitch her onto the dance floor — or the pavement.

Freddie had set them up a tour of drag clubs, gay bars, and what he called *normal, boring cis bars*, and she had at least one drink at each of them. The last stop was a gay bar that had male strippers whose moves aroused everyone with a pulse.

Saoirse was astounded when her sisters were the ones making the loudest catcalls at the dancers. They pushed their way to the stage to stuff money into bulging *banana hammocks* in return for some quick groping of tight asses and thighs — or for a sloppy kiss from the cowboy with the hat or the Scottish highlander with the micro-kilt.

Saoirse was about ready to pass out by three in the morning, so Freddy said goodnight to all his friends who had joined them and corralled the women out the door and back into the limo. Saoirse's sisters and Jerene had snuck their drinks out with them, so the partying continued during the ride home.

Freddie challenged those who were still awake to play poker with him. But first, he gallantly offered his king-sized bed to Saoirse, and she invited Jerene to share it with her. Saoirse smiled to herself as she pulled off her clothing, knowing a good time was had by all. She passed out in just her underwear almost as soon as her head hit the pillows.

Diego's bachelor party started with a thrill-ride. He, John, Nathan, and some of the other men took the limo into Augusta. The group feted him with skydiving out of a private plane owned by one of the affiliate members, who also wanted to join the party. Since none of them had ever jumped out of a plane before, it was a fun and challenging experience for everyone.

Afterward, they went out for dinner, then hit a few bars, ending in a strip club. Diego smiled as other men cheered the dancers on, but kept his hands to himself, despite the women who offered him lap dances. After a few hours, they headed back for the compound and used one of the smaller conference rooms to play poker, smoke cigars, and drink large quantities of whiskey. Porn movies played in the background, which were mostly ignored — until the scenes of bestiality involving wolves and humans. That got everyone's attention, and they yelled and threw peanuts and popcorn at the screen.

"No, that's not how you get a female wolf receptive!" someone yelled.

"That wolf's dick would fit in easier if she changed position," one man observed loudly, as they all laughed.

"We could make better wolf porn than that crap," another one of the men yelled.

Others challenged him to prove it with his girlfriend. That might have led to a fight, but Diego moved to stand in front of him to calm him down. Instead of escalating the argument, they all agreed that another round of shots was in order.

At one point, some of the men decided to shift and run outside. Diego joined them, outrunning most of them. When he stopped to howl at the moon, his wolf reminded him, *Soon she will be ours . . . forever.* The sheer bliss they both felt in that knowledge made for a joyful run that ended when the sun was coming up. The few men that hadn't run ended up passing out in the chairs they sat in, or on nearby couches. But Diego and most of the other men made it back to their own beds before they gave in to their tiredness.

None of the men had bothered with clothing since no one else was expected to be awake. Diego strode naked into his quarters and fell facedown onto his bed. He was asleep even before he hit the pillow. But when he awoke, he hugged the pillow that Saoirse slept on, to inhale her scent and build his anticipation for when he would see her again.

Nathan was left in charge of security when Diego and those attending the wedding left for the airport in Augusta. John was the best man, so he accompanied Diego. Very few of the security guards chose to go, since they preferred to maintain vigilance while the pack leader was gone, especially so close to a change in leadership.

The report Diego received from Nathan after settling into his hotel in Boston mentioned some of the pack members traveling into town to do some holiday shopping. Since this was to be expected for the time of year, he gave it as little attention as Nathan had.

CHAPTER TWENTY-FIVE

Sunday was a day of rest for Saoirse and her group of partiers. *Thank God I finally get a morning to sleep in! And Freddie knows the owner of the place he's taking us to breakfast at, so whenever we get there, will be fine.*

Once they were seated at the table, there was a lot of good-natured teasing. Those who had foggy memories of the night's late activities were told of their outrageous behavior by others who had stayed sober enough to remember. Pot after pot of coffee was brought to their table, and they didn't leave until well after the place closed, at three in the afternoon.

Soon after they got back to Freddie's place, he turned and exclaimed, "You know what day this is, right?"

Saoirse raised an eyebrow. "Um, Sunday?"

"That's right, Sam! And what does Jorge's favorite bar have every Sunday night?"

"Oh no! Not karaoke! You know I can't sing! I can barely carry a tune in a bucket."

"Ah, but what about the rest of the wedding party? Ladies, are you up for showing everyone what you've got?"

Everyone else was enthusiastic about it, so Saoirse bowed to the majority consensus. The group hit the bar and spent a few hours making each other laugh as they all tried to prove they could sing . . . with varying degrees of success. The celebrating ended early since few had gotten much sleep the night before. But all agreed that Freddie threw the best parties, and they were glad he was *the man of honor.*

Saoirse's sisters had gone back to their hotels to shower and change after their brunch. They returned to Freddie's that night for the partying, then returned to their rooms to get in enough sleep before facing their husbands and children the next day. And so their parents, hopefully, wouldn't suspect they had partied for two whole days and nights.

The next morning, the rest of Saoirse's family started to check into the two hotels that had offered group rates. Saoirse, Jerene, Monique, and Freddie grabbed a taxi and went to one of the hotels after breakfast. Jerene and Monique checked into their rooms, while Saoirse checked into the *Honeymoon Suite*. She and Freddie checked out all the amenities, laughing at the size of the California King four-poster bed. Freddie nicknamed it *the gymnasium*. He commented on how *he* would indulge in some light bondage using neckties if he was the lucky one getting to enjoy the enormous bed.

Suddenly the door opened, and Diego called out, "Where's my woman?"

Saoirse ran over to him and jumped into his arms, wrapping her legs around him. He held her ass with both hands as they kissed as if they'd been separated for years, completely oblivious that they were being watched.

Freddie shook his head, grinning at their display, before turning to talk to the man who had followed Diego into the room. Suddenly, it felt like all the air had been sucked out of the room, and he stopped breathing, to stare open-mouthed at the most gorgeous man he had ever seen.

The man approached with a casual smile, extending his hand for a shake. "Hi, I'm John Johnson, the best man."

Freddie held out his hand, trying to stop his arm from shaking. When their palms met, John's eyes widened in surprise, and Freddie felt a tingle race through his whole body, to end up centered in his groin, making his jeans suddenly way too tight.

"I'll say you are," he stammered, feeling himself blush uncharacteristically. He recovered quickly. "I mean . . . hello, I'm Freddie Landon. I'm the maid . . . I mean, *man of honor.*"

"So you're Saoirse's best friend from back when you were little kids?"

He nodded. "Yup." *And you're the man she told me was closeted so tightly the door has never been opened? Sam, we're not even anymore. I owe you big time for this gorgeous man that I'm going to seduce as quickly as possible!*

Freddie waved at the wedding couple. "Maybe we should give them a little privacy?"

John glanced at them and nodded.

Both men made for the exit, and Freddie announced as they opened the door, "You guys really need to come up for air, or you're going to pass out from lack of oxygen. John and I are heading down to the bar in the lobby. You can meet us down there when you're . . . um . . . done."

Diego growled when the door closed behind them.

"I need you naked. Now!"

He put her down, and they both stripped as quickly as possible. Diego picked her up again and pushed his way into her. To his great joy, he discovered their passionate kissing and groping had made her slippery enough for him to seat himself fully in her slick channel.

"We . . . *I* have missed you," he growled, his wolf asserting itself.

"Wait till you see the bed," Saoirse panted.

Diego looked around over her head and saw the bed through the doorway she'd approached him from. He carried her toward the bedroom while still inside of her. Saoirse squeaked from an orgasm his walking movements had apparently caused.

When he reached the bed, he turned to sit on the edge, his hands still gripping her ass, kneading the muscular globes, while he withdrew and then plunged himself back into her. She began to do a belly-dancing roll that ensured every part of her was stimulated by his cock. It didn't take long before he lost control, despite his best efforts to hold out. He howled as her orgasmic spasms pulled him along on the roller-coaster ride of blissful mindlessness. Eventually, he lay back on the bed, trying to regulate his breathing back to normal.

She fell forward onto his chest and panted. "Welcome to Boston, honey." She raised her head and smiled at him.

He opened his eyes to stare into hers. "I felt incomplete without you. As if a part of me had gone missing. I never realized how much I could need another person. This mating bond is stronger than anything I've ever felt before."

"I missed you too," she murmured. "If I hadn't been drinking so much, I'd have called you each night. As it is, Freddie has kept us partying for the whole time we've been here."

"Do I need to kill anyone?"

She grinned. "Uh, no. Freddie may be gay, but he's still a man, and he has a wicked right cross—which I taught him, by the way. He would've decked any guy trying to touch me. The ones he might have missed would have been flattened by Monique. You know that. And if by any chance they didn't stop the guy, I'd have neutered him myself before I'd have let him touch me. I'm a one-man, one-wolf woman now."

"Thank you for acknowledging both of us."

"But we do need to keep an eye on the time. The rehearsal is at the banquet hall, starting at four. We'll be going to a nearby Italian restaurant for homemade pasta after. I'm sure everyone is congregating in the bar downstairs, where Freddie and John escaped to, to avoid having to witness our . . . um . . . extreme joy at being reunited." She giggled.

He rolled his eyes. "I've never come so close to losing control over myself with others watching."

"Me neither, big guy. But then I've never been engaged before. And we haven't spent any time apart since our first time together."

"I'm just glad it was John, whom I trust implicitly, and your friend Freddie. I assume he can keep a secret?"

"Yeah . . . until he wants to tease me unmercifully. Then he'll remind me of my indiscretion. But who cares? I'm in love and getting married tomorrow."

Diego let out a low growl. "Yes. Tomorrow."

She gently slapped his arm. "Let's go shower, so we don't smell like we just had sex. Then we can get dressed and go downstairs. I've got a whole lot of relatives who will be expecting to meet you, and they'll be insulted if we spend all our time up here. There'll be plenty of time for this kind of thing on our honeymoon. Which reminds me, you still haven't told me where we're going."

"You'll find out when we get there. Just trust me on this, you're going to love it."

Reluctantly, Diego pulled himself out of his woman, and they got up to head for the shower.

Many hours later, after the rehearsal was done and dinner had been enjoyed, people lingered in the hotel bar once again, talking in small groups. Saoirse jumped up from chatting with her brother to hug Freddie, who was making his way back from the bathroom.

"Freddie, you've done a marvelous job!" She hugged him fiercely.

"Sam, nothing is too good for you, my sweetie." He grinned at her.

"But you set all of this up by yourself. I have the greatest bestie that anyone could ever have. And you've been the best *man of honor*. I don't know how to thank you for all you've done."

Freddie glanced over her shoulder. "Oh, I think you've taken care of that just fine."

She followed Freddie's gaze to see John, who was sitting next to Diego, chatting with her parents and grinned. "Yeah, he *is* your type, isn't he?"

He nodded. "But you're right about him being wound tight. I know he's interested, but I'm trying to figure out how to seduce him."

"Just be careful, please. He's Diego's second . . . um . . . best friend. And he's a close friend of mine also. I don't want him to be hurt."

Freddie's eyebrows rose. "I don't plan on hurting him . . . unless he asks me to."

"Ha, ha."

"No, really. And I don't plan on doing anything that will spoil your joyous occasion."

She sighed heavily. "Fine. Just try to remember what your first time was like, and don't push him into anything he's not ready for."

"Honey, my first time was so long ago I can't even remember what that was like."

She stuck her tongue out at Freddie, then noticed Diego beckoning for her to join him.

Freddie sat quietly when John got up and headed toward the bathroom, waiting until he returned, then waved for John to join him at his small table. As John sat down, the waitress put two drinks on the table, and Freddie paid her for them both.

"How did you know what I'm drinking?" John asked.

"I've been watching you all evening," Freddie replied,

careful to keep his voice casual.

"Why?" John took a sip from his drink.

Freddie leaned closer, keeping his voice low. "Because I know you felt the electric shock when we shook hands, just as much as I did."

John met his gaze steadily. "I'm not sure what you mean."

Freddie took a deep breath. "You're a gorgeous man, John. I'm very attracted to you. Normally, I'd invite you back to my place, but you have a hotel room right upstairs. What say we bring our drinks with us, and go find a more private place to talk?"

"Are we going to do more than talk?"

Freddie looked deep into those light brown eyes and almost swooned. "That depends on you, John."

John glanced around the room before meeting Freddie's gaze. John's pupils were so enlarged with excitement, the color was almost not visible anymore.

"Let's go," John whispered.

Freddie had to resist the urge to jump up and pump his arm in celebration. Instead, he picked up his drink and followed John out of the bar.

Saoirse watched Freddie and John leave, breathing a silent prayer that they would find some measure of happiness together. Then she concentrated on trying to rein in her parents. They were busily grilling Diego about every detail of his life, from his birth up to now, to ascertain if he was good enough for their baby girl.

The door was barely closed in John's room before he grabbed Freddie and pressed him against the wall with his hips. He leaned forward and enjoyed his first real kiss. They were close to the same height, so there was no danger of cricks in any-one's neck. They were perfectly matched. Erections rubbed on erections, and zippers became instruments of torture.

The kiss escalated when Freddie licked at John's mouth and got their tongues involved. John groaned, as years of pent-up passion threatened to overwhelm him. They groped each other, and he enjoyed the feel of the hard muscles under smooth skin. Their hands slid under each other's shirts to stimulate sensitive areas. Then shirts were torn off as they both sought more skin-to-skin contact. They moved further into the room until he was backed up to the side of the bed.

John tried to remember *how* to breathe. He started getting frustrated when he didn't know how to ask for what he wanted, then sighed when Freddie took the lead and opened his pants. John obliged by opening Freddie's, also. He grasped Freddie's hard cock, moaning at the pleasure of that first feel of hardness in the palm of his hand.

Freddie sank to his knees, looking up with glazed eyes. "May I?"

"Oh, my God . . . yes." John could barely get the words past his dry throat.

Freddie pushed John's pants down and used both hands to fondle his erection. John felt his balls move upward and tighten as Freddie palmed the tender globes.

Freddie lowered his mouth to lick at the drops of pre-come leaking out and groaned. "You taste so good."

John's hips automatically thrust forward at the sensation of Freddie's tongue, and the man obliged him by relaxing the back of his throat and swallowing him whole.

John's eyes rolled back in his head when Freddie started bobbing up and down. Freddie swallowed forcefully each time his nose nestled at the base of John's cock. Then he'd lick his way back up to the tip, only to take him even further into his throat the next time. It didn't take long before he grabbed

Freddie's hair with both hands and held his head firmly against his body, growling as he came. Freddie enhanced his pleasure by easily swallowing, despite the force of the stream from his orgasm, which seemed to go on forever.

John's legs gave out, and he collapsed backward onto the bed. Freddie grinned when he stood and finished undressing. He reached over and pulled off John's shoes and socks, then grabbed the ankles of his pants and eased them off also.

"Are you ready for the next round?" Freddie asked with a mischievous grin.

John got lost in the inky depths of Freddie's eyes. The man crawled onto the bed to lie next to him, one hand trailing circles around his closest nipple.

"Will it be as good as that?" John asked in a husky whisper.

"I'll do my best," Freddie said, licking his lips.

"There's so much I want to try . . ."

"We may have to limit things, since I don't have any supplies with me."

"Like condoms and lube?"

Freddie's eyebrows expressed his surprise.

John smiled shyly. "There's a drug store right down the street. I may be inexperienced, but I have watched some porn. I know how things are done — just not how they feel."

"Are you a top or a bottom?"

John shrugged. "I dunno. Never been either."

Freddie leaned over for a kiss with a long, lingering caress of his lips. "Then we'll have to try it both ways. Maybe more than once . . . just so you can be sure."

"We should probably get some sleep . . ."

"We will . . . eventually."

And many, many hours later, they did.

Chapter Twenty-six

The weather cooperated, offering bright sunshine in the morning. Saoirse and Diego ordered breakfast up to their room and made love while they waited for their food to arrive.

"Our last time as single people," Saoirse panted, trying to recover from one orgasm before the next one blasted through her.

Diego growled, shaking his head. "No, not single. Mated, but not yet married. My wolf is happy, but I need a ring on your finger."

They both stayed naked while they enjoyed their food. Saoirse was just pouring more coffee into Diego's cup when his phone suddenly insisted that he answer it immediately.

"Damn! Where did I put it?" He jumped up to look for the pants he'd discarded the night before. He found the pants and pulled the phone out while it was still ringing. "Hello?"

Saoirse watched his face reflect a myriad of emotions.

"Oh, hi, Mom. So you've arrived? You're staying in one of the penthouses? Great. Are the girls with you? Both of them? Good, very good."

He took a sip of the coffee she passed to him as he listened. "No, I'm not too busy to come up to say hello. Yes, I will bring my fiancée with me so you can meet her. No, we're not staying in separate rooms. That would be silly. We're in the Honeymoon Suite."

He sighed heavily. "No, Mom. I don't think that's bad luck. And I don't care if I see her in her dress before the wedding.

We make our own luck, Mom." He rolled his eyes. "Look. We just finished breakfast in our room. We'll get dressed and see you up there in about twenty minutes. No, that won't make us late. The ceremony isn't until three, and it's only . . ."

Saoirse checked her phone, then held up ten fingers plus one extra.

"It's only eleven o'clock. There's plenty of time for you to get to know Saoirse before we have to get ready." He closed his eyes while he listened quietly for a moment.

"Yes, you tell your security people to expect us. You know what I look like, and Saoirse is the most beautiful red-headed angel you've ever seen."

He smiled as she blew a kiss at him.

"Yes, I love you too, Mom. See you soon."

He hung up and shook his head. "She seems to be in a good mood, so that's something. She says the paparazzi were fooled by her sneaking into the hotel via the kitchen entrance, and they think she's at the hotel across the street. It won't take long until they realize their mistake. But hopefully, we can lose them on the way to the wedding."

"I've never met a celebrity before." Saoirse got up and walked over to the bathroom. "Whatever should I wear?"

"No matter what it is, you'll always be the most beautiful woman in the room to me."

She grinned at him. "Good answer, lover. Now let's wash the sex-smell off ourselves before we go meet your famous mom."

He growled at her and chased her as she giggled her way into the bathroom.

They had to go through a phalanx of security before they could even knock on the door to the penthouse suite. The door was opened by a young blonde woman, who hugged Diego in a restrained manner, then waved her arm to indicate they should enter.

"Hi, Vanessa," Diego said. "This is my fiancée, Saoirse McColl. Saoirse, this is my sister, Vanessa. She's the older one. The other one is" — he looked around the room — "over there."

As they walked in, Saoirse noticed suitcases of clothing all over the living room, looking as if they had exploded with sequins and glittery fabrics. High heels were scattered all around the room. In the middle of the mess, Valerie Vargas sat at a vanity while a young woman applied cosmetics to her face. In the chair next to her, a younger version of the woman was also having her face done. When Valerie saw Diego in the mirror, she pushed the makeup woman away and jumped up out of her chair.

"Diego! My first child! My baby boy! Just look at you! You've changed so much since the last time I saw you."

She grabbed his shoulders and pulled him close for an air kiss. "Don't smudge Mommy's makeup, darling. I've been in this damn chair for hours already. You know I want to look perfect for the wedding photos."

As she released Diego, he gestured for Saoirse to join him. She'd been standing by Vanessa, who fidgeted with some makeup, apparently waiting for her turn in the chair. When she stood next to him, he took her hand and kissed her knuckles. She tried to ignore the tingle that shot through her body, arousing places that always responded to his touch.

"Mom, this is my fiancée, Saoirse McColl. Saoirse, this is my mom, Valerie Vargas."

"Please to meet you, ma'am," Saoirse began.

"Oh, God no! You can't call me that!" Valerie wailed dramatically. "I'm not old enough to be called that." She glared at the cosmetician. "You're supposed to ensure that I don't look old. I don't care how long I have to sit in this chair, you need to make me look too young to be called *ma'am*."

Saoirse stammered, "I . . . I didn't mean anything by

that . . ."

Valerie turned and approached her to give her the same kind of impersonal hug and air kiss she'd given her son.

"Of course, you didn't. I know that. It's just that Diego is my oldest, so he's the first to get married." She waved a dismissive hand.

She turned back to her son. "She's lovely, Diego. But such a weird name. You'll have to spell it more than once for the reporters, I'll bet. Is it Irish or something? Such bright red hair, such a nice smile. Of course, we'll have to tone down the hair so it doesn't look orange in the pictures. But that's easily done, right, Melba?"

The cosmetician nodded.

"Uh, Mom, she's not doing anything with her hair. I like it the way it is."

"Oh, darling. You say the nicest things. But of course, she'll take my advice. After all, I know about how to get the best pictures taken. I've been doing it for years," she added in an aside to Saoirse, with a wink.

"Besides, now that we're friends again, you'll need my advice so that only the pictures you approve will appear in any of the tabloids. There'll be wedding pictures, honeymoon pictures, then, of course, when any baby bump might appear, there'll be pictures of that, and of the eventual grandbaby. Oh my God! I'm old enough to be a grandmother! Holy shit! Melba, I need my highlights done again. My hair is looking brittle and old. I don't want to look old enough to be a gramma. I want people to wonder if I had Diego in my teens—which actually, I did. Of course, I was nineteen at the time."

Diego shook his head. "No, Mom. There are *not* going to be any pictures of our wedding in the tabloids. I forbid it. I won't sign any releases, and neither will any of our guests. This is not a publicity stunt for your career. This is my life, and it will be done my way."

"What? Victoria, see how he talks to me?" She fell back dramatically into the chair she'd been on and wailed to the girl sitting in the other chair, who glanced up briefly, from playing games on her phone, to shrug.

"Diego, you know that everywhere I go, paparazzi follow me. I can't help that my public wants to see me in my private life."

"No, Mom. You don't have a private life. You never have. You gave that up a long time ago when you signed that contract with Satan to be a pop singer."

She glared at him. "It kept you fed when you were little, mister. Remember that."

He reached for Saoirse's hand, and when she squeezed his, he took a deep breath.

"Mom, I told you when I invited you that this is a private ceremony. If you think that pictures are going to go out whether or not I approve them, then maybe you shouldn't attend the ceremony."

There was a long, extended silence. Saoirse held her breath, looking around in dismay at the dysfunctional grouping that was Diego's only family.

"You hear how he talks to his mother," Valerie shrieked. "Such disrespect! How long will it be before he treats you like this too?"

Saoirse cleared her throat to speak soothingly. "I don't think he means disrespect, Valerie. But we live a very quiet life these days. We're not public people. None of my family was expecting to be in tabloids, so no one will agree to it. We already have a photographer hired, and she's the only one we will allow to take pictures. We run a school, after all, and we don't want any publicity to detract from the important work we do with our students."

"School?"

Diego sighed heavily. "Yes, Mom. I told you when I moved out east that I'm the principal of a private high school."

"What's the name of it? Just one mention of it associated with my name, and you'll be turning the students away while their parents offer to pay you double or triple the usual tuition."

He shook his head. "No, Mom. I'm not telling you the name just for that reason. And as for the rest of the details of my life, they're not for sale. And when we have children, they won't be, either. When I ran away from you, it wasn't *you* that I was escaping from, but your publicity. I love you because you're my mom. But I don't want any part of your lifestyle."

She scrutinized him, still glaring. "Then why did you invite us? You know what it's like to be me."

He shrugged. "Maybe I hoped it would be different . . . just this once. But I can see that I was wrong."

Suddenly her eyes filled with tears. "All right. If that's how you feel about it. I can tell when I'm not wanted. You don't want your mom to be a part of your life. You've made that perfectly clear. I don't want to be where I'm not welcome. I'll take your sisters and leave. And I'll try to forget that I ever had a son. Will that make you happy?"

"No," he began, but his voice cracked. He cleared his throat. "No, Mom. It won't make me happy. But I was never happy when I was a part of your public life. And the problem with you is you aren't any different in private. There *is* no private *you*. There's only your public persona. And I don't like her much."

Valerie sniffed audibly, then leaned closer to examine her face in the mirror. "Shit! Now, look at what you've done. My makeup is ruined. But I guess it doesn't matter because I won't be going to any wedding today." She got up from the chair and waved her arms towards her daughters. "Girls. Pack up your things. We're leaving. If your brother doesn't want us at his wedding, then we'll go."

Victoria looked up from her phone and got up from her chair. "Mom, can we go to New York? I want to do some more Christmas shopping. They have the best stores there."

Vanessa chimed in, "Yeah, and there are holiday shows everywhere. I'll bet we can get into lots of them, because they'll be thrilled to have you make a surprise guest appearance. Won't that be great? It'll be a huge Christmas present to everyone there who didn't expect to get to see Valerie Vargas when they bought their tickets."

Valerie's eyes sparkled anew, not with tears, but with excitement. "Yes, you're so right. Ooh, I wonder who's in town now? I'll bet there are some bitchin' parties planned." She turned to bark out some orders. "People, people. You heard me. We're leaving. Get all of this shit packed and make arrangements for us to fly to New York. We're going to do up Christmas right this year."

She turned back to look at Diego, who was watching her silently, and Saoirse, whose mouth had fallen open.

"And you, Diego. You've always been such a disappointment to me. You go back to your boring little life, with your boring little wife-to-be. And don't worry about me. I'll be fine. Congratulations on your choices, you two. I'm sure you'll be very happy together."

With that, she turned and swept out of the room, slamming the bedroom door behind her.

Diego started towards the door to leave, still holding Saoirse's hand. She turned to look back at his sisters, but they were both busily ordering the servants around, getting them to pack up all the clothing. Neither of them even looked in their brother's direction.

Diego opened the door, and they walked through past the security guards to the elevator that would take them back to their floor. Diego's back was ramrod stiff until the door of the elevator shut. Then he slumped back against the wall, closing his eyes and rubbing his temples.

Saoirse moved in front of him and pulled him close for a hug. "Diego, I'm so sorry."

He looked into her eyes, and she hurt from the pain she saw there.

"Why? You didn't make her this way." He sighed. "It's the way she's always been."

"Then why did you invite her?"

He shrugged. "It's been over ten years. Maybe I hoped that age might have mellowed her. Maybe I hoped that she might have missed me and might want to be a part of my life. But I was wrong. She's the same as she ever was."

Saoirse just held him as their breathing synchronized. Suddenly he reached behind her to hit the button that stopped the elevator, just short of their floor. She looked up, questioningly.

He met her gaze steadily. "Now that you know what I come from, do you still want to marry me? I wouldn't blame you if you wanted to run as far away from me as you can."

She shook her head. "No, you silly man. I love you even more, now that I see what you've had to overcome. I'm awed by the strength that you have to reject your dysfunctional family and your even more dysfunctional father. You found a place in the world that allows you to be the leader you were meant to be. I'm honored that you want me to be your wife. And I know that I will always be able to depend on you. And I want you to know that you'll always be able to depend on me. I love you, Diego Vargas, *both* of you. And you know, I hope, you're *already* a part of my family. We don't have any money, but we have lots of love. And my mom and dad told me they approve of my husband-to-be. So you don't need her and her baggage anymore. You have a new family to belong to—a real one."

There were tears in Diego's eyes. His voice was hoarse with emotions. "I have always seen myself as an emotionally broken man. But with your love, I feel healed and whole. I love you, Saoirse McColl. And I can't get that ring onto your finger soon enough."

He lowered his head for a kiss in a solemn vow for both of them. Then he pushed the button again, and they rode down to their floor. They smiled at one another as the door opened, and they both took a deep, cleansing breath and returned to the reality of their lives.

CHAPTER TWENTY-SEVEN

The guests all found their seats, and the procession began on time. Saoirse peeked into the chapel area while she waited. Diego and John stood at the flower-covered arch, looking handsome in their suits. The music started, and it was time. Freddie walked out first with her mom, followed by her dad walking her down the aisle. The love that shone in Diego's eyes as he awaited his bride was evident even from the back of the gathering.

The ceremony itself was non-denominational, centering on the role of love in creating families, and in keeping all family members strong. The woman's words struck home, making Saoirse and Diego smile as they gazed into each other's eyes.

They had written their own words to say to each other, and to those unaware of Diego's alter-ego, *her* words were merely a quaint turn of phrase. Hopefully, for those who knew *why* she said what she did, it was a point of pride for them that she totally accepted every part of him. Surely they could sense her devotion to making their marriage an example of the joy to be found in truly loving every aspect of another person.

Diego's voice broke more than once. His words professed his undying love and adoration for the woman who made him whole, and to whom he would devote even his last dying breath to pleasing.

They placed rings onto each other's fingers, then they were told to kiss. Before the words had even left the lips of the officiant, Diego swept Saoirse into a passionate embrace.

When they turned to the audience, Diego called out

triumphantly, "She's mine!"

It was obvious to Saoirse that some of the audience were fighting their resulting desire to howl in acknowledgment of Diego's elation. Instead, they settled for clapping and cheering, just as Saoirse's whole family was doing.

Endless pictures followed for the wedding party and their friends and relations. As each group of people was released from posing, they joined others already working on the canapés and drinks. Finally, even she and Diego were able to join them. Soon after that, the owner of the banquet hall announced that it was time to file into the next room to find seating for dinner. In one corner, a DJ was setting up his equipment. The bar was open, and the entire room was festooned with red and white flowers, with pine branches for contrast.

It was a perfect setting for a Christmas wedding celebration. The food was fabulous, and the cake was extraordinary, thanks to another close friend of Freddie's. A good time was had by all, and no one was allowed to sit when there was music playing. The DJ said goodnight at midnight, but the hall stayed open until one, to allow everyone to gradually make their after-party plans. Many people headed back to their hotel bars, to continue their revelry long into the night.

"After all," Saoirse told Diego with a smile as they got back into the limo Freddie had hired for the day. "We *are* Irish, you know. We wrote the original book on partying."

Diego groped her in the limo. "All I can think of is making love to my wife," he growled into her ear.

"Later, lover. We have relatives who've come a long way to be a part of our joy. We have to at least make a quick appearance in the hotel bars. We can have a quick drink in each one, then excuse ourselves early. No one will question why we want to get back to our *Honeymoon* Suite."

So they chatted briefly with many of the people in each bar. They personally thanked all their friends and relatives for attending their wedding, reminding them of the day-after brunch the next day.

The last two people they approached were Freddie and John, who were slow dancing in a dark corner of their hotel bar. Saoirse tapped Freddie on the shoulder, and when he turned, she was amazed at the supreme happiness on his face. She looked at John and saw a mirror-image on his face as well.

Feeling like an intruder, she teased. "I was going to thank you for all you've done for me, Freddie. But one look at you two, and all I can think of to say is, *Get a room!*"

"We have one. Are you two heading upstairs now?" Freddie asked. The dreamy tone in his voice was hard to miss.

"Yes, and you should also, lest you embarrass any of the children."

John looked at his watch and snorted. "It's after three. There shouldn't be any children still up. And we're in a bar."

Saoirse pointed at a couple of nearby tables occupied by some of her cousins, who were teenagers playing lively games of poker with a pitcher of coke close by.

"Okay, okay. We'll head upstairs, too," Freddie said.

Diego's eyes were unfocused while they were waiting for the elevator.

Saoirse poked him in the side. "What?"

"Oh, nothing. I just can't wait to get you alone, Mrs. Vargas."

She grinned at him. "Talking to your wolf, were you, Mr. Vargas? Well, tell him I've got some surprises still in store for you tonight."

His eyebrows rose. "You do? Like what?"

"Just you wait and see, husband."

When they got into the elevator, they were accompanied by Freddie and John. Some drunken businessmen who were not a part of their party also stepped in. Everyone kept their hands to themselves. Freddie and John got off on their floor, saying goodnight. The drunken businessmen ogled Saoirse, still in her low-cut dress.

"Jus' married?" one asked.

She nodded. "Yup."

The other man addressed his words to Diego, "Why do we keep on doing it?"

"Doing what?"

"Putting on the ball and chain on purpose. Why do we let them trap us like that?"

Diego's eyes narrowed. "Because I want her to myself. If any other man so much as *looks* at her with lust in his heart, I'll rip it out of his chest and eat it for breakfast."

Saoirse had to muffle her squeak of laughter as the men's eyes widened in shock. They mumbled words about needing some exercise, so they'd walk the rest of the way up to their rooms. They punched the button to get off on the next floor.

Diego had a self-satisfied smirk on his lips as they rode the remainder of the trip up to their floor. Finally, the door opened, and they made their way to what truly now was the Honeymoon Suite, to officially begin their married life.

Diego grabbed for Saoirse as soon as he had locked the door to their room.

She pushed back gently. "No, husband. I need to use the bathroom. You just make yourself comfortable on the bed, and I'll be right out."

He grinned, nodding as she headed into the bathroom. He took off his tux jacket and his tie, opening the top few buttons on his shirt and kicking off his shoes. He moved over to the bed and lay on his back, lacing his fingers behind his head.

After a few minutes, he called out, "I'm not a very patient man right now . . ."

The door opened, and Saoirse sashayed in, using the remote to dim the lighting and turn on some music. The room filled with the sounds of a sexy saxophone playing bluesy jazz. She swayed her hips to the rhythm as she made her way further into the room, stopping near the foot of the bed. As she moved, she reached behind herself and unzipped her dress, letting each side fall off her shoulders, and holding the front up against her breasts.

Diego was trying to remember how to breathe as he watched, spellbound.

Saoirse turned around and continued to rotate her hips, slowly letting the dress fall around her feet. Diego gasped at the sight of her smooth skin covered with only a lacy bra with a matching thong, a garter belt, and nylons, along with her high heels. His nostrils flared as he scented the moisture that wetted the little patch of lace between her thighs. Still, he somehow managed to remain on the bed, merely watching.

She continued to sway in rhythm to the slow, sexy beat of the music while she removed her strapless bra. As she turned, she pushed her breasts up and together, an offering Diego couldn't ignore. He moved to sit on the edge of the bed and replaced her hands with his own, caressing her breasts lovingly, then he licked at one and then the other. With a growl, he fastened his mouth on one nipple, to torture her with suction and licking. He then released it and did the same for the other.

His hands were busy, too, kneading the round globes of her ass. Then with a quick flick of his wrists, he tore at the interfering thong. Shredding sounds fill the air as he pulled the stitches apart and discarded the lace on the floor. He slid his hands along her upper thighs in a moment of reverence. With a low groan, he pulled her closer, then twisted to toss her into the middle of the bed.

Then things became wild as they both tore at his clothing

to get him naked, too. Once he was, he crawled onto the bed, spreading her legs with his knees. He stopped for an instant, and she opened her eyes to catch him staring intently at her.

"What?" she asked him in a husky whisper.

"I can't believe what a lucky man I am."

He maneuvered himself into place, rubbing the head of his cock against her clit, mingling their juices together. Then he pushed his hips forward and impaled her and stopped, enjoying Saoirse's happy sigh as he stretched her to accommodate him. When he didn't move right away, she peered into his face, her eyebrows raised in question.

"I want to savor this moment," he murmured. "The first time I enter my *wife*, to make us one. Our union is complete. I will remember this for the rest of my life."

Saoirse smiled dreamily at him, "So will I, my love. But I can't help myself. *You* might be able to stay still, but not me."

She squeezed him with her inner muscles, tightly, then released, then tightly again. Her breathing sped up as she brought herself closer and closer to her completion. When she froze, holding him tightly, he surged forward with a howl. "Mine!"

They were both suspended for a moment, staring into each other's eyes. Then their bodies took over, and they spiraled together into multi-orgasmic bliss. Saoirse's eyes squeezed shut as they both enjoyed the rising and falling of the tidal waves they rode as one.

At some point, he collapsed onto her and struggled to re-learn how to breathe. Eventually, he pulled himself out of her and rolled off to lie on his side, pulling her into his arms. She snuggled in with a contented sigh, licking at the salty sweat on his chest.

"Can we get some sleep now, husband?"

He nodded. "For a while. Until I wake up hard again."

She giggled. "You always wake up hard."

"When my senses are overwhelmed with your scent while I sleep, yes."

"Then let's rest, and dream about the next round."

He smiled, kissing the top of her head.

He reached for the remote that she'd tossed onto the nightstand and turned off the music and the lights. Then he wrapped both arms around his wife, smiling when he heard her snoring softly.

My life is complete.

Yes, she belongs to us now . . . and forever, his wolf replied in a soft, contented purr.

He sighed with satisfaction, barely noticing that the first rays of daylight were beginning to peek through the blinds, as he drifted off to sleep.

CHAPTER TWENTY-EIGHT

As Saoirse told Diego to expect, the brunch the next day was pleasant and subdued. A large number of people were eschewing any alcohol, due to having over-imbibed at the reception and after-parties. Some brave souls did expound on the *hair of the dog* theory, ordering a mimosa or Bloody Mary along with their omelets. Conversations were easy and companionable, since most of the guests sat with their relatives or friends. After a couple of hours, everyone took their turn in leaving to head home for their Christmas celebrations. Planes needed to be caught, and goodbyes were hurried but sincere.

Diego had made their traveling arrangements. Saoirse was delighted to discover their flight was booked for mid-afternoon. Almost all their guests were already gone by the time they left for the airport. They flew back to Augusta, accompanied by the others who had flown out to Boston with them.

"For security reasons, of course," Monique said with a wink.

Once they got off the plane, however, their paths diverged. The others were met by Nathan and the limo. But Diego mentioned he had rented a car, so they made their way over to the rental agency, where they were given the keys to a shiny, new sporty sedan.

"So, where are we going?" Saoirse queried as they put their luggage into the back seat of the vehicle.

Diego smiled. "It's a surprise. But I guarantee you'll be pleased."

When they drove out of the airport, instead of heading northwest, they headed almost straight west. The sun was out, making the snow sparkle like diamonds. They settled into an easy, relaxed mood, switching radio stations to avoid songs they didn't like. Saoirse sang loudly along with the ones she knew most of the words to.

The sun was beginning to set when Diego turned off the highway, driving down a long, two-lane road. They had only passed one small sign along the way, so Saoirse still had no idea where their destination was. But she perked with interested when they pulled up to a well-maintained building. Even in the harsh Maine winter, it appeared inviting.

She accompanied Diego into the lobby with a large fireplace, comfy sofas, and a wall of books waiting to be read.

"Hello, and welcome to Dreamers Inn," the receptionist said as they reached the check-in desk.

Diego gave their names and signed in, then was given a key, along with a small map of the grounds.

"Dinner serving begins at seven," the young man said. "And tonight, the chef is preparing Beef Tenderloin plunged in merlot with shallots and tail of veal."

"Wow!" Saoirse said when they got back into the car. "That sounds like a very fancy dinner."

Diego smirked. "Of course it is. We're on our honeymoon, remember? And we're staying here through Christmas and into next week, so we're going to get to have quite a few of the chef's specialties. Breakfast will be delivered to our cabin every morning."

"What kind of place is this?"

He handed her the brochure, and she paged through it, looking at the pictures of the various amenities.

"It's a part of a national group of very elite places," he began.

"I'll bet it's expensive," she remarked.

Diego shrugged. "I suppose it is. But one of our affiliates wanted to express how happy he is for us, though he wasn't able to be at the wedding. He's a part-owner of this place, so we're staying in his cabin. All of the places have a view of the lake, along with fireplaces and indoor hot tubs. But some of them are close to other cabins. We'll be more remote and closer to the woods."

Saoirse smiled at him. "So no one will hear me when I scream your name?"

He shook his head. "Nope."

"It's perfect!"

The week passed too quickly for Saoirse. She sighed with happiness, though, as Diego started the car and began to pull away from the cabin they'd dubbed as their *love nest*. She relaxed in her seat, reminiscing all the things they had enjoyed during their stay.

We were pampered at dinner every day, with staff that anticipated our every need. They produced wines that complemented every part of the meal, ending each meal with superb desserts. We ordered breakfast on cards left on the porch and were awoken each morning by a discreet knock on the door that signaled our food had been delivered.

Since there had been so much snow, we borrowed snowsuits from the main desk and rented cross-country skis one day, snowshoes the next, from the amply supplied boathouse. We explored the extensive grounds until we were tired, then we warmed up in the hot tub in our cabin, soaking aching muscles. And we continued to find new ways to express our undying love and passion for each other, falling asleep from exhaustion each night, in each other's arms.

What a honeymoon!

Now they were driving back down the road to return to their lives. Saoirse glanced at Diego and smiled.

"I think I'll give our affiliate a huge discount on his dues for next year," Diego remarked. "After letting us enjoy this place, he deserves it."

Saoirse nodded a hearty agreement. "While I'm sad to be leaving paradise, we can't live here. We need to get back to where we belong, and to the lives we've chosen."

When they got back to Augusta and dropped off the car at the airport, Nathan met them with the limo and drove them back to the academy.

Much of their remaining time off during the school holiday was spent moving into the newly emptied penthouse. While Diego caught up with what had happened in his absence and got back into his responsibilities, Saoirse busied herself with plotting out the new semester of work for her students.

I wonder if they'll want to call me Mrs. Vargas now? I'll be fine with being Miss McColl in school — at least for a while. Funny how a small thing like being married changes so little, and yet everything. And for the better!

CHAPTER TWENTY-NINE

Diego sighed heavily as he regarded the large piles of papers strewn about on his desk in the principal's office. He had half-heartedly moved some of them around when he first sat down, but now he was wallowing in feeling overwhelmed.

There was a quick knock on the door, and he looked up to see who was disturbing him.

Monique smiled at him from the doorway. "Okay if I come in, boss?"

"Sure. There's a chair on the other side of this desk somewhere. Probably under those piles of folders."

She grinned as she picked up the folders and placed them on top of the nearest pile of papers. "Guess when you take time off, things accumulate, huh?"

He nodded ruefully. "Yeah. And the knowledge that there are even more urgent things in my other office that I should be dealing with makes me anxious to be done here. But I'm not even sure where to start."

Monique took a deep breath. "Would you like some help organizing things?"

His attention quickly returned to Monique. "Are you offering?"

Her lips curved in a smile. "Yup. I'm pretty good at wading through piles of papers and rendering them into usable piles, like semi-urgent, urgent, and *house-on-fire*."

His shoulders relaxed, just the tiniest bit. "I'd really appreciate any help at all, but I honestly didn't know who to ask.

Everyone around here is always so busy already, and I figured it was my problem."

Monique shook her head. "First, boss, you're now the pack leader, so any problems that are yours belong to all of us. I'm only too happy to help. Second, I'm not so busy these days. My kids are older now, and a new family that joined us right before you became leader includes a woman who is elementary-certified. She's been running some classes for the younger kids in the old meeting house next to the chapel. She's pregnant with their first child, so classes may be halted for a while after she gives birth. But since my strong-arm duties don't keep me busy all day, and my kids don't need me to home-school them anymore, I've got time on my hands."

She waved at all the papers with one arm. "And third, I've always loved the challenge of creating order out of chaos."

She leaned an elbow onto the nearest pile of papers. "I'm not sure if you're aware, but in addition to my experience being the wife of a pack leader, I'm also ABD for my MBA, so I know stuff about being in charge of things."

Diego frowned. "What? Could you say that again in English, so I'll know what the hell you're saying?"

"I was in grad school when I met my husband. We both knew right away what we had in common, and that we were meant to be mated. I got pregnant quickly, and we got married to make things legal. We visited his pack soon after that, so he could introduce me to them. And Tim was named leader by the old one before he died. That's when we both dropped out of college. No need for an advanced degree to be either a pack leader or his wife."

"So?"

"ABD means *all but dissertation*. And of course, MBA means Masters of Business Administration."

"So, in other words, you're ready, willing, and able to help me clean all of this up?"

"Sure thing, boss. I stopped by earlier, looking for you, and saw what condition your desk was in. I didn't want to move anything around until you were here, but if you'd let me help, I can take at least part of your burden off your shoulders."

He eyed her speculatively. "How would you feel about being the new principal?"

She grinned. "One step at a time, okay, boss? Let me see what the job entails, and I'll let you know. I'll organize stuff and let you review what I think needs to be acted upon urgently. Deal?"

He heaved a massive sigh of relief. "Great. Now I can head back to the equally daunting piles of things on my other desk."

"Sorry, but I can't help with those. That's pack leader business, boss, and not for us mere mortals to view."

"That's fine. But do you mind if I ask you a personal question?"

Her face grew solemn. "I guess not. I reserve the right to not answer if it's too personal."

"You're not the only one who's been calling me *boss*. John and Nathan have been doing it, too, as well as some of the teachers."

"But not Saoirse, right?" When he opened his mouth, she held out a hand, shaking her head. "No! I don't want to know what she calls you. Especially not during *those* moments."

They shared a quick smile.

"But really, why?"

Monique leaned back in her chair. "What did you call Joe?"

"I called him Joe sometimes. But most of the time, I called him *sir*."

"Right. That's what all the rest of us called him, too. Partly because he was so much older than us, that it felt kind of weird calling him by his first name. But also, because he was so noble and so powerful, that *sir* just felt right . . . like he had earned the right to be honored by his people."

"But I haven't earned that right yet?"

Monique shook her head. "It's not *only* that. It's partly because *sir* is what we called Joe, and we're not over grieving for him yet. Also, you're the same age or younger than a lot of us, so giving you that kind of honorific feels odd. But we do want to set you apart, based on your station around here. You are the pack leader, so calling you Diego is okay for social occasions. But when there's work to be done, *boss* honors your position, while being casual enough to feel more comfortable."

"Okay. I think I can understand that. And thanks for your honesty."

"Hey, just like it takes a village to raise a kid, it also takes a pack to teach a new leader how to lead. And might I add, *boss*, that you're already doing a fine job."

Diego rolled his eyes. "There hasn't been that much to deal with . . . yet."

"And let's hope it stays that way. You've only been our leader for about two months. You've been married for a few weeks. And now you're going to let me do the heavy lifting for your job as principal. That's a whole lot of changes to go through in a short time. There will be plenty of times to *try a man's soul* in the future. Let's not wish for them now." Monique shooed him away, then sat in the chair behind the desk.

"Okay," Diego said, feeling a massive sense of relief as he walked to the door. "Once you're done sorting through everything, organizing stuff, let me know, and I'll come back to talk with you about how things need to be handled."

"Sure thing, boss."

"I'll be in the pack leader's office when you need me."

"Of course," Monique said, sounding distracted. She was already reading and sorting paperwork.

That was almost too easy. Diego walked quickly through the halls, heading back to his other office. *I hope she decides to take my old job, so I can give all of my attention to pack business.*

At the January monthly pack meeting, Diego happily announced he had appointed Monique Martin as the new principal for the academy. There was the formality of a board vote, with the expected approval quickly recorded.

And later that evening, Saoirse teased him while getting ready for bed. "I'm so glad that Monique is the principal now. I can't be accused anymore of getting away with murder because I'm sleeping with the boss."

Diego growled, chased her over to the bed, and threw her into the middle of it. He climbed on, stalking her slowly, licking his way from her toes to her mouth. He paused at some of his favorite places in between, resulting in a vigorous encounter that left them both exhausted. They slipped off to sleep still in each other's arms.

CHAPTER THIRTY

January and February passed quickly, with Saoirse and Diego kept extremely busy with their jobs, both of which often lasted long into the night. Saoirse suggested to Diego that Valentine's Day should be a night they both shut off their phones and had dinner sent up to the penthouse for some alone time.

That way, we can celebrate our love all night. She smiled as she shook the wrinkles out of a new negligee that she had ordered for the occasion. It was a dark maroon color that, oddly enough, complemented her coloring.

"After all," Diego remarked to anyone who questioned his choice, "we're still newlyweds. We deserve some time to focus on each other."

Janine agreed, telling everyone, "A strong leader needs to have a strong marriage. That's what keeps a pack healthy."

Most of March flew by also. But Saoirse was unprepared for the festivities that were planned to celebrate the spring equinox. "After all," she noted, "the snow is still falling around here. How can you even tell it's spring?"

Diego grinned. "Our wolves know. It's part of the natural cycle of things, and we feel it in our bones. It's a time for renewal, for rebirth, and for new life."

Since the beginning of spring had never had any special meaning in her life other than as the harbinger of Easter, Saoirse didn't give any special notice to Diego's words.

On the last Friday in March, she and Diego were soaking in the *Jacuzzi* to relax after a long, hard week. He was sitting behind her, massaging her shoulders when he suddenly stopped.

"Why did you stop?" she asked.

"Please turn to look at me, Saoirse," he said.

The tone in his voice made her obey quickly. "Is something wrong?"

He shook his head. "No. But I have to ask you something." His look turned serious. "Have you ever considered having your IUD taken out?"

She didn't even try to hide her surprise. "Why? It's good for another two years before I have to replace it."

"But I don't want you to replace it."

"No?"

He shook his head decisively. "No. We're married now. Haven't you ever thought about having children?"

She smiled. "Of course. I'm from a big family, remember? But I always figured that would be sometime in the future. Even now that we're married, I thought we'd at least get a year or two to get used to being husband and wife, before we have to become Dad and Mom."

He leaned forward, his hands tracing her curves. "I don't want to wait. You're mine now. And it's only natural for me to want to watch my seed grow in your body."

She made a face. "Come on! You're kidding, right? I mean, we're not just talking about growing a house plant here. You're asking me to grow a new person inside of me, then to spend the rest of my life taking care of it. That's a huge decision, dude. Not something to be entered into lightly. Or without talking about it long enough to get used to the idea."

"I don't need to talk about it. I'm already used to the idea. In fact, it's about all I've been thinking about lately."

"What?" She scooted over to the other side of the tub.

Diego's eyes were almost black with his passion. "Ever since the wedding, I've wanted to talk with you about this. But there never seemed to be a way to work it into the conversation. So now I'm just blurting it out. I want to get my wife pregnant. I want to watch as your belly grows and know that it's my child doing that."

"Whoa! Was asking me what I thought about the whole idea any part of what you've been thinking about?"

"Of course. But in my fantasies, you are as excited about it as I am. Somehow, I'm sensing that's not the reality, is it?"

Saoirse sighed heavily. "It's not that I don't want to have your child. Actually, I'd like to have three or four of them. Just not ten!"

He smiled. "I don't want that many either. But just enough to know that our love has produced new lives. I need that. *We* need that." He gave her a significant look.

"Um, let me ponder this a bit, okay? I'm due for a pap smear soon . . . like in a couple of months. Can I at least have that long to think about it?"

Diego's frustrated growl let her know that neither of his personas was happy with her answer.

Suddenly feeling awkward with each other was not a fun way to end their evening, either. Their lovemaking was less than spectacular, and she swore she saw his wolf looking at her as they watched each other reach orgasms.

He doesn't look happy with me. A terrible feeling of alarm fluttered in Saoirse's stomach, and she wondered what that meant and how she could make things right again.

Saoirse was so concerned about her husband's new obsession with creating a baby that she wracked her brains about whom to talk to about it. Jerene was out because she was married to a non-lupine. Janine had the experience, having been married for many years to a pack leader. But Saoirse felt odd talking about something so personal with someone even older than her own mother.

So she was pleasantly surprised when instead of Diego,

Monique showed up at the head of the trail she was going to run, one Saturday afternoon.

"Hey, Sam." Monique smiled as she approached. "The boss man has all kinds of top-secret meetings going on today. There's been some unrest among some of the affiliates and their pack-lettes. He needs to deal with it right away. So he asked if I could take his place running with you today."

"Pack-lettes?" She headed towards the trailhead.

Monique nodded. "Yeah. Some of them are families, but others are small groups of shifters that band together for protection. They're not big enough to be called a pack, but they don't have shared blood, so they're not a family. They pay a stipend, like some independents do, to be able to run on our grounds. The arrangement means that if they have any kind of issue with the pack, they need to hash it out with the leader. This has been pending for a while, so I'm glad he's finally getting it done."

As they reached the beginning of the trail, Saoirse asked, "Diego isn't in any kind of danger, is he? I mean, no one will challenge him or anything?"

Monique shook her head. "No. It's not that kind of issue. If it was, I'd be there, instead of getting to run with you. Besides, John is there, and so is Nathan. Even Janine is sitting in on this one. She knows them all and is respected by all of them."

She stretched her arms up high, twisting her body to the right, then to the left.

"Ready?"

Saoirse nodded. "Let's do this."

They took off at an easy lope, with Monique leading and Saoirse following close behind her. It was a rare sunny day after so many cloudy, rainy, and snowy days recently. Saoirse enjoyed the warm sunshine as they trotted along through grounds, just beginning to show signs of life.

Someone had thoughtfully put a picnic table at the furthest

point of the trail. It was obviously for the comfort of runners who wanted to stop and have a drink or a snack before running back along the same path. It was still far too wet and messy to sit on the ground.

"Wow, this table is a great idea," Saoirse observed.

They both sat on the bench with the sun at their backs, facing the trail they had just run. No one spoke as they leaned against the table and drank the water each had remembered to bring.

After Saoirse's breathing returned to normal, she took a deep breath and broke the silence. "Can I ask you something personal?"

Monique smiled and shrugged. "I guess. But I think I know what you're going to ask me about."

"What?"

"Just ask away."

"You were married to a pack leader. Did you get pregnant right away?"

Monique shook her head, grinning. "No, because I was already pregnant when we got married."

Saoirse's eyes grew wide with her surprise. "You were?"

Monique nodded. "Yup. We met when we were still in college. We were both trying to finish our MBAs. We met in the middle of the fall semester, and by Christmas, we knew we were mated."

Saoirse waited patiently while Monique took a quick sip of water before she continued.

"We were having a whole lot of sex, as I'm sure you know, being married to a pack leader and all. Our men have really high sex drives and know how to satisfy a woman. Am I right?"

Saoirse felt the telltale heat on her face and nodded quickly. "Oh yeah. That's for damn sure."

"But not too long after Valentine's Day, he got even more

persistent. I'd be trying to get some schoolwork done, reading some intense book, or typing a paper, and he'd attack me. Not that I'd offer much resistance, of course. But it made it very hard to keep my grades up. And the first time I realized he hadn't used a condom, I got very upset with him. I told him there was no need to trap me, since both my wolf and I already agreed that we were mated. And I wanted to finish the degree that I had worked so hard on for so many years."

"Why was he like that?"

"Springtime. It does that to a wolf, but especially to the males."

"Really?"

"Um-hmm. It makes them want . . . no . . . *need* to get their mates pregnant, so the pups will be born early in the summer. That way, they'll have time to teach them what they need to know before the snow returns. It's part of the cycle of life that our wolves are attuned to."

"But we're talking about men here, not wolves. Pregnancy lasts a lot longer for humans, so the babies wouldn't be born until the next winter."

Monique shrugged. "Who knows how much sway their wolves have in making them feel this way? Maybe all human males feel this way about their mates, but they don't say anything because they're too civilized. Maybe it's only *some* of the shifter males who are like this, but I know that my Tim sure was. So that's how I got pregnant before the end of the semester, and despite having been an A student, I barely limped by with B's, which ruined my GPA . . . if I still cared about it. But I didn't. I was in love, pregnant, and the man I loved was called home to be there when the pack leader lay dying, to pay his respects. And, as it turned out, to be the one chosen to be the new leader."

"So you're ABD?"

"Yup. Someday I might try to finish my degree. Or maybe

not. I haven't decided yet. But it can wait until my kids are old enough to take care of themselves. And until after I find out if any of them are gonna take after Mom and Dad and get hairy to howl at the moon sometimes."

Saoirse panicked. "I never even thought of that. When and if I get pregnant, that's always a possibility, isn't it?"

Monique patted her leg. "Actually, it's not really that much more likely than if you were both non-weres. Lots of weres have non-were kids, and lots of weres are born to families who have no idea why their kids like to spend so much time away from home, late at night, during certain times of the year." She drained her water bottle. "So, did I answer your question?"

"Yes, and thank you. But I still don't know how I'm going to deal with this. I have so much going on right now, and he wants me to allow him to plant a new life inside of me, that I will have to love and raise when I have no idea what kind of a mother I will be."

Monique laughed as she got up from the table. "Honey, none of us have any idea before the baby is born. Even after the baby is born. Even after multiple babies are born. You just fumble your way through it, because you love your man, and it's a part of life. The love will be there, and that's really all babies need. They need to be loved and cherished and made to feel important. Everything else is just style." She grinned. "Ready to head back?"

"I guess so. You won't tell anyone what I asked you about?"

"Of course not. You're not only my pack leader's wife, but you're also one of my only female friends in the pack. I like Jerene well enough, but she knows I like skinny white guys, so I always feel like she's keeping an eye on me when her husband is around."

Saoirse laughed at that. "But Arnold isn't a skinny white

guy. He's huge!"

"Yeah, but I bet I can bench press as much as he can. And you're right. He's not skinny enough for me."

"There's always Nathan."

Monique shook her head. "Nah. We got to be friends when I first got here. He helped me get settled in and introduced me around. He feels more like a brother to me, so I don't see him that way. And both of our wolves feel the same way, so I figure he does, too. We've been alone, had opportunities, but neither of us ever acted on it. So, no. For now, I'm a vol-cel woman—voluntarily celibate. But I'm all right with that. Like I said, I've got kids to raise. And I'm still mourning my Tim. The bonds between a male and a female are very strong among our kind."

Saoirse couldn't hold back her bark of laughter. "Hell, I'm not one of your kind, and even *I* know that! It's only been a few months, but I can't imagine my life without Diego in it."

"Then you know what I'm saying." Monique inclined her head to the trail, "Now?"

Saoirse nodded, and they took off along the trail to return to the campus.

At least now I know I'm not going crazy, and neither is Diego. But I still don't know how I'm going to deal with him and his incessant demands for a baby. I guess I'll figure it out. Soon, I hope.

CHAPTER THIRTY-ONE

Diego sat in his office, listening to the drone of information. He was having a hard time concentrating, his mind preoccupied with thoughts of Saoirse and the yowl of his wolf.

"So that's about it, boss," Jerene said as she concluded her report. "She's been accepted by the teachers, by the students, and by their parents. And personally, I think Monique is doing a great job. In fact, there isn't any reason for me to keep filling you in on things because she's handling everything so well."

He had his hands steepled on the desk in front of him, tapping his fingers lightly against each other, a self-soothing habit he'd carried over from childhood.

Jerene shifted around in her chair, "Is there anything else, or can I go help my poor husband wrestle the kids into their jammies?"

"I . . . uh . . . well. What I mean is, there *is* something I wanted to ask you about."

Jerene leaned forward expectantly. "What? You can ask me anything, boss, you know that. Not only are you my pack leader, but you're also my friend. Remember, I was one of the first ones to accept you when Dad welcomed you into the pack."

Diego nodded. "And don't think I'll ever forget that. And you were the one to warn me when Stacy had decided we were mates, without even asking me what I thought about it. So I know I can trust your discretion. It's kind of a personal question."

"About you and Sam?"

He smiled at her use of Saoirse's nickname. "Yes. She's . . . um . . . not very open to the idea of having kids. At least not now."

Jerene laughed. "Dude! You two have only been married for, what? Three months?"

"Almost four." Even to his own ears, he sounded defensive.

"Okay, four months. But she hasn't even been living here for a year yet. And look at what she's had to deal with since she moved here. She had to learn how to be a teacher. She had to learn how to live in a very remote, albeit beautiful area. And soon after that, she had all of her scientific notions upended when she had to learn to deal with the fact that werewolves really exist. That, in fact, many of her new friends and acquaintances here are weres. Then she realized she'd fallen in love with a shifter. And soon after that, she had to watch you fight a challenger, both of you as wolves. And still, she didn't run screaming out of the state. Instead, she married your ungrateful butt. So now that you and your wolf have everything you want, you're gonna start to strong-arm her to get knocked up? Can't you let the girl catch her breath first?"

Diego frowned. "But you know how it is with us. It's spring. You know what that means."

Jerene rolled her eyes. "Don't I know it! Arnold couldn't figure out why I was jumping his bones three or four times a day the first spring we were together. We weren't even married, yet since our wedding was in June. But I was voracious! Not that he minded, of course. What man would?"

Diego could help but snicker.

"And it didn't stop until my periods did, and I knew I'd been successful and was thrilled. But Arnold was not. He had expected to be able to enjoy life as a newlywed for a while, maybe to travel the world. And then, not even two weeks after our wedding, I was telling him I was pregnant like I was giving him the best-ever present, expecting him to be thrilled. But he wasn't ready for that kind of news. We had some unpleasant scenes until I'd finally talked with my mom, who explained why I had been acting like that. Then I had to explain it to him. Not the best way to start married life, let me tell you."

"That's why I wanted to ask you about it. You're the only one I know well enough to ask, who is married to a non-were. So eventually, you made peace with each other?"

"Duh! We've been married almost seven years and have two kids already, so yeah, we've made peace."

Diego leaned back and sighed.

"So she's not crazy about the idea?"

He shook his head. "No. In fact, she's getting more obstinate about not wanting to even talk about it anymore. Yet my wolf is pestering me almost non-stop. It's hard enough to concentrate on what I need to do as a new leader, but now both my wolf and my wife are not happy with me."

"Life's a bitch sometimes."

"Yeah. But what am I supposed to do about it?"

There was silence for a few minutes until Jerene leaned forward. "Have you ever shifted in front of her?"

Diego furrowed his brows, confused. "Of course. You know she was there when I fought the challenger. But even before that, she saw me as a wolf standing next to my pile of clothing, which is what made her finally realize what was staring her in the face, though she didn't want to accept it."

"No, I mean, have you ever changed *just* for her. In front of only her? In your penthouse, when there's no one else around?"

"What difference would that make?"

"Believe me, it made all of the difference in the world to Arnold. When I told him that I was a werewolf, he laughed, thinking I was joking. When I shifted in front of him, it freaked the hell out of him. But there was no way to deny what he had seen. He was scared out of his wits, so I ran off into the woods we were camping in, and howled at the moon all night long, thinking I had lost his love. But when I got back to the campsite in the morning, I didn't find it empty — he had a pot of coffee on and was cooking bacon. We talked a lot, over breakfast, since he had lots of questions. Then, since neither of us had slept all night, we took a long nap. When we woke up, he asked me to shift in front of him again. I didn't know what he was going to do, but he wanted to touch me, to stroke my fur, to convince himself that I was real, and he wasn't going crazy or delusional. And that's how he truly accepted that he was going to marry a woman who had a wolf living inside of her. And that the wolf sometimes likes to take over and go for a run in the woods."

"So you think that if I shift in front of her, that will make a difference?"

"It might. I mean, you're not only asking her to let you plant a child in her but to accept that the child might end up being a were, also. Of course, it might not. But that's got to be something she's thinking about. If you shift just for her and let her touch you, and really see for herself what your wolf is like, maybe she'll relax a little, and be more receptive to your request to put a *wolfy*-bun in the oven ASAP."

Diego rolled his eyes. "Honestly, you can be so wise, with such good advice, then you ruin it by saying something crass like that."

Jerene grinned. "Part of my charm. Just ask Mom . . . or John . . . or Arnold. And cut me some slack, dude. I have to watch what I say most of the time. Little ones repeat everything they hear — especially when it's something Mom or Dad said. And I have to be *teacher-y* in front of the students. So I don't get much chance to just be myself. Sorry if it bothers you, but it's the real me."

"No, it's okay. Really. I didn't know who else to ask. And obviously, it's kind of embarrassing to talk about with any-one—even you."

"So did I help at all?"

"I think you did. It never occurred to me that she might feel so disconnected from my other half. But it makes perfect sense. So I'm going to try it and see what happens. If you hear screaming and see her running down the hall, you'll know it didn't go well."

"You're being silly, Diego. She loves you. Give her the chance to process things in her own time. Then romance her into bed and amaze her with your charm. That should do the trick. If not, you may just have to teach your wolf patience."

"Yeah . . . right."

Jerene giggled.

"Are you laughing at your pack leader, young lady?"

She shook her head, "No, boss. Just at the look on your face. And you know I love your lady as much as I love you. Maybe even more."

"You're a brat, sometimes."

"Yup. Comes from being the youngest in the family. Now am I excused?"

"Yes. Get out of here. Go back to your husband, who has totally accepted you just as you are, and to your two beautiful kids. And leave me to my misery."

Diego could still hear her giggling after she closed the door and was walking down the hall. He stared out of the window for a long time, thinking about what she had said.

Well, what have I got to lose? I'll try it.

Later that night, while they were spooning in bed, drifting off to sleep, Diego took the first step in trying Jerene's suggestion.

"How about we have dinner up here tomorrow night? It's a Friday, and we've both been working so hard. I'd like for us to have some privacy, so we can relax."

"I guess so." Saoirse sounded guarded. "But you're not going to keep talking *at* me again, are you? Can we talk about something else other than your incessant desire to make a baby?"

Diego nodded against her hair, trying not to sound disappointed. "Yes. I won't even mention it. Promise."

"Then okay. I'll look forward to it all day. I like having you to myself, and not having to share you with your pack . . . even if just for a little while."

"It's a date." He had a smile on his lips as he kissed the top of her head.

Soon after that, he heard the regular breathing that let him know she had fallen asleep. He lay awake for a while, wondering if his plan would work.

Will getting to touch my wolf, to experience me as an animal, help in my quest to have a child with her? Or will it scare her even more? He stared into the darkness for a while, before closing his eyes and joining her in sleep.

CHAPTER THIRTY-TWO

Why are Fridays always so manic? Saoirse did her last walk around the lab, making sure that everything was turned off, unplugged, and put away. *Or is it worse now because of the craziness that all wolves feel due to springtime? Does it even affect the young ones that are in my classes? Or are they just going stir-crazy, since it's almost finals week, and the school year is almost over?*

She carefully locked the classroom door and headed down the hall toward the stairs for the penthouse. The hallways were deserted. *Not only is it close to dinner, but I suppose some of them are out running. It's a gorgeous sunny day, and nice weather is supposed to last for the next few days. Finally, we have something resembling real spring weather! I wonder if Diego will be able to go for a run with me.*

When she got into the penthouse, there was a note left for her on the dining room table.

Meeting with affiliates until 6. Asked for dinner to be here by 6:30. There is a bottle in the fridge that will go well with the dinner I special-ordered for tonight. Go ahead and open it. Will share the rest with you when I get back. No other meetings for tonight. Just me and my lovely wife.

XXOO

She smiled to herself. *Okay, then. I wonder what kind of wine goes with a special-order dinner?*

She walked over to the fridge and looked inside. There was a small bouquet of flowers on the top shelf in a vase, next to a bottle of *Tattinger Brut La Francaise.*

French champagne? He's making this a special occasion for sure! Oh, Diego, I really do love you so much! I hate to disappoint you in any way, but I'm just not sure if I'm ready to be a mom yet.

She looked at her watch and smiled. *Only five? Plenty of time for a nice, long soak in the* Jacuzzi!

She got the water running in the tub before opening the bottle with a large *pop*! She poured herself a glass and put the bottle back into the fridge. She took the flowers out and placed them in the middle of the dining room table, so she could inhale their fragrance. She picked up her flute of sparkling wine and carried it into the bathroom, then stripped and stepped into the tub. She lay back, pushed the button to start the bubbles, and took a sip of her sparkler. She sighed, contentedly.

Ah, relaxation at last. And might I add, yummy! Thanks, my love.

After her long soak, Saoirse took extra care with her appearance. She chose a teal-colored knit dress.

Hell, it's spring. I might as well dress like it, even if it's still too cold this late May to go outside wearing only this. But inside, I can even wear sandals, since I have a pair that matches this dress. I remember falling in love with them and getting them super-cheap on sale a couple of years ago but having nothing to wear with them. I've got this new dress I ordered online, and I've been waiting for it to be warm enough to wear it. Now's as good a time as any to try to wow my husband with how well I clean up.

She applied minimal makeup but left off lipstick since Diego didn't like kissing her when her lips were what he called *slimy*.

After all, I plan on doing a whole lot of kissing of his various parts. Don't want to slip off any of them. She smiled at herself as she heard his key opening the door.

When she emerged from the bedroom, Diego was putting a second bottle into the fridge. He turned when he sensed that she was behind him. His eyes widened, and he sucked in an audible breath.

"*Díos mío*," he said in a low tone. "Just when I think I know how lucky I am, you appear to me like that—the most beautiful woman I have ever set eyes on. And once again, I realize that you are too good for me."

Saoirse grinned. "And here I was, thinking nasty thoughts about how fine your ass looked while you bent over to put that bottle into the fridge. I guess we're two of a kind, eh, *señor*?"

He approached so quickly she didn't even see him move. One minute he was standing still, the next he was holding her in his arms.

"I certainly hope so," he murmured into her hair.

He tilted her head and covered her lips with his, inhaling deeply as if he was absorbing her. She pressed herself closer, but he gently pushed her back.

He took a deep breath. "No, not yet. I'm going to take a quick shower. Hopefully, by then, our dinner will have been delivered."

"Can you at least tell me what we're having?"

He shook his head. "It's a special thing I asked Janine to make just for us. But you could pour me a glass of champagne."

He turned and strode quickly into the bedroom, and soon she heard the shower running.

Wow! A second bottle of this expensive champagne! He's really trying to woo me this evening with a special dinner, and special wine. I sure hope he keeps his promise and doesn't follow up all of this with another pitch for getting me with child.

She got out a second flute before pouring herself more champagne from the bottle she'd already opened. *This is so delicious! Dry and light . . . hints of fruit . . . I'll bet dinner is going to be some kind of seafood.*

The shower noises stopped, and soon after, there was a

discreet knock on the door. Saoirse opened it, and John walked in carrying their dinner tray.

"You're the delivery man tonight? Kind of a demotion for you, isn't it?" she teased.

John returned her smile. "Nope. It was the only way to get Mom to make some of it for me, also. So I've got to run back quickly before anyone else realizes she made extra and eats it before me."

He quickly returned to the door, turning briefly to wave at Diego, who had just reappeared wearing only a pair of silk lounging pants. Diego walked into the dining area, where the tray was on the table.

"Enjoy!" John said as he closed the door behind him.

Diego walked over to the door and locked it.

He turned with a smile. "Now we can enjoy being alone, just the two of us. On a date, actually."

Saoirse held the second flute out to Diego. He took the glass and clinked it against hers gently.

"Cheers, my love."

"To us," she returned, as they both took a sip.

"Just as wonderful as I'd hoped it would be." He lifted the lid on the tray to check their dinner.

Saoirse inhaled deeply. "Smells delicious! What is it?"

"A specialty of Janine's," he answered. "It was Joe's favorite dish for spring when there isn't any fresh seasonal local produce yet, but the fishing is improving. It's broiled haddock fillet, with spinach and tomato, baked together in a light sauce that she won't share the ingredients or recipe for, with anyone. I see she made a dark chocolate flourless cake also."

"And is that raspberries and whipped cream to top it with?"

He nodded. "Apparently, in a nod to your cravings for red fruit and cream. And there's a pot of coffee to go with dessert."

"Let's eat! Smelling that has reminded me how hungry I am, and how long it's been since I scarfed a quick salad for lunch."

He put the plates onto the table while Saoirse put the champagne into a marble ice bucket, then brought it over and sat down.

Diego lifted his glass again. "To my beautiful wife. May we always be as happy as we are tonight."

Saoirse clinked her glass against his, and they both took a drink. Then they applied themselves to their dinner, not stopping until their plates were empty. They put fruit on their slices of cake, topped it with the whipped cream, then carried their dessert plates, along with their champagne glasses, over to sit on the sofa. Diego went back once, to grab the smaller tray that held the coffee and the creamer, along with two mugs.

Saoirse let a tiny piece of the cake dissolve on her tongue. "Oh my God, this is delicious!"

Diego sat and picked up his plate.

"It's my personal favorite. I was hoping you'd like it."

All too quickly, the cake was gone, and Saoirse leaned back against the sofa cushions. "I don't think I could eat another bite."

Diego smiled, "I agree. In fact, as much as I want to express my undying love and devotion to you, I think even I have to allow for dinner to digest a bit first."

They spent some time enjoying their coffee, alternating with small sips of the champagne. Diego asked how Saoirse's research into finding a hint to the werewolf anomaly was going.

"Not so well. I haven't been able to find any markers in the blood. At least not with the equipment that I have . . ."

Noticing that he was going to object, she quickly added, "It's not that I don't have everything I asked for, and more.

It's just that the markers might be so tiny as to require more magnification than can be achieved in the kind of lab we have here. Or it might be on a gene. I don't know how I'm going to be able to test for that. I'm still working on it. But I won't give up."

"Good. It would relieve the minds of a lot of folks if they could have a way to predict which of their kids is going to have a sudden awakening of a wolf. Teen years are turbulent enough as it is, without surprises like that."

"You don't worry that it would reduce the number of students we have here?"

Diego paused a moment before responding. "I doubt it. We often have to turn away many who want their children to come here due to lack of room. We don't want to get any bigger than we already are. We have a family-type atmosphere here, and that's how we all want it to remain. That's why we don't do any advertising."

"I thought that was to keep the academy a secret, so our location is unknown."

"That too. But what I mean is that there will always be more students whose parents want them to come here than we can allow. So no, I don't think if you can isolate what the cause is, that we won't have students anymore. We might even have more applications."

Saoirse asked how Diego's meetings with other packs and affiliates were going. They spent some time discussing the enormity of the scope of his responsibilities, which he had never realized were a part of the pack leader's role.

While they talked, they gradually cleaned up after dinner, putting all the dishes back onto the huge tray. Then Diego replaced the cover and put it outside of the door. After that, he excused himself to use the bathroom. When he got out, it was Saoirse's turn to excuse herself.

She got back out to see that Diego had lit a candle and

turned off all the lights.

His face glowed in the soft light, as he rose to embrace her. He kissed her gently, then his lips trailed a path along her chin to her neck, where he inhaled deeply. He nipped at her earlobe, then his tongue poked into her ear.

Saoirse twitched. "That tickles!"

His gaze burned into hers as he led her back to the couch. He had refilled their champagne flutes with the last of the wine from the first bottle.

"Come, sit with me, my wife. Let me devour you and excite you in ways you've never even thought of. Let me love you." His voice ended in a low growl.

Diego's kisses alternated, first gently, then with insistence, as his tongue plundered her mouth, demanding she return his passion. Meanwhile, his hands roamed all over her body, proving to her that there were no places on a woman's body that couldn't be considered erogenous zones. Especially with the right touches, by the right partner.

Saoirse had to keep forcing herself to remember to breathe as his touch aroused her nerve endings. She also explored his body, caressing places she knew would excite him further, thrilled with his reaction.

Diego growled. "Too much clothing! We're both wearing too much clothing."

"What should we do about that, my love?"

He stood up quickly, pulling her up with him, then swept her into his arms, his lips demanding her surrender as he carried her into the bedroom. He sat on the edge of the bed and put her down in front of him.

"Just stand here," he commanded. "So I can unwrap my present."

Saoirse had spent many years picking her own body apart, finding areas she thought were presentable, and others she agonized over. She had always felt no man would ever be able to accept her almost translucent skin, her freckles, or her huge feet, topped with what her sisters called her *cankles* – calf-ankles. She bemoaned her many imagined deficiencies.

But at that moment, she felt like a goddess. Diego's eyes were black with arousal. He leaned forward to cover her nipples with his mouth, blowing hot breath onto them without touching her dress as his hands reached behind her to slowly unzip it. His touch was reverent as he slid the straps off her shoulders, kissing and licking at both, staring intently as he lowered the top below her breasts.

He inhaled deeply before gently growling. "Even more beautiful. Each time I look at you, I fall more deeply in love with you. I desire you even more. Having you as my wife completes me in a way I never dreamed was possible."

Saoirse was having trouble standing still when his every touch excited her skin, making her twitch and writhe with his passionate tickling.

Saoirse stepped out of her dress, and he lay back on the bed, pulling her on top of him. He began to move her back and forth, stimulating them both. She undulated her hips, rubbing her clit against his engorged cock, teasing and frustrating him. When he tried to surge into her, she moved just out of reach of his insistent organ.

"Why do you torture me like this?"

She smiled dreamily. "To make you work for what we both want so badly."

"Like this?"

He raised his hips, flipping her over onto her back next to him. He loomed over her, holding both of her wrists above her head and started licking her. He began with her elbows, then gently nipped at the tender skin under her arms, until he neared her breasts. His soft growl vibrated across her chest, increasing her arousal.

"My woman. Everything about you intoxicates me. Your

every smell . . . your every twitch when I touch you . . . every scream when I make you come."

He continued to move lower on her body, licking at her skin along the way. When he reached her belly button, he poked his tongue into it, making her giggle. Then he lowered his head further, to nibble at the inside of her thighs, first one and then the other. He inhaled deeply, raising his head to smile at her. "Your scent makes me crazy! It makes me want to bury myself in you, any way that I can!"

His fingers blazed a trail across her skin, sensitizing everywhere he touched. One hand spread her labia as his tongue began its delightful torture of her clit. He suckled on it, then nibbled it gently before licking the entire length of her. He poked his tongue into her opening, swirling it around, before lapping at her like he was slurping on an ice cream cone.

Saoirse writhed on the bed, unable to stop her movements. His mouth and tongue brought her to the brink, then moving away, causing a constant state of arousal, with no relief. Finally, he took pity on her, concentrating on her clit for an extended licking, allowing her to move around to find just the right position.

She exploded with a small scream, feeling herself gush on his face. He continued to lap at her, a continuous low growl vibrating from his throat. When he raised his face, his mouth was shiny with her juices, and he looked almost feral in his passion. He quickly moved himself up and pushed his hips forward, burying himself to the hilt in her slick channel. He stopped, as he had done on their wedding night, to watch her writhe beneath him.

"Diego, you know I can't stay still when you're filling me up like that! I have to move . . . to get you right where I want you to be . . . right . . . there!"

Her entire body tensed for an instant before her hips jerked uncontrollably. She squeezed her eyes shut as her inner muscles once again exploded in orgasmic bliss. Diego let out a low groan, his fingers digging into her hips, holding her still as he rapidly plunged himself into her, over and over. He soon reached the point of no return and stopped moving, staring into her eyes and gasping as his orgasm blasted out of him . . . then he howled.

His orgasmic throes sent Saoirse off on another roller-coaster ride, climbing up, then plunging into even more bliss. Their multiple orgasms became kinetic, each one setting the other off on another round of shaking, pulsating pleasure.

When their passion finally cooled, Diego collapsed on top of her. Her breath *whooshed* out of her with his sudden weight.

"Sorry . . . can't move yet . . . soon," he gasped.

She rubbed her hands across his back, lightly stroking his shoulders, gently running her nails down his spine, kneading the tight muscles of his glutes. After a few long moments, they were both breathing easily again. Diego rolled onto his side, pulling her along until they were facing each other, still entwined in each other's' arms.

"Is the top of my head still here?" Diego asked, his voice hoarse from all his growling.

"Yes. Why? Did you think it exploded off of you?"

He nodded, stroking her face with his free hand. He wrapped his fingers in her hair and pulled her head close for a lingering kiss.

"That's how you make me feel, every time, my woman."

"Good. I want to be the best you've ever had, my husband."

He searched her eyes intently. "Can there be any doubt?"

She sighed contentedly. "No. We were made for each other. We fit together perfectly. I miss the feeling of being complete when you're not inside of me."

"Then rest in my arms, knowing that you are my world," he murmured into her hair.

With a long sigh, she closed her eyes, drifting off on a cloud of satisfied bliss.

The howl of a wolf woke Saoirse from a light nap. The moonlight streaming through the open balcony doors offered enough light to realize Diego was also awake and watching her closely.

"That's kind of freaky," she remarked. "I don't like it when you watch me sleep. What if I drool, or snore or something gross like that?"

He shook his head. "There's nothing that you could ever do that I would find unattractive. Drool would be magical if it came from those lips that I love to kiss. All I would be able to think of is how much I love to plunge myself into your mouth and feel the slippery touch of your tongue on me."

He leaned forward and kissed her, increasing the pressure until she felt him growing hard against her leg.

"Again? Let me use the bathroom first." She pushed herself away up and padded to the door.

She frowned when she returned to find the bed empty. She cocked her head a moment, then heard Diego in the next room. She entered the kitchen just as he was adding cream to a cup and stirring it.

"So I take it, we're not going back to bed just yet?" she asked.

He held up the cup, and she walked over to take it from him.

"No, I have something else in mind for now," he said.

"Like?"

He inclined his head towards the balcony's open doors.

"You're going for a run?"

He nodded. "Even now, the pack is scattering through the woods, enjoying the feel of the soft grass under their paws. My wolf chafes to join them."

She smiled. "Then go."

He shook his head. "Not yet. There's something I want to do first."

"What?"

He walked over to take her free hand and pull her to sit on the couch next to him.

"I want to shift in front of you—just for you. I want you to watch me and to touch me when I'm a wolf. Any questions you have will have to be asked now, or some other time, of course, since I won't be able to answer you when I'm shifted. Different vocal cords and all."

Saoirse gaped with her surprise. "I didn't expect this. Why do you want to do this?"

"Because you are my wife and my mate. And in choosing me, you have also chosen my wolf."

He gently placed a finger on her lips as she opened her mouth to object.

"No, my wolf doesn't want to have sex with you as a wolf. He prefers female wolves. But he's content knowing how happy I am with you, to observe and participate with us, as we pleasure each other, as humans."

"He's not going to want to have sex with a female wolf, is he? Which, of course, would be all right since *he's* not married to me. And I'd have no way of knowing, anyway. But it wouldn't be like *you* were cheating on me, would it?"

He took her coffee cup and set it on the table, then clasped both of her hands, placing them over his heart. "There's so much that we need to talk about. You only recently discovered what I've known for much of my life. I have a wolf living inside of me, who likes to make my body change, so he can take over and be *the driver* for a while, running through the woods and howling at the moon."

He looked toward the moonlight streaming in when another wolf howled right under their balcony. "They will all be running tonight."

"Since you're their pack leader, you should be out there too."

"I will be. Soon. But you're wrong, my love. It *would* be cheating on you for my wolf to mount a female wolf. He loves you as I do. You married both of us. It's . . . it's kind of hard to explain. But he was sure that you were the one for us the first time I smelled your scent. You reminded both of us of wildflowers and grass. He urged me to take you many times before I had even kissed you. I had to keep reminding him that you're a human and that things aren't that simple for humans. That we had more courting to do before we could have sex. So he waited. Now that we are mated, neither of us wants another female. You belong to us, and we belong to you."

Saoirse spoke softly. "I *have* been worrying about that. I guess I don't have to worry anymore."

"No. You don't. Is there anything else you want to ask me before I shift?"

"You said it hurts."

He nodded. "Yes. Every time."

"But it makes you stronger, gives you longevity? Does that mean you'll outlive me? Or I'll be a decrepit old hag, while you're still young and hot?"

"No. I prefer to think of this as my insurance that I'll still be able to satisfy you, into old age and beyond. Nothing but death will separate us, my love. And I'll do everything in my power to ensure that you are kept safe. Even though I have an entire pack to protect, my first thought will always be your safety—even before my own."

Saoirse took a deep breath. "Then, I think I'm ready to watch you get all black and furry."

Diego stood in front of her, as naked as he had been when they'd fallen asleep. As her eyes roamed over his body, he started to harden under her gaze.

She giggled. "Is that going to make it . . . ahem, *hard* for you to change?"

He shook his head. "No. It's just how I react any time I'm near you, whether you are naked or clothed. Makes it kind of distracting when we're in a crowd. But I'm working on learning to control myself in public."

"I just like to look at you, Diego. You're a magnificent man, with hard lines and muscles all over your body. Every place I look, I see more proof that I'm the luckiest woman in the world, because I get to touch you whenever I want to, and it's me that your glorious body pleasures."

"If I don't start to shift soon, I'll have to have sex with you again, first," he said through gritted teeth.

"Okay. I'll be quiet. Now do your *thang*, sweetie."

He closed his eyes for a moment, and he seemed to be swelling in size. Then he began to shimmer. The lines of his body blurred, and his skin began to bulge in some places as bones shifted underneath it. His face became a grimace as he dropped to all fours. It seemed as if there were living things under his skin, moving and stretching in ways that must have caused immense pain.

The air filled with the sounds of bones cracking as joints popped out of place and reset themselves in different ways. A low, inhuman growl came from Diego's throat as he began to change. His nose extended forward to form a muzzle, his ears shifted to the top of his head, and black fur quickly covered the new body as it reformed. A tail had grown out from his spine, and his paws fully formed. When the change was complete, the wolf lifted his head and howled, then turned his head toward her.

Saoirse shrank back against the cushions, taken aback at being noticed after the upheaval of the last few minutes. The wolf walked over to stand in front of her, staring with Diego's dark eyes.

"What are you waiting for? I thought you were going for a run . . ." she began in a shaky voice. "Oh, right. You said I was supposed to touch you. I've only touched one other wolf before, only for a minute, and I had no idea at the time that it was one of the students. I'll feel stupid petting you like a dog. But I do want to feel your fur. It looks so soft. I always thought wolves had bristly fur, like bears. I touched a baby bear once, many years ago, when I was camping down in the Smoky Mountains."

She reached forward, and the wolf remained still as she touched his head.

"Listen to me! I'm babbling like an idiot to cover up being scared. But I don't have to be afraid of you, right?"

The wolf shook its head, still watching her intently, without moving.

"Okay, then. I'll touch you further back. Wow! Your fur is kind of bristly on top, but there's softer fur underneath that. What a luxurious feel there is to you!" She moved forward to kneel on the floor next to the wolf.

Awed, she ran her hands across his back and sides. "You have strong muscles as a wolf, just like you do as a man."

The wolf slowly sat down, apparently content to let her explore.

"The fur on your chest is much softer—more like dog fur. And your belly fur is the softest of all . . . oh my!"

She gasped when the wolf's cock began to push its way out of the protective sheath. She heard a strangled noise and pulled her gaze up to his face to see what appeared to be a grin on his face.

"You're laughing at me, aren't you?"

He nodded his head.

"You're a big, bad wolf, mister. You're just as much a horn-dog in wolf form as you are as a man. But then, I guess if I'm married to both of you, I should expect that."

He nodded again, baring his teeth.

She put both of her arms around his neck and hugged him, whispering into his fur. "I love you, Diego. All of you. And thanks for letting me watch up close how you become your other self." She let him go and stood up.

"But now, I'll go open the door for you, so you can join your pack out in the woods. Then I'll read for a while. If I'm asleep when you get back, feel free to wake me up—you know, in that *special* way that you do, when you come in all frisky from your run." She snickered.

She padded over to the door and unlocked it. She jumped in surprise when the wolf brushed her legs, rubbing himself against her and licking her thigh. She bent forward, and his raspy tongue laved her face quickly before he turned and bounded down the hall to the stairs.

She watched until his tail disappeared around the corner. She closed and locked the door before walking over to the fridge to open the second bottle of champagne.

No. I'll save that for another night with Diego. I still have part of a bottle of Prosecco, which has a screw top. I'll just have a glass of that, to help settle my nerves. After all, it's not every day that a girl gets to watch as her husband turns into a wolf.

She carried her glass to the bedroom and reclined on her side of the bed, picking up her reader and sipping the wine as she dove back into the sci-fi novel she'd been reading. She finished her glass of wine, then before she realized it, she dropped off to sleep, the reader slipping down onto the floor.

When Diego returned, it was still dark, but his enhanced faculties told him dawn would be arriving soon. He shifted back to human shape and joined the others streaming into the mansion after a long, very satisfying run.

When he got up to his room, he opened the door and made his way quietly into the bathroom. He took a quick shower to get the dirt and mud off his body, then crawled into bed next to his gently snoring wife.

As he snuggled up close to her, he breathed in her scent. Combined with the events of the evening, his cock hardened to an almost painful size. He slipped one hand underneath her, stroking the wetness still between her legs from their earlier encounter. His other hand reached around in front of her and began to twist and rub her nipples.

With a small sigh, she woke, turning her smiling face to receive his ardent kiss. His stroking became more intense, then he pushed his hips forward to slide himself into her from behind.

She arched her back, welcoming him into her warm depths. He began stroking in and out of her with real purpose, forcefully claiming her as his own once again. It didn't take long before his balls tightened, and his orgasm pulsed inside of her. She soon joined him in his pleasure, trembling in his arms.

Diego lay his head on the pillow close behind hers and sighed contentedly as he drifted off to sleep, just ahead of the first fingers of dawn appearing in the sky.

CHAPTER THIRTY-THREE

"I'll be in meetings all day," Diego said as he walked with Saoirse down the hall towards their respective jobs.

"And I'll be rechecking the finals, running the bubble sheets, and getting the lab essay questions labeled for every class. Guess neither of us will get much of a break today, my love."

They got to where they needed to separate, and Diego pulled her into his arms, covering her lips with his. She melted into his embrace, running her hands up and down his spine.

"I live for tonight," he whispered into her ear as he nipped at the lobe.

She smiled at him, "Me, too."

After another kiss, they both headed down the halls to jump into their workdays. Diego smiled, still brimming with the satisfaction of the sexually sated.

Many hours later, Saoirse put a sticky note on the last pile of tests and sighed with satisfaction.

Done! Now even a monkey could give the finals, since everything is labeled and ready for each class. Guess being anal-retentive can be a good thing – at work, anyway. Damn, I'm good!

Her phone buzzed to indicate a text, and she pulled it out of her back pocket and swiped the screen, finding a message from Diego.

Called a twenty-minute break. Have to see you, now. Meet me in the chapel.

She shook her head, grinning. *You bad boy! You'd better not expect me to desecrate a holy place by having sex in there. You might not have been brought up Catholic, but I was.*

She locked the door to her classroom to keep nosy students away from her tests, which were safely locked in her desk drawers. She headed down the stairs and out the back door toward the chapel.

As she pushed open the door, she breathed in the familiar smell of incense and dust that she always associated with the peace and quiet of a church. She walked into the big room and turned slightly to dip her finger into the holy water.

She briefly glimpsed a movement behind her when she felt a prick on her upper arm. She glanced down to see a needle jammed into it. She tried to turn, but whatever she was injected with acted very quickly. Her last coherent thought was for her husband. *Shit! Diego, I'm sorry! I love . . .*

Her mind went blank as she collapsed.

Diego walked out of the meeting room, yawning and stretching as he moved into the late afternoon sunlight streaming in through the huge windows in the foyer. He nodded at some of the people he'd been meeting with and shook hands with others. The day produced a general feeling of accomplishment with everyone happy to have old disagreements settled, petitions in consideration, and trust in their new pack leader finalized.

He made his way up to his room, thinking of a hot shower. *And maybe a quickie before dinner, with my gorgeous wife!* When he walked into the penthouse, he searched with his senses for any sign that she might already be there. But there was no discernible scent of her, which was disappointing. *Maybe she'll get here while I'm in the shower. That would be fun.*

When he got out of the shower and she still wasn't there,

he began to wonder where she might be. He picked up his phone from the nightstand, but there wasn't any message on it. *Where are you, my sweet?*

He quickly pulled on pants and a t-shirt, then went out to check her classroom, to see if she was still working. When he got there, the door was locked, and he began to feel a sense of unease.

He glanced down the hall and walked quickly toward the one open door. He poked his head into the classroom and saw Jerene perched on her lab chair, tapping away on her laptop.

"You know you don't have to work so late," he stated, trying to keep his voice conversational.

She looked up. "I know, boss. But I'm almost done with my finals. I got a late start since Jonas puked up his lunch today. Not sure if it's a bug, or he just didn't like tuna salad."

"You don't know where Saoirse is, do you?"

She shook her head. "Nope. Haven't seen her all day. Why?"

"She's not in our place."

She shrugged. "Maybe she went for a run?"

"Don't think so. Usually, she waits to run with me. At least she leaves a note if she's going out alone. Besides, her running shoes are still in the closet. This isn't like her."

Jerene frowned, then closed her laptop with a click. "Then let's go see if she told anyone else where she was going." She led him out of her room, locking it behind her. "I'm sure there's nothing to worry about, but two people can do more checking than one person can."

An hour later, Diego met with Jerene and Monique in the foyer. Diego noticed their grim faces and had to force himself not to give in to the panic he felt growing in the pit of his stomach.

"Nothing?" he asked, afraid the answers would verify what he already suspected.

They both shook their heads.

He started pacing back and forth. "She can't just have disappeared. Someone must have seen something."

Diego stopped, his heart pounding in his chest when John walked in. But one look at John's face dashed his hopes.

"The only ones who saw her were the people working on the flowers out back," John said. "They saw her walking toward the chapel, but they didn't see her come out. Remember, there are doors on the back side that they wouldn't have been able to see from where they were working."

"When was that?" Diego tried to keep the panic out of his voice.

"They guessed about two, maybe three o'clock. The sun was still hot and bright. But it was definitely after their noon lunch break, and before their quitting time of four."

"So no one has seen her for over three hours?"

Jerene spoke up. "Maybe she sent you a text before she went to wherever she went."

Diego pulled out his phone. "I didn't see any text or voicemail when I checked it before."

"Let me have a look at it, boss. Maybe there's something you missed," Jerene suggested.

He handed his phone to her, turning with everyone else when Nathan jogged up to them from the back of the house.

"News?" Diego asked.

Nathan shook his head. "News, but not good. There is a car missing—one of the Suburbans. And a few people are unaccounted for. They could be out running, but no one has seen any of them for most of the day."

Jerene paused her scrolling through Diego's phone. "Damn! Here's a text that *you* sent to Sam at three-fifteen today."

"I was in meetings all day and didn't have my phone with me."

"Where did you leave it?"

"In the penthouse, of course."

She read aloud. *"Called a twenty-minute break. Have to see you, now. Meet me in the chapel."*

Diego swore under his breath in an angry stream of Spanish profanities.

Monique turned to Nathan. "Who are the people unaccounted for?"

Nathan held up a hand, taking a step back. "Don't shoot the messenger, boss. Vernon Tate, his wife Pearl, and the midwife, Stacy."

This time Diego's swearing was in English *and* Spanish.

"They've got a head start on us, so we'd better get going," John announced.

"To where? We have no idea which direction they'd be heading," Monique countered.

"I figure they'd probably pick somewhere close by," John suggested. "Somewhere the other three could meet with Virgil yet be back here before anyone noticed."

Nathan cleared his throat. "They . . . uh . . . that is, Pearl and Stacy have been sitting together for their meals since around Christmas. I noticed it but didn't think it was significant. I'm sorry, boss. I should have told you and let you decide if it was worth investigating. I just figured you already had so much on your plate . . ." His voice drifted off.

Monique shook her head. "How could you know? Besides, they'd have denied they were plotting anything."

"What should we do?" Jerene asked in a small voice.

They all turned to Diego, who suddenly felt twice his age. "I don't know. But we have to find her. Options, people. What are our options?"

The planning meeting moved into one of the smaller conference rooms. It eventually involved the entire security force, as everyone who had had any contact at all with the missing three people was questioned.

Through it all, Diego was haunted by self-recriminations.

This is my fault! I didn't kill him when I had the chance. That allowed him to plan this. I have endangered my wife. ¡Díos mio! Lo siento, mi corazón. *I will not make the same mistake twice. When I find him, I will rip his throat out and eat his heart!*

CHAPTER THIRTY-FOUR

Saoirse gradually drifted back to consciousness. Her head throbbed, her throat was parched, and her body felt unresponsive. *Oh my God! What happened? Am I paralyzed?*

Her pulse and breathing sped up, and fear caused bile to rise in the back of her throat. No! I can't panic! What did Shamus and Sean teach me? When faced with an unknown threat, the first thing is to take stock of the situation. And not to lose control over yourself.

She forced herself to modulate her breathing, taking deep, calming breaths until her pulse slowed down. *That's better, Saoirse, me lass. Now assess the threat. Am I really paralyzed, or is my body unresponsive due to whatever fucking drug they pumped into me?*

She concentrated on trying to move her fingers. Sweat broke out on her forehead from the exertion it took to fight for even the smallest of movements. When the numbness gave away to a burning, prickling sensation, like her fingers were waking up from being asleep, she pushed even harder. She almost cried out in triumph when one and then another finger responded by twitching.

So I still have both arms! Fingers on both hands are moving, thank God! Now do I still have legs to control? I can't feel them, but are they there? Toes, you're next. Move for me.

She almost wept with happiness when her toes began to wriggle. Her breathing slowed when she stopped exerting herself, and her panic subsided.

Okay, so where am I? And what the fuck happened? I felt a prick in my arm, so I know I was drugged. Someone was waiting for me in the chapel, and it wasn't Diego. That's right! He was in those high-level meetings. I didn't even notice, but I'll bet, as usual, he didn't take his phone with him. That means that someone else sent that text to me, to get me out to the chapel. But who?

Her entire body started prickling as her other body parts *woke up.* She tentatively opened her eyes and was disappointed to find it was too dark to see anything. *Shit! Not going to learn anything that way. It smells musty in here, so the room has been closed up for a while. Feels kind of damp also. Wonder if I'm in a basement? That would explain the chill also . . .*

She tuned in to her hearing, trying to locate any identifiable noises. Suddenly, she heard voices, and she resisted the urge to keep her eyes open. *No! Got to let them think I'm still asleep. I need to know who they are and what they want. If they think I'm still unconscious, they'll talk more.*

She worked at keeping her breathing slow and steady, while her ears were on full alert.

There was the sound of a door opening. The voices got louder as they got nearer. There was the sound of footsteps on stairs. *Yes, I'm definitely in a basement.*

A light switch clicked, and Saoirse fought to not show any physical reaction to her eyes being assaulted by so much light after the darkness. She recognized the first voice immediately. The man who had challenged Diego sounded angry.

"How much drugs did you pump into her? I told you I wanted her out, but not for days."

A woman answered him. "I didn't give her that much. We needed her to be out until we got her here and into the cage. But she's a redhead. They overreact to a lot of drugs. It could still take a while before she comes out of it."

I don't recognize her voice, but I'll bet she's the nurse who wanted to be Diego's mate.

"Yeah, but what I still don't know is if she's a natural red-head. I want to see if the carpet matches the roof."

There was some gruff male laughter, which meant there were at least two men in the room.

"Why?" the female whined. "You don't need her. You've got me now."

"Sure, Stacy, baby. I know I got you. But part of beating that asshole when I challenge him again is letting him know what a lousy lay his wife is. Plus, I figure if I fuck her two or three times a day for a coupla days, that oughta get her knocked up, so I can tell him she's pregnant with my kid."

The other male spoke. "Yeah. Once he hears that, he won't be able to think about anything else. Then you can take over the pack like you deserve to. It needs a new direction."

The other male must be his brother, Vernon. They have the same slight drawl to their voices.

"You bet your ass it does! Old Joe was a good man, but not a forceful leader. He was too lenient on a lot of shit. Plus, he had rules about behavior that shouldn't apply to wolves. We don't need to follow the same rules that normals do. We're better than them. We make our own rules."

"Then will you kill her after you take over?" The female voice sounded hopeful.

"Depends."

"On what?"

"On whether or not she really *is* a lousy lay."

He and his brother laughed long and hard at that quip.

Another woman spoke up. "Maybe someone should go in and shake her. I bet that would wake her up."

That's Pearl's voice! And after I gave her such a nice Christmas gift! Saoirse decided to speak up, so no one would feel the need to enter her cage—*cage?*—to touch her.

"Seriously? How the hell is anyone supposed to get any sleep with all of you yakking so loudly out there?"

She opened her eyes to see Virgil walk closer to the bars they had erected on the doorway, to leer at her.

"So you're awake now. How much did you hear, while you

were pretending to still be out?"

She sniffed. "Enough to know that you'd be wasting your time trying to knock me up."

"And why is that?" His voice sounded dangerous.

"Because I won't let you get your disgusting dick near me. And even if you managed to, it wouldn't do you any good. You're too late. I'm already carrying Diego's baby."

He whirled around to glare at the two women, who both shrank back under the ferocity of his gaze.

"Is that true?"

"How should I know?" Stacy looked irritated. "She hasn't come to see any medical people that I know of."

He turned to Pearl. "Do you know if she's lying or not?"

She shrugged. "No."

"You clean their place. Have you seen any cunt-plugs lately? Any sign that she's on the rag?"

"I'm only allowed in there once a month." Pearl defended. "No, I haven't seen anything lately, but the last time I was in there was three weeks ago."

He turned his glare back to Saoirse. "I say you're a lying bitch."

She sat up, then had to take deep breaths when the room swam and her head throbbed even more.

"We just found out. The pee test was just positive a couple days ago. We hadn't told anyone yet. Diego's been too busy doing pack leader business. You know, meeting with other leaders, gaining their respect—the kind of things you aren't capable of doing."

He slammed his fist against the wall next to the bars, and the throbbing in her head got worse.

"Then maybe I'll just fuck you so I can tell him all about what a lousy lay his wife is."

"You can try."

"What's that supposed to mean? You think you can fight

me off?"

"Yes, I do."

"I don't know if you paid any attention, but I'm ex-military. I think I can handle one little woman."

"My oldest brother, Shamus, was in the Marines. When he came home, he taught us girls how to defend ourselves. I was always a good fighter, so I picked up most of what he showed us how to do."

Virgil sneered. "I was a jar-head, too. There's nothing he could have taught you that I won't know about."

She held her ground and continued to meet his leer with her own steady glare.

"My other brother, Sean, decided that Marines were pussies. So he joined the Navy and became a Seal. When he came home, he had even more tricks to teach us. Between them, they made sure that no guys would be able to rape their sisters. Instead, they'd have to learn to sing soprano."

"Thanks for letting me know you'll go for the balls. Not a smart move, little girl."

She shrugged. "No matter. They will have to be exposed for you to get your little pencil dick close enough to try to stick me with it. And once testicles are mashed that hard, they never recover. It will probably be the last hard-on you ever get, so better enjoy it."

Saoirse kept a cautious eye on Virgil as he paced back and forth, raging impotently in front of the bars. The other people in the room, who watched quietly, were easily ignored.

I hope Shamus and Sean were right! They said to always try to psych the man out first with words. If you tell him you're waiting to cripple him, ready to fight, most men will reconsider. They want compliant victims. Rape is a crime of violence, not of sex. So a woman who will fight back is less attractive, since she might actually hurt you.

Virgil stopped in front of the bars with an evil glint in his eyes. "Maybe I'll have Verne come in with me to hold you down. He can even have sloppy seconds."

"No!" Pearl shouted.

"Aw, baby," Vernon soothed. "I won't fuck no one but you. You know that."

"Fine," Saoirse spit out. "But since you can't kill me before you get me back to the pack, I'll be sure to tell everyone that you needed help to rape me. You weren't man enough to do the job by yourself. What kind of leader is that gonna make you? A strong one that others will obey and follow? Or a poser?"

He grabbed hold of the bars, the heat of his focused hatred palpable. "Maybe I'll drug you again. You're like most bitches. You talk too much. Drugged, you'll be more cooperative."

"Yeah, and I'll tell everyone *the only way that asshole was able to fuck me is he drugged me.* And they'll wonder what kind of man needs to drug a woman to get between her legs."

He slammed his fist into the wall again. "You know what? On second thought, I don't think I want to fuck your disgusting hole. Not after that Spic has been spraying his brown jizz in there. See, the thing is, once a white woman lets any kind of colored man take her, it ruins her. She's not clean and pure anymore. She's too dirty to touch. So I wouldn't fuck you even with someone else's dick."

Abruptly, he turned and strode across the room, then stomped up the stairs. Vernon was right behind him. After a hate-filled glance at Saoirse, Stacy trailed the men up the stairs. Pearl started to follow.

"Hey! Can I at least get a glass of water? That drug you put in me gave me serious dry mouth. And I'm kind of hungry, too. If you're going to keep me here until your brother-in-law challenges Diego again, you need to be sure I'm healthy enough to walk by myself. Otherwise, there might be trouble with the security people when you get there."

Pearl turned, glaring with hatred in her eyes. "Sure. Water and some food. Will there be anything else for your majesty?"

"Why are you doing this? I've always been nice to you. I thought we were friends."

"Friends? Ha! You're the pack leader's bitch. I clean up after you. How is that *friends*?"

"Okay, maybe not friends. But friendly. What did I ever do to you to deserve this?"

"You married the pack leader, but you're not one of us. That's a big one right there. And I don't need any other reason. Virgil wants to challenge that filthy Mexican again, and this time he'll win. Verne will become his second, and I'll be living in a much nicer place, with a maid who cleans *my* messes up." With that, she whirled around and followed the others up the stairs, slamming the door to emphasize her anger.

Left alone, Saoirse's thoughts wandered to her husband. *Diego, I don't know how you'll be able to find me. But I don't think they'll kill me before he challenges you. And they'll have to bring me there to show you that I'm still alive. I just hope I can keep him off of me until I see you again.* She looked up when the door at the top of the stairs opened, and Pearl walked down, holding a tray.

The bars in the doorway ended about six inches above the floor. Pearl slid the tray into the gap and pushed it. Then without a word, she turned and stomped back up the stairs.

Saoirse forced herself to get up, holding onto the wall while the room spun around her. She walked over to the toilet next to the sink and fell onto it. *Got to get my body under better control. I don't think I could fight anyone off right now. I hope there's something edible on that tray.*

She looked around, realizing Pearl had left the light on, though the outer area was still in darkness. *This must be a bathroom that they converted into a cell. The cot with the mattress on it must be where the tub was supposed to be. Thank God, at least I have a toilet and a sink. And toilet paper. There's even a tiny sliver of soap. Of course, a toothbrush would be nice.*

She stood up carefully, glad to notice the room didn't spin quite as rapidly as it had the last time she got up. She walked slowly over to look down at the tray. It held three bottles of water lying on their sides, an apple, a banana, a granola bar, and a small can of peanuts.

Great! All of the important food groups. Hopefully, I won't be here long enough to need more food. Please, God, help Diego find us! Or at least, let the challenge be soon. He's got to be going crazy with worry. So am I, honey . . . so am I!

CHAPTER THIRTY-FIVE

Diego spent the next two days in a daze. He directed groups to leave the grounds to search, but with no idea where to look, they always returned with no news. No one in the local towns seemed to have seen any of the perpetrators, and no one noticed one more Suburban driving around in a rural area. The GPS on the car had been dismantled, so there was no way to track it. And they discovered that all of them had left their cell phones in the chapel in a back pew, along with Saoirse's phone.

Though he forced himself to lie down, sleep eluded him as anger and fear fought for dominance in his brain. He wanted to kill but had no target . . . yet. Affiliates were contacted, and everyone was glad to help with the search, but no trace of them could be found.

Diego was sitting alone in his office with his head in his hands, early on the second morning, when his cell phone rang. He automatically checked the number and didn't recognize it, but he picked it up anyway. He knew the drawl immediately, and his wolf joined him in instant alertness.

"How y'all doin', *Señor* Pack Leader? Missing somethin' . . . or is that someone?"

"If you have harmed her, I'll torture you *before* I kill you."

"Yeah, right. About that. I claim the right to another challenge. That means we get safe passage onto the grounds, and to the battlefield. And to ensure that, we'll bring your whore with us, but she will be guarded at all times, so no one better try anything sneaky while I'm busy killin' your ass."

"I need to hear her voice."

"Sure thing, *señor*. She's right here, close by. Of course, she's nekkid, like she's been all the time she's been here. But I get tired of pounding her loose cunt, so I gotta take a break now and then. Hey honey, talk to your husband a minute."

He heard footsteps, then the angry voice of his wife yelling over the phone.

"Diego! I'm fine! He's a lying *pendejo*!"

There was an audible *slap*, then Virgil's drawl returned. "She's kind of feisty when she doesn't get enough dick. You might have a big cock, but me and Verne have been doin' our best to keep both her holes plugged, double-timin' it. Now about that challenge . . ."

Diego was grinding his teeth so hard he could feel the pain up into his brain.

"When?"

"I was thinking later today. Say about five? We'll get to the main gate about four. Tell the guards we get safe passage, or I'll kill her and bring her to you in pieces."

"Done."

"I wish I could say it was a pleasure doin' business with you. But it *will* give me pleasure to kill your ass and claim my rightful place as pack leader. Later."

The line went dead. Diego stared at it for a long moment, then began to make calls to get things ready.

Diego growled as Jerene fussed over him like a mother hen.

"Are you sure you don't want Rachel to give you a shot of adrenaline, or something? You look like shit, boss. You obviously haven't gotten any sleep. And you need to be at your best, because he's gonna be coming for blood."

He shook his head. "No. I won't need any drugs to kill him. My wolf and I can take care of that just fine."

"Um, not to be too indelicate and all, but you're not gettin' any, and you *know* he is. Isn't that going to weaken you in the fight?"

Diego glared at her.

"Whoa, boss! You're setting my hair on fire! Okay, I get it. You'll handle things. I'll just shut up now . . ."

He looked up as John and Monique came into the room.

"All of the arrangements made?" he asked. "Everyone knows what to do, and affiliates who want to observe have been notified?"

"Yes, boss. There will be representatives from most of the small packs." Monique gave him a tight smile. "You've made a lot of friends already, Diego. They're all anxious for this to be over."

John nodded. "They want to see for themselves that you are the leader they believe you to be."

"A killer. A murderer." Diego grimaced. "What I was trying *not* to have to become. But he forced my hand, and I will rip him to shreds for endangering my woman."

The others in the room nodded.

Janine walked in with some of her cooks, carrying food trays. They all dug in, but Diego had to force himself to eat, reminding himself that he needed to have maximum energy and stamina to right this terrible wrong.

I didn't kill him the first time. My mistake, Saoirse, my love, and you had to pay the price. I will make him suffer before I kill him.

He could have been eating sawdust. Nothing had any flavor to him. But it was useful fuel, so he chewed slowly and carefully, plotting moves in his head, to ready himself for, literally, the fight of his life.

Just slightly after four, the Suburban slowly approached the main gate, which was opened quickly. Saoirse fidgeted a bit when the guards came out to check out the car. Virgil drove, with Vernon in the passenger seat. Pearl and Stacy sat on either side of her in the back. Her wrists were bound with plastic cuffs, and her mouth was covered with duct tape. *They don't want to hear what I have to say.*

Pearl blatantly displayed the handgun on her lap, pointed at Saoirse.

"Weapons are not allowed," one guard instantly pointed out.

"Then we're leaving," Virgil said, putting the car into reverse and starting to slowly back away.

The guard looked around for support, but the other guards shook their heads.

"Why do you need a weapon?" he asked.

Virgil stopped the car and snorted, "Why? Because we're strolling into a compound where we're not welcome, to challenge the pack leader, and we're holding his bitch hostage. He needs to see that no one can try to help her escape while we fight. Once I've killed him, I'll decide if I feel like killing her too. But until then, she's my prisoner."

One of the other guards had been talking into her COM link, and she moved forward now. "Let them pass."

"With the gun?" the first guard asked.

She nodded. "Yes. Pack leader's orders."

The first guard shrugged, then moved back as Virgil put the Suburban into gear again and started driving in through the gates.

Once the vehicle had passed, the gate was locked again, and the guards—two males and two females—all resumed their places.

"Wish I could watch this time," one of the males said.

"I missed the last time," a female responded. "I was on guard duty then, too."

"I don't want Virgil to win. He's a dick. He always acts like he's better than everyone else, and he fights dirty. I don't want him to be pack leader," the first male growled.

There was a general murmur of agreement.

"The last time it was a brutal fight. But Diego didn't go for the kill at the end like he should have," the second male added.

The second female nodded. "I think he's learned his lesson. I expect there'll be blood on the ground today. Either way, a wolf will be getting buried in the woods."

With that, they all resumed their vigilant stance while praying for the outcome they desired.

When the Suburban reached the front of the mansion, it stopped. A crowd was already there, surrounding the battlefield. Like before, many had already shifted into wolf form, but others maintained their human shape, to help keep everyone under control. Diego was at one end of the field, pacing. He stopped when the doors to the vehicle opened and his enemies got out of the car. When he saw Saoirse, handcuffed, he sucked in a breath, his upper lip curling in anger.

Monique spoke in a low voice to keep others from hearing. "Don't let it get to you, boss. He's trying to bait you. She looks fine. And knowing her, I'm sure if he tried to touch her, she fought like a banshee. She doesn't look too bruised, so my guess is he was bullshitting you."

Diego met Saoirse's stare, and he tried not to project his emotions across the distance—fear fought with anger, anxiety with determination. But above all, the abiding hatred that filled him made him gnash his teeth.

"He will regret this," he growled.

"Yes, he will," Monique said. "But concentrate on him, not on her. I will work my way over to her while you're fighting. She will be freed by the time you are done."

He straightened up and nodded briefly. "I always forget, you've been through this before."

"Yes. Multiple times. It still hurts. But I don't intend to be on the losing side ever again. That's why I stand with you."

He turned to watch John and Nathan accompany the kidnappers into the opposite side of the battlefield. They took up their positions as observers, with John on one side of the group, and Nathan guarding them from the other side.

Diego strained to see Saoirse and was heartened by the quick, defiant nod she gave to him, which he interpreted as *Kill him for me, my love.*

Just like the last time, Verne was the second for his brother. Virgil tore off his clothing quickly, turning around slowly to let everyone see his hardening cock, winking at some females and sneering at nearby men.

He turned back and yelled, "Hey, *Señor*! Your *puta* didn't want to *put-a* out for me. But once she got a look at what she could have, she changed her mind!"

Virgil laughed loudly at his own wit, his brother the only other man to join him. They both looked around in surprise at the staid expression on many around them.

"What? A couple of months of him being pack leader and you're *all* pussies now? Some of you were on my side the last time. You'll want to be on the winning side this time, so show some respect for your new pack leader."

"He's just talking shit to get to you," Monique said in a low voice, as she handed over a bottle of water.

He nodded. "I know."

Diego grimaced as Pearl reached over and tore the tape off his mate's mouth. Saoirse didn't make a sound, but defiantly raised her head and stood tall. Diego was heartened when their eyes met, and she gave him an almost imperceptible shake of her head.

He nodded back, then took a deep breath, relief filling his lungs, and he began to strip.

John walked into the middle of the grassy area being used, once again, as a battlefield. "No one else is allowed to participate or help either of the combatants in any way. According to tradition, the winner is pack leader. No objections will be allowed." He glanced at both men, waiting for an acknowledgment.

Diego nodded at John.

Virgil growled, "Let's get this over with!"

John backed out of the center as Diego and Virgil dropped to all fours for their change.

Saoirse was hyper-aware of Stacy's wolf crowding her on the one side, while Pearl held the barrel of the gun jammed into her ribs on the other side. *I'm not sure which of them I should be more afraid of. Stacy, whose jaws are right next to my wrist, ready to clamp down and chew off my arm, or Pearl, who might be trigger-happy.* The wrist-cuffs added to her discomfort. Never-the-less, she was determined to watch the entire battle this time, without closing her eyes. She leaned forward to get a better view.

"Don't get any ideas," Pearl muttered. "Make a move, any move, and I'll blast you."

Saoirse gave her a quick, withering glance. "I wonder if he'll let you live once he wins."

"Virgil will. Your dead Mexican will be left out for the critters to eat."

Saoirse ignored the woman and turned her attention back to the fight, forgetting even to blink.

The combat was intense and blood-filled. Both wolves fought brutally. Teeth and claws were doing maximum damage, and before long, both were covered with blood and foaming at the mouth. First, Diego would appear to have the advantage, then Virgil. There was a deathly silence surrounding them, as the audience bore witness to the intensity of the hatred between the two.

Saoirse lost track of time. All she knew was that both the wolves were fighting more slowly now, their previous injuries clearly affecting them. They were still vicious, but more wary of each other, each having gotten a taste of the other's fighting style, and both favoring their own injuries.

Virgil's wolf made a sudden feint to one side. When Diego countered, Virgil spun in mid-air and clamped his jaws down on Diego's front leg. The crunching sound was horrifying as bones splintered. With a howl, Diego swiped with his other paw, raking his claws across Virgil's face. Virgil's wolf yelped as one eye was torn out of the socket, and the other was blinded by the blood streaming into it from above it.

Diego moved back, the broken leg useless, limping as he watched for an attack. Seeing that his opponent was blinded, he leaped forward and clamped his jaws onto Virgil's' neck. Virgil twisted and turned, but the more he tried to shake off Diego, the tighter Diego's jaws closed.

Copious amounts of blood oozed out of Virgil's neck as his movements became slower. Diego held on, grinding his jaws together, effectively shredding whatever was left of Virgil's jugular vein. A burbling sound came from the remains of Virgil's throat as he collapsed onto the ground. Diego rode him down, then unhinged his jaws and stood, staring down at the other wolf. For an instant, it looked like Virgil was struggling to rise again, but Diego immediately clamped his jaws hard on what was left of Virgil's neck. He shook his head back and forth, tearing Virgil's head off, then tossed it onto the ground and stood, panting, on his three good legs.

Diego glanced around the assembled pack, then tilted his head back and howled his victory. A chorus of howls joined him, and the noise of the celebration was deafening.

Saoirse heard the click of the gun and remembered Pearl's orders to shoot her if Virgil lost. She quickly jabbed an elbow into Pearl's side before deliberately ducking forward as the gun went off. When she turned around, Stacy's wolf was frozen in place, staring wide-eyed at Pearl for a moment before toppling to the ground. Pearl gasped, her mouth agape as she realized the bullet had gone through her friend's head.

Monique moved in quickly and punched Pearl on the side of the head, knocking the gun onto the ground. Pearl collapsed in a heap, almost landing on top of Stacy.

Monique reached down and helped Saoirse up, quickly using a small knife to cut the restraints from her wrists.

"Welcome home, Sam."

Saoirse reached forward, hugging Monique tightly, never so happy to see someone in her life.

"Thanks!" she squeaked.

"Can you walk?"

She nodded. "I have to. I have to get to my husband."

Saoirse followed Monique, threading their way through the pandemonium of humans shifting into wolves and joining the howling. At the far end of the field, Nathan and John wrestled Verne to the ground and were cuffing his hands behind him.

Saoirse finally broke through the crowd to where her battered and bloody wolf-husband sat. One front leg hung useless, and the other three were shaking from the effort of holding him upright. She fell to her knees and wrapped her arms around his neck, sobbing into his thick fur. Not only could she feel his exhaustion, but also his underlying exultation.

Suddenly, an eerie quiet surrounded them, and she raised her head, looking around. All the wolves had both front paws extended, and their heads bowed down, and the few remaining in human form had dropped to one knee. Every one of them facing Diego. Then, as one, their voices howled a cacophony of what Saoirse could only assume was a celebration that their leader had prevailed once again. And that this time, the challenger was dead.

Monique gently grasped Saoirse's arm and pulled her up. "He needs to shift, Sam. Give him space."

She held her breath as he shimmered into the shift. Some of the damage to his body was repaired as she watched. But once he was fully human again, his left arm hung useless in front of him, bones sticking out, blood oozing from many places. Rachel rushed to his side, wrapping a large cloth around the arm to stanch the blood and temporarily restrict any movement.

Diego glanced around at his pack and waited. One by one, the voices died down, until there was only the absolute silence of the early evening.

When he finally spoke, there was a new layer of authority in his tone. "I, Diego Vargas, am still leader of the Northwest Maine Pack. Does anyone else want to challenge me?"

There were no sounds, as respectful poses were held by all.

He nodded. "I have killed Virgil Tate. Does anyone object?"

"You killed my brother! I'll have you arrested!"

Verne had been pulled to his feet by Nathan, and he stood defiantly glaring at Diego.

"The police will find only a dead wolf buried in the woods. How will you explain to them that he's your brother?"

Verne spat on the ground.

"I, Diego Vargas, pack leader, declare that you, Vernon Tate, and your wife, Pearl Tate, and your co-conspirator Stacy Black, are sentenced to death. You will be restrained until the arrangements can be made. Then you will be hunted and killed."

Pearl, who had regained consciousness and been dragged to her feet and cuffed, began to wail. "That's not fair! Just let us leave! We won't cause no more trouble!"

"Shut up, woman," Verne growled.

"No! He's going to hunt us and have us killed!"

She turned to Saoirse and pleaded, "Don't let him do this to us! We won't ever come back. Just let us go!"

Saoirse did not reply. She just stared coldly at the woman who had willingly participated in her abduction.

Pearl's screams could be heard for some time as she and Vernon were dragged away toward the jail cells in the security building.

Saoirse turned her full attention to Diego, who was swaying so much she was afraid he'd collapse. She moved to his good side and let him lean on her. They walked proudly yet haltingly toward the mansion, with Rachel on his other side and Monique right behind them, ready to catch him if he fell.

It took a while, but they eventually reached the penthouse, where Diego was eased onto the bed on his back. Rachel immediately went to work, cleaning around the broken bones and resetting what was left of them, as he groaned and gnashed his teeth in pain.

Saoirse held his other hand, ignoring that he squeezed her hand so hard she was afraid he'd break *her* bones unintentionally.

Finally, Rachel stood with a sigh. "I've done all I can do for tonight. Don't let him move that arm. It needs to stay still. I've strapped it to a board, which should keep it straight. Tomorrow I'll be able to tell if it's healing okay. If not, I may need to re-break it and reset it again. But it's such a mess now that I can't tell."

Saoirse nodded, wiping at the tears streaming down her face, with her other hand. Diego had stopped crushing her hand, but his face still reflected the immense pain he was in.

"Is he awake?"

Rachel shrugged. "Maybe. I didn't knock him out. I just gave him some painkillers in those shots. Here's a bottle with some pills in case he needs them during the night. No more than two, every four hours."

"Can I clean him up a little bit? Get some of the blood off him?"

"Sure, as long as you don't move that arm." She paused for a moment, scrutinizing the situation. "Are you going to be able to stay awake all night, or should I send someone else in here to spell you, so you can get some sleep?"

Saoirse raised her head defiantly. "My husband just fought to protect me and his entire pack. I think I can stay awake and care for him through the night. It's the least I can do to prove my love and loyalty to him."

Rachel nodded. "Good." She headed toward the bedroom door but looked back before passing through. "He chose wisely. The pack salutes you both." Then she walked out of the room.

Saoirse heard Rachel speaking to someone in the next room, then the main door open and close. She was not surprised when Monique walked into the bedroom seconds later.

"Can I do anything to help, Sam?"

"I want to clean him up a bit—get some of the blood and gore off of him."

"Go ahead and get what you need. I'd be honored to stay and watch over him while you do that. Then I'll be outside the penthouse all night, guarding both of you."

"Thank you."

Saoirse quickly found the basin she used to soak her feet when she gave herself pedicures and filled it with warm, soapy water. She grabbed a few towels and washcloths and brought it all back into the bedroom and set it on the nightstand. Once everything was set, she carefully began to clean off the worst of the evidence that he'd been in a fight to the death.

"Can I bring you anything before I leave?" Monique queried.

"Maybe some water? I know I'm parched, and he probably is also."

Monique walked out, but quickly returned with a tray holding a pitcher of ice water and two glasses. There were also some grapes, a few chunks of cheese, some mixed nuts, and two containers of pudding, along with a spoon.

"Why pudding?" Saoirse asked.

"After a challenge, my Tim was always seriously depleted, but his jaws would be too tired to chew much. Pudding always perked him up." Monique brusquely wiped at her face. "Got something in my eye," she muttered.

Saoirse put down the cloth and got up, then pulled Monique into a tight hug, fighting back her own tears.

"Thanks for everything," she said. "This must be so painful for you. Please know how much I appreciate your caring soul."

Monique sniffed. "I'm just glad you had a better outcome. Now I'm off to work some crosswords outside your door. Call me if you need anything at all."

She padded silently out of the room, and only then did Saoirse realize that while Rachel had been dressed, Monique wore nothing.

She must have been a wolf while she moved through the crowd to get to me, then shifted back to punch Pearl. I guess I'm getting so used to people being naked around me. I don't even notice it anymore.

She returned to her husband's side and resumed gently washing him, careful not to disturb the broken arm. She took extra care around the stitches and bandages to clean off as much blood as she could.

When she was done, she emptied the basin into the toilet and flushed it. Then she washed her hands and returned to pull a chair next to the bed, within easy reach of the nightstand. She moved the tray Monique had prepared onto the stand and poured herself some water. She sat down and took a long drink, then began to nibble at some of the food.

She leaned back in the chair and rested her feet against the side of the bed. And she studied her husband's face, still set in a rictus of pain, even in his sleep.

I don't know if I'll be able to stay awake all night, Diego. But I'll sure try. I hope your super-human body repairs most of the damage while you sleep. I want to feel your arms around me again. I love you so much!

Diego woke a couple of times during the night. The first time, Saoirse had gone to the bathroom to splash cold water on her face. When she returned, she saw that his eyes were open, and he was gritting his teeth from the pain.

"Do you want pain pills? Rachel left some for you."

He nodded. "Water. I need some water, too."

She got out two pills and poured some water into the second glass, then sat on the bed, taking care to not disturb the immobilized arm. She placed the pills in his open mouth and helped him raised his head up to drink the water. He emptied the glass, then lay back with a long sigh.

"Better?"

"Will be soon, I hope."

She put everything down and turned back to see him staring at her.

"I have to know." He hesitated for a moment. "Did he?"

She gave him a small smile and shook her head. "No. My brothers beat me up a lot, but they taught me how to fight. A large percentage of that is psychological. If you let your opponent know that you won't go down easy, sometimes, if they're cowardly enough, they back down. Like he did."

He nodded, But his grimace let her know the move caused him pain

He took a deep breath, his eyes full of regret. "I'm so sorry, *cariña.*"

"For what?"

"It's my fault, what he did to you — what he tried to do to you."

"You didn't plan it. *He* did."

"No, but I didn't kill him the first time. That left him able to plot revenge. And hurting you would have killed me. He knew it. That's why he took you. That's why he said you'd be killed if I won. He wanted me to know those things, so I'd lose concentration."

"It didn't work, did it? And he never raped me. Hit me a few times, but nothing more than that. So I'm okay."

"Still, I feel responsible."

"No. I won't allow you to feel bad that you didn't want to be a killer. I was so proud of you then."

At his look of distress, she tried to reassure him. "But I'm prouder of you now. You did what you had to do. He won't be able to threaten anyone ever again."

"One down, three to go . . ." His voice was a mere whisper as his head fell to the side, and he began to snore softly.

She sighed and reached out to move the hair from over his eyes and caress his cheek. *That's a discussion for another day, Diego. For when you're healed. Then you can decide to maybe show mercy for Verne and Pearl. But later. Once cooler heads have prevailed.*

A few hours later, she yawned and stretched as the first rays of dawn sneaked in through cracks in the blinds.

Diego moaned, then woke again, gnashing his teeth.

"More pain pills, my love?"

He nodded. "And more water."

She gave him the pills and held the glass for him again. This time he fell back asleep as soon as his head lay back on the pillow.

Saoirse curled her feet underneath her and leaned back into the cushions behind her head.

Maybe I can just shut my eyes for a minute or two . . .

CHAPTER THIRTY-SIX

Saoirse woke to the sound of Diego's voice talking to Rachel. She was embarrassed to have them both know that she'd fallen asleep. When she reached out to grab a glass of water, they both turned to her.

Diego spoke first. "Good morning, my love. Thanks for staying awake for so long, looking after me."

Rachel nodded. "He said you gave him pills a couple of times. Good for you. He really needed the sleep."

Rachel turned back to Diego, shaking her head. "And you, mister. I'm always amazed at your recuperative powers. I'm used to quick healing, but you're the master at it. Of course, your arm bones will take some time to heal. But most of your other wounds are closed and healing. The itching will start soon."

"It already has," Diego grunted as he reached down to scratch a particularly large gash just below his belly button covered with stitches.

Rachel slapped the offending hand away from the stitches. "Not so fast, sir. I said everything was healing, but it's still going to be a long process. Not nearly done enough for you to scratch any itch yet."

She gave Saoirse a significant look, indicating her seriousness. "I mean *any* itch." She made her emphasis clear. "You need at least a couple of days of intensive healing, Diego. Your body has taken a real beating, and even *you* will need time to be back on your feet again."

Diego shook his head. "Sorry, Doc. Not possible. I have a

pack to run. I have decisions to make about some traitors and arrangements to make. I can't be lying around here in bed while there are things I need to do."

She gave an exaggerated sigh. "If all of my patients were like you, I'd hang up my stethoscope and call it quits."

"So what's the story on the arm?" Saoirse asked.

"It looks to be healing as well as can be expected. The bones were shattered by powerful jaws. I set the larger parts together, but the smaller shards are somewhere on the grass outside. That's what will take so long to regrow. I'm afraid your arm is going to have to stay immobilized for quite a while, Diego. And even then, I'm not sure how much use it will be to you."

Saoirse gasped. "Do you mean he might not be able to use it?"

Rachel shrugged. "I won't say *yes*, I won't say *no*. I *will* say that I don't know. Shifters heal quicker than normals. If he wasn't a shifter, I'd have amputated what was left of the arm last night to stop it from getting gangrene. But his shifting helped start the healing process. Now we've just got to wait and see." With that, Rachel stood. "Janine is sending breakfast up for you both, and it should be here soon. Make sure he eats."

Rachel left the bedroom, and Saoirse heard a knocking at the main door, then voices. Seconds later, John and Nathan walked into the room. Nathan was carrying a food tray, and John had a laptop tucked under his arm.

"No Monique?" Saoirse wanted to know.

Both men shook their heads, but John was the one to answer.

"She was the night shift. Besides, she had to go to her other job. We're the day shift. We've come to help him eat, and to talk about . . . uh . . . unfinished business."

Saoirse looked at Diego, who struggled to sit up, using only one arm. "It would be better if we eat out in the dining room. You'll need to help me get out there," he said with an apologetic tone. "But after that, you can get me over to the sofa, and I'll stay there for the rest of the day."

"I think I'll take a quick shower. Make sure he doesn't move that arm," she cautioned. "Rachel says it could mean the difference in how much use of it he'll have once the healing is done."

She got up and went into the bathroom and closed the door. She turned on the shower to let the water heat up, then walked over to the sink to brush her teeth. She winced at her reflection in the mirror. *God! I look like shit! Bags under my eyes that I could use for luggage. Bruises on my cheek where that asshole hit me. And my color has never been so pale or puffy. Good thing Diego is in bad shape also, or he might have second thoughts about being married to such a sad excuse for a woman.*

She finished with her teeth, then stuck out her tongue at herself. Steam filled the room, and she pulled off her clothes and threw them into the hamper. *I may burn those clothes, since they'll always remind me of having to live in them for so many days. Or maybe I'll keep them in a bag in the back of the closet, just to remind me of what happens when you let your guard down.*

She reveled in the feel of the hot water as it pounded onto her from the three spigots in the shower stall. Washing her hair had never felt so wonderful before, so she followed the oft-ignored directions of *wash, rinse, and repeat*. And once she was clean, she still lingered, enjoying the feel of the heat soothing her tired muscles.

When she finally got out of the shower, she dried off with a large, fluffy towel, then looked around and realized she didn't have any clothing in there with her. She wrapped the towel around herself and moved over to the door, opening it slightly. The male voices were far enough away that she knew they must have all moved out of the bedroom. Cautiously, she stuck her head out of the door and saw that not only were they out of the room, but they had also closed the door behind them.

She grinned as she darted into the bedroom to quickly pick out some clothing and get dressed. *Casual nudity is such a non-deal around here that I'm surprised they would be so thoughtful of my feelings. But then, I'm not a shifter, so no one except Diego has ever seen me naked. It must have been his idea. Thanks, sweetie!*

As she dressed, her stomach growled, which reminded her how hungry she was. She pulled a brush quickly through her hair, then tied it back with a clip. Making another face at herself in the mirror on the back of the door, she opened it and joined the men in the living room.

Three sets of eyes looked up as she entered the room, and they all smiled at her.

Diego's smile was the broadest. "You look lovely, wife. I'm such a lucky man."

She rolled her eyes. "Apparently, you're not a very picky man, then. I look like shit right now. But it does feel good to be clean again. And after I have something to eat, I'll feel more human. So continue with your business. Pretend I'm not here."

The men resumed their talking while Saoirse helped herself to eggs and bacon, along with a blueberry muffin, and sat at the dining room table to eat. All the food was quickly devoured, and she was enjoying her second cup of coffee when Diego addressed her.

"You need to come over to be a part of the conversation now, my love."

She rose and walked over to the sofa, carrying her coffee along with the pot so she could refill Diego's cup.

"Why? You're talking about pack business. That doesn't involve me."

"Yes, it does. You're my wife, so you're automatically the fifth in command. For official business, you need to be a part of decisions and, um . . . rituals."

She set the pot down and sat on the chair that Nathan had just vacated for her. Something about the tone of Diego's voice made her uneasy. His worry for her was evident in his expression.

"What kind of ritual?"

He sighed heavily. "You're not going to like it. I don't like it either. But it has to be done. I've been told that Stacy was guarding you as a wolf when she was shot by Pearl. She and what's left of Virgil have already been buried in the wolf cemetery near the woods. But Verne and Pearl need to be dealt with as soon as possible."

"But they're harmless where they are, right? And they both worked here long before Verne's asshole brother joined the pack. Why not just let them keep working here?"

"Because they betrayed the pack twice already. I can't allow that to happen again."

"Why would they?"

Diego winced. "There's the little matter of my having killed Verne's brother."

"But he knows why you did it. It was a fair fight. Maybe he can let bygones be bygones." She looked around, but no one except Diego would meet her eyes.

"Honey, I tore out his brother's throat and ripped his head off after a brutal fight. That's kind of hard to forgive."

She swallowed hard as memories of what she had witnessed the day before suddenly threatened to make her breakfast reappear. "Then send them away. What harm can they do?"

The other men remained silent as Diego answered patiently.

"They can enlist the aid of other shifters. There are many un-affiliated small packs, some of which are run by would-be alphas who think just like Virgil. They would be glad for the insider knowledge that Verne and Pearl could supply about our security, our routines—even our weaknesses. Do you really want to take the chance that our pack members, or even our students, might be hurt or killed because you wanted to show mercy to those who had none for you?"

Saoirse felt ill as the truth of his words sank in, but the thought of what must be done rankled.

"But you're talking about murder. What you did yesterday was a fair fight. But you're not in any condition to fight anyone right now. Killing them will be murder. Who elected you judge and jury?"

John interjected. "Actually, we all did when we approved him as pack leader."

Her brain whirled. "So you're all right with this? You're all in agreement that he can pass sentence on them and have them killed?"

John nodded. She glanced at Nathan, who also nodded.

"There will have to be an official vote, of course," Diego said. "All of the hierarchy of the pack has to be unanimous in this vote. But the arrangements have already been made. The vote will be later today. The sentence will be carried out tomorrow."

"How?" she snapped. "Firing squad? Lynching? Stoning? Something the children can all enjoy watching, as an object lesson for why not to ever cross the pack leader?" Her voice ended on a hysterical note, but she didn't care.

Diego sighed heavily. His expression showed her that he would absolve her of this responsibility if he could. When he spoke, it was with sad gentleness. "No. They will be forced to shift into wolves. Then they will be given an injection of a substance developed by one of our affiliates, a psychologist who dabbles in pharmaceutical chemistry. It will keep them in wolf form, unable to shift back, for up to forty-eight hours. They will be allowed to run into the woods, and no one else will be allowed to shift or go running until they are found."

"By whom?"

"There is a family of hunters who live up in Canada. They often enjoy our hospitality when they venture this far south. And they have done this kind of service for our pack before, long before I was here. Joe was challenged once, early on in his leadership. After that, no one else ever dared. I'm hoping for the same results."

Her eyes grew large as his words sank in. "So the hunters will comb the woods for them, hunt them like animals, and kill them? Are they shifters also? That still seems like murder to me."

"Yes, they're shifters also. But loyalty is a very valued trait among us. If your pack leader can't count on his own people to support him, he'll have to learn to sleep with one eye open. That's not the kind of future I want for *us*." His expression pleaded for understanding.

Saoirse realized her horror must be reflected on her face because when she glanced at John and Nathan, they still didn't meet her eyes. They both glanced at Diego, then out the window. Only Diego looked back at her, clearly begging her to see the wisdom of his words.

She was quiet for a long time before she spoke. "What if they refuse to shift? I'm sure they will know why you want them to. What then? You can't force them to, right?"

Diego's face was as emotionless as his voice. "No, I can't. But my wolf can. He is pack leader to their wolves. He will call them to appear, and they will have no choice. It's a strain—on all of us, but especially on me. They will be fighting against the change. I will have to be able to retain my human vocal cords to command them, but still shift enough to allow for my wolf to speak to theirs. It's not something I've ever wanted to learn how to do. But now I have no choice. Hopefully, it will be the only time I ever have to do it."

"Why do I have to be there? I don't want to be any part of

this . . . this *murder*."

"Because you have a vote, and you have to be there to witness the sentence carried out."

"But we won't be out in the woods. How will we know it's done?"

"The hunters will bring the dead wolves back, and we will bury them with Virgil and Stacy."

"What if I vote *no*?" Saoirse murmured.

Diego pleaded in an equally quiet tone. "Please don't."

Saoirse got up and paced to the window and back, then stopped, staring into Diego's eyes. The room was so silent a pin dropping would have been loud.

Tears brimmed in her eyes, but she shook her head. "I'm, um . . . I'm going for a walk. I need some fresh air. See you later."

She strode quickly to the door and walked through it, then stopped, unsure of which direction to take. She walked down the hall to the stairs, stopping on the floor for the school. She passed the classrooms and her lab, where she could see students taking her final. She hoped the door she was headed for being closed wasn't a bad sign. She paused a moment, then knocked on the entrance to the principal's office.

"Come in," Monique answered.

Taking a deep breath, Saoirse entered the office and collapsed onto the chair in front of the desk. She met Monique's questioning gaze bravely, then burst into tears. Monique handed her a box of tissues and waited for the worst to be over. Gradually, her sobs turned to sniffles, and she took cleansing breaths to get herself under control.

"He told you, then?" Monique asked.

"It's that obvious?"

"To me, yes. I know what he had to tell you, and what you will have to do. And I know you."

"Do you? Because I'm not even sure that I know myself

anymore. I was a happy woman at the start of the week. Then I was kidnapped, threatened, beaten, and almost starved. Then I was almost shot while I was watching the most gruesome murder I've ever seen. And the worst part of that was it was real. And it was my husband, the man that I swore to love forever, who did the killing."

Saoirse stopped to blow her nose, and Monique offered her a bottle of water from the mini-fridge behind her. She opened it and took a long drink, then set the bottle down.

"I thought once I was back here, that I would be that happy woman again. Now my beloved wants me to vote *yes* on the killing of two more people. And I'll have to watch while he forces a change on them, then they'll be hunted and killed. And he says I have to be all right with that because I married him, and as the pack leader's wife, I have to do it."

She shook her head, bitterness creeping into her voice. "But I didn't sign on for any of this! I fell in love with him. With the man that he is . . . or was. Not the man he's becoming in front of my eyes. And there's nothing I can do to stop the change. I hate what he wants me to do, since it suggests that I condone what's going to happen. I don't! But I will have to vote for it, or risk . . . what? If it's not unanimous, will they still do it? He says the hunters are already on their way here. What am I going to do?"

Monique leaned forward, tapping a pencil on the desk, absent-mindedly. *"Take this cup away from me, for I don't want to taste its poison."*

Saoirse gaped. She knew those words.

"Yes, I was raised in the church," Monique said. "Not the Catholic one, like you were. Gramma was a Baptist. But I had to memorize Bible verses, and be able to repeat them to her, as well as discuss what they meant."

"How do I get out of this?"

"Simple answer? You can't. You don't have the liberty of

just being yourself anymore, and he's not *just* Diego anymore. He's the boss now, and you're his lady. And there are things that have to be done, and only you can do them."

"He . . . he wants to have a child with me. How can I bring a child into this kind of life? Where people are casually written off as disposable? Where's the justice?"

"Hold on, now," Monique snapped. "This isn't the kind of thing that happens regularly around here. This hasn't happened in our pack for over fifty years. When a pack leader dies, there is always a period of upheaval and unrest. Diego has had to fend off a challenger, not just once, but twice. And the first time, he tried to stay true to his own personal beliefs, and that allowed for the challenger to try a second time. Along with, I might add, kidnapping the leader's mate. That's not the kind of thing that can be allowed to go unpunished."

"Virgil's dead. Decapitated, if you didn't notice."

"I did. And while it was nauseating to watch, it was necessary. This last step is necessary, too. Virgil's brother supported him twice against Diego. He will try again, no matter whether he's kept in captivity here, or allowed to leave. And in case you haven't thought about it, captivity can be worse than death. I'm sure it wasn't any fun for you."

Saoirse shook her head.

"It's even less enjoyable for us. We put up with the pain of shifting in order to allow our inner wolves the joy of running freely through the night, with the soft grass under our paws, and the moonlight showing us the way. Being captive for any length of time would seem a fate worse than death for those two. Both their human and wolf sides would suffer."

"I guess. And Diego said they know too much about the inner business of the pack to be allowed to give that information to anyone else."

"You know he's right. We have hundreds of people, families with children, who live in the compound. Then add in the students whose parents trust us to keep them safe. How can he take that kind of chance with all of their lives? What kind of leader would he be if he was willing to risk all of them? And for what? Principles? Morality? Tell me, what do you think he should do?"

Saoirse's throat ached from crying and from tears unshed. Numbness crept through her body, and Monique's voice seemed to be coming from a long way away. She stared down at her hands, clenching each other so tightly that her knuckles were white.

Finally, she replied in a flat monotone. "I don't know."

"Then you have no choice. You have to support him because you love him. You have to choose the health and safety of the pack because you are also partly responsible for all of us. We are all your family now."

Saoirse got up from the chair.

"Feel better?"

She shook her head. "No. I'm going to go for a walk. I need some fresh air."

"Do you want some company?"

"No. I need to think." She walked over to the door, then turned back with her hand on the knob. "Thanks for listening, and for advising me. I didn't know who else to turn to."

Monique nodded with a small smile. "I've been in your place. What you need to realize is how dependent we all are on each other. A family, as large as a pack, needs a strong leader to make the unpleasant choices and do the things that protect us all. And *he* needs a mate to support him in public, and then to hold him at night and love him for being the man that he still is, under the layers of hardness that he's still busily constructing right now."

Saoirse opened the door and let it close behind her. She quickly walked down the hall to the side stairway, which led outside using a less-frequented passage, to avoid having to talk to anyone else. Her strategy worked, and within a few minutes, she was outside the mansion. She got her bearings and walked in the direction of the chapel. *Stupid, I know, since the last time I was in there was the unpleasant beginning to this whole nightmare. But I refuse to let the actions of a few jerks deny me the comfort I've always found in God's house. Because, Lord, I need you now, more than ever!*

And though she'd never have thought it possible, Saoirse knelt for so long, with her hands folded in prayer, and her head resting on them, that she actually fell asleep for a while. When the sounds of children laughing nearby intruded into the chapel, she looked at her watch and was surprised at how long she'd been in there. She sat back onto the pew and stretched her legs, which ached from having been on her knees for so long.

But when she got up, she knew what she had to do. It had all been decided. Resolutely, she walked out of the chapel and back to her life.

Chapter Thirty-seven

When Saoirse got back to the penthouse, the other men were gone, and Diego was asleep on the couch. The bottle of pills was nearby, next to a nearly empty glass of water. The late afternoon sun was streaming in through the windows, and she stood watching him sleep for a long time.

Unconscious, his face lost the newly acquired lines of responsibility that had aged it recently. He was truly the most attractive man she had ever seen, and the knowledge that he belonged to her used to make her heart swell with love and pride. Now she took in staggered breaths, as she thought of what the next twenty-four hours held for them. His unruly black hair reminded her of times they had marathon erotic sessions, both panting with exhaustion and satisfaction. His long, curly black eyelashes fluttered as a grimace of pain shot across his face.

Forcing herself to act, she moved into the bedroom and used her laptop to go online and book a flight. She dashed off a quick email before taking down a zippered tote bag, then putting some clothes and toiletries into it. When Diego's phone rang, she heard him answer it. She placed the bag in the back of her closet and went in to talk to him.

Diego looked up with a small smile. "That was John. We will meet right after dinner, in the small conference room. There will be witnesses, but it won't be a large group. The meeting will be called to order, the vote will be taken and recorded, then we will adjourn."

She tried to keep her face neutral as he studied her closely.

"Will you be all right?" he asked.

"Don't you mean, will I vote the way you want me to?"

He shook his head. "No. I know you will make the only possible choice—the right choice to keep everyone safe. But are *you* all right? When you left, I was concerned. I wanted someone to follow you, but John said that I should give you time to assimilate what had happened. He reminded me that as difficult as this is on all of us, it must be worse for you. You spent the last few days as a captive, and the lack of sleep is probably combining with delayed shock." His voice trailed, his worry at her lack of emotion was evident.

"I'm fine." Her voice reflected the numbness she felt. "I'll vote the way you want me to. And I'll witness what you do tomorrow. But after that, I think I need a break from pack business."

A look of panic flashed across his face. "A break? What do you mean?"

"I'm . . . um . . ." Her voice broke, and she coughed to clear it. "I'm going to go spend some time at home . . . with my parents."

Diego tried to get off the couch, but without being able to move his arm, and still feeling weak from his other injuries, he struggled and flopped back.

"You don't have to get up on my account," she said. Don't bother to try to talk me out of it. It's just something that I need to do right now."

"I want—no, I *need* to hold you in my arms right now."

"You mean in your arm—singular. You can't move the other one. And remember, Rachel said no sex, so there's really nothing you need me for right now."

Diego swore softly, a stream of Spanish words that she didn't understand, but could guess the gist of by the wild look on his face.

"How can you say I don't need you? You are a part of me.

Not having you here . . . Not knowing what was happening to you, and being unable to do anything to rescue you, damn near killed me. I was only half-alive without you by my side."

"This will be different," she said in a flat, cold voice. "You'll know where I am. I will be at my parents' house in Chicago. And no one will be hurting me there."

"But why?"

"Because I'm already hurting so much, I don't think I can take any more."

Diego's gaze reflected so much confusion. "But why are you leaving *me*? I love you. I need you. I don't want to live without you."

"Then let me go. This is something that I need to do . . . for me. I'm in so much pain that I've shut myself off for self-protection. I can't process what I'm thinking or experiencing. I need to be somewhere that I can totally relax. That's why I'm going back to my childhood home, to sleep in the bed I grew up in."

Tears brimmed Diego's eyes as he stared at her as if trying to will her to change her mind. Saoirse returned his stare impassively, her face as calm and emotionless as she felt inside.

Finally, he took in a staggered breath, his voice almost a whisper. "*Mi corazón. Eres toda mi vida.*"

"*¿Ingles, señor?*"

"*Lo siento.* I'm sorry. When my soul speaks, it uses the language of love. You are my heart, my love. You are all my life. I'm nothing without you. Please don't leave me."

"There's an old saying that goes something like, *If you love someone, let them go. If it was meant to be, they'll return to you.* I can't stay here right now. I have to remove myself to somewhere neutral. Somewhere safe."

"*Will* you come back to me?"

This was the question she'd been dreading. Emotion threatened to overwhelm her as tears filled her eyes. When she spoke, her voice was ragged, as if torn from her soul. "I don't know."

His face was stricken. "Do you still love me?"

She nodded, tears now streaming unheeded down her face. "I just . . . I don't know if I can live this life anymore."

"I have no choice. I must remain here." The croak in his voice betrayed his sadness.

"And be the pack leader they all need you to be. I know. But that's not the man I married. The man I fell in love with."

They were both crying now, and Diego held out his one good arm in supplication. With a small cry, Saoirse flew to the couch and wrapped her arms around him, sobbing into his chest. He stroked her back and buried his face in her hair, inhaling deeply with staggered breaths that reflected the depth of his emotions.

After a long time, they both calmed, still clinging to each other. Their heartbeats and breathing synchronized, making them one being, despite their separate bodies.

Finally, Diego pulled back slightly, lifting her head so he could gaze into her eyes. "I won't be whole without you."

His lips touched hers gently before resting his forehead against hers and closing his eyes.

"I won't beg you to stay. I won't try to stop you. But I will only be half-alive until you return. Remember that." He lifted his head, his eyes liquid pools of infinite sadness.

The signal from his cell phone made them both jump. Diego reached for it, and Saoirse got up.

"I've got to use the bathroom," she mumbled as she almost ran into the other room. She splashed cold water onto her blotchy, puffy face, and her red swollen eyes. As she stared at herself in the mirror, she could feel the coldness filling her heart, numbing her to the pain. By the time she got out of the bathroom, her face was emotionless again, and her determination strong.

Diego looked up as she entered the room. "Janine asked if we wanted dinner to be sent up here."

"What did you say?"

"I said I wasn't hungry. She said that Rachel had insisted that I'm not allowed to skip any meals. So she's sending our tray of food to the conference room."

"Do you need help getting off the couch?"

"Yes. And I'll need to use the bathroom. Then we can go down."

They made their way down the hall to the elevator that would require less physical exertion for Diego's condition.

When the doors had closed, Saoirse asked in a bland conversational tone, "What will you tell the others?"

Diego looked at her and quickly masked his despair. "That you have gone to spend some time with your parents. Nothing more needs to be said. Then I will visit the chapel every day, to pray for your quick and safe return."

The doors slid open, and they headed down the hall to the small conference room. He didn't taste any of the food he forced himself to eat, nor did he attempt any small talk.

Promptly at seven, there was a discreet knock on the door. When he called out, "Enter," the other members of the pack hierarchy came in, along with a small contingent of witnesses, and the meeting was called to order. Since there was only one order of business, it didn't take long.

Diego cast the first vote for the sentence of death by hunting. John seconded the vote, Monique agreed, and Nathan added his assent. When it came time for Saoirse to cast her vote, her gazed flitted around the room, as if looking for someone to give her a way out. At last, she turned back to him with empty eyes that hurt his heart.

"Yes," she said with a voice barely above a whisper.

As soon as the meeting was adjourned, John released the witnesses from their duties, and they left the room.

Saoirse asked to be excused. Diego nodded, and she followed the others out of the room.

The others apparently waited for Diego to say something. But he remained silent, staring at the door that had closed behind his wife. After a long silence, he shook off his misery when he realized everyone was watching him.

"I . . . um . . . suppose I should let you all know. Saoirse will be leaving tomorrow afternoon after the sentence is carried out."

No one said anything.

"She . . . uh . . . will be spending some time with her parents."

"It'll be okay, boss," Monique said with quiet conviction.

He gave a quick emotionless nod. "It has to be."

John cleared his throat and opened his laptop to begin a discussion about some semi-urgent pack business. They continued working for a while, distracting Diego from his pain.

It was almost ten o'clock before the meeting ended. John volunteered to help Diego back to the penthouse. He unlocked and opened the door, and helped Diego to the couch, where he collapsed, spent from his exertion. John refilled the water pitcher and got two pills out of the bottle left on the table. He gave them, along with a glass of fresh ice water, to Diego, who swallowed both gratefully.

"Do you need anything else from me, boss?" John asked, trying to keep the worry from his voice.

Diego shook his head. "I just need to sleep."

"Do you want me to help you into bed?"

"No. It's too hard for me to reach anything there. Here, the water and the pills are handy. I slept here all afternoon, and it's comfortable enough."

John helped him get adjusted to support the broken arm on the splint and pulled the light blanket over him. Then he walked over to the door, turned out the light, and locked the door from the inside before pulling it closed behind him.

Monique was already sitting on the couch in the hall, right across from the door. John sighed as he sat down next to her. Monique patted his leg.

"I know," she consoled. "It's a shock, but not surprising. She's been through a lot this last week. She just needs some time to process it all."

He frowned, his own emotions in turmoil. "I don't know how he's going to cope. I mean, the only person I've ever felt anything like love for lives in Boston. I've only seen him once since the wedding. I can't allow him to come here because he's not pack. And I can't tell him about what I am because that would endanger all of us. So no matter how much I feel for him, I'm unable to act on any of it. It's torture in the utmost. I can't even imagine how I'd feel if we were married, and he left me."

Monique stared at the door across the hall. "Let's just hope she doesn't stay away too long. He needs to heal, and having her gone is going to slow that down."

"Do you think she'll come back?"

She shrugged. "I hope so. She has to know that she's made a lot of friends here. And she's a great teacher. I hope she realizes how much she belongs here while she's away."

"And how much Diego loves her. We need him whole. He needs her."

"Amen, son. Amen."

John made a face. "I'm almost as old as you are."

A brief grin flashed across her face. "But I feel so old, sometimes." Her expression turned serious again. "I've been through so much upheaval, what with pack politics and challenges. I just want some peace and quiet for a while."

John nodded. "We had over fifty years of peace, with Dad in charge."

"That's something to focus on and hope for."

"Amen to that, sister."

He got up, yawning. "Now I'm off to bed. Good night, *she-who-never-needs-sleep.*"

Monique chuckled. "Remember the lyrics to that Warren Zevon song? *I'll sleep when I'm dead.* Words to live by."

In the darkened bedroom, Saoirse lay alone, staring up at the ceiling, trying to feel something . . . anything. But she was numb and cold, and no amount of blankets helped to warm her. So she lay still and watched as the moonlight moved across the sky. Only when the first streaks of light were making an appearance did she finally close her eyes, from sheer exhaustion.

Chapter Thirty-eight

Saoirse slept later than she intended to. Voices from the next room woke her. She glanced at the clock and realized that if she wanted any breakfast, she'd need to get up soon. She sighed and rolled over to hug Diego's pillow and breathed in deeply. But the creeping numbness reasserted itself, so she rolled back over and got out of bed.

After she took a quick shower, she got dressed. When she left the bedroom, Diego was on the phone. He looked up at her and waved toward the dining room table, where breakfast had been sent up. She walked over and poured herself some coffee, then checked to see what breakfast was.

The small omelet had white cheese visible on the edges. An English muffin with some raspberries and whipped cream sat on a plate off to the side.

Way too much food. I'm not even hungry. But thank you, Janine, for sending up all of my favorites.

When she lifted the plate, there was a small piece of paper folded over with her name on it. She picked it up and read Janine's cramped, old-school handwriting,

Safe travels. I hope you find what you are looking for and return home soon.

From one pack leader's wife to another.

A lump formed in her throat. She put the note into her back pocket and sat down, taking only small bites of the omelet, trying to swallow it down around the lump that was threatening to make her cry. She forced herself to remember what was going to happen today, and the threat dissolved as the cold numbness returned. She tasted very little, and only ate half of what was there.

Diego was done on the phone and looked up.

"That was the Canadians. They've cleared customs and will be here within the hour."

"How do they get across the border with weapons? Or do you keep a stash of them here for situations like this?"

He flinched at her cold tone but answered calmly. "The only weapons on the grounds are for security. They're kept locked up and guarded. The Canadians bring their own supplies. I don't know how they get them across the border, and quite frankly, I don't care. The sooner this is all over with, the better."

She sipped her coffee slowly, looking at him over the brim.

He squirmed a bit on the couch, obviously uncomfortable. "When is your flight?"

"At three. I'll need a ride to the airport about one-thirty."

"I'll arrange it with Nathan."

"I can ask him myself. After all, I'll see him at the . . ." She paused. "What should I call it? The execution?"

He stared at her. "You will witness the forced change and the injections. No more. Everything else is in the hands of the hunters."

"And the rest of you can get back to your lives as if nothing is happening."

"Yes. But we will know that this latest threat to the safety of our community has been neutralized."

They continued to lock gazes until she finally sighed and looked away.

"Oh, Jerene called," Diego said. "She gave the last of your finals yesterday, ran the bubble sheets through, and aggregated the grades. She was wondering what to do with the short answer lab questions."

"Where are they?"

"She left them locked in your desk, in the lab."

"I'll head down there now and pick them up. I can grade on the plane and at my parents' house. If I can't access the grading program from there, I can email her with all the results and ask her to input them."

She got up and started toward the door.

"You could tell her to leave them until you get back."

She stopped. Without turning around, she replied. "That wouldn't be a good idea, since I don't know when I'll be back. It wouldn't be fair to my students. They deserve to know their final grades as quickly as possible."

She opened the door and went through it, letting it close behind her.

Damn it, woman! Diego gnashed his teeth, which reminded him how sore his jaws still were. *You're not going to give me any hope at all, are you?*

Saoirse sat at her desk, using her key to open the drawer. She pulled out all the essays and found a copy of the totals for each class's multiple-choice test grades paper-clipped to the first essay test for each class. They were rubber-banded together by class, with a note from Jerene on top.

Be safe! See you soon. XO

She heard Jerene's polite cough, announcing she'd entered the room. Saoirse turned and smiled at her friend.

"Did you and your mom conspire to both leave me notes, or is it just coincidence?"

"Why? She gave you a note too?"

"Yes. Under the plate that held my white cheddar omelet."

"You got a white cheddar omelet? The rest of us got veggie scrambled eggs."

Saoirse felt the lump beginning to form in her throat again, so she swallowed hard to make it go away. "I think she was trying to remind me how good the food is here, so I'll come back for more." She choked back a sob and put her head in her hands to hide her face from her friend.

Jerene quickly moved over to hug her from the side. "Aw, honey. We all know *why* you're leaving. We're just worried that you might not come back."

"Because you'll miss *me*? Or because you need Diego to be strong?"

"I won't lie to you, Sam. Both. But you're a part of the pack now. Any time we lose a pack member, it hurts all of us."

"But not if they've been tried, convicted, and sentenced to death."

"That will still hurt. Mom and a few of the older members are the only ones who were around the last time this had to happen. They will all be there to witness and lend support to those of us who might need it. That's what a family does, Sam. We take care of each other."

"I know. That's why I'm going back to Chicago. So I can spend some time with my family—*my real family*—being taken care of."

"I know you don't mean that. Because we're your real family now, also. We danced and partied with your family as our two families became one. As you two became one."

"I wish I was already on the plane."

"I know. But we have to be a part of this ritual, Sam. You, especially. You have to be strong. From what Mom says, it's going to be disturbing—even more so if they fight the shift. But it has to be done. They betrayed us, and we can't allow that to go unpunished. A pack with a weak leader is seen as easy prey. We had many years of peace with Dad in charge because he was strong enough to make the hard decisions and carry them out. Diego is still finding his way—*his style* if you will. But he's doing the best he can with the difficult role he's been given. A change in pack leadership is never easy."

Saoirse allowed the numbness to creep over her again. She tamped down the panic and fear she felt, which made her want to run, screaming, all the way to the airport to avoid what she was going to have to witness.

Jerene's phone buzzed. She pulled it out of her pocket and looked at it. "Mom says the Canadians are here, and things are going to happen very soon. We all need to gather out on the battlefield again."

Saoirse got up, holding her papers to her breasts like a shield of protection. "Then I'd better get these into my luggage, so I don't forget them. I'll email you the grades when they're done."

Jerene gave her a quick, searching look, then nodded. She obviously was fighting the urge to say more. Instead, they walked quietly out of the lab and into the hall. They split up, with Jerene heading to the main stairway to go outside, and Saoirse going to the side stairway, the more private one, to head back up to the penthouse.

Diego was already gone when she got there. When she went into the bedroom to put the essays into her luggage, she could smell his soap and aftershave drifting in from the bathroom. Her breath caught in her throat when she realized she might not ever smell that again. She resolutely zipped the bag closed, then turned with the bag on her shoulder, and glanced around at the bedroom. She had found such delirious joy in this room, which now felt like a prison. Much like the tiny bathroom she'd been held in by the people whose execution she was about to witness.

Then she dropped the bag on the dining room table and left the penthouse, to walk down the main stairway. Along the way, she invited the cold, numbness to completely envelop her so she wouldn't feel anything, no matter what she saw. And she prayed to God to ensure that she wouldn't remember anything. But the image of Diego tearing out the throat of his rival flashed before her eyes in full color. She knew this was bound to be yet another horrible memory, haunting her sleep for the rest of her life.

Once outside, Saoirse was surprised by how few people were gathered in the field. She'd been expecting it to be as crowded as it was when the battle for pack leadership raged. But this time, there were only a few witnesses besides the hierarchy and some security guards. Jerene was there, standing next to her mother, who had her arm around her daughter protectively.

That's what I need! I need to feel my mother's arms around me. I need to hear her tell me that everything's going to be all right — even if I know it's a lie. I need her to protect me from the monsters, including my own husband.

Diego stood next to Janine, talking to a small knot of strangers, all of whom were wearing forest green, camo-colored clothing. There were three very tall young men, two of whom had hipster-style facial hair, and a young woman, obviously a sibling to the other three. As she got closer, she could see another woman with iron-gray, very short hair. The younger female had her long, blonde hair braided and twined around her head. They all carried serious-looking weaponry, but they were smiling and chatting amiably with Diego, Janine, and Jerene.

Once she was close enough, Diego waved for her to join them. Reluctantly, she forced her suddenly heavy feet, one at a time, to carry her over to the gathering.

"This is my wife, Saoirse," he said to the newcomers.

There was a general murmuring of greetings, and the older woman waved around to introduce her family.

"I'm Gertrude, mother of these miscreants. This is my daughter, Griselda, my oldest, along with her three brothers, Grant, Glen, and Guy."

Saoirse felt dazed as she looked around at the smiling faces, nodding to each one to acknowledge meeting them. *Almost like this is a family reunion and not an execution! So surreal!*

The older woman must have read her mind.

"Sorry we have to meet under such terrible circumstances," Gertrude said. "We know this is a difficult time for all of you. I hope the next time we're down here for a visit, we'll be able to get to know you better. Diego is a wonderful man. I predicted that he'd be the next pack leader here back when I first met him, didn't I?"

There was a general nodding of heads in agreement, with lots of smiles directed toward both Diego and her. She felt like she was standing in molasses, with no way to direct her own movements.

She was saved from having to make an actual response by the approach of a man carrying a medical bag.

"Ah, Dr. Sullivan. Prompt as usual," Diego greeted him with a handshake, using his good hand.

"I heard about your injuries from the challenge, Diego. May I say how pleased I am that you were victorious? Hopefully, you will have a quick and total recovery. And I'm happy to do my small part to put this unpleasant business to rest."

He put his bag down and pulled out a container that held two syringes. "Ready whenever you are."

As if on cue, John and Nathan appeared from behind the security building, leading Verne and Pearl over to them. Both had their hands plastic-cuffed in front of them. Verne looked angry, while Pearl looked terrified.

When they got close to the small group, they stopped. A security guard walked in front of them and used a knife to cut the cuffs off. Other security people now joined John and Nathan in guarding them, to keep them still. Diego addressed them.

"Vernon Tate and Pearl Tate. You have been convicted of conspiring to depose the leadership of the Northwest Maine Pack, and of kidnapping the leader's wife. For your crimes, you have been sentenced to death by hunting."

"No!" Pearl cried out, her knees buckling.

Nathan held her upright, but she fought his grasp.

"You can't do this! It's murder! We have rights!"

She looked around wildly, then fixed her gaze on Saoirse.

"Saoirse! Please don't let them do this to us! It's inhuman! We're not animals! Make them stop! Have mercy!"

"Like the mercy you showed her, by trying to shoot her after I killed Virgil?" Diego spat out.

"Quiet, woman! Can't you see it's been decided? And she voted for this also, or we wouldn't be here. The vote had to be unanimous. She's as bad as all the rest of them." Verne spat onto the ground in Saoirse's direction.

Saoirse could feel herself shaking from nerves. She reached within herself, looking for the numbness to keep her safe.

Janine and Jerene helped Diego out of his shirt, then he walked over to stand in front of the prisoners. Through a haze, Saoirse saw the doctor moved behind the prisoners and take the syringes out of the container. He held one in each hand, cocked and ready to administer. She focused on her husband so she wouldn't have to witness what he was about to do.

Diego was shimmering, but not as violently as in the past. His face was set not in pain, but in concentration. Signs of movement appeared under his skin, but the only change that happened was the slight alteration of his face as his wolf rose to the surface. And when he spoke, his voice sounded strangled, like a cross between a human voice and a growl.

"I am your pack leader. I command your wolves to appear. I command you to change and appear before me as the creatures that you carry within you."

Verne started to shimmer and shift, but Pearl was fighting against the change, twisting and turning in Nathan's grasp.

"No! I won't change! You can't hunt me and kill me if I

don't change! I won't! I won't!"

Diego moved so his face was right in front of Pearl's, concentrating directly into her eyes.

His growl got deeper and harder to understand. "You know what you have done. You know what must happen. I command you to take over this body. Become the wolf. I, your pack leader, command it. Do it now!"

Her voice began to change as the shimmering started. It started to sound less like a woman's cries, and more like the feeble whimpering of a subordinate wolf. Within minutes, both of them dropped to all fours on the ground as their bodies remade themselves into wolves. Verne finished first, and as soon as the fur covered his entire body, the doctor jammed a syringe into his back haunch and injected the full dose of the serum. Verne turned and snapped at him, but the doctor had anticipated that and moved quickly to the other side of Pearl, who was shifting more slowly.

She continued to fight against her own wolf as the bones reset and her face elongated into a wolf's muzzle. She was still crying *No! No! No!* until her throat was completely changed and fur covered her body. She snarled with rage as the doctor jammed the other syringe into her haunch and injected her also.

He jumped back, free of both sets of snapping jaws of the now-trapped wolves, who looked like they were preparing to attack everyone there. Monique had appeared in front of them as her wolf, and she growled at both of them, putting her body in between them and Diego and Saoirse.

Diego looked exhausted, but he still commanded their attention with his inhuman growl. "Hear me and obey your leader. You need to start running. These hunters will track you. The quicker they do, the sooner this will be over. Now go!"

Without another look around, they both took off into the

woods, running so quickly they were a blur of legs and fur.

Saoirse realized she had been holding her breath for a long time and forced herself to breathe. But when Diego almost fell forward, she jumped in front of him to catch him. She was shocked by the depths of exhaustion she saw on his face. He was still shimmering slightly as he forced the wolf to retreat once again.

John moved quickly over to help support Diego from the side with the good arm. Saoirse stayed on Diego's injured side so he could rest the splint on her shoulders as he trudged wearily toward the front stairs.

Saoirse glanced back to see the hunters disappearing into the woods, already tracking their prey. Then she had to concentrate fully on helping Diego manage his way into the mansion and onto the elevator. Nathan had joined them, and together they got Diego into the penthouse and over to the bed. He collapsed onto his back and was already snoring before his head hit the pillow.

Monique joined them, once again oblivious to her own nudity. Saoirse grabbed a pair of running shorts and a t-shirt from her dresser, handing them to Monique, who gave her a nod of thanks and pulled them on.

Saoirse turned to Nathan. "I need a ride to the airport."

A look of pain flashed across his face, but he quickly arranged it to be neutral. "When?"

She looked at her watch. "Now."

He nodded. "I'll get a car and meet you out front."

He left quickly, and Saoirse moved to go after him.

"Sam?" Monique called.

She turned and accepted the hug Monique gave her, feeling, once again, like she was moving in slow motion.

"Come home soon," Monique whispered into her ear.

John moved in for a hug and shook his head sadly. "We're all going to miss you. Come back as soon as you can."

Monique nodded. "At least before the school year starts. I don't want to have to find a new science teacher. I'm happy with the one we hired last year."

Saoirse felt the lump returning to her throat, so she just nodded and moved quickly out of the bedroom. She grabbed her bag from the table, checked to be sure her phone was in the outside pocket, then almost ran to the door to leave.

Once the door closed, Monique and John looked at each other over the sleeping form of their pack leader.

"Now what?" John asked.

Monique shrugged. "Now we wait. And hope that her love is stronger than her fear, so she comes back to her husband."

John waved toward the door. "I'll take the day shift."

"And I'll take the night shift."

"You must be part vampire."

"They don't exist."

A quick grin shot across John's face. "Neither do werewolves. So, yeah . . . maybe."

Monique's eyes sparkled before her gaze fell on the exhausted Diego. "Take care of him."

Then she walked out of the room and went to her quarters to hug her children very closely and tell them she loved them.

CHAPTER THIRTY-NINE

Saoirse only got a few papers graded as she waited on the tarmac for the plane to take off. Once in the air, her exhaustion took over, and she slept for the rest of the ride. The flight attendant had to shake her awake when they were landing at O'Hare.

She was still groggy when she got off the plane, her bag over her shoulder. She went through the gate and headed for the exit, calling her mom as she walked. From long experience, she knew her dad would be driving.

"Mom? I'm just getting to the pick-up area now."

"Wonderful, Saoirse. Your dad and I have been playing cards, sitting in the *kiss'n'ride* section at the River Road parking lot. We'll jump right onto the highway and be there in a few minutes. I can't wait to hug you!"

Tears stung her eyelids, but she fought them back. *Time enough for tears when I'm home, in bed. I don't want strangers to see me cry.*

It wasn't long before she saw her parents' Ford Escape approaching. She waved to catch their attention, and her dad expertly maneuvered his way to the curb. She pulled the back door open, threw her bag into the seat, and climbed in.

"Saoirse! It's so good to see you!"

Her mom turned around, trying to hug her between the seats, which made her smile.

"Save the hugs. Seatbelts, please, ladies." Her dad, always the voice of reason.

Her dad's voice was brimming with love, but they all knew

that he was a stickler for seatbelts. She clicked hers on, and he took off from the curb, cautiously re-entering the airport traffic.

Within minutes they were on the Kennedy Expressway heading into the city, and to the home Saoirse was longing to see. Every familiar sight made her happy. She could feel the knot of pain and tension beginning to unravel, the closer they got to home.

Once her dad pulled into the driveway, her mom barely waited until the car had stopped before she jumped out and pulled Saoirse's door open.

"Give me a hug, sweetie!"

Once her arms were around her mother, the dam broke. All her resolve flew out the window, and Saoirse burst into a torrent of tears, huge sobs wracking her body.

Her dad flew out of the car and wrapped them both in a group hug. "My God, honey. What's wrong? Did he hurt you? What happened?"

She shook her head, trying to get herself under control. "Let's go into the house," she blubbered. "I don't want the neighbors watching."

They let her go, and her parents walked with her into the house. Her dad took her bag, saying, "I'll toss this into your room."

Her mom led the way to the living room. "What can I get for you? Coffee? Wine? *An IV of my blood*? Whatever you want is yours."

Saoirse offered a tiny smile at the obvious *mom-ism* she'd heard her whole life. "A glass of wine would be great, Mom."

"Red? White? I think we even have sparkling, since I bought some with a screw top. I don't know how much sparkle it still has in it, but it should still be good, since I opened it yesterday, to celebrate that you were coming for a visit."

"Anything, Mom. Red or sparkling. I don't care."

"Be right back." She bustled into the kitchen, returning seconds later with two flutes of sparkling white wine and a small dish of cheese.

"Did you already have this cut up?" Saoirse asked.

Her mom nodded. "Yup. I wasn't born yesterday, you know. When my newlywed daughter emails me to say she's *dropping in* for an unexpected visit, all the way from the east coast, I know that there's something she needs to talk to me about."

"Is that why Dad disappeared?"

"Of course. So we could have some *girl-talk*. So tell me, my *Sha-sha*. What is it? Why did you come home?"

Saoirse smiled at the use of her childhood nickname, given to her by her younger siblings. She glanced around the room with a sense of satisfaction. "I just wanted to be home for a while, Mom. To be a daughter again and not a wife."

Her mom took a sip of her wine, and popped a piece of cheese into her mouth, chewing slowly. "So what you mean is, you can't, or won't, tell me anything about it. But you need a shot of Mom and Dad loving, the way that only we can do, right?"

She nodded, taking a drink of her wine. "It's just that . . . being married isn't what I expected. It's a lot harder than I thought it would be."

Her mom watched her closely, taking another sip.

"It's just that . . . you and Dad are so good together. We grew up watching how you always had each other's backs, and you are so protective of each other." She stopped suddenly, surprised by her own words.

"Go on." Her mom offered a small smile of encouragement.

"But you always made it look so easy. Like it was the most natural thing in the world for you to be so happy together."

Her mom threw her head back and laughed. "Easy?

Natural? Child, you should have been there when we were first married! Or first had kids! Or lots of time when it was anything *but* easy."

"Really? You've never even had any disagreements, let alone fights."

"Not where you children could see or hear. That didn't involve you. It was between us. But Lord, yes, child, we've had our bad times, as well as our good times."

Saoirse chewed slowly on a piece of cheese. Her mother leaned forward and patted the back of her hand.

"Just tell me one thing, Saoirse. He didn't hit you, did he? Or hurt you in any way?"

"No, of course not."

"The bruises on your face are from . . ."

"Someone else hit me."

Noticing the look on her mom's face, she grimaced. "It's a long story, Mom. But Diego wasn't involved, except to punish him for it."

Her mom shook her head. "I always said your brothers shouldn't have taught you to like fighting so much. You never were much for acting like a lady."

Saoirse managed a small grin. "It's the red hair."

"Mine used to be red too, you know. But if he didn't hit you, any trouble you are having is just what I call *adjustment time*."

"Adjustment time?"

Her mom nodded. "Yup. You see, honey, when the whole two-become-one thing happens, it's much easier for the man. He's never had that kind of emotional support before, so for him, it's a major relief. He now has someone to express his emotions to, to share his inner thoughts with. Someone he can be vulnerable with, and not fear that you're going to hurt him. A man can only find that with the woman he marries."

"What if he's gay, like Freddie?"

Her mom shrugged. "Well, then I suppose he will find it with the one man he's meant to share his life with. But most men don't trust each other enough to let their hair down that way with another man. Of course, your brothers do with each other. But that's different. They don't worry about being stabbed in the back, simply because they've all cried and laughed together for so many years. Family is different. Family is everything."

"I know that, Mom. But there are parts of him that I didn't know about before. Parts that I'm not sure I can live with."

"Honey, we all have parts of ourselves that we're not proud of. We all have our little foibles and idiosyncrasies. Things we never share with anyone, because we don't like to admit them out loud. It's too embarrassing." She chewed on another piece of cheese. "But remember, we don't get to choose the cards we're dealt in life. None of us do. Our only choice is how we play those cards."

Saoirse sipped her wine, listening intently because her mother was in full-on *mom mode* now.

"To continue the comparison, for us women, the adjustment time is much harder. We are more emotionally centered, so we don't need that kind of support from our men. Of course, it's going to be necessary in the long run, for a good life together. But initially, that's not the first thing we notice. And we've shared intimate details with our sisters and our close girlfriends, so we're not quite so quick to need to do it with our new mate.

"What two-becoming-one means for us is that, in a very real way, we lose our identity. Whereas before, we were assertive and supported ourselves, now we're expected to concentrate more on making our man happy. Whereas we could take care of ourselves very well—thank you—now we're expected to let our man take over our protection. It's not really his fault either, my dear. He's been fed the same load of crap that we all have since we were babies. So he doesn't realize how much of your agency he's taking away from you, in his zeal to show you that he can totally take care of you and that you can depend on him."

Saoirse leaned back, shaking her head. "I thought it was weird taking his name because I had a perfectly good name already. I resented it, but it's tradition, so I did it. Of course, the kids at the school kept on calling me Miss McColl, but that's because he wasn't there to hear it."

Her mom snickered. "Husbands tend to get kind of upset when you seem to reject the whole name change thing. Because to them, it's no big deal. Of course, it's not them having to do the changing. They get to stay who they are, and you're expected to become an extension of your husband . . . like another appendage . . . like a new arm or something."

"Why didn't you tell me any of this *before* I got married?"

"Because it wouldn't have made any sense to you then. Your brain and body were flooded with *bonding* hormones, and all you could think about was having sex, sex, and more sex."

Saoirse blushed. "Oh, Mom!"

"Don't you *Oh, Mom*, me, young lady. You know I'm right. I saw the way you two looked at each other at the wedding. You had it bad, and it was so, so very good."

They both looked at the clattering noises coming from the kitchen. Saoirse's dad poked his head through the doorway.

"I've got the coals going, my sweets. What should I put on for you? Burgers, chicken breasts, or pork tenderloin?"

"Pork for me, Dad. And thanks."

"Burger for me, honey. And could you grill up some veggies also?"

He nodded. "Already got them out on the counter. I know my women-folk." He smiled and retreated into the kitchen.

"See? That's what I mean," Saoirse observed. "Everything

is so natural and comfortable with you two."

"Honey, we've been married for almost forty years. If we hadn't worn off the rough edges so we could fit together smoothly, we'd have split up a long time ago. For instance, your father does the driving around town, especially to the airport, because I don't like driving in traffic. I get too angry and frustrated, and I tend to swear at people out the window. But when we're going on long trips, who drives?"

"You do, Mom. Always."

Her mother smiled with pride. "It took me years of crabbing and complaining about how bored I was and how much I wanted to drive. Now I've got him to the point where he automatically gets into the passenger seat. On long trips, it's a mutual expectation that I will drive. Oh, I offer to let him spell me if he wants to, but you know what? He never wants to. He actually prefers to read, or nap, or look out the window at the scenery. So with time, we've gotten to a compromise that suits the both of us very well."

"So Diego and I just need time? Is that what you're saying?"

"*Sha-sha*, I don't know what it is that precipitated your coming home, and I don't care. It's not my business, and I won't pry. But if you're thinking that marriage is all *beer and skittles*, you're wrong. It's a lot of hard work. It will cause buckets of tears and many hurt feelings. You will learn that your love ebbs and flows like a tide. Sometimes you'll look at him and wonder what you ever saw in him and question your own sanity for marrying him. Other times, you'll feel so deeply in love that you'll be drowning in a pool of attachment hormones. Making you feel like you're nothing when you're not together because you'll feel so . . . so *empty* without him." Her mom waggled her eyebrows, followed by a wink.

"Mo-om!" She grinned. "You're outrageous! Aren't you too old for that sort of thing? Other moms don't talk about sex like you do."

Her mom huffed. "Dad and I may be old, but we're not dead yet. And more's the pity for their children that they don't. I won't ever lie to you, *Sha-sha*. I tell the truth. Marriage is like getting older—it's not for *wussies*. You have to be strong, to knit two lives together with threads of steel so the bond can't be broken. Trust me on this. I know of what I speak."

"Oh, Mom!" Saoirse fell forward into her mom's embrace. The cold, numbness around her heart started to melt as the love she'd depended on from her earliest memories washed over her and wrapped her in a cocoon.

She held onto her mother for a long time. Trying, yet failing to be sneaky, her mom started to sniff her head. "Mom! What are you doing?"

"I love you. I'm smelling your scent. It comforts me. My daughter is home. I'm going to enjoy hugging and sniffing you as long as I can because, eventually, you'll go back to your husband. And you live too far away for my taste. But that's life. You give birth in agony, then feel the most extreme bliss when you hold them. You nurse them, comfort them, raise them, and give them a shove. Then they leave you and wonder why you miss them so much. You'll know what I'm talking about someday, my girl. Then you'll understand why I like to sniff my children."

There was a crashing sound from the kitchen, followed by audible swearing.

"I think we'd better go in there and help with dinner, don't you?"

Saoirse grinned. "That's probably a good idea."

Her mom grabbed the cheese plate and her glass, and Saoirse grabbed hers, and they made their way in to join in preparing their meal.

Before she went to sleep that night, Saoirse sent a quick text to Diego.

Got here safely. Feel better already. Talk soon. XO

She smiled as she hit *send*, thinking her message would bring him comfort.

Diego grimaced as he reached for the phone. His arm was on fire, and the pills he'd just taken were not working their magic as quickly as before. And his extreme exhaustion still had not subsided. He felt as if he'd run a marathon with every part of his body tired and in pain. He gritted his teeth, ignoring the pain in his jaws, and read the message.

Great! She feels better because she's away from me. I hope she's not telling her parents why she left. I won't tell anyone if she does because I won't let anyone hunt her down. But she's there and feeling better, and I'm here and miserable. I need my wife, and she left me. I don't deserve her. I deserve to be alone. No matter how hard I try, nothing I do is ever enough.

He tossed the phone onto the floor and lay back down. And for the first time in a great many years, he cried himself to sleep.

CHAPTER FORTY

If Saoirse's sisters and brothers were surprised that she was home for an unexpected visit, they had the good manners not to show it. Many of them had been married for a long time, and they wisely asked no questions. They just enjoyed spending time with her. She *oohed* and *aahed* over how big their children had grown in the months since she'd seen them, and they exchanged lots of hugs.

Saoirse spent a few hours each day grading labs, but she went out to lunch with her siblings and spent time at some of their houses for dinner. She had arrived in Chicago on a Saturday, and before she knew it, it was Thursday. She had sent a text each night to Diego but thought it would be unwise to talk to him. She assured her conscience that she was thinking of his feelings, but still had a nagging feeling that she wasn't. She ignored it.

Thursday was her mom's grocery shopping day, and though they had gone together when she was younger, Saoirse opted to stay home. She had to finalize the grading of the essays and email the results to Jerene. She had just finished sending them, along with a note telling Jerene that she was feeling a lot better and would talk to her soon, when her dad poked his head into her old bedroom.

"I made some fresh coffee. Want to come sit on the patio and enjoy the gorgeous day with your old dad? Or are you still busy?"

She got up and stretched. "No, Dad. I just finished. What a relief! And I'd love to come and enjoy coffee and conversation with my daddy."

She followed him downstairs, and when they reached the kitchen, he grabbed her for a huge hug.

"I don't tell you I love you, often enough," he murmured. "But I do. I think of you all the time, and like your mom, I miss you terribly. But you have your life to lead, and I know that. I'm just glad you still think of the old folks, now and again, and toss us a bone by coming to visit."

Saoirse returned his hug. They both got their coffee, and her father grabbed a plate of shortbread, and they headed out onto the patio.

"What would you think if I said I was thinking of staying here for a while longer?" Saoirse asked, tentatively.

Her father's regard turned grave for a few minutes. "Is it that serious?"

"Is what that serious?"

"The reason that you left him and came home."

"Dad, I don't really want to talk about it . . ."

"Fine. Then just listen while I talk. With all you females around here, I don't get a chance to do that much. But every once in a while, you need the male perspective. So here it is."

He finished chewing his bite of shortbread and swallowed, then took a deep breath. "Did your mother ever tell you about the time she left me early in our marriage?"

Her eyes widened, and she shook her head.

"Well, she did. You weren't born yet. We only had our two wee boys, and they were about three and two. I was working three jobs at the time, and your mom was doing home day care for other neighborhood kids to bring in some extra money. We didn't see each other much. When we did, I was usually too tired to do much other than play with the boys. But I was a happy man, loving my family. The only fly in my ointment was that for my jobs, I sometimes had to do things that I didn't want to do. Things that I wasn't proud of . . .

things that made me want to quit. But we really needed the money, and I was over a barrel."

He took a sip of his coffee and leaned back, his eyes clouding over, clearly lost in his memories. "Despite having two babies, your mom and I were still in our newlywed phase. We both still expected the other person to be everything we ever dreamed that we'd need. So I made a huge mistake. I told her about some of the things I was ashamed of doing, but that I had to do to help feed my family. I don't know why I did that. Maybe I was just looking to share my feelings with someone. Maybe I was hoping for absolution of some kind . . . that she'd tell me it was all right, and that she forgave me and loved me anyway. But that's not how she reacted. She was shocked, and we argued over why I had to keep doing those jobs. She said she'd get another job outside the house, so I could quit. But we both knew that would be impossible, since we had no money for daycare, and two babies to think of.

"I could hardly sleep that night. We had never gone to bed angry with each other before, but I couldn't understand how she could reject me when everything I was doing was to take care of her and our babies. She didn't talk to me over breakfast the next morning. She just focused on the boys. I gave her a kiss as I left for work, but she didn't return it, and her eyes were sad.

"When I got home that night from my second job, the apartment was so very quiet. I figured they must all be sleeping, so I moved around quietly, trying not to wake anyone. But when I went to peek into the boys' room, they weren't in their cribs. Then I went into our bedroom, and my wife was gone, too. There was a note left on the nightstand."

Saoirse reached over to pat the back of his trembling hand resting on the table, offering what comfort she could.

"Even after all these years, it still hurts. The agony was unbearable. In the note, she told me she'd gone to stay with her parents, and that I wasn't to follow her. She said she needed time to process what I had told her and her own reactions. She said that she still loved me, but she had to decide if that was enough."

Saoirse's eyes grew wider at her father's words, and she kept forgetting to breathe. The lump was back in her throat, and she fought back her own trembling.

"The next two weeks were horrible. I went to my jobs, did what I had to do, and returned home to an empty place. I'd eat dinner at the local pub, so I could at least have someone to talk to, even if it was the bartender I was paying to feed me the drinks I needed to be able to sleep. And every night, I'd hug your mother's pillow, just to remember her smell. And sometimes I would cry myself to sleep."

Tears were flowing from Saoirse's eyes, dropping unheeded into her coffee. Her hand trembled as she took a sip before putting the cup down. "Oh, Daddy, I never knew. How awful for you!"

He nodded, forcing a small smile. "Yes. But it was awful for both of us. We loved each other so much, yet there was a wall between us, and neither of us knew how to break it down. I respected her too much to disobey her wishes, even though I wanted to race to her parents' house and drag her back home to me. And it turns out that her parents were getting so old that they really needed some help around the house, so having her stay for a while made things easier for them. So there wasn't anyone arguing for my side with her. I was afraid that she'd never come back."

"What happened?" she whispered.

"You happened," he said with a shrug.

"What?"

"Turns out that your mom's period was late, and when she went to the doctor, she found out that she was pregnant again. That made her realize that she was responsible for the health and wellbeing of others besides herself. And now there was going to be another one to take care of. When her parents heard that, they both told her that her place was at home with her husband. They thanked her for all of her help, but basically told her it was time for her to leave."

She scrutinized him closely. "Have you told this story to anyone else in the family?"

His eyes sparkled with his sheepish grin. "Maybe I have. But you don't need to know whom I told it to. Sometimes marriages are rocky in the beginning, but when the love is strong enough, things get worked out. And the fewer people who know about the hard parts, the fewer people there are to sit in judgment. So my lips are sealed on that subject."

"So what happened?"

He took a deep breath. "The day I walked back into the apartment and smelled dinner cooking was the happiest day of my life. I almost collapsed with emotion before I even got the door closed. Then when my two boys raced over, yelling *Daddy! Daddy! We're back!* I kneeled down to hug them both and cried into their hair. They both danced around me, giggling because they had never seen me cry before. But I told them that it was happy crying because I was so glad to see them.

"I looked up then, and your mother was standing in the kitchen doorway, smiling at me. I walked over to take her in my arms, and I cried into her hair, also. I don't remember what we ate for dinner because I didn't taste anything except love. And when the boys were in bed, and your mother and I were alone, she told me that she had assimilated everything I said and decided that if that was a part of me, she had to accept it, because she loved me so much. She said that what we had together was worth preserving, and she would work to be a better wife to me. I couldn't stop crying as I told her how empty my life had been without her, and how much I needed her love to make living worthwhile. The rest of that night is between your mother and me." He waggled his eyebrows and winked.

"Oh, Dad! You're as bad as Mom. She says you two may be old, but you're not dead yet."

He grinned. "She's so right. To me, she's still the most attractive woman I've ever had the honor of kissing. And doing lots of other stuff with also."

Saoirse's face warmed with her blush, but the heat also melted what was left of her cold numbness.

They both chomped on shortbread for a while, sipping their coffee and breathing in the warm breeze laden with lilacs and magnolia blooms.

"Your yard is really beautiful," she said.

"Thanks. Now that I'm only working one part-time job, I have time to do things right around here."

"Did Mom tell you anything about why I'm home?"

"No. All she said is that you needed some parental love time because being a married woman was more work than you expected it to be. I just want to let you know that even the best of marriages can have rocky starts. But that doesn't mean you give up on them. It just means that you have to work harder to remember why you are together. But if your love is strong enough, and you both want it badly enough, you can make it work."

Saoirse stared off into space for a while as her dad chewed more shortbread. She watched a male cardinal land nearby, singing for them, and a hummingbird briefly flitted over to the feeder, then disappeared.

Saoirse took a deep breath. "You know, I think I may have stayed around long enough. I don't want to impose on your hospitality."

"You're not imposing. You're our daughter. *Mi casa es su casa*. Isn't that how it's said?"

She giggled at his Irish accent pronouncing Spanish words. "Yeah, Dad. Close enough."

The Escape drove along the alley and pulled into the garage. Her dad pushed himself up from the table. "Your mom's back with the groceries. I better help her get them into the house."

Saoirse got up and grabbed him for a big hug. She snuggled into his chest, breathing deeply.

He patted her back. "What are you doing, girlie? Don't tell me you're going to be like your mom, sniffing everyone all the time?"

She looked up, smiling. "I love you. I just want to have your smell deep in my mind, so when I'm back home, I'll remember it."

Her mom approached from the garage, carrying a bag of groceries and a gallon of milk. "Is anyone going to help me, or do I have to do all the work around here?"

Her dad let go and stepped back. "Coming, my love. I was just having a chat with our daughter."

Her mom gave Saoirse a long look, before nodding and smiling.

"That's fine, dear. But let's get this stuff into the fridge before it melts."

"I'll take those, Mom. Dad can help you with the rest. I'm going upstairs for a while. I've got some things I need to do."

She turned and walked into the house. As she opened the back door, she set it so that it stayed open to make it easier for her parents to get in with bags of groceries. She put the bag on the counter and the milk in the fridge, then she headed up to her room.

Colleen poked her husband in the ribs as he reached into the trunk.

"The story about when I left you?"

He nodded. "It seemed like time for her to hear it."

She smiled, reminiscing. "It was the worst of times, followed by the best of times."

"Not exactly the way Dickens wrote those words, honey."

"No. But it's true, isn't it?"

He smiled at her, putting the bags of groceries down as he took her into his arms.

"No. The best is yet to come, remember? Every day I get to be your husband is the best of times."

They shared a passionate kiss. She broke it off, grinning as a car drove by in the alley and beeped at them.

"We're shocking the neighbors again."

He shrugged. "After all of these years, you'd think they'd be used to it by now."

They picked up the grocery bags again and carried them into the house.

Saoirse was tapping single-handed on her keyboard, holding her credit card in the other hand. Then she closed the laptop and picked up her phone.

When she got downstairs, her parents were starting the preparations for dinner.

"So soon?" she asked.

"Corned beef has to be cooked for a long time on the coals," her dad reminded.

"I remember. Um, can I borrow the car for an hour or so this afternoon?"

"Who are you going to see?" her mom asked.

"Nobody, Mom. I have a doctor's appointment. Just a checkup. I've been so busy, with the end of the school year and all. I haven't had any time to do anything else."

Her mom's gaze assessed her closely as she nodded.

"Of course. The keys are hanging where they always are."

"Thanks. Oh, and could one of you give me a ride to the airport tomorrow afternoon?"

Her parents exchanged a significant look that Saoirse pretended not to see.

"Can we take you out to breakfast first?" her mom asked.

She nodded. "Yeah. My flight is at two, so I should probably be at O'Hare by noon at the latest."

"There's this great little diner that has the most excellent omelets," her dad said. "And it's on the way to the airport."

"Great. Now I'm going upstairs to get some laundry put together, so I can wash stuff before I pack it."

Her parents waited until they heard their daughter's footsteps on the stairway. Then they grinned and high-fived each other.

CHAPTER FORTY-ONE

The next morning, Monique was in a meeting with Diego, John, and the head of their IT department. They were discussing some changes that had to be made in their technology to update their security system. When her cell phone buzzed to let her know she had a text, she glanced at Diego, who was answering a question that John had just asked. She figured it was safe to glance down to see who might be texting her while she was at work.

It was from Saoirse.

My plane gets in at 4:00. Can you have Nathan take one of the smaller cars and pick me up from the airport at 4:30? And ask Janine to send dinner up to our penthouse by 7? I want to surprise Diego with my return. Thanks.

She looked up when Diego cleared his throat to get her attention.

"What do you think of that idea, Monique?"

She worked hard to keep her face neutral, saying, "Sorry, boss. Text from one of the kids. I didn't hear what you were saying. Can you explain it again?"

The rest of the meeting took way too long, as far as she was concerned. But finally, they were done, and Diego released them for lunch. He and John walked down with the tech engineer, but under the guise of checking on her kids, Monique went the other direction.

As soon as she was out of their hearing, she called Nathan.

"Where are you?"

"Washing the cars, why?" Nathan asked. "It's a gorgeous

day, and I've been spraying some of the little kids with the hoses, so it's all good."

"I need a favor."

"Anything for you, Monique."

"You have to keep it quiet."

"Okay," he sounded mystified.

"You need to be at the airport at four-thirty."

"Who will I be picking up?"

"Saoirse."

"Thank God!"

"I know, right? But she wants it to be a surprise, so you can't tell anyone where you're going."

"No problem. I will suddenly remember that I need to pick something up, and I'll head into town for it."

"Thanks, dude."

"Glad to help. Hopefully, this will help him recover faster."

"I expect it will. Remember, tell no one. Bye."

Nathan put his phone back into his back pocket and resumed washing the cars and spraying the kids, who were supposed to be helping him. But he had a new spring to his step, and he was smiling a whole lot more than before, which of course, none of the kids noticed.

Monique went into the kitchen to speak to Janine personally. She had just finished with lunch preparations and was drying her hands when Monique walked in.

"Can I have a minute?" Monique asked, trying to sound casual in front of those still in the kitchen.

Janine nodded. "Sure. Want to go into my office?"

"Yup."

Janine led the way and closed the door behind them. "So

what's up?"

"Saoirse texted me. She's coming home today."

"That's a relief. He hasn't been doing well with her gone. He's got way too much healing to do, and he's not taking care of himself the way he should. He's not eating much at all. It's like he doesn't care about his own health anymore."

"She wants it to be a surprise. I swore Nathan to secrecy when I asked him to pick her up at the airport. She thinks she'll be back here by six-thirty or so. She asked that you send dinner up to the penthouse by seven o'clock. That way, they can eat while they talk."

Janine snorted. "I'm sure. I'll send something up that will taste all right reheated. Both you and I were married to pack leaders. We both know damn well that talking is not going to be the first thing on his mind."

Monique winked. "Ah, I remember those times well."

"You're too young to be alone forever, dear. You need to think of yourself."

"I will. But my kids are still young, and they need me to be mother *and* father to them right now. Maybe when they're a little older, I will have the time to think about that."

"You do that."

"I've got to get out to lunch now. I sure hope the buffet hasn't been totally depleted."

"I've been making less food since the students aren't around acting like a ravenous horde of locusts. But if there's slim pickings, you just let me know, and I can whip you up something special."

Monique gave her a grateful look. "Aw, thanks."

"We pack leader widows have to stick together, you know."

Janine sat at her desk after Monique walked out, making some notes on the paper in front of her, smiling. *So, what should I make to send up to the happy couple?*

Saoirse waved at Nathan when she saw him driving up in one of the newer, smaller SUVs. He drove close to her and stopped to get out. He grabbed her bag and threw it into the back seat, then he turned to give her a hug.

"Welcome home," he said.

"I'm glad you didn't bring a limo. Can I ride in the front with you?"

"Of course."

He opened the door for her, and she slid into the seat and clicked on her seat belt.

Once on the highway, Saoirse casually asked the first question on her mind. "So how has Diego been while I've been gone?"

Nathan shot her a quick look before returning his attention back to the road.

"Not good."

"You have to tell me more than that."

"He's supposed to be getting a lot of rest, but he's working all of us hard, trying to deal with everything all at once, having lots of meetings that last way too long. Especially considering that it's the summer, and we finally have some nice weather to enjoy."

"So if he's not getting enough rest, he's probably not recovering as quickly as he should be, right?"

He huffed. "He's not sleeping much either, judging by how tired he looks. I know he's not eating much, because I've sat with him at meals, and he mostly pushes the food around, then gets up to leave. He still has so much healing to do, but it's been slowed down by his general lack of attention to his health. And obviously, he can't run with the pack, since as a four-legged animal, he would need that front paw to run on.

So he's kind of majorly-stressed, with no way to relieve the pressure."

She stared out of the window in silence for a while. "Verne and Pearl?"

"Caught within twenty-four hours. The next day, we buried them in the wolf cemetery behind the chapel, close to the woods."

He glanced at her, then looked back at the road.

"Is that's why you left?" he asked.

She shook her head. "That's not the only reason. There were a whole lot of things." She studied the man's profile. "You've never been married, have you?"

He shook his head. "No. I haven't found my mate yet."

"It's so weird to me that you all think of it like that. Like there will be some magical sign that this is *the one*, and you'll know."

He shrugged. "I've heard that's what it's like for us. Somehow our wolves know before we do. I'm hoping that's right. I'm not the most self-assured kind of man around women I find attractive."

Saoirse smiled. "My brothers used to complain about that when they were dating. It's a lot harder on the man than on the woman—initially. You are supposed to do the pursuing, putting yourself out there to be rejected. It's assumed we women get to do the choosing, since we're literally sitting on what you want."

Nathan snorted. "I never thought of it that way. And I sure never expected my pack leader's wife to say something like that."

It was Saoirse's turn to shrug. "I was raised in a big family with six brothers. We talked about lots of stuff, and no one pulled any punches. I will never actually get to *be* a man, but I shared what the female experience was, and they shared the male experience. We figured that gave all of us an edge since we were at least aware of how *the other side* thinks."

She returned to staring out the window in silence, but from the corner of her eye, she caught Nathan glancing her way.

After a long while, she sighed. "But that doesn't mean I have any advantage in something that I've never done before . . . like being married. It's a whole lot more work than I expected it to be. Going home to talk with my parents was a real eye-opener. I thought all you needed was to be really in love, and things would work out easily. But my parents have been married for almost forty years and raised ten kids, and they both told me that there are bad times, along with the good times."

There was a longer silence in the car this time, but it was companionable.

Finally, Nathan spoke up. "I'm glad you're coming home. Everyone else will be too."

She smirked. "Because you missed my sterling wit and personality? Or because you need a healthy and happy pack leader?"

"Both."

"Thanks for being honest."

They spent the rest of the drive mostly in silence, occasionally talking about the scenery or the weather. But the time passed quickly, and soon Nathan pulled up to the gate to be admitted. When the guards saw who was in the car with him, broad smiles spread onto all their faces.

Saoirse held her finger up to her lips, cautioning everyone. "It's a surprise, people. Please don't ruin it by telling him that you let me in."

One of the guards saluted, but the rest merely nodded.

"Understood, boss-lady."

She grinned at their name for her as Nathan drove into the compound.

As the huge gate closed behind them, Saoirse glanced

around the grounds, surprised to find herself smiling. *It's good to be home.*

CHAPTER FORTY-TWO

Diego was getting really annoyed at how everyone was trying to boss him around. When John suggested they really needed to be done soon or they would all miss dinner, he almost demanded they continue. A working dinner could always be delivered up to them.

As if sensing his irritation, Monique spoke up. "Janine asked me to tell you that she's sending dinner up to your penthouse, so you need to be up there by seven. She says you haven't been eating enough, and she's making you something special. You don't dare hurt her feelings by not eating it all. So John's right. We need to wrap this up. We can always finish with this business tomorrow."

Diego sighed. "Oh, all right. I can see that no one wants to get anything done around here right now anyway. So, go. Meeting adjourned."

"And you need to get up there before your food gets cold," Monique reminded.

"Fine," he snapped. Then he shook his head. "I'm sorry, Monique. I've been kind of stressed lately."

She nodded. "We understand, boss. Go up and have some dinner and try to relax."

The others walked out of the conference room together, then Diego headed toward the elevator. He'd been using it instead of the stairs to conserve his energy.

Monique waited until she was sure they were well out of

Diego's hearing, then turned to John.

"This better go well tonight."

"Their reunion? How could it not?"

She rolled her eyes. "It's obvious you've never been married, mister."

He shrugged. "Since the one man I'm interested in isn't a shifter, that's a given."

"But they love each other a lot, so I'm keeping my fingers crossed."

"I will too, then. Buy you a drink for dinner?" John offered.

She pretended to start running down the stairs. "Not offered very often. Must get there quickly before he changes his mind!"

Laughing like children, they raced each other all the way down to dinner.

Diego opened the door to the penthouse and sighed. With heavy steps, he walked over to the dining room table, where the huge tray of food waited for him, emitting tantalizing aromas. He lifted the cover to see that Janine had made one of his favorites—meatloaf made of beef and lamb, sliced then grilled and made into an open-faced sandwich, with slices of fried potatoes. She had garnished the plate with mango chutney and grilled asparagus. And for dessert, she had made a chocolate mousse, with raspberries and whipped cream.

Suddenly, Diego's tired brain started screaming three things demanding his full attention.

His wolf told him, *We are not alone.*

His brain registered, *There are two plates of food on the tray.*

And finally, his ears picked up that someone was in the next room, singing an off-key version of one of Saoirse's favorite songs.

He was rooted to the spot, unable to move. He even forgot

to breathe.

Saoirse suddenly appeared in the doorway to their bed-room. "Oh, good. You're finally here. I told them to be sure you were up here by seven."

He stared at her, stunned silent by her presence. *Am I hallucinating?*

She moved closer, smiling. "Don't blame any of them. I wanted to surprise you. It took a bit of finagling, but judging by the look on your face, it worked."

"When . . ." His voice broke, so he coughed and started again. "When did you get here?"

"About twenty minutes ago. Nathan picked me up at the airport. I snuck up the side stairway, and luckily, since it's dinner time, no one saw me."

Diego felt the haze he'd been in for so long, closing in around him. Dumbfounded, he couldn't form words to re-spond.

Saoirse studied Diego's face for a moment before sighing and shaking her head. "Nathan was right. You haven't been tak-ing care of yourself. You're slowing down your own *magical-wolf-y* healing powers. That ends now."

Her husband was pale and looked as though he'd lost some weight. His good hand clutched the back of the dining room chair so tightly his knuckles were white with the strain.

"Diego, I'm sorry I left you so suddenly. But I had to. I was freaking out about a lot of things. I needed to get away and think things through. And I needed to talk with my parents. By the way, they both send you their love."

He winced, then stuttered. "Y-you didn't tell them . . ."

She grinned. "That I'm living in a community of were-wolves, and I'm married to their pack leader? No, silly, of course not. They'd never have believed me anyway. But they didn't pry. Mostly they just talked to me. And I needed to hear what they said."

Diego's nostrils flared when Saoirse moved even closer to him. He inhaled deeply, and his wolf rejoiced at the familiar scent of wildflowers and grass. She stopped just shy of being able to touch him and started talking again. He snapped himself out of his reverie, realizing he needed to listen carefully and focus on her words.

"They told me that marriage is a lot of work. See, I had this idea that if you really loved someone, things should be easy. There shouldn't be any problems that make you feel like you can't handle things. Everything should just work itself out, with no effort. Turns out, that's not the way it was for my parents. Things are easy and natural for them now, but they've had forty years to buff at the hard parts that used to cause friction between them. They fit together well because they've both worked at it for so many years."

Diego felt compelled to say something. "I had no idea."

"I know. You were never part of a family. I was, but they never let us kids see any of their conflicts. So we didn't realize there were any."

She took another step closer. "When I started feeling overwhelmed, I thought it was because something was terribly wrong with *us* . . . with me, anyway. I thought we had made a mistake. That we got married too quickly. So I ran away, to give myself a breather. Turns out, I ran to the right place. I slept in my childhood bed and ate familiar foods they cooked. And I found out that a good marriage isn't easy, but it's worth the effort. And I realized something else."

"What?" His voice was little more than a raspy whisper.

"That no matter how unhappy I might sometimes feel with you, that's only temporary. But I'm not happy *at all* without you. So I guess you're stuck with me, husband."

His eyes brimmed with tears, and his whole body flooded with relief.

Saoirse reached into her pocket. "Oh, and I brought you a present."

She handed him a tiny jewelry-style box.

He finally let go of the chair and reached out with his good hand to flip the top open. He stared at what was in it, then gazed into Saoirse's glistening eyes.

"You had your IUD removed?" he whispered.

She nodded with a slight smile. "Yeah. I was going to wait for you to find out for yourself. But then I realized that knowing us, it would probably take until the third or fourth time before you even realized it wasn't poking at you anymore."

He put the box down and held out his one good arm.

Saoirse quickly closed the remaining distance between them, pressing herself against him. Her arms twined around his back, while her hands caressed from his shoulders to his butt and back again. His one arm held her tightly, and he buried his face in her hair.

His tears wetted her hair, but that was okay. Her eyes were also streaming tears. She rubbed her face against his shirt, inhaling deeply and rejoicing in the smell of the man she loved. His arousal became evident with the hardening of his cock. She massaged her pelvis against him, adding to the intensity of the moment.

Diego's voice, hoarse with emotion, murmured, "Please don't ever leave me again."

Saoirse lifted her head, shaking her red curls. "Sorry, but I can't make that promise. You married a feisty, red-headed Irishwoman. We're notoriously hard to tame."

She stared into his eyes, more pupils than color now, and she felt like drowning in the liquid pool of love that they reflected.

"But I do promise you this. I love you so much, Diego Vargas, that I will *always* come back home to you."

He bent his head and laid claim to her lips, first gently, then with increasing pressure as they both responded to their deep emotions. They spent a few moments of fiery heat and passion before Diego pulled his head back, resting his forehead on hers.

He cleared his throat. "Dinner first?"

Saoirse shook her head. Though her lips felt puffy, and her eyes were lidded from the passion of their kisses, she managed to speak in a breathy voice. "No need. Janine sent reheating directions."

She backed away from Diego slightly, clasping his good hand in both of hers. She took a step backward, giving him a sly smile.

"Come with me into our bedroom, husband. My body has missed the feel of you inside of me. Make love to me and make me scream."

That was enough to get Diego moving. He quickly led them into the next room. They helped each other to strip— clothing torn, buttons flying without care of where they landed. Soon they were both naked.

"How can we do this while protecting your arm, my husband?"

He backed up to the bed, pulling her with him. "You get on top of me, my love. That way, I can watch as your orgasms spread that beautiful flush all over your skin, which lets me know that we are one again."

He lay back, and she crawled over to him, her tongue giving light licks and kisses to various parts of him, as she continued to inhale.

"I've missed your smell," she confessed.

"You *must* be part wolf," he growled.

She moved on top of him and began to swirl her hips, soaking him with her juices as she teased him. He moaned in frustration.

Gradually, she lowered herself onto his huge cock. She inched herself down slowly, as he stretched her, opening her up for him. When he was inside of her completely, she stopped, gazing down at his wide-opened eyes. Once again, she could see both of his personas staring back. The man *and* the wolf.

"This is what I've been missing," she gasped. "I need to feel you inside of me. I'm not whole without you anymore, Diego. I love you."

They moved together, slowly, then more quickly, as their passion grew. Diego barely contained his reaction when Saoirse started to scream. He managed to hold himself back until her pleasure resulted in almost continuous orgasms. Finally, with a howl that came from deep in his soul, he spread his hand wide, gripping her ass to hold her down as he shot blast after blast into her. In wonder, what was left of his conscious brain realized it was indeed possible for men to have multiple orgasms. He rode the roller-coaster of pleasure with her, each bringing the other to shuddering climaxes, repeatedly.

Finally, she collapsed on him, his barely softened member still inside of her. It took a moment for them to relearn how to breathe separately and for their heartbeats to gradually slow down. His good arm was draped across her back, and he idly fondled her hair as they lay in blissful exhaustion.

When he could speak again, he said in a low voice, "My wolf is glad to have you back."

He could feel her smile on his chest.

She raised her head, her eyes sparkling with amusement. "I know. He told me."

"I wonder, will sex always be this good, now that each time might be the time that we get pregnant?"

She shrugged. "Who knows? Maybe. But it's going to be a whole lot of fun practicing until we get it right."

As they gazed into each other's eyes, they could hear the sounds of wolves howling outside, some sounding as if they were right under the windows.

"Listen," he said. "The pack is celebrating that you're home."

She giggled. "That's because they all know what we're doing right now."

"Probably. But a happy pack leader makes for a healthy pack."

"Good. Because I'm happy to be back where I belong. With you."

He pulled her head down for a long, luxurious kiss, full of promise and love.

You may also enjoy the following from eXtasy Books Inc:

Blood Immoral
Astrid Cooper

Excerpt

In the dark alley, something was dead. Mirra rarely hunted in alleyways, but some of the others did. Especially the vampires—no accounting for taste there, Mirra thought. Vamps enjoyed the twisting shadows, the concealment, the certainty of cornering one's prey.

She halted, scenting the alley. This dead thing had nothing to do with her, but instinct, a compulsion—something—drew her down the narrow lane. She cursed as she saw the spreadeagled body. This was a complication she did not need.

Mirra bent over the prostrate figure and gently turned it. The woman was dead, beaten and shot. And raped. But none of these had killed her. The woman's throat had been torn apart and she had been drained of blood. A messy killing, no finesse, just flesh ripped open, peeled back like a tin can and the contents devoured.

If one had to kill, then it should be done cleanly. This was a butcher's work. If it wasn't for the after-scent, and the psychic vibration in the alley, Mirra would have said that the woman had been human-killed. But that tendrils of aura wafting around her wasn't human. A Blood had been there. But not just any Blood. A rogue vampire.

"Just what I need!" Mirra whispered.

The victim was cold, but her killer's taint was starkly fresh. As Mirra probed the energy currents she sensed that somewhere nearby, the rogue vampire fed, ignoring all restraint.

But worse, the vamp had ignored the one rule that bound the Blood Hunters—never leave a victim to be found. By so doing, humans, with their increasingly sophisticated forensic science might begin to suspect the truth and that truth was dangerous. Deadly to all Blood-kin.

The vampire who had fed was shockingly vicious. Mirra had seen frenzied killers' handiwork before, but this was by far the worst she had encountered. His taint was impaled through the battered flesh. He'd fucked her properly, his blood and seed saturating his victim. All these in combination meant that the woman would resurrect in the worst possible way. Mirra retreated. She had to get away. Fast. A creature that did this to his prey would have no compunction about chewing on a succubus. Succubus sex-magic was coveted by the vamps, when they could get it. She wasn't about to go on any damn menu. She looked down at the twisted body and shuddered, swallowing against the gorge rising in her throat.

"Don't move!" a male voice shouted behind her. "That's right. Now real slow, you stand up, turn around and put your hands behind your back."

Mirra obeyed, curiosity overcoming caution because she liked his voice. A deep voice, harshness hiding the gentleness. A voice of contrasts, like the man—this she knew in a moment. So, she obeyed.

She heard his footsteps on the pavement and looked over her shoulder. A man, dressed in black leather, dark hair, a gun . . . a Colt Python levelled at her. She hated guns. They were clumsy, killing tools for cowards who didn't want to get their hands bloodied. The moonlight highlighted him, and the gun—large and lethal, like its owner.

As he glanced down at the body, she saw his jaw tighten. His gaze lifted to Mirrazan.

"Up against the wall, face first. Don't make me use this." The gun waved her forward.

His hand pressed her hard against the bricks, her cheek scraping the rough masonry. She gagged at the mouldy stench. It filled her nostrils and her mind, the uncounted grime and disease of generations of thieves and scum who had used the alley, done unspeakable things, leaving their psychic imprint before moving on . . .

His hands moved quickly. With a sharp snap, heavy cold metal was fastened around her wrists. She was pivoted around to face him.

She tested the handcuffs. She could easily break them, but for the moment, only for a moment, she would indulge him. Bondage was a game she enjoyed, but she was never the one restrained. And she preferred to use silk cords and ribbons, occasionally a strand of pearls, but never anything as coarse and barbaric as handcuffs. She twisted her wrists, the metal chafing. Interesting. But now wasn't the time to be thinking of sex games. Handcuffs might be something for the future, though . . . on her prey's wrists, never her own.

She watched as he knelt beside the figure, a finger caressing the dead woman's cheek. His touch was one of familiarity, of love. Mirra frowned. He knew the victim, she realised. Sorrow filled him, but was quickly replaced by burning fury. He pushed himself to his feet, all whipcord and anger.

He dug into his leather jacket and flashed a wallet before her eyes. A police badge . . . Oh great! A cop. Trouble of the worst kind. She stared at the gun.

"You're no cop!" she challenged.

"No?" He frowned, his gaze intense.

"Adelaide cops don't use a Colt Python. Against the rules."

"I make my own rules. I'm Detective Ric Rodrigeuz and I'm arresting you for murder."

"I didn't kill her."

"You're covered in blood."

"I can explain."

"Yeah, you can try."

ABOUT THE AUTHOR

I've been an avid reader since I was five, when Mom taught me to read. I've always written stories in my head when bored or occupied with some other task—like baking or cooking, driving, and even sleeping. I've even woken up with entire story arcs and well-developed characters demanding my attention. I used to think that everyone had characters talking to them all the time.

A few years ago, I decided that my head was getting too noisy and crowded, and that some of the people and their stories had to be written—so they could live in books, and readers' heads. I feel like they are telling me their secrets. Once the book is done, they are happy to have been heard, so they are quiet. But then the next characters start to talk, demanding their turn. I enjoy the noise.

I write contemporary romances involving a strong, independent woman who enjoys casual flings. Enter the equally strong, independent man who decides this is the woman for him. He has to convince the heroine that he's the one for her. I love happy endings.